CAITLIN SWEET
THE FLAME
IN THE MAZE

An imprint of ChiZine Publications

CAITLIN SWEET

THE FLAME
IN MAZE
THE

FIRST EDITION

The Flame in the Maze © 2015 Caitlin Sweet
Cover © 2015 by Erik Mohr
Cover and interior design by © 2015 by Samantha Beiko

Distributed in Canada by
Publishers Group Canada
76 Stafford Street, Unit 300
Toronto, Ontario, M6J 2S1
Toll Free: 800-747-8147
e-mail: info@pgcbooks.ca

Distributed in the U.S. by
Diamond Comic Distributors, Inc.
10150 York Road, Suite 300
Hunt Valley, MD 21030
Phone: (443) 318-8500
e-mail: books@diamondbookdistributors.com

Library and Archives Canada Cataloguing in Publication

Sweet, Caitlin, 1970-, author

    The flame in the maze / Caitlin Sweet.

Issued in print and electronic formats.

ISBN 978-1-77148-326-1 (pbk.).--ISBN 978-1-77148-327-8 (pdf)

    I. Title.

PS8587.W387F53 2015   jC813'.6   C2015-903048-X

                                  C2015-903049-8

CHITEEN
Toronto, Canada
www.chiteen.com
info@chizinepub.com

Edited by Samantha Beiko & Sandra Kasturi
Proofread by Elisabeth Nielsen

Shelfie

A **free** eBook edition is available
with the purchase of this print book.

CLEARLY PRINT YOUR NAME ABOVE IN UPPER CASE

Instructions to claim your free eBook edition:
1. Download the Shelfie app for Android or iOS
2. Write your name in **UPPER CASE** above
3. Use the Shelfie app to submit a photo
4. Download your eBook to any device

Canada Council Conseil des arts
for the Arts   du Canada

We acknowledge the support of the Canada Council for the Arts which last year invested $20.1 million in writing and publishing throughout Canada.

ONTARIO ARTS COUNCIL
CONSEIL DES ARTS DE L'ONTARIO
an Ontario government agency
un organisme du gouvernement de l'Ontario

Published with the generous assistance of the Ontario Arts Council.

Printed in Canada

Emma wanted more Icarus.
This book is for her.

The Door in
the Mountain

Second Athenian
Sacrifice

First Athenian
Sacrifice

Third Athenian
Sacrifice

The Flame in
the Maze
Book One

Book Three

Book Two

Book Two

Book Four

Book Five

Book Four

First Athenian
Sacrifice

Second Athenian
Sacrifice

Third Athenian
Sacrifice

THE STORY SO FAR...

Princess Ariadne of Crete has no godmark. Ariadne's mother Pasiphae can make water seep or flow from her skin, and Ariadne's father, Minos, is marked with flame, which spits and leaps from his body and makes his palm warm when he lays it against Ariadne's cheek. Two of her brothers can summon wind. Their friend Icarus is sometimes almost a bird, though he can't fly. And her half-brother Asterion, son of Pasiphae and a Priest of Poseidon—*he* turns into a bull. He is worshipped and praised for this. He is the son of a god.

Ariadne has no godmark—but she'd planned nearly everything.

When Minos's eldest son was murdered in Athens, the king demanded fourteen young Athenians as tribute, to be sent to Crete every two years. It was Ariadne who suggested to the king that the great Daedalus carve a labyrinth beneath the Goddess's mountain, where the Athenians would wander and die, according to the Goddess's desire. It was Ariadne who suggested to the king that Asterion, whom Minos hated as much as she did, be placed inside the labyrinth, too. The people would imagine this a great honour—the divine bull-boy, receiving sacrifice—but that didn't matter. He would be gone forever, soon forgotten. That mattered—and Ariadne planned it well.

But when the second group of Athenians arrived, bull-god Asterion's name was everywhere: on banners and in songs. He was more adored than ever, and Ariadne more overlooked. So, four years after Asterion and the first Athenians had been imprisoned beneath the mountain, she sent a letter to Prince Theseus of Athens. She implored him to disguise himself among the next group of Athenian sacrifices. She promised she would show him how to slay the beast beneath the mountain—and in exchange, he would take her back to Athens with him as his queen. She planned this, too.

What she didn't plan for was her father's mark-madness: the flames that once gave him power began to eat away at his flesh and his mind, and soon he became more monster than king.

And she didn't plan that Chara, palace slave and Asterion's best friend, would switch places with one of the Athenian girls and disappear into the mountain, along with Theseus.

In *The Door in the Mountain*, Ariadne thought she'd planned it all.

Now, as *The Flame in the Maze* begins, her plans are beginning to unravel, like a ball of godmarked string.

PROLOGUE
Late summer
Four years after the first Athenian sacrifice
Three months after the third

The sky above the Goddess's mountain was on fire. Manasses saw it first.

"Papa!" he called from outside the hut. "Come and look!"

Alexios set down the bowl of curds he was holding and stepped out of the lamplight and into the night. His godmark always turned darkness to silver-tinged day, for him—but *this* darkness was different. A sheet of red-orange threaded with silver lightning hung to the south. It rippled slowly and silently, blotting out the stars.

"It's fire," Manasses whispered. He was tipping his head back, and his eyes were wide and nearly unblinking. "Godmarked fire: I can tell, because of the silver in it."

Alexios put his hand on the child's shoulder; Manasses backed up and leaned against him. Below them in the paddock, a sheep bleated and quieted.

Alexios felt him draw a deep breath. "Is that where 'Tiria was running away from?"

After a moment, Alexios said, "I imagine so"— though she hadn't told him much more than she had his son.

"Is it where she went back to, when she left here?"

"Child," Alexios said, too roughly, "enough questions." He remembered how she'd tried to calm him, when he was hard on the boy. How she'd squeeze his hands and make funny faces until he smiled. *I only knew her for two months*, he thought, as he already had so many times before. *How can I love her?*

"I don't know," Alexios said, as gently as he could.

She'd put her slender, scarred arms around him, the night she'd left with the bird-man, and said, "Someone needs me. An Athenian. I have to go to him."

"Come back," Alexios had said, his lips moving against hers with every word. "When you've healed him." His godmark showed her to him with such beautiful, helpless clarity in the dark.

"Tell Manasses goodbye for me," she'd said, and kissed him, and slipped away.

Manasses squirmed around to face him. The lamplight from the hut played over his forehead and cheeks. "I want her to come back, Papa. I want her here."

Silver lightning spread like a spider's web across the flame. *Godmarked fire*, Alexios thought, and fear froze the breath in his chest.

"So do I," he said.

BOOK

ONE

ARIADNE & PHAIDRA

Midsummer
Four years after the first Athenian sacrifice
Two months after the third

CHAPTER ONE

"Princess."

The first thing Ariadne thought, as she struggled awake, was, *Theseus—oh, thank the gods, I hear you; it has been far too long.* But even before she opened her eyes, she knew it wasn't Theseus—for the word had been spoken aloud, not in her head; because he'd been silent for ages, and something was definitely very wrong.

The second thing she thought, as she sat up and her vision wobbled and cleared, was, *Chara. Chara, thank the gods you're back*—but it wasn't Chara, either. Of course it wasn't: Chara had run into the labyrinth months ago, along with Theseus and the Athenian sacrifices.

All Ariadne had heard of her were some garbled words Theseus had sent her at the very beginning: *::Chara is here and says you . . . Chara knows the . . . ::*

No: this would be the other slave, who hardly ever said anything and lurked in corners, staring with her dull, close-set eyes. The other slave, whose name she didn't know.

But it wasn't.

"Ariadne," Queen Pasiphae said. "Get up and follow me."

Ariadne remembered another night when her mother had needed her; just the one, so many years ago, when Ariadne had been six. Pasiphae had been in the Goddess's altar room, naked, straining to birth a baby. Ariadne's half-brother, Asterion, who was half-bull, half-boy. Asterion, marked from the beginning by his god, when none (not gods, not goddesses) had given Ariadne anything.

"Mother," she said now, sitting up, reaching for skirt and jacket, "what is it?" She couldn't help it; her voice shook with eagerness or anger or dread or curiosity—one, all of these.

"Your father," Pasiphae said. *Her* voice was steady and hard. "His mark-madness is worse."

Ariadne stood up. Her vision was entirely clear, thanks to the moonlight that streamed down through the roof of the corridor beyond her chamber. She could see the painting on the wall behind the queen, though the green plant spirals looked black, and the brown fauns and hares were blurry, as if they were moving. She could see her mother's eyes glinting, along with the gold at her ears and throat. She could see her long fingers, curling and uncurling around the flounces below her girdle.

"Why do you care?" Ariadne said, steadily this time. "You haven't cared about him in years. About either of us. It's Phaidra you favour—why is *she* not helping you?"

Queen Pasiphae turned and took a step toward one of the pillars that framed the doorway. She looked over her shoulder at Ariadne. A coil of dark hair slid from its knot and settled on her shoulder like a snake on marble. "The king is a danger to all of us, now more than ever. I am thinking only of my people." She looked away. "He refuses to speak to anyone, including me, of course. And he used to listen to you. Never to Phaidra."

Ariadne smiled and stretched her arms above her head, because her mother was gazing at her again. *You stupid woman*, the princess thought as her heart stuttered and sped. *He promised to make me queen. He broke his promise. He burned me when I protested. How can you possibly imagine that I'd help him? And yet.* She smiled again—a true smile, this time. *There just may be some new thing to find out.*

"Very well," she said, running her fingertips lightly over the scars on her arms. Puckered pink ropes, scored by godfire. "Take me to him."

——— · ———

Minos was standing between the stone horns where Ariadne had stood, years ago, the day he and his army had returned from the war in Athens. He was leaning out into the air above the gate, just as she had. She remembered how he'd looked that other night; the flame-bright lines of him sharpening as he drew closer. The loincloth, hair, beard and skin that hadn't burned, because his mark had protected him, even as it seared holes into the earth.

He was naked now. The loincloth had long since blackened, curled and fallen away. His jaw and cheeks showed in livid red patches through the remnants of his beard. His skull was blistered and smooth, though there were wisps of charred hair just above his ears. His godmark was consuming him because he could no longer contain it—or perhaps because he no longer wanted to.

"Husband!" Pasiphae called. He strained even farther into the wind, which whipped the flames in long, streaming lines behind him. Ariadne saw a knot of people on the steps far below, craning, staring: High Priest Hypatos; another, shorter priest; a man with a bow in one hand and an arrow in the other. "Husband, I have brought someone. Turn around. Come down from there."

He didn't. Ariadne climbed onto a slave's shoulders, and from there to the roof. She stepped up level with the horns and laid her fingertips on one of them. It was as hot as sun-baked sand. She eased her head around the front of it and saw the king's face. She'd imagined he'd be smiling, exulting in mark-madness as she'd seen him do before—but his eyes and mouth were holes, black and gaping and wild with pain.

Father, she thought helplessly, as if she were again the child who loved him. Then she pressed her hand against the pillar, forced the heat to clear her head, and thought, *Good*. "Look at me," she said, over his crackling and the wind.

He turned to her. His hole-eyes didn't blink—no lids, she saw. His raw, oozing lips shaped her name, though he made no sound.

How long has it been since I saw him? she thought. *How much longer can he possibly live?* "Come down," she said. "Please."

He gave a whoop and she stumbled backward. As she steadied herself, she saw the guard below nock the arrow to the bow and raise them both.

"Ariadne!" Minos bellowed. Gouts of flame spewed from his mouth and into what was left of his beard, and Ariadne choked on a waft of burned hair and flesh. He leapt down from the horns' pediment to stand before her; he seized her hands and she gasped, though she wanted to scream—*Not again, not again; no more burns!*

Pasiphae was between them both, suddenly. Her own hands were silver and running with water, and she wrapped them around Minos and Ariadne's. Ariadne felt the godmarked moisture drip and seep and numb; she moaned with relief and then with anger. *Why didn't you do this for me when he hurt me last time? And why did you tend to Asterion's burns whenever he changed from bull back to boy? You hateful, cruel woman.*

"Minos," Pasiphae said in a low, urgent voice. "One of your men is below us with his bow trained on you. Others will join him soon, if you do not come down—all the way down, to the ground. We will talk more there."

He stared at Ariadne with his empty eyes. They were weeping a thick, yellowish fluid, she saw, and she drew her hands away from her parents' so that she could wrap her arms around herself. He stared and stared, until she said, "Yes. We should get down now." The moment the last word was spoken he was past her— two long strides and a leap, and a hissing plume of flame that faded to smoke as Pasiphae and Ariadne gazed at it.

Ariadne fell to her knees and peered over the edge of the roof. She'd never seen anyone jump, or jumped herself; she'd always clung to a pillar with her hands and feet and eased herself down with her dancer's muscles. Minos was beneath her, face-down, his limbs outstretched. "Do not fret, daughter," Pasiphae murmured at Ariadne's shoulder. "He will get up."

Ariadne tried to relax her clutching fingers and thought, *I don't care if he gets up.*

He did, of course. His limbs twitched and snapped, and he raised his head and stared at her. His blistered lips moved. She heard nothing but wind, and her mother's breathing, but she understood.

Ariadne. Come down to me.

She slid down the column, unaware of muscles or effort. She knelt at his head. Tendrils of her father's smoke wove through her fingers. He laughed a spray of sparks.

"Your mother . . . wishes to speak to me of weighty . . . things."

"I do," Pasiphae said, above Ariadne's left shoulder.

Minos wrenched himself up—a molten caterpillar on a leaf, hovering and clinging at the same time. "Speak, Wife. It has been a long time . . . after all."

Ariadne glanced up at her mother. The queen was bending down, her green eyes even greener in the light from his fire. "Minos. Minos King. Even your priests are demanding that you be put out of the palace. Exile on an island, they say, and my priestesses agree. Karpos is begging me to summon the kings of Phaistos or Mallia, to get their advice."

"Karpos?" He was panting. His lower lip was dripping blood slowly onto the ground. "Who is that?"

Ariadne bit her own lip so hard that there were bits of skin between her teeth when she let go. She didn't make a sound, though, which pleased her.

"Daedalus's apprentice," Pasiphae said, her voice suddenly very low. "The young man you have made your heir, thereby humiliating your own two sons, and me."

And your daughter, Ariadne thought. *Your daughter most of all.* Her scars seemed to throb, suddenly: on her arms and hands, her chest and belly. Her hands twitched to touch them but she kept them still.

"Karpos," Minos said, his breath whistling as he

panted. "How odd. What does Daedalus . . . think of this?"

Pasiphae sucked in her own breath and coughed. Ariadne dug her fingernails into her palms. "Daedalus is dead," the queen said at last. "Are you truly so far beyond this world? Do you not remember? He and Icarus and everyone else who worked on the altar within the Great Goddess's mountain—they all died in a pirate attack more than four years ago."

"Did they," he said, in a low, smiling voice. "Did they indeed, Daughter?"

He swung his sightless eyes toward Ariadne, whose head spun with words: *You and I and that horrible Theron are the only ones who know they didn't die, and you know it very well; you'd be* winking *at me now, if you had eyelids—gods, no one else must know! Not my mother; not anyone. It's our secret and I've been keeping it close, waiting to make use of it . . . soon, perhaps, if Theseus's silence continues.*

As she waited for her voice to stir in her soot-thickened throat, he waved a hand. "Never mind, my dear, never . . . mind. And what of you, my water lily, my seahorse, my Queen? What do *you* think . . . should be done with me?"

"I think," said Pasiphae, "that you are a king, not a lizard. I think that you should get up and come with us to your Throne Room, where we will continue this discussion."

Minos sat up, very quickly. Ariadne heard a wet ripping sound, saw gobbets of what had to be flesh glistening on the dusty ground. She tried not to look at his chest and thighs. "I will speak with Ariadne now," he said to Pasiphae, so sharply that he almost sounded like his old self. "And I will speak with her here. Leave us."

Water flowed from Pasiphae's hands—from all her skin, Ariadne knew, because the queen's jacket and skirt had begun to cling to her, and because her curls had gone flat against her neck and back. Her moist lips parted; Ariadne saw the tips of her perfect teeth before her lips closed again. The queen whirled and walked away from them, toward the staircase that would lead her to the royal apartments.

Minos growled a laugh, and it, too, sounded so terribly familiar. *It's just the two of you,* Ariadne thought. *Just like before, when he loved you and promised you the queenship, and you loved him. Only it's not. Remember: he betrayed you, and he is mad, and you* do not love him.

When his laugh had faded into tendrils of silver smoke, Minos said, "They are all right—the people who worry about me. I *am* mark-mad. And my god and father, Lord Zeus, no longer wishes me to live in the world of men."

He wasn't breathing hard, anymore. His words slid out of his cracked, blistered, bleeding mouth and he could have been sitting on his throne, leaning toward Ariadne with his fists on his knees, as he had so many times before. She closed her eyes to quell this image, or to pull it closer; she didn't know which.

"So I am going to give myself to my god."

She opened her eyes. "When?" she whispered, when he said no more.

"In two months, on the festival of his birth."

"Where?" Though she knew, of course.

"The place of his birth, child. The Great Goddess's mountain." This time his laugh trembled a bit, and a tongue of silver-blue flame slithered out between his teeth. "Since Daedalus built his box inside it, the mountain has belonged more to your mother's god than it has to mine—and more to Athenians than Cretans. It is time that the people remembered Zeus. And they will, as they watch me burn myself to ash for him."

He stood up so quickly that Ariadne had to scramble to rise with him. He moaned and doubled over. His flesh seemed to fade and thin, until it looked transparent. Rivers of fire branched and boiled and overflowed; he was Zeus's lightning and Apollo's sun, silver and gold, red and white. She felt the heat of him pulse against her own scarred skin.

"What if there is no need?" she said. "What if the power of your godmark"—*your madness*—"passes? What if you could live quietly, as some others do, when their gods give them rest?"

He straightened and snorted, and fire trickled from his singed nostrils. "Rest? No. Their gods leave them—they remove their blessing, and their marks. A more desolate life I cannot imagine—to be pitied and feared, not for power, but for loss of it. No: my god feeds my strength, and demands my sacrifice. And I will obey."

Good, she thought. *Though I'd rather have seen you pitied.* "And what of the Athenian sacrifices, when you go?" These words rushed out as if she'd planned them. "You speak of fear—but King Aegeus will no longer fear us, then. He will stop sending the youths of his city here—and then the priestesses will demand that Asterion be freed. Who will do that? Where is the key?"

Thick, rank-smelling fluid dribbled from Minos's mouth when he smiled. "Your sister is the only key," he said. "I commanded Master Daedalus not to fashion any other."

"What?" Ariadne forced herself to press her lips together, so that she wouldn't gape. "But that is ridiculous! I—"

"My King?" High Priest Hypatos was standing between the pillars of the gate, the bowman behind him. Ariadne blinked at the priest. His honey-coloured eyes looked like tiny, unlit coals. His beard, wrapped in golden thread, was so slick that Ariadne imagined she could see the olive oil dripping from it to the front of his black tunic. He could summon lightning and earth-cracking thunder, when Zeus wished it. Even when Hypatos wasn't using his godmark, he was storm, lowering and dark.

Minos's bald head spewed flame as he turned. He lowered himself into a crouch as if he meant to spring, but he didn't; he shimmered, still and silent.

"My King," Hypatos said again, stepping forward. "Please. Let us escort you somewhere—a place where you will be able to rest, beyond the prying eyes of your people."

"They fear me." Minos spoke so quietly that even Ariadne, who was so close to him, had to strain to hear him. "You fear me. Perhaps even my wife fears me. None of you will *make* me go; none of you would dare provoke my god or me that way. Isn't that right, Hypatos?"

Minos's light reflected off the priest's eyes and turned them from coal to liquid gold. The two men stared at one another for what seemed like a very long time, until Hypatos blinked and looked down at his feet. "It is," he said. Such short words, but it took them a while to rumble into silence.

"My Lord King," Minos said, as if instructing a child.

Ariadne fell back a pace, dizzy with heat and dread

and even excitement, because this almost always came with dread. Just as Hypatos opened his mouth to say something, though, her head filled with another voice.

::Princess! Listen . . . see what we . . . ::

Suddenly it was not just Theseus's words, throbbing behind her eyes and along her veins: it was images, too. This had never happened before, in all these long months, and he'd never warned her that it would, and she felt herself fall as the pictures came: *a vast cavern ringed with pillars and gaping corridor mouths and no ceiling; a girl—no, a woman who* was *a girl, the last time Ariadne saw her, but who was now changed, except for the wild fall of her red hair; and Chara—Chara, by the gods, her own hair just a dark fuzz; Chara, crouched with her dirty, bleeding hands held before her . . . And something—something enormous and distended, with horns that shone bronze in a strange, rippling light—*

Asterion, some part of Ariadne breathed.

Theseus said, *::We can't keep him a . . . why did you not tell me what you* did *to . . . ::*

*Chara was crying; her freckles looked smudged and blotchy. The red-haired woman was screaming, though Ariadne couldn't hear her: just Theseus, shouting words that crackled and hissed and fell away as the bull-boy—the bull-*man—*who was her half-brother lowered his horns and charged—*

"Daughter? Ariadne? Little Queen?"

She was curled on her side. She heard whimpering and knew it had to be from her, because Theseus's voice was silent and Minos was talking—talking, talking as his godfire lapped at her skin. She didn't open her eyes, which were full of wavering, dying lines that might have been a pillar or a horn.

"Princess? Ariadne? Can you hear me, little love? I heard you—heard you cry out and fall—Ariadne?"

Theseus hasn't killed Asterion, as I commanded him to, she thought dimly. *So I must get into the labyrinth. He promised to take me away with him. I need him. I need to get in—and I need to get* up, *right now.*

She opened her eyes as she pulled herself to her knees. The world tipped and steadied. Sickness bubbled into her throat when she stood, but she swallowed it. Her father gazed up at her with his black, unblinking eyes.

"I am fine," she said loudly, so that Hypatos and the bowman would hear her. "It was just the heat, making me weak. Your godmark, Father—it is a powerful thing. You know this."

No, she thought, *oh, no indeed: I was listening to Theseus. Theseus, son of Aegeus, king of Athens, whom you blame for your own son's murder. Theseus, who will get me off this island. Would you kill me, if you knew? Would you burn me to ash, then yourself?*

"Yes," Minos said, so gently that she felt like his child, again. "I know this. I have hurt you in so many ways, and do not deserve your forgiveness. When I am gone, you will no longer have to endure it. The gods will soon grant all of us peace."

I'll be gone long before then, she thought. "Yes," she said. "I am sure they will." She smiled at him, though he couldn't see it, and she smiled at Hypatos, who did, and then she walked away.

CHAPTER TWO

Phaidra was asleep. Ariadne had known she would be: it was the middle of the night, after all, and Phaidra had always slept so soundly that Deucalion had declared this her true godmark, to everyone's great amusement. Ariadne stared down at her now: long, moon-silvered limbs; hair, both silver and gold, that flowed over the edge of the bed.

"Phaidra. Get up."

The girl murmured and rolled onto her back. *Fine little breasts*, Ariadne thought. *And a fine little belly. I would smother her, if I didn't need her fine little godmark.*

"Sister. *Get up.*" Ariadne tugged on a lock of Phaidra's hair and she sat up, moaning and rubbing at her eyes.

"Ari?" Her voice was muffled and rough, but when her eyes opened they were clear. "What do you want?"

Ariadne walked to the window, which overlooked the road and the ragged hills and the glint of sea beyond them. Phaidra had a better view than Ariadne did, at the summer palace. *Everyone* had a better view than Ariadne did.

"I need you to open a lock for me."

Phaidra stood up. *When did she get so tall? She looks like one of Karpos's statues: made of marble, but breathing and warm. Godsblood, I hate her.*

"You've never come to me before," Phaidra said. "You've never asked me for anything."

Ariadne smiled. She made sure that the moonlight

was falling on her face, so that Phaidra would see it. "Get dressed."

"I'll do nothing for you." Phaidra crossed her arms over her ribs, which made her breasts higher and fuller. "I can't imagine why you think I would."

"Indeed." Ariadne walked slowly back and forth in front of the window, her skirts whispering on the stone floor. On her third circuit she stopped and laid her hand on a pillar, which was cool and polished, painted with ferns and thistles that almost prickled her skin (Daedalus's work, no doubt, or perhaps Karpos's). She turned her face to the moonlit sky. "And what if I told you this lock would lead you to Icarus?"

She had expected a gasp, or a *thump* as Phaidra fell to the floor. Instead there was silence. Ariadne glanced at her sister and saw her standing straight and pale, her gaze steady.

"Icarus." Phaidra's voice was also steady.

"Yes."

"Icarus is dead. He drowned more than four years ago when his ship was attacked by pirates. I was in the Throne Room when the messenger brought the news. Remember, Ari? I was there." At last, a tremble. A tensing of the muscles in her arms.

"I remember." Ariadne crossed her own arms and took three steps toward Phaidra. Their elbows were almost touching. "But oh, Sister: there is so much you do not know."

She watched Phaidra swallow.

"Tell me, Ariadne. It's what you came to do. So do it."

Ariadne turned and walked to the doorway. "No, Phaidra dear. I'd rather show you. Follow me."

After a long, long moment, Phaidra did.

Phaidra didn't seem at all put out by the underground tunnel, which annoyed Ariadne, even as it relieved her. She couldn't have borne a hysterical, snivelling companion—but Phaidra's calm made Ariadne remember her own panic, the first time she'd crawled into this place. The damp earth, the skittering creatures, the sneer of Minos's man Theron, who'd wanted to put his filthy hands on her, and taunted her because he couldn't.

"Faster," Ariadne hissed. The tunnel's walls sucked her voice away, but Phaidra heard her. Even though she said nothing, Ariadne was certain she'd heard her. Her lantern swung, and their shadows twisted together on the earthen walls.

When she finally opened the trapdoor at end of the tunnel, the air was so fresh that Ariadne whimpered. She'd imagined this moment so often, in the years since her father had first brought her here. She'd imagined pulling the lever behind the great storage jars and striding the length of the tunnel and thrusting open the trapdoor that would lead to the pasture, the cliff, the ledge—but these were fantasies, only. She hadn't needed to do it—not until now, when Theseus's voice was silent again and Icarus and his father were the only people who could show her the way, once the door in the mountain was open.

"Careful," Ariadne said over her shoulder as she pulled herself up and onto the grass of the pasture—but Phaidra was already there, bending and straightening as if she'd been scrambling up out of tunnels all her life. They stood facing each other. A sea wind lifted their hair—the dark and the golden.

"Take me to him, then," Phaidra said, in a voice that was child's and woman's, both.

"Stupid girl," Ariadne said. "*Impatient* girl. I would make you wait—"

"If you did not need me so much. Yes. So take me to him."

Ariadne wrenched herself around and walked toward the place where cliff met sky. Phaidra's footsteps scuffed along behind her. *She's not a dancer like I am*, Ariadne thought. *Daedalus never made her a dancing ground in front of the palace at Knossos. She may be young and lithe and lovely, but she walks like an old man.*

Ariadne's hands and feet found the cliff steps as if it hadn't been years since the last time. She gazed up at Phaidra's pale, open-mouthed face, said, "Come on, then. He's down here."

The ledge was still sickeningly narrow. The sea still roared below it, hungry and dark. Phaidra's eyes darted from her feet to the empty space that yawned just past them, and Ariadne smiled. *Not as confident here as you were in that tunnel. Good.* She pulled Phaidra down to crouch by the small, round, rusted door. "Here," she said loudly, over the pounding of the waves. "Open it."

The girl leaned forward on the balls of her feet. She laid her hands on either side of the lock. She was shaking from fingertips to forearms.

"Do not make me wait." Ariadne pushed her words through gritted teeth. A trembling had begun in her own belly, though it had nothing to do with a fear of falling. "Phaidra. Do not."

Phaidra turned to look at her with a calm that she couldn't, mustn't be feeling. "I know how to get here now," she said, her words measured and slow. "After I let you in, will you kill me?"

Ariadne's laugh trembled, but it didn't matter; the wind snatched it away. "Godsblood, Phaidra: of course not!"

"And what if I tell someone?"

"Even if it was not him you told," Ariadne said, with exaggerated care, so that she wouldn't shriek the words instead, "our father would find out. It was he who put them here—yes, *them*," she went on as Phaidra's eyes widened. "Daedalus, too. And the king shared this secret only with me. He wanted no one else to find out. He's mark-mad, little sister—utterly without reason. He would likely kill them, if you told, and perhaps you, too."

"I could come back alone. I could set them free." Phaidra was thrusting her pointy little chin toward Ariadne as she had when she was a child, clinging as ever to their mother's skirts.

Ariadne laughed again, more loudly this time. "Ah, Phai; so silly! The king sends a man to them every month with food. Their disappearance would be discovered—and where would they have gone, by then? Where would they go that the great, mad Minos could not find them?" She put her hands on Phaidra's shoulders and clenched her fingers to keep them from shaking. "You will not speak of this. You will not come back. But by the gods, you *will* open this lock—and if you do not hurry, I will knock you senseless, when you are done, and leave you here, and only *I* will see him."

The wind gusted; water crashed and foamed below them. *My mother's god*, Ariadne thought. *Lord Poseidon, ramming his childish fists against the cliff because I don't revere him.*

Phaidra turned back to the door. Her hands hovered

for another endless moment, and then they touched the rust-thickened lock. Silver godlight blossomed from her palms and fingers and spread like spider's web across the metal. Even though wind and waves filled her ears, Ariadne heard the *click* as the lock opened. She lunged forward and pushed and fell into the passage she remembered, with its smell of wet earth and stale air. Her lantern dragged on the ground; when she lifted it, she saw an insect rippling up toward the ceiling, its transparent body joined to too many legs. She looked past it and saw the opening that would lead to him.

"I did this for you," Phaidra said from behind her. "Now take me to him."

It took no longer than a breath or two. The passage opened into a roofless cavern that flickered with light: one of Daedalus's old shell inventions, sitting on the stony floor, bathing the cavern in pink, then blue, then green, then gold. The stench of sweat and excrement made Ariadne recoil and press a hand to her nose and mouth. Phaidra straightened up behind her, apparently unaffected. "Icarus?" she called, into the gold-tinged darkness. "Icarus: it's Phaidra. Where are you?"

A shadow stirred, at the edge of the light. It was hunched and tall, spiky with feather ends and a beak— no: something between a beak and a nose. Ariadne hadn't seen him in four years, but he was so familiar: he had just dropped down from the roof above her bed chamber; he was rocking back and forth between the stone horns above the courtyard at Knossos, and there was a honeyed oatcake in her hand for him, which she didn't want to deliver.

"Phaidra." He didn't sound the same. His voice

had always been pinched and thin, but now it was splintered, too. Broken.

He dragged himself into the guttering light. Phaidra took two paces and held out her hands to him and he stumbled, shambled, took them and leaned into her as if she alone could hold him up. He bent and touched his forehead to hers. "Phai," he murmured, "gods, how you've changed," and Ariadne just had time to think, *When did he ever notice her? It was always me he watched,* when he spun and cried, "Ariadne! Show yourself!"

Phaidra pulled her hands free and backed away from him. Ariadne stepped forward. "Here I am," she said. Her voice remembered him—remembered how to be sweet and smooth and deep. *You've missed him, gods help you; you've missed this—*

Icarus shouted. It wasn't a word, but it echoed, and Ariadne understood it. She took three more paces and stood before him, bathed in the light that was green, now—as green as new olive leaves, or the stone at the centre of her dancing ground.

"Icarus," she said. "I am sorry it has taken me this long to return to you."

His thin, misshapen lips parted and curled. "Ah, Princess. Imagine how sorry *I* have been, not to have seen you all this time! For when last you were here, you took my ball of string—oh, and you broke my father's hands with a hammer, and watched as *your* father cut his tongue out—oh, and then you watched my mother throw herself into the sea."

Yes, Ariadne thought, as Phaidra gave a wordless cry, *and all of that sickened me*—but then she thought, *I was sharing a secret with my father, and I revelled in it. As I do now.*

"I have longed to visit you, and why not—for how

well you speak! The palaces have not been the same since you left them."

She was going to say more, but she heard a sound: a long, slow dragging. Breathing that was raspy and moist. She didn't want to look, but did—and Daedalus drew himself up from the floor, hairy and ragged. For a moment she remembered how tall he'd been, and how he'd smiled at her the day he finished making her dancing ground, and how his hair had been close-cropped black, threaded with white.

He sprang at her with his mutilated hands extended.

Icarus threw himself between his father and Ariadne. She caught a glimpse of Daedalus's fingers, which *weren't* fingers—tiny spears, maybe, or tree branches tipped with claws longer and sharper than Icarus's. "No, Father," Icarus panted. "You leave her to me." He clutched Daedalus's strange, warped hands and turned to her. "Princess. Why are you here?"

Phaidra had retreated and was standing by a rock. Ariadne noted this, even as she straightened and slid her gaze to Icarus. She noted, too, that Daedalus was sinking to the ground. "My old friend," she said, "I need you."

Icarus laughed and said nothing.

"Yes. I need you—for my father is mad, and intends to give himself to godmarked fire at the door in the mountain. The door *you* made, Master Daedalus"— she glanced at the man curled like a sleeping child on the earth—"and I cannot bear the thought that the place will be destroyed, because there may be people living within: Athenian sacrifices, and my brother, of course." She drew a deep breath. "Only you and your father can show me how to find them, once my sister has opened the door. Only you can lead me to them *quickly*, so that they may be saved."

No laughter, this time: just silence. Water dripped somewhere, regular as heartbeat.

"You cannot bear the thought," Icarus said at last. He drew a shuddering breath. "You, Princess Ariadne . . ." He made a muffled noise and spun in place, feathers rustling and whining in the wind that was hardly a wind. One of his feet sent the lamp scudding into the rock where Phaidra was; the light went from pink to blue to gold to green in a breath, then died entirely. Ariadne held up her own lamp, whose glow seemed very dim.

"You wish to save them," Icarus gasped as he stopped spinning. He pointed his taloned fingers at her and waggled them. *He's gone mad*, she thought. *I suppose I shouldn't be surprised.* "The Athenians whose entry into the mountain was so dull to you that you watched the sky instead. And your brother! The boy you set on fire when he was, what? Two years old? Yes, Chara told me—and she told me much else, besides. About how much you hated him. And now you cannot bear the thought that he might die?"

Phaidra had sunk into a crouch. Her hands were clasped; her eyes darted between Icarus and Ariadne and Daedalus. *I should've knocked her senseless after all*, Ariadne thought. *She shouldn't be hearing these things, seeing . . .*

"I am glad you mentioned Chara," Ariadne said, making her voice catch a little. "Because she, too, is in the labyrinth. Yes," she went on, as his mouth-beak fell open, "she is. She disguised herself as an Athenian, and I noticed her too late—as she was leaping through the doorway. Two months ago, Icarus. And in barely two more the mountain will be on fire."

He went to Phaidra and hunkered down in front of her. "Phai," he said quietly. "Is it true? Is Chara inside too?"

Phaidra nodded. "Though I didn't," she began, and cleared her throat, "I didn't know about Father's plan." They gazed at each other, as unblinking as Minos, until Ariadne said, "So, Icarus?"

He glanced over his shoulder at her. "Your mother will put the fire out."

"She will try. But this will be like no other fire. Her power may be no match for his." She put her lamp on the ground and walked around Daedalus. She set her hand on Icarus's hair, which was smooth, not matted with filth, as she'd expected it to be.

"It should not matter why I want in," she said. "You should not care." She drew her fingertips down through his hair and felt him shiver. "Four years ago you would have longed to do my bidding."

She knelt behind him and wove her arms around his chest. His shoulder blades were sharp against her breasts, and the tips of some of his feathers were sharp too, but she didn't flinch. She pressed her skin against his and breathed slowly, grateful that for some reason he didn't stink too terribly; grateful that his own breath shuddered and rasped. *He still wants me— of course he does, probably more than ever, because he's seen no one but his poor, ruined father, all these years.*

He stood, drawing Ariadne up with him, and turned in the circle of her arms so that he was facing her. "And what will you give me, if I help you?" She did flinch a bit, this time; his twisted lips were very close and she smelled the old, stale air that seeped between them.

She slipped out of his arms and took two paces back. Undid the clasp of her jacket and pulled it open, and watched his eyes travel from her face to her breasts, and stay there. It didn't matter that they were lumpy with old burns—nor that her arms and hands were. She saw him drink her in as if he were dying of thirst.

Phaidra rose and ran for the mouth of the corridor, but Ariadne hardly noticed her, nor Daedalus, who stirred and moaned. She lifted her hands and ran her middle fingers around her nipples, and as they hardened she began to untie the girdle at her waist. *Think only of Theseus. Think only of Icarus leading you to him. Think only of Athens, where you will be queen.*

"No."

She barely made out the word, because just then the outer door screeched open and clanged shut.

"No," he said again, in a voice that she was sure meant *yes*. His tiny round eyes were still on her breasts, so she cupped them and stepped toward him. Her thumbs made languid circles on her own skin.

"Yes, Icarus. You will have me here, now—perhaps again at the mountain, under the open sky? Put your hands on me and—"

He walked to where she stood and stopped with his thin, feather-splotched chest almost touching her. "No," he whispered, and smiled, and walked away from her.

He knelt beside Daedalus. She whirled to look down on them both. There was a pressure in her belly, rising, squeezing her breath away—but her voice rang out anyway. "So your hatred of me is stronger than your desire to help your friends."

Icarus shrugged a bony shoulder. "The gods will see to their fates. And yes."

Daedalus's dark eyes watched Ariadne fumble with the clasp of her jacket. "Then your father will help me," she said, "because I'll make sure neither of you gets any food; I'll starve you, and he'll beg to show me the labyrinth—you will both—"

"Starve us?" Icarus said. "In the two months before the king gives himself to the mountain?"

The pressure was inside her head, throbbing, turning her vision flat and white. When it cleared a little she saw Daedalus, straining up from his knees. "Ih-oh," he said, with his tongueless mouth, and she knew with a horrible, vivid certainty that the word was "Minnow"—that name he'd called her, in his workshop without a roof, and in the sunlit corridors of Knossos, when she was a child and he was the master with hands of godmarked silver. "Ih-oh"—beseeching, sad, not quite hopeless.

Ariadne picked up her lamp and went to the corridor. She moved with a care that she knew looked exaggerated, but it was better than running. She crawled to the door and seized its handle. For a long, cold moment she thought that Phaidra had locked her in, but then the door swung open with a scream that made her grind her teeth. She crawled more quickly, because the wind was so fresh, and Icarus might be behind her, reaching out his talons to push past her into the night.

Ariadne stood up on the ledge, as shakily as a child learning to walk. When she turned back to pull the door closed, Phaidra was in front of it, her arms spread wide.

"He didn't want you, did he?" Phaidra's fingers twitched. Golden hair blew against her cheeks and across her lips.

"Oh, he wanted me."

Phaidra continued, as if Ariadne hadn't spoken. "And he wouldn't help you, just as I won't."

"Close the door," Ariadne snapped. "Do it now, before one of them attacks us and gets free." Phaidra narrowed her eyes and half-smiled. Ariadne had never seen this expression on her sister's face before: quiet and calculating; older.

"Close it or by all the gods and goddesses I *will* hurt you."

Phaidra's arms dropped to her sides. She bent over and pulled hard on the handle. "Good," Ariadne said. "Now lock it—quickly."

The silver from Phaidra's hands lit the ledge and the cliffside and the air above the sea. It flowed from skin to metal and stone, and Ariadne drew closer so that it fell on her, too. It blazed so suddenly that she was blinded. She heard the metal within the lock *click*, and her eyes cleared.

The godlight had already dimmed. Wisps of it flickered along Phaidra's fingers and pooled in her palm, then snuffed out. The girl rose and went to the cliff steps.

"Phaidra! Wait!"—but Phaidra didn't.

Ariadne tucked her skirts up into her girdle and followed her, very slowly; the lantern left her with only one hand, and the moments when it was only her feet that held her to the cliff left her breathless and dizzy. By the time she reached the top, her sister was already far away, and Ariadne had to run to catch up.

"Wait, I said!" She put out a hand and grasped at Phaidra's arm. Phaidra halted but didn't turn. "Remember," Ariadne continued, trying to sound as if she hadn't had to rush, "if you tell, if you return to him, he will only end up suffering. Swear to me you will not do these things."

At last Phaidra looked at her. She was still wearing that half-smile; still a woman, not a child, considering something clever and secret. She said nothing—just shook Ariadne's hand away and slipped off again, like godlight fading in the grass.

CHAPTER THREE

Ariadne heard Karpos before she saw him: the ringing of his chisel on marble; the tap-tap of his hammer—and, somehow, the silver of his godmark, twining through the other sounds. *A statue*, she thought as she walked toward the doorway of his workshop. *A big one; I can hear it in the way he strikes the stone.*

This workshop was much smaller than the ones Master Daedalus had left Karpos at Knossos; he'd had to push workbenches and stools and strange metal machines aside to make room for the block of marble. He was kneeling at its base, resting his forehead against it. His bare back was to her; it was streaked with sweat-darkened dust, and his brown loincloth had turned white with it. One of his hands was resting on the chisel he had laid on the ground. Hand and chisel glowed with silver, as did the three toes that he had already drawn from the marble.

"Princess," he said, without moving.

Ariadne's pulse quickened, though she'd told herself sternly that it wouldn't. *See how well he knows you?* she thought. *The gods wish us to be together; now they must tell* him *so.*

"Who will this be?" she asked, as carelessly as she could.

He turned his head so that she could see half of his face. His eyes were closed; perhaps he was still seeing the vision his god had shown him, of the figure within the stone. "Your father the King."

She was glad he couldn't see her startled blink. "But he forbade any images of himself to be made—forbade it as soon as his mark began to scar him!"

Karpos shrugged. He opened his eyes but didn't look at her. "He wishes one final likeness to be made." He paused. "He has demanded that it be a true likeness."

At last he looked at her, and she gazed back at him, and between them was an image of Minos as he was: eyeless, blistered, bleeding, a patchwork of crimson and black.

"He means to give himself to Zeus." She hadn't intended to speak so quietly, but the words came too swiftly for her stop them. "At the Goddess's mountain."

"Yes," Karpos said. "I know. What I do *not* know is why you're here now."

She smoothed away a scowl. "For your help."

He stood and stretched his arms up over his head. His right hand brushed the marble once, twice, trailing silver. "You must have exhausted all other possibilities, to be coming to me."

You have no idea, she thought. She said, "And why would you think that?"

"Because you wanted me to marry you and I said no. Because you do not allow '*nos*,' unless they come from you. So. What do you imagine I might do for you?"

"You need to convince him not to do this thing. Tell him that he must wait, to see if his godmark cools or dies."

"And why do you imagine he would listen to me?"

"Because he made you his heir. Because you crafted a statue of his beloved son Androgeus, and he has just asked you to craft another of himself. He respects you. Perhaps only you, now."

"Princess. Do you truly think I have not already tried to speak to him?"

"Try again."

"Why would I do this for you?"

"Because it is in the interests of the people you will rule. They are in danger now; imagine what will happen when his godmark consumes him! Imagine the injuries, the deaths—the riots that will happen when the priestesses' followers realize that their precious bull-boy god has been killed!"

Karpos smiled. "How delightfully surprising it is, Princess, that you have decided to be a loving sister to Asterion!"

"You insult me."

"I distrust you." No smile now; just a line of lips, pressed tight.

She closed the space between them in four paces. She put both her hands on his chest and dug her fingers into his skin. "You wanted me, once," she hissed. "I know you remember. 'I'll carve your likeness at the summer palace, Princess! I will, I will!'"

He placed his hands over hers and held them there. His palms were cool and rough with dust. She wanted to keep touching them until they warmed—only no, she didn't: all she wanted was Theseus and Athens and anger.

"I was more taken with my godmark than I was with you," he said. "And I was so young—anything beautiful was a thing to be pursued. I am wiser now."

Her hands twitched with the desire to claw at his calm, lovely eyes, but his own hands kept them still. Before she could command herself to move, she heard a whistling, coming from the hallway. Closer, closer—the rising and falling music of wind blowing over the mouths of empty shells.

The sound stopped. "Karpos!" a voice called, and Karpos stepped away from Ariadne.

She turned toward the doorway to look where he was looking—at her older brother Deucalion, who was gaping at her.

"Ari!" he finally said. "I didn't expect . . . well."

Karpos smiled at Deucalion, who smiled back at him. Ariadne felt her stomach twist, then flushed so deeply and quickly that sweat broke out on her palms and on her neck, beneath her hair.

"Ah," she said after she'd swallowed carefully, to ensure that her voice wouldn't crack. "I see, Karpos. I see. If you could, you would make my *brother* queen. How terribly sweet. How happy I am for you both."

"Ari," Deucalion began, but she was past him before he could say more. The wind of his godmark tugged at her heels as she walked away.

———— · ————

The moon was waning when Phaidra returned to the prison. She'd wanted to go back the very day Ariadne had taken her there; she had, in fact, made her way as far as the underground storage jar chamber and put her hand on the latch before thinking, *No—not yet— she'll expect this. She* won't *expect you to be patient.*

As Phaidra was walking back up the stairs toward the courtyard, Ariadne's slave found her. "My Lady Phaidra? My mistress is looking for you."

Of course she is, Phaidra thought, with grim, amused relief. She followed the slave to Ariadne's chambers.

"You wanted me?" Phaidra said, widening her eyes to questioning innocence.

Ariadne narrowed her own. "Yes," she said slowly. "I wanted you . . . to talk to our mother about the king. She has always preferred you to me. Talk to her. See if he has spoken to her about his intention to give himself to his godmark."

Phaidra smiled at her. "Very well," she said, and left the chamber before her sister could think of more to say.

Phaidra *had* spoken to Pasiphae about Minos, simply to keep busy. Her mother, it turned out, did know about the king's plan, for Hypatos had overheard him telling Ariadne about it. The queen had said, "The gods will decide his fate, as they do all of ours," and turned her face away.

"But Mother," Phaidra said, "what if the mountain explodes in fire? Asterion is—"

"Asterion is beyond us." Pasiphae's eyes were back on Phaidra; they were dark, their green nearly vanished. She lifted her hands from where they'd been pressed, in her lap, and Phaidra saw that they'd left wet, silver prints. Her mother's godmark, belying her words? Phaidra didn't—couldn't—care. She was already up and walking; measuring out her steps, because soon they'd have to lead her back to Icarus. And, two weeks later, they did.

It was day, this time. Phaidra couldn't find Ariadne—not even in the baths, where Ariadne had told her slave she'd be. And when, on impulse, Phaidra asked a kitchen slave about the princess, the slave told her that Ariadne had been seen leaving the palace, on foot and alone. Phaidra said, "Surely not! My sister would never do such a thing!" But the slave bowed and insisted. *Very well*, Phaidra thought, *it must be now*, and she walked down into the cool shadows of the storeroom, before she could be afraid.

She thought of Icarus as she tripped the latch and crawled into the tunnel beyond the jars. She'd tried very hard *not* to think of him, these past two weeks, because it made her want to cry, or run straight to him without caring about discovery. Now, though, stumbling beneath the ground with a lamp clutched in her hand, she remembered it all: how he'd looked years ago, crouched on Knossos's roof. His skin had glinted with half-grown feathers, but she knew that they'd vanish once he swung back down to the earth on the length of metal string that Daedalus had made him. He'd known she was watching, and gazed back at her with his bright, round eyes. He'd smiled at her: Princess Phaidra, six years old, holding onto Pasiphae's skirts because that was the only way she could feel safe from Ariadne. Sometimes he'd taken the western road away from Knossos with Asterion and Glaucus and the slave-girl Chara. Phaidra had watched then, too, burning with jealousy but afraid to leave the walls. She'd squinted at the strange, lovely shine of Icarus's feathery hair and Asterion's horns until they were all out of sight.

I've finally let go of Mother's skirts and got down from the wall. She felt a little sick as she thought this, but her pace didn't falter.

She left the lamp on the ground beneath the trapdoor that led to the pasture: the day was bright, and she would need both her hands for the cliff stairs. She should have brought a length of rope, she realized. Icarus would be able to climb, but Daedalus, with his broken hands, would not. *Stupid girl!* she thought. *You've had two weeks, yet you couldn't come up with a decent plan—just that you'd lead Icarus to the ruined temple near the town and bring him food and watch him turn his face to the open sky. I'll come right back,* she decided as she slid her feet onto the top step. *I'll get Icarus settled and return for Master Daedalus tonight, when Ariadne's asleep.*

Last time the moonlight had made the sea look blurred and far away; now she stood frozen on the ledge, staring down at water that seemed far closer and hungrier. She shifted her eyes from the base of the cliff to the island that lay just off the shore, and this made her feel steadier. It was green and red, scattered with tall, scraggly trees. Birds wheeled around the treetops: gulls, smaller ones that might have been swallows, and, abruptly and noisily, an eagle, beating its way up out of a nest to scatter the others.

Phaidra swallowed and hunkered down carefully before the door. Her hands shook, even as silver blossomed in the threads of her palm and flowed to the ends of her fingers. *Thank you, Apollo,* she thought, as she always did when her godmark filled her with its cool ache. *Thank you for helping me bring your light into closed places.*

Except that this time, the silver sputtered and died as she touched the lock. *No. How can this be?*

The door was already open.

She pushed it, flinching at its rusty shriek even though she knew it would come, and crawled into the corridor. She hardly glanced at all the details that had been so vague during the night: the sprays of stones on the ground; the roots braided into the damp earth of the walls; tiny white lizards, fleeing daylight. She was panting by the time she reached the cave.

"Icarus! Daedalus!" She scrambled to her feet. The air in here was dim; she opened her eyes wide, trying to find them. "Icarus?" The rock threw her voice back to her again and again.

There was another passageway on the far side of the cave. It was much narrower and lower, but she thrust her way along it, scraping her shoulders and palms, which she used to feel before her in the darkness. Water dripped and dripped. She whimpered and this sound, too, echoed, though only within her head.

Time passed; hours, maybe. The passageway ended. She leaned her forehead against the stone, which was cool and slick (that dripping, on and on), then squeezed herself around and stumbled back the way she'd come.

The cave seemed very bright, after the tunnel. She sat down heavily on the boulder in its centre and watched droplets falling from a stalactite. They were forming a conical mass underneath, she noted dully. A terraced lump that glowed faintly green.

"Icarus?" she called once more, hopelessly, to the emptiness.

CHAPTER FOUR

Ariadne couldn't stop thinking about the mountain, in the two weeks that followed her visit with Phaidra to the cave. She waited for more of Theseus's mind-images, or for his mind-voice, at least—but there was nothing. No voice except her own, in her head, chattering and frenzied: *I can't just wait; he's not coming out; Icarus and Phaidra won't help me; I'll have to go to the mountain myself.*

This last thought was so alarmingly simple that she stopped her pacing of the hall above the courtyard. She laid her palms on scarlet columns and gazed down at her father, who was still there, below, naked and flaming, his eyeless face turned up to the sky. His people came and went around him, raising their hands to ward off the heat and the smell.

Yes. I'll go to the mountain myself—when the priestesses deliver food. Maybe I'll be able to figure out how to get inside; maybe I won't need Phaidra, after all. I'll bring string to mark my path once I'm in, at least until I find Theseus, and Icarus's godmarked string. It will take much longer than if Icarus had led me, but so be it.

When one of Poseidon's acolytes told her that the next food delivery was a mere three days away, Ariadne thought, *Yes. The gods are making the way clear for me.*

"I will join the priestesses at the mountain," she said.

The girl bowed her head. "It is not a thing that we share . . . that is, there is no need, Princess."

"I will join the priestesses at the mountain," Ariadne said briskly. "My mother need not be told, nor Karpos. I simply wish to observe how Poseidon's daughters are attending to his son."

The acolyte's head was still bowed. Her pointed chin was pressing against the hollow of her throat. "Very well, my Lady," she whispered.

Three days later, Ariadne informed her dull-eyed slave that she'd be in the baths all day. "Wash the walls while I am gone," she said, and the slave nodded slowly.

The road to the Goddess's mountain was wide and hot and nearly empty. She saw two shepherds and a child, who was attempting to drive a flock of geese with a long stick and a dog with tangled black and white fur and a hoarse bark. Mostly, though, Ariadne was alone. Her heart hammered with this solitude, and sweat pooled in the small of her back.

I'm not afraid, she thought—though she was, a little. The slopes that fell and climbed and fell, the glint of sea, the shimmer of heat that blurred everything ahead and forced her to squint—these things made her long for the crowded courtyard and faces turned up to her.

She'd never been to the mountain by herself. It looked different, as she approached it at last: it seemed to grow more slowly on the horizon than it had during the processions, and to be much larger, when she was finally beneath it. The broad path up to the door was eerily empty, and the place where children danced in their bull masks was springy with grass and flowers that didn't *fit*, somehow. Even the sky was strange:

larger and lower, layered with fog. *Keep walking*, she told herself. And, when her legs did not obey, *Stupid Princess—why so meek, when all of this belongs to you? Imagine everyone is watching.* She forced herself up the path, but the bright, empty silence still weighed on her.

Master Daedalus's doors were the same: the towering one and the waist-high one set in it. She crouched with her hands against the metal of the smaller door. Her palms warmed, as they used to when she laid them on her father's arm. Long ago, when his fire was all beneath his skin.

Hurry, she thought as the mountain quiet settled around her. *Hurry, you priestesses of the Goddess: your bull-man is hungry. And my Athenian king-to-be is hungry, too, though you don't know it.*

The sun was starting to slant toward afternoon when she finally heard voices and the creaking of wood. A few moments later, an enormous bird's head rose above the line of the road. Ariadne scrambled to her feet, breathless, sweating again. She hadn't ever needed to think about how the priestesses delivered food into the mountain. It occurred to her only now to wonder why she hadn't thought about it anyway— only now, with the wooden bird looming, lurching toward her. It was much taller than the top of the great metal door. Its head, neck and wings were painted red, its body green, its long, straight beak yellow. She saw gears turning within it. Wheels rolled beneath its splayed, taloned feet. Six priestesses held onto cables strung from its wings; the cables were taut, but Ariadne didn't think the women were pulling on them. It was as if the giant bird was pulling *them*.

By the time the priestesses reached her, Ariadne had

schooled her expression to its customary smoothness. "Sisters," she said, as the bird creaked to a towering, tilting halt. "I have come to observe, at my mother the Queen's command. To ensure that her beloved son is receiving all the sustenance he should."

One of the priestesses held up her hands in the sign of the Bull. "We will be glad to have you here with us." Her brow was shining with sweat. She licked her lips; Ariadne thought they must taste like salt, as hers did. "Follow us, Princess. But take care: the way is very steep."

"Of course it is," Ariadne snapped—and yet moments after she'd started off after the bird, up the rocky slope, she was gasping with effort. She'd watched Chara climb this slope, after Asterion had disappeared into the mountain. The king's flame had been burning up rocks and grass; the queen's rain had been coursing down, but not heavily enough to quell the fire. And Ariadne had glimpsed Chara, when the water and smoke parted for a moment—scrabbling like a beetle up a stem, though Ariadne couldn't imagine why.

She was looking for another way in, the princess thought now, as she paused with her hands on her knees. Her breath burned in her throat, and it was nearly all she could hear when she resumed climbing. Even the grinding creak of the bird-thing faded to a murmur. But after a time she began to hear another sound: a high, whistling song. She straightened and stared.

Black pipes jutted in a ring from the rock just below the mountain's jagged peak. Glass? Polished, smooth—even the openings. The singing, she realized, was wind, blowing across these openings. She glanced at the priestesses, who were standing with their heads lifted to the wind, eyes closed. They'd positioned the bird-thing so that its beak was pointed down, nearly touching the highest of the pipes. She noticed suddenly that its wings were shifting gently: rows of scarlet feathers with graceful golden tips. *Icarus*, she thought, and felt a strange, sudden pang that she immediately twisted into scorn.

"Receive our gift," one of the priestesses cried, opening her eyes and lifting her arms as the others did the same. "Great Mother, receive this food; bestow it upon the Bull's child; bestow it as you will."

One of the women pulled a lever that lay along the bird's leg. Cables moved, beneath the wooden pieces. New noises began: a swishing, a whirring. Mere moments later, the bird's beak swung open and something thumped and rattled down into the pipe.

"Salt fish," said a priestess from beside her.

"That is Master Daedalus's work, I presume," Ariadne said. Her words were clipped, but the priestess kept smiling. The ones by the bird were singing a song without words, which sounded like waves on shore.

"Yes. Minos King demanded a conveyance worthy of the Goddess, and Prince Asterion. We are honoured; this mighty creature was the Master's final work before his death."

Priestesses hauled on cables. The bird swivelled; its beak lined up with another pipe. A different lever screeched.

"Figs," the priestess beside Ariadne said serenely, as they began to tumble from beak to pipe.

Concentrate, Ariadne told herself. *Think only of how you might use that thing to get inside.*

"So," she said, trying to sound indifferent, "why do you not leave it here all the time?"

The priestess turned almond-shaped brown eyes on Ariadne. "It is part of the honour we do the Goddess. Part of our obeisance. We must struggle to do her bidding, every second month: that is just. It is required."

"And do you ever think what it might be like to climb it yourself? To see the mountain from above?"

The priestess was beaming, now. "I *did* climb it, four years ago, just after Master Daedalus presented it to us—the wood was still a little bit silver, from his godmark. He urged us to. It was remarkable. Looking down on the mountainside—I could see forever. To the sea! Chrysanthe said she thought she saw a dark line that was Athens, but I think she was just imagining it."

Ariadne raised her brows. "Indeed! And what of those black glass pipes? What did you see in them?"

"Oh," said the priestess, in a quieter voice, "nothing except darkness. Daedalus told us to take care; he said that if we tipped and fell inside one, we'd break all our bones when we stopped falling. He told us the pipes are smoother than any metal we know, and slipperier than oil. And he said that this was good, because otherwise people might try to get in and disturb the sanctuary."

"Indeed," Ariadne said again. She spun so quickly that her skirts lifted and tangled briefly between her shins.

"Princess? You will not wait for the end of the song, at least?"

"No," Ariadne said, over her shoulder. "I have seen enough. I will tell my mother that the Goddess's work is being done well."

As she slid down the slope she thought once more of Chara climbing it. She imagined Chara craning up at the black pipes that would never lead her in, or out. Imagined the way her tears would have looked, clinging to her splotchy freckles.

Even if you could have got in, Ariadne thought, *how did you think you'd get* out? And then, so abruptly that she tripped over her own feet, she remembered holding Icarus's ball of string out to Theseus in his cell; she remembered Chara's still, quiet presence behind them. *Clever thing,* she thought, flushing as if she were admitting aloud how foolish she'd been. *Clever slave. And yet Theseus has gone silent, and no one's come out. I'll think of a way, though. I will—and I'll be in Athens before the month is out.*

She stood still for a bit, her arms outstretched to keep her steady in the wind that had risen. Her stomach growled and twisted, and she swallowed hard. The stones and tufts of dried-up grass looked huge; the sky looked huge. *I couldn't dance here,* she thought. *Everything's too big; I'd fall.* She pushed herself down the mountainside before the fear could hold her still.

———·———

The chattering in Ariadne's head wouldn't stop. *Phaidra's your only chance; you'll have to involve her after all, and hope you'll be able to get away with Theseus before she can make trouble. Go find her,* now—*and don't forget to bring your own ball of string.* She'd only just returned from the mountain, but she nearly ran from her chambers. Her steps faltered when she saw people clustered by Phaidra's doorway.

"Daughter," Pasiphae said. "I was about to call for you. It seems the High Priestess wishes to speak to me of the king. I imagined you, too, would wish to hear what she has to say."

Karpos was beside the queen; Deucalion was a few paces away, leaning on a column overlooking the courtyard. Ariadne knew what he was seeing: their father, lit by the fire coursing over and through him. Their eyeless, bald, blackening father, who yesterday had shouted, to everyone and no one, his words as rough as coal, "My Father Zeus shall send me a sign! He has told me this! I shall not leave this place until then." She saw that Deucalion's lips were pursed and threaded with silver; he was making a wind, to carry the flames away from the courtyard and into the sky.

"I see," Ariadne said. She glanced between her mother and Karpos, at the entrance to Phaidra's rooms, then forced her gaze back.

"Speak, then," Pasiphae said to the High Priestess, who inclined her head and smiled a thin, unhappy smile.

"It is difficult, my Queen, Master Karpos: it is difficult for me to say this—and yet Lord Poseidon no longer permits me to be silent. King Minos, and his intention to sacrifice himself at the Goddess's mountain . . . my Lady: he must not do this."

Pasiphae's plucked brows arched. "Oh? But it is the king's god who drives him to do it."

"Zeus has removed his grace from Minos and replaced it with madness. Zeus no longer cares for him; you know this. Perhaps the madness will fade in time, and his mark will leave him forever, as others' do—but it comes down to men, now, to stop him. Men, and women."

Karpos went to stand beside Deucalion. He put his hand on Deucalion's shoulder; Deucalion covered it with his own. They both looked down on the king.

"We will not be able to stop him," Karpos said. "We will not even be able to get near him."

Pasiphae said, "And surely, my Sister, you are not suggesting that someone dispatch him with an arrow or a spear?"

The priestess shook her head, and her black hair rippled. "Of course not. But if we cannot stop him, we can save Asterion the Bull, at least. The Princess Phaidra could open the door in the mountain—soon; now, even. The king will not know."

"And then what?" Ariadne said. Everyone turned to her, and she stood taller, gazed at them one by one. Her pulse hammered in her head. "Master Daedalus and all the men who made the labyrinth are dead. Who would go in and find my brother?"

I would, I will—just let me get to Phaidra's rooms first. "And do not tell me that your god would lead you through the maze. Surely it is plain to you that Lord Poseidon cares nothing for his own spawn."

They stared at her. She thought she saw Karpos frown, before he looked back down into the courtyard.

"*Princess,*" the High Priestess snapped, "how dare you speak thus of—"

"I shall deal with my daughter."

Her voice is actually trembling, Ariadne thought— and then, in a surge of strength that swept away her fear, *But it doesn't matter: I'll be leaving here soon; she won't be able to punish me for long.* "Leave us, now," the queen continued, waving her hand at the priestess. "I shall consider what you have said. I shall—"

Just then the world lifted.

It's like being on a ship, Ariadne thought as the stones beneath her rippled and rose. After the ripple there was a sickening, lurching fall. She was on her knees; Pasiphae was standing, her arms flailing wildly; the priestess was on her back; Deucalion and Karpos were clinging to pillars, which were swaying back and forth like masts. *A ship in a gale*—and the wind *was* screaming, tearing at hair and clothing, and at the breath that Ariadne wanted to be a scream of her own. Great slabs of stone shifted, atop the columns; they teetered and plunged down into the courtyard, where other people had begun to shout. Minos's fire billowed up and out, surging through the tipping columns.

Ariadne tried to cry out again as flames licked over her old scars. She crawled. *Phaidra, Phaidra—must get her* now; *must get out before the palace crushes all of us*—

She scrabbled to her feet, once she was past her mother. Two long, unsteady strides brought her to Phaidra's doorway; two more carried her inside.

"Phaidra!" she shrieked, above the din of wind and stone. "*Phaidra!*" No answer. No one. Just crumpling painted walls—green sprays of fern and purple thistles, cracking apart and raining down on the ragged floor.

She turned and stumbled back out to the corridor— and as she did, the wind died and the ground steadied. Stone continued to fall, in the stillness: blocks and shards of it, thudding or pattering like hard rain. Screams turned to sobbing and moaning and shouted names that sounded like questions.

Ariadne stepped over a gaping rent in the floor. The High Priestess hadn't moved—she was on her back, her arms flung wide—but now a slab of stone hid her from the waist down. Her mouth was working soundlessly, trickling blood. Deucalion was bleeding too, from a gash on his forehead; he was wiping at his eyes with a crimson hand while Karpos held both his shoulders. Pasiphae was standing tall and straight. Only her earrings were moving—swinging in arcs that grew smaller as Ariadne watched; glinting in the quiet sunlight.

"People of the Father!"

If Ariadne hadn't known better, she'd have thought that Minos was himself again. His voice was deep and smooth, which made her think, dizzily, of the polished black pipes in the Goddess's mountain.

"People of the Father, come here to me!"

Pasiphae and Karpos glanced at each other, then picked their way over the rubble to what remained of the steps.

Ariadne followed them. *Maybe Phaidra's down there too; we'll leave while everything's still in chaos.* She stood on a slanted step near the bottom and scanned the crowd that was gathering around the courtyard's edges, away from the king's fire, which sprang from his reaching arms in pulses like breathing.

"It is Zeus!" he cried, as Pasiphae went to stand as close to him as she could. "He has called to me, as he promised he would. This was his sign, and his punishment; I have waited too long. I cannot wait until the festival; I must give myself to him *now*."

"But Husband, you—"

"Make the procession ready immediately."

The king walked past Pasiphae, leaving black, smoking lines in the fallen stone and churned earth. She raised dripping hands but didn't touch him; the black lines smudged and ran. When he had gone out under the remnants of the gate, she called, "Hypatos!

Come!" and the High Priest stumbled after her.

"Sister." Ariadne sucked in her breath when Glaucus spoke, from right behind her. She glanced at her brother over her shoulder. He was digging the end of his painted stick under a piece of stone: the tip of one of the horns had that lined the palace's top storey. *Stupid stick*, Ariadne thought. *I hope it snaps.* But it didn't, and Glaucus kept chipping at the dirt under the stone, his eyes darting and wide. Blood was dribbling down his nose from a cut on his forehead, but he didn't wipe it away.

"You'll come, won't you?" he went on. "To the mountain?"

She coughed dust and smoke from her throat. *Oh, I'll go. I'll be there long before you are.* "Yes. Why wouldn't I?"

He scowled. "I just . . . you know. Our father hurt you. I wasn't sure you'd want to see this."

"Oh, but I do." She smiled. Someone was calling to her in a soft, sad voice, from somewhere close: "Princess—help me . . . help . . ." Ariadne didn't look around. She held up her own arms so that the cloth fell away from them; she gazed at the scars that still seemed to be bubbling, alive on her skin. *How I'd love to watch you burn, Father. But I have a prince to rescue.*

When she lowered her arms, she saw Phaidra crawling up from the shattered staircase that led to the storerooms.

CHAPTER FIVE

Phaidra had only just ducked out of the tunnel behind the great jar when the earth began to shake. She stood up and took a single pace. The jar shattered behind her, then another, and another; shards pelted her, cutting the backs of her legs and her neck as she fell; grain pelted her too, hard and stinging as hail. She lay on her side with her arms over her head, watching the floor ripple away from her in a long, straight line, like a snake preparing to strike. People were screaming, somewhere above her.

First the empty cave, she thought. *Now this. What are you planning, gods and goddesses of Crete?*

As she huddled away from the heaving, cracking earth and the gouts of steam, she tried to remember leaving the cave. She couldn't. She *did* remember saying Icarus's name over and over, in her head or maybe aloud, probably as she followed the tunnel back to the palace. She didn't remember the tunnel, either. *I'll likely remember* this, she thought, and a strange laugh rose and died in her throat.

After the ground quieted, she sat up. Pain tore up her back and arms and neck; when she reached behind her to pat at these places, her hands came away slick with blood. Her breath hissed through her gritted teeth. She eased herself onto her uninjured hands and crawled carefully over tumbled stones. Dust hung in the air, and sunlight shone through the dust in places that had been closed, before. Holes everywhere, above and beneath her. Patches of sky, and cracks so deep she imagined she'd fall out the bottom of the world, if she slipped.

By the time she'd crawled to the top of the steps to the courtyard, the pain was a dull throb. She paused, her gaze skittering across the wreckage: churned earth and slabs of stone; her father's burning body; other people, crying, groaning, gabbling, or still.

Then Minos's voice silenced everything. Phaidra didn't watch him as he spoke; she watched the queen, who stood near him, holding out her godmarked skin to his. *Mother*, Phaidra thought, when Minos finished talking and limped away, out beneath the western gate (one great scarlet pillar fallen; the frieze above shattered and partly gone). *Mother—why do you still love him?*

"Phaidra!"

Gods and goddesses of Crete, Phaidra thought as her body sagged, too late, toward the ground. *Please don't let this happen.*

Ariadne's shadow fell across her. "You're bleeding."

"Yes," Phaidra said. She struggled to stand and managed not to moan. "I noticed."

Her sister's eyes narrowed in that way that used to turn Phaidra's insides to water. "Why were you down there?" she said, gesturing to the remnants of the steps. "No, wait: I know. You went to see *him*, though you swore to me you wouldn't."

"Ariadne," Phaidra began, cursing her fear, groping for words, "I was only—"

"Never mind," Ariadne snapped. "I have no desire to think of him, or his crippled father, ever again. You and I have to go, now. To the Goddess's mountain."

Phaidra gaped at her sister, blood and pain forgotten. "Why now? Why not wait and go with everyone else in Father's procession?"

"Because we're going to get that door open by ourselves. We're going to rescue our brother before *Father* can destroy everything."

Phaidra felt her rebellious insides tighten. "You're a liar, Ariadne. You have no desire to save Asterion. What's really going on?" Her shoulders hunched, her body reacting to words she hadn't even known she was thinking. She waited for a slap, or a sharp tug on her hair, or fingernails raking more bloody lines into her flesh—but Ariadne just frowned at her as if she weren't really seeing her.

"Does it matter?" Ariadne said. Her voice was as far away as her gaze. "We're going to help. Icarus and Daedalus didn't care at all. We do."

An almost unbearably vivid certainty gripped Phaidra: *They do care, even if Icarus said they didn't. Maybe he and Daedalus escaped somehow, right after Ariadne told them about Asterion and Chara. Maybe they've gone to the Goddess's mountain. And now I will go there, too.*

"Very well," she said steadily. "How do you intend to get Asterion out, once I let you in?"

"This." Ariadne's eyes were keen again, as she drew an enormous ball of string from beneath her girdle. When the cloth fell back over it, stone dust puffed and scattered. "We'll attach it to the entrance and let it out as we go. It's not godmarked, as Theseus's is, but it may be long enough, and lead us back again."

Someone screamed from across the courtyard. Silver-gold light bloomed a moment later; a godmarked, healing light, perhaps, or a numbing one, at least. The pain of Phaidra's own wounds returned, throbbing from the surface of her skin deep into everything that lay underneath.

"Was it ever the gods' will, to build the mountain temple?" She could barely hear herself. Ariadne's chuckle, though, seemed loud.

"Not for you to know, Sister. Now, let's go."

The statue of Androgeus had fallen face-down onto the dancing ground. One of his arms was bent at a terrible angle; if this hadn't been Karpos's work, the marble would have shattered."No," Ariadne whispered. She was staring at the dancing ground: its uprooted, broken stones, jumbled among the clods of earth in a meaningless pattern. Her eyes shone.

Tears? Phaidra thought incredulously—though what she said was, "Hurry! Before he sees us, or Mother comes out." She tugged at Ariadne's skirt and her sister started, as if she were waking. She dragged a hand over her eyes.

"Yes," she said, her gaze once more sliding past Phaidra, to some invisible place inside her own head. "Hurry."

———— · ————

They didn't speak, on their way to the Goddess's mountain. Ariadne walked ahead, kicking up puffs of dust that stung Phaidra's eyes and nose. The morning sun slanted to afternoon. The sea turned from smooth, polished gold to angry grey as a wind blew up, gathering clouds. Ariadne stopped once or twice, hands on hips, cursing under her breath.

She thinks she should be in a palanquin, thought

Phaidra. *She thinks slaves should be sweating so that she wouldn't have to.*

When they came to the place where the path branched away from the road, Phaidra saw that the path had become churned earth—rocks and dirt loosened by the quake. Ariadne picked her way onto its grassy edge. Phaidra lengthened her stride until she passed her sister. It was the same as it had been the other two times, even though there were no musicians or dancers now, no banners snapping or Athenian slaves shuffling along in their masks and robes. The mountain door called to her, as it always had. She felt her blood stirring to silver, as she got closer: her god urging her to go to the lock and wish it open, as she had the one on Ariadne's puzzle box, so long ago. The one Daedalus had made for her. Icarus had been beside Phaidra that day, gangly and young, the layers of his strange hair dimming and brightening in the light that had streamed into the palace after the storm. Asterion had been there, too. And Chara, dressed in unaccustomed finery so that she could be given as a birthday gift to Ariadne. They'd watched as Phaidra's godmark had flowed through her fingers for the first time. There had been a tiny metal bull at the centre of the puzzle box. Phaidra had opened it; she'd seen it first.

She was nearly running as she crested the rise that she knew would bring her within sight of the great lock.

Icarus was standing in front of the doors. Icarus: the lines of his body blurred and sharpened by feathers. She stumbled to a halt and saw that there was someone with him. The someone had short, dark hair and was wearing a woman's skirt and jacket. Phaidra looked at her, at him, at the big door and the small one and the lock that lurked above everything. The edges of both doors were warped, and strips of metal had been sheared into coils that hung down— but the lock was intact.

"Godsblood," Ariadne whispered from right behind her.

Phaidra walked. She felt her sister drawing up beside her; she saw her at the edges of her vision, smudged by the shadows that were more dusk, now, than storm. They arrived at the door together, both of them skirting the saw-toothed rocks that had been stripped from the mountainside by the quake.

"You," Ariadne said. If she'd lifted her hand she could have clawed at Icarus's downy cheek. He wasn't looking at her, though: he was gazing at Phaidra. His eyes were so bright that she wanted to close her own—but she didn't. She looked back at him, as the lock sang of silver and promise.

Ariadne rounded on Phaidra, her eyes alight with rage. "And *you*! You let them out after all!"

Icarus stepped forward with a hissing of feathers. "She didn't. We got out ourselves. We planned it for years." He squawked a laugh and tipped his head up at the mountain's peak. The smoke was white against the darkening blue of the sky. "We thought we'd fly together to the island, then away."

"And you still may," the girl said. Phaidra's chest ached when she saw the girl's gentle gaze on his face, and her soft hand on his shoulder. Scars crisscrossed this hand, and her arm. Her other hand, Phaidra noticed, was swollen and lumpy, its knuckles a raw, bloodied pink.

"And who are *you*?" Ariadne snapped.

The girl's large eyes rose to Ariadne's. "Sotiria."

The princess frowned. "I remember . . ." She sucked in her breath. "You're an *Athenian*—Chara and I visited your cell the night before the third procession! Your hair was long and tangled then." She laughed almost as Icarus had. "She switched places with you. She went to you to plan it, even as I went to him."

"To him?" Icarus repeated. The second word cracked. Phaidra thought, *Ah—so he's not in love with this Sotiria girl; it's still Ariadne he wants. You should have known. Do* not *be a weakling about it.* She squeezed her eyes shut.

Ariadne reached up and touched the edge of the lock. "And why did you come here, bird-*man*?"

His lips and shoulder twitched. "The earth moved. I thought . . . I hoped the lock would have broken. I hoped the door would be hanging open; that we'd be able to go inside and find them."

"And it isn't," Ariadne said, waving her free hand. "It isn't hanging open. So we need to *get* it open, and see whether Zeus's earth-shaking has made a way for us, inside."

"Why so desperate, Princess?" Icarus said.

And Phaidra said, as steadily as she could, "Yes— why, Sister? I'm not sure you really answered, when I first asked you this."

"How *dare* you?" Ariadne said. Her hand clenched on the lock. "How dare you ask me to explain myself? You—"

"Stop." Sotiria spoke quietly, but they all turned to her. She was looking back down the path, and they followed her gaze. The sky behind them was throbbing with orange.

"The procession," Ariadne said. "The king. Already?" She gripped Phaidra's wrist and dragged it up to the lock. "Open it *now*."

Phaidra glanced at Icarus, who smiled at her with his twisted, purple lips. She smiled back, then stood up on her toes and placed her palms and fingertips on the lock. The silver flowed immediately. It coursed over the metal and into the air around it; it shimmered when the lock sprang open. The low door opened too, with a muffled *clang*.

"Yes!" Ariadne tugged on it until it swung wide. She knelt, her hands out, seeking air, and the others crouched behind her.

There was no air. No opening. The doorway was blocked by three slabs of stone that might have been placed deliberately, so neatly did they fit together. No space atop or around them; no spaces between—just seams to show they were separate pieces.

"No," Icarus said. He put a hand on Phaidra's back and pressed. She could feel it shaking. Its stubby feathers prickled her, reminded her that she was covered in cuts. She didn't move.

Ariadne lunged forward with a shriek. She pounded her fists against the stone, growling and panting.

"Stop," Sotiria said again—loudly, this time. She hunched over, curling her fingers (even the broken-looking ones) into her palms, flinching every time Ariadne's hands hit the stone. *She looks like she's in pain*, Phaidra thought. *Ariadne's pain?*

Ariadne kept hammering at the blocks. "I need him!" she cried, and the stone darkened with her spit. "Gods*blood*—let me in! *I need him!*"

Who? Phaidra wanted to ask—but instead she turned and took Icarus's hand in both her own.

"We have to go," he said.

Phaidra nodded. "Where?"

"There are lava tubes near the top—pipes. I tried to reach them once, with Chara, and it didn't work—but the earthquake may have loosened things, up there. It has to have *somewhere*." He glanced back down at the orange stain in the sky. "Yes. We go up. And we leave your sister here—because if I have to have anything more to do with her, I'll probably kill her."

He was still shaking—all of him—and despite the mountain and the fire that was coming, Phaidra wanted to laugh. *He doesn't love her,* she thought; *he hates her.*

Sotiria was smiling at her—a lovely, sad, knowing smile.

"Let's go, then," Phaidra said.

BOOK

TWO

POLYMNIA

First Athenian Sacrifice

TWO

CHAPTER SIX

Polymnia remembered, as she fell. She didn't want to, but she remembered, in images so quick that she could barely see them, and so bright that she saw nothing else behind her squeezed-shut eyes.

The voyage from Athens: the storm that tossed the ship around on the first night; the Cretans lined up along the cliff, all of them cheering their triumph and our death; the boat their priestesses used to take us from our ship to the shore, its prow a living, snorting sea monster's head on a scaly neck; the tiny flowers growing beside the cliff path I tried to throw myself off; Princess Ariadne making cow eyes at Kosmas; the procession to the Goddess's mountain only yesterday: dust in my mouth, and the brown leather mask that stank of death and home; the girl Chara, who spoke to me; no clouds, when they opened the mountain's door and pushed us in; that prince of theirs, shouting, on fire, turning into a bull; blue sky in the doorway as I fell, wind and screaming in my ears—

She landed. She had no breath; then she did, and she wheezed, arching her back, twisting and bucking like a fish on a line. Her fingers clutched at something that felt like springy moss; her nails chipped on the stone beneath.

The screams trailed off slowly. She heard someone sobbing, someone else gibbering about a broken ankle. She heard water dripping, and metal whining against metal.

She whimpered and opened her eyes.

A wall rose above her. It was studded with small golden lights that didn't flicker, and lines of carving: blue waves and purple tentacles and tall, scarlet, winding flame. The wall rose into the darkness high above, where the mountain door must be.

Move! she told herself. *There are still some more up there!*—but before she could summon the strength to roll over again, one of them fell. Theodosia. She fell silently, her body spread wide and still; Zenais, who came after her, shrieked and flailed. They landed together, their limbs tangled, cracking, popping. Polymnia raised herself up on her elbow, still whimpering, not sure if she were steeling herself to crawl the short distance to the other girls, or preparing to throw herself over the lip of the ledge she now realized they were all lying on. It didn't matter— because just then, there was a screeching of metal so shrill that she cried out. The portion of the ledge where Theodosia and Zenais lay shuddered. The wall began to move—except that it wasn't the stone itself: it was cables, strung taut among all the carvings. Three rows of them, shining like bronze as they slunk downward. A portion of the ledge detached from the rest and plunged. Polymnia scrambled to her hands and knees and leaned over; she saw the girls' faces—pale, open-mouthed, plummeting away from her and into a bank of thick, firelit steam.

She wanted to scream, but her throat was too tight and dry. Her muscles and bones, though, had turned to water; she flopped back onto the ledge, panting. Her eyes leapt again to the wall. The three cables continued to move; somewhere very deep, gears kept grinding. The cables strung by *her* piece of ledge were motionless. *Good*, she thought, *good, good yes—stay here; stay quiet*—but then another figure came hurtling down toward her. This one didn't scream; it roared. Its misshapen limbs trailed fire, and the horns on its great furred head shone so brightly that she almost had to look away. But she didn't—she didn't move at all. *Too late. This is how my god has decided that I'll end.*

She hadn't been truly afraid of the bull-boy when they'd been outside the mountain's door, because she'd been halfway inside already, and she was sure he'd stay behind, under the sky. But now he was here, a writhing, bellowing mess of blistered flesh and spreading fur, and his huge, round eyes were on her, and she could hardly breathe. *Sing*, she thought. *Quickly. Your godmarked voice will calm him as it's calmed so many other beasts; maybe this* won't *be the end.*

"Asterion." She'd heard the Cretan queen call out this name; Polymnia remembered this, and was surprised that she remembered, even as she sang it. "Asterion, be still, be safe, be calm."

Usually, after these many words, the slaughterhouse beasts would be sagging to the ground, their gazes fixed and far away. This one shook his head and roared again, and her voice faltered. Silver puffed from her lips and vanished. *His godmark's too strong; so much stronger than mine.*

"Back!" someone shouted, and she watched the beast's eyes and body swivel toward the sound. She turned too, and saw Kosmas clinging to one of the cables, well up the wall. Blue-eyed, unmarked Kosmas, whom the Cretan princess had fed with her own fingers. Now he let himself slowly down—because he hadn't fallen as the rest had. Somehow he hadn't fallen.

"Get away from her!" he yelled, in his deep, ringing voice—and the creature backed up a step. It snorted, and a gout of bloody mucus sprayed Polymnia's face and robe. She retched at the feel of it, and its iron stench. She would have whirled and run, if there'd been anywhere to go—but as she stood in place, throbbing with fear and the shame of her failure, Kosmas cried out more words, and the beast's fur smoothed back into flesh, and its hooves into fingers. Asterion dropped to his knees, panting, just as Kosmas landed on the ledge.

"I'm . . ." Asterion said, thickly, as if his tongue were reshaping itself, too. "I'm sorry." He raised his head slowly—the horns hadn't changed—and gazed at her and at Kosmas. The bubbling had subsided, but the skin on Asterion's arms and chest was livid. She didn't want to look, but couldn't help it: she saw how the fresh marks were laid over older ones. Wounds over scars. Pity tugged at her, beneath the shame and fear.

She turned to Kosmas as Asterion's breathing slowed. "Thank you," she whispered. Kosmas shrugged. His blue eyes looked even clearer and lighter, in the glow of the lamps that lined the wall. Blood was dripping from his palms; when he saw her gazing at it, he closed his hands and grimaced.

"Anything for a lady," he said, and she had sudden, choking desire to laugh. *That princess was a lady,* she thought of saying. *That Ariadne who fed you honeycomb. But even when I was in the merchant's big house, I've only ever been nothing.*

"Princeling," he said to Asterion. "I'd push you off this ledge right now, except that I need to know: why did your own people do this to you?"

Asterion eased himself down until he was sitting with his raw legs straight. He shook his golden-haired head; his horns made faint silver arcs in the air. "I don't know." His words were ragged, and leapt from low to high.

He's just a boy, Polymnia thought. *That's what he is, really.*

"So you didn't expect this."

Asterion sniffled and rubbed the back of his hand under his nose. "They told me . . . the priestesses. They told me I'd be taken to see the first Athenian sacrifices. Maybe they didn't know, either. Maybe it was just the king who knew I was to be a hunter. Though if the king knew, so did Ariadne." He sniffled more violently than he had the first time, though this time Polymnia thought the noise might be laughter. "Godsblood— what am I saying? It was probably her idea in the first place."

"A hunter," Kosmas said, his voice gone very quiet. Somewhere close, gears bit; the cables directly above them moved and the ledge shuddered down. Asterion scrabbled at it with his fingers, and Kosmas and Polymnia sat so they wouldn't fall—but after a moment that couldn't have been longer than a few breaths, the movement stopped.

"As I was saying," Kosmas continued, between clenched teeth, "a hunter?"

Asterion tilted his pale, gaunt face up to look at Kosmas. "It's what my father said, up there. I'm here to hunt you down—the ones who survived this part, anyway. I'm here to kill you for the Goddess."

Polymnia thought, *And now he changes back into the bull and gores us with those horns, and it doesn't even*

matter, because we're just going to die falling, otherwise.
Only he didn't change. He sat and stared, his scarred palms turned up on the stone.

Kosmas crouched. "So," he said, his face not far from Asterion's, "I suppose I should push you over, after all."

"You should," Asterion said. "Or I should jump." He licked his lips, and Polymnia saw that the lower one was oozing blood. "Except that I don't want to die. And I don't want anyone else to, either."

Kosmas glanced at her. "What do you think, my Lady? Should we be merciful?"

She couldn't speak, and didn't know what she'd have said, if she could. All her bones were juddering; everything beneath them was slipping. Shock, some part of her knew.

"Very well," Kosmas said, as if she'd replied. "We all live. For now, anyway."

Asterion smiled a strange, sad smile. "We'll probably all regret this."

"Probably," Kosmas said. "Now let's see if we can't let ourselves off of here." He turned and wrapped his hands around one of the cables that ran up from the ledge. Polymnia's vision was suddenly awash in red and speckled with black dots that leapt and wriggled; Kosmas's body warped into an impossible shape. She squeezed her eyes shut and listened to the uneven hammering of her heart for one long moment, then another.

"It won't work," Asterion said. "Daedalus built this place."

She opened her eyes. The red haze was gone. Kosmas was clutching the cable, one foot braced on the ledge, the other on the wall. He grunted and hauled himself up. Beneath them, metal whined. The cable moved and he let go of it with a grunt. He pulled himself up on it again, and this time when it moved, so did the ledge; it juddered upward and then it dipped, ending up farther down than it had been before. Polymnia cried out.

"Even if you *could* get up there," Asterion said, "what would you do? Wait for two years until the next sacrifice, then run out as they're coming in? And what then?"

Kosmas nodded. "You're right. That's not the way out."

"There won't *be* a way out."

How can they be this calm?—but as soon as she thought this, Polymnia saw that Kosmas's hands were wrapped so tightly around the cable that she could see the bones in them, and that Asterion's eyes were rolling as they had when he was the bull.

"At least," Asterion said, "there'll be food. Somewhere. They didn't put me in here to die. The priestesses wouldn't let that happen."

"Good," Kosmas said. "We look for it. At least we know how to get *down*, now. I'll take this cable; you take that one. We'll pull on them at the same time and let go—let's see if it moves up and then down again."

"I can't," Asterion said, holding up his hands. His fingers were still fused into a shape between hand and hoof.

Polymnia said, so softly she could hardly hear herself, "I will."

"You?" Kosmas eyed her appraisingly, a little frown between his brows.

"Yes," she said, more loudly now that she knew what to tell him. "I spent years in a slaughterhouse, butchering and hauling. I'll be able to do this." *I spent years after that in a big house, singing for rich people, eating well and sleeping on a soft bed*: this, she didn't say.

"All right, then," he said. "With me, then. Ready and *pull*."

The cable cut into her palms but she pulled on it, biting her lip to stop herself from whimpering. The grinding gears sounded very far away because her blood was roaring. "Now let go!" she heard Kosmas call. She did, and the ledge dropped. She squeezed her eyes shut as hot air gusted against her skin. Sweat snaked down from her forehead; she felt it on her eyelids and nose and cheeks—everywhere on her head, front and back, because she had no hair to soak it up. None of them did, except Asterion. "Pull . . . let go!" Kosmas called. "Again! Again!" And, finally, "Stop!"

As soon as Polymnia unclenched her hands, they began to burn.

The platform that had carried Zenais and Theodosia down was now level with theirs. Kosmas leapt to it. He landed with a grunt and dropped to his knees between the girls.

"She's dead," Zenais said. Her teeth were chattering so hard that it took a moment for the words to make sense to Polymnia. "Dead. I heard her neck snap." Zenais was sitting with her legs extended. The right one was bent strangely at the bottom, and covered in blood; when Polymnia stared at it, she saw that the skin above her ankle was jutting, as if the bones beneath had shifted.

"Put your arms around my neck," Kosmas said. "Quickly, now. Good. Hold on."

Zenais's skull was streaked with scarlet. Her lips

were smudged with it. She lifted her eyes to Polymnia's; they were all white and black. Kosmas crouched, his arms wrapped tightly around Zenais. Her shattered leg stuck out in a way that reminded Polymnia of the slaughterhouse, and the animals who'd fallen, broken their bones, screamed and bellowed until she sang them to silver sleep.

"Ready?" Kosmas didn't wait for an answer. He leapt and landed on the other platform. Zenais screamed as she fell from his arms and sprawled in front of Polymnia. Blood spattered. *Just like home*, Polymnia thought again. When Zenais lifted her head and saw Asterion she went very still.

"Polymnia." Kosmas's voice was both deep and sharp. "Pull again, when I say so."

She did, because he spoke with a voice that wasn't her father's; because he spoke with strength, not impatience or anger. She wound her torn-up palms around the metal and tugged, when he told her to. Their stone platform dipped again. It thrust its way down into the heat-bent, light-speckled darkness; when it finally hit something solid, its cables screamed. It shuddered and stilled.

Polymnia turned to Asterion. Wreaths of smoke hid his face, but his horns swept back and forth, making clear trails that filled in as she blinked. "I can't," she thought she heard him whisper, and then he stumbled off the ledge. She followed, sucking in her breath as her bare feet touched the ground. It was hot stone, a straight path carved with tiny spirals. The path was painted bright blue; she could see this, in the light of the lamps that lined it, flickering moonlit-silver through the smoke. The tiny spirals were gold. She coughed; the air here felt thick and smelled of fire.

Kosmas set Zenais gently upright and she leaned heavily on a painted urn. It was waist-high, covered in designs of looping green seaweed and bronze-scaled fish. There were others, set along the path at regular intervals, each with different patterns: octopus, jellyfish, swirling lines that made Polymnia dizzy.

Zenais clutched the urn's lip, her back hunched. She was staring at Asterion, who was staring at the ground. One of his feet had pale, digging toes; the other, a circle of hoof, yellow-hard and fringed with dark brown fur.

"What's your name?" she said, only a little shakily. *How is she so bold?* Polymnia thought, with a surge of envy and shame that made her feel, briefly, as if everything were just as usual.

He blinked at Zenais. "Asterion," he said. "Son of Queen Pasiphae."

"So you're a prince." Her eyes were wide but she didn't sound afraid.

"Not anymore," he said, and started blindly off along the corridor. They straggled after him, Zenais leaning on Kosmas, but they'd only gone a few paces when a scream stopped them all. A human scream, this time, not a metal one—though Polymnia couldn't tell if it were a male or female voice. It was shrill and far away, at first; a moment later, it sounded much closer.

"What?" she heard someone say, in the quiet after the scream. Again the voice was close—right beside her ear—but none of them had spoken. "Arkadios: where are you? Stay; say something else so I can find you." A whimper, which wound like an eel through the air between Polymnia and Zenais, and away.

A wolf howled.

"That's Ligeia," Zenais whispered, and Polymnia

thought, *Gods forgive me—why her?*

"Who *is* that?" Ligeia called, from wherever she was. The words were rough, as they always were after she used her godmarked howl. "Is that Zenais?"

"Yes," Zenais whispered. "What's going on?"

Asterion's gaze skimmed up and back down, past all of them, into the steam-wreathed corridor. "I've been in caves before. They twist sounds. There's no way to know where anyone is unless they're right in front of you. Two other people are here somewhere—but we might never find them."

"I'm coming!" the invisible Arkadios cried. "I'll keep talking so that you—" The voice didn't fade, this time: it stopped.

"Arkadios?" Kosmas shouted. "Ligeia?"

Silence, until Kosmas said, "Let's go."

"Wait." Asterion sounded stricken. He was staring at the wall, which Polymnia saw was painted red and covered in gold writing. She and the others gathered behind him.

Daedalus, Master Craftsman of Athens and Crete, begs forgiveness of you who walk this path. His blood was strong; the will of Minos King was stronger.

Kosmas blew his breath out. "He could have done something secret, if he felt so badly. Put in a back door; made one hallway and closed off the ends off all the others, so we could escape. The king would never have known, and Master Daedalus would have had his freedom anyway."

Asterion shook his head. "Didn't you see that boy who showed everyone what the labyrinth looked like? I know that's what he did; I was still shut away in the litter, but I heard what Minos said, and I heard everyone gasp and shout. I'm sure the king had people like that boy spying on Daedalus. People who'd show the king what was being built. And if anything looked wrong, he could still deny him his freedom, or hurt his wife and son—something like that. Maybe." He paused. "Minos is cruel and clever. He could scare anyone, even Daedalus." Another pause. "Or maybe Daedalus just didn't care enough. But he felt guilty anyway, and left this message." He stared off into the distance. "I don't know. It doesn't matter."

——— · ———

Hours later, they found Ligeia—or she found them. This time there was no screaming or howling; she simply walked into the chamber where the blue-painted path had ended. They were sitting with their backs against the pillars that ringed the circular chamber. Smooth obsidian pillars with no open space between them: just bands of crystal-layered stone. No way out except the way they'd come.

"Well," Ligeia said as all of them except Zenais scrambled to rise. "This is it, then." Her eyes glinted in the coppery light of five spherical lamps that hung from the ceiling, which was almost low enough to touch. "This is everyone. Polymnia the Meek, Kosmas the Handsome, Zenais the—"

Her gaze fell on Asterion as he edged into her sight. She cried out and lifted her hand, which was wrapped around a large, pointed obsidian flake.

"Don't be afraid," Kosmas said, as the muscles in Asterion's shoulders twitched. "He's fine. He won't hurt you."

"He's a monster," Ligeia hissed. "He changed when the king touched him with flame. He's a creature warped by his own god." The obsidian shard shook in her hand. Asterion raised his face to look at her. His cheeks were scored with pink, rising burns. "I was marked by the gods to mimic the *voice* of a beast, but this—he—is a monster."

Zenais heaved herself away from her column with a grunt. Polymnia remembered a sheep that had tried and tried to walk, on its broken leg; it had bleated and stumbled and gazed at her with wild, helpless eyes before she'd sung it to sleep. Zenais's eyes were steely in the pulsing light; Polymnia thought, *I could sing to her; she'd be happier for a time.*

"'Geia," Zenais said between her teeth. "He has a name." She nodded encouragingly at Asterion, who clenched his hands and stared at his feet (the hoof had turned back, sometime, as they walked).

"I'm . . ." His voice cracked, and Ligeia let out a sharp laugh. "I'm Asterion."

"Huh," Ligeia said. "A monster with a name. How very odd."

Fall now, Polymnia commanded the ground. *Fall, right beneath her; carry her into the flaming depths and let her breathe only smoke and fire, and make her suffer as even* innocent *beasts are made to suffer.*

"I'm sorry." He spoke steadily now. "I didn't know what would be done to you. To us. I didn't . . . I have to get away from here. From you." He lurched back toward the corridor.

"No," Zenais called, "don't—wait—come back," and he slowed, stopped, turned.

"She's right," he said, his head dipping and swaying as if it were still as heavy as the bull's. "I'm a monster, here. The heat; the hunger—they won't let me be anything else. So I have to leave. Otherwise I might hurt you."

Polymnia wanted to go to him and say, quietly but firmly, "No. Don't be silly. You must stay with us." But she couldn't. She stood, unmoving, while Zenais dragged herself to him, her arm reaching even as her broken leg trailed.

"No," Zenais said. "You don't want to harm us; I can tell. We'll need each other."

He turned to her. "Maybe," he said. "I suppose I could stay for a bit, anyway—see if I get worse," then, all in a rush, "Thank you; I don't really want to be alone. . . ."

"Lovely," scoffed Ligeia. "But don't expect me to let go of *this*." She brandished the obsidian again, and its many facets winked. "Now, let's see what else this charming place has to offer."

"Nothing," Kosmas said. "There's no way out of here except by that corridor."

Ligeia snorted. "You think so? Have you heard nothing of the skills of the Great Master Daedalus, Athens' most dearly missed exile?" She ran her hand up each column in turn. She squinted at the walls between them, patting and poking. "Ha!" she said at last, and pressed her fingers against a knob of crystal. Metal ground together and a hinged stone door opened in the floor directly beneath her with a *crack*. Ligeia shrieked as she vanished. Her obsidian blade remained behind, glittering on the ground.

"Come on!" she called up after a moment. "It's smooth—you'll slide. There's another chamber here—another tunnel." Her words and footsteps faded.

Zenais winced as she sat down at the edge of the

trapdoor. "I'll go first," Asterion said. "I'll catch you." Envy stirred in Polymnia's belly again as he sat, slid, disappeared and, finally, cried, "Ready!" Zenais bit down on her lip and disappeared after him.

Kosmas was tapping a finger on a column, looking down at the obsidian. "I want to know how to get back to that first corridor," he said, as if Polymnia had asked him what he was thinking. "At least we know it's directly underneath the mountain door." He picked up the obsidian and drew it along the column. It made a creaking noise and left a thin, pale line. "You see? I'll scratch every surface I can, as we go." He smiled at her.

She wanted to say, *You poor, stupid boy: how can you feel any kind of hope?* She lowered her gaze to her own feet. They were so dirty that she thought she should be a child again, picking her way across the slaughterhouse floor toward whatever beast needed to die, as her father bellowed curses at her back.

"Come on," Kosmas said, and she heard a hiss as he followed the others down the slide. She stood motionless. Turned her head to look at the tunnel that had led them here. *Go back*, she told herself. *Find somewhere to die. No one will miss you; no one ever does. Not even your Mistress, who gave you to the king. No one.*

"Polymnia?" She lifted her head at Asterion's voice. "Polymnia!"

Her mouth was dry and tasted of smoke. She swallowed. "Coming," she said.

CHAPTER SEVEN

So many tunnels: tunnels cut out of rippled bands of rock, with ceilings of transparent crystal that glowed as white as moonlight; tunnels lit by tiny lamps embedded in the walls, or what seemed to be fireflies, flitting always above their heads; still others that were completely dark. Different lights, like the ones far, far up in one great cavern: spots that looked like blue-green stars, sprayed in constellations that Polymnia learned to recognize during the interminable time she walked below them. Strange shapes, like the steps that were actually jutting, frozen runs of the mountain's lava; other steps that were even and squared-off, smoothed by men as they would be in any palace or temple beneath the sky. A cavern ablaze with jewelled stalactites that tugged at their hair and bone-white stalagmites that tripped them and sliced the bottoms of their robes into ribbons. Water dripping somewhere, nowhere, everywhere.

They shuffled and limped; once Kosmas had to crawl, to see if there was anything at the end of a narrow fissure carved with bunches of gaping clams. "Huh," he said. "There's a seat with a hole—by the gods, it's a *latrine!*"

"Of course it is," Ligeia said. "The Great Daedalus would have hated the idea of the Athenian sacrifices defiling his work."

"And water," Polymnia whispered—because there it

was, at last: mere threads of it, wending down the wall. Ligeia fell upon it first, with her hands and mouth; Kosmas held Zenais up against the stone so that she wouldn't fall, as she lapped, and he drank after that. Asterion nodded at Polymnia.

"You saw it," he said. "I'll wait."

The water was colder than any she'd ever tasted before. Her head swam with numbness and relief that passed far too quickly.

"Come," Kosmas said, after they'd all taken several turns at the wall. "We have to keep moving." They shuffled after her, licking the last of the moisture from their hands.

Kosmas's obsidian got smaller and smaller as he drew it along the endless stone, but they found a fresh pile of shards in a black chamber, and each of them took some. Soon Kosmas couldn't use his at all, because Zenais grew so weak that he had to carry her.

"How can this place be so big?" he gasped once, after he'd set her down by yet another set of corridor mouths.

Zenais lifted a hand and gestured vaguely. "What we see of the mountain from the outside isn't all of it. We climbed and climbed out there, to get to the door; imagine—now we're under everything. The earth could be hollow all the way through."

"Enough of your prattling," Ligeia said, stepping around Zenais to reach the closest doorway. "Kosmas: pick her up. Bull-thing: you'd better be right that there's food somewhere here. Food, and a whole lot more water."

Their pace slowed to a shamble, which seemed to prove that days were passing. Zenais claimed she felt them. "It's been six days, now," she said once—but sometime later she mumbled, "It's been three, now," and Polymnia heard Ligeia hiss to Kosmas, "You see? She has no idea. The fever's addled her brain. Or the hunger. Or the thirst."

Not long after that, they stumbled across a bridge suspended between two tunnels. The one they left was lit with blue and silver; the one across the deep cleft was a crimson that undulated in waves along the walls. They rested here, because Kosmas had to put Zenais down again, and the others were weak as well. Polymnia's body throbbed with dizziness and pain.

"So how did they find *you*?"

Polymnia sucked in her breath and glanced at Ligeia, who was scowling at her. The crimson light turned her lips black. "What's wrong with you?" Ligeia snapped. "Why aren't you answering me?"

How are you so energetic? Polymnia thought. "Because," she said slowly, "you never said a word to me on the ship, or here. You've barely even looked at me."

Ligeia cackled. Red danced across her teeth like flame. "Oh, I looked at you. When you tried to throw yourself off the cliff, for example. When you cried like a baby at dinner, the first night on the island, and snot ran into your mouth. We all looked at you."

"'Geia," Zenais whispered, "don't be cruel."

Ligeia tossed her head and the golden stubble on it glinted. "And you, Zenais! They found *you* in the whore's quarter—Theodosia told us this one night on the ship, when you were asleep. One of King Aegeus's men fell in love with you, he thought, and brought you to the palace. And they found *him*"—a tilt of her head at Kosmas, who had walked ahead with Asterion—"in with the boys who clean the athletes' weapons during the Games. I just want to know how *she* came to be among us."

Polymnia traced a vein of crystal and imagined what she might have said, to someone else. To Zenais, maybe, if they'd been alone.

They came for me the morning after I turned fourteen, on a hot day at the end of summer. I was sitting outside the slaughterhouse, fanning myself with the cloth I'd been wiping my hands on. I smelled the blood on it, every time I waved it, but I also smelled the salt of the harbour and the pink flowers that hung over the wall across from me. I was tired. My sister had been sick all night, whimpering and whining like a puppy. I'd had no sleep but once I got to the slaughterhouse I sang (the cows would sleep, anyway, before they died). My father was in a foul temper. I knew, as I sat outside, that he'd be angry when he found me gone from the killing floor. I knew he'd probably smack me with the haft of his knife, in front of everyone. But then a man came up to me—a slave, he said, except that he was dressed in dyed cloth, and had a bronze ring around his arm. "My mistress heard you singing in the market," he said. "I'm here to take you to her."

"For how long?" I asked.

"Forever," he said, "if you like."

I stood up. I thought, Say farewell to your mother and sister, at least; go home, even if just to do that. But I didn't. I followed the slave. I sang for his mistress, that day and for months after. They dressed me in cloth finer than the slave's, and fed me meat from animals I hadn't had to kill. They cooed over me like a pet. I slept in a clean bed and didn't let myself think of my whimpering sister. Months after that, I sang for the king and Theseus, his son, and my mistress gave me to them, even though I didn't want to go. She gave me away. And now I'm here, with you and Ligeia and a bull-boy, and I'm not sure which one of them is the beast.

Polymnia looked at Ligeia. "It doesn't matter now," she sang, and then her weariness returned, and she closed her eyes on Ligeia's startled face.

———— · ————

Polymnia was dreaming about the slaughterhouse, so at first she didn't realize it was Ligeia screaming. Instead it was cows—cows, and her father, shouting that she must sing, quickly, or he'd bring the knife's hilt down on her flesh until it was flayed as the cows' should be flayed, except that she wasn't singing—godsblood, why would she not open her throat and *sing?*

Ligeia's scream was much shriller than a cow's.

"What is it?" Zenais, of course, trying to make things right, even though her leg was foaming and stinking and her skin burned with fever. "What, 'Geia?"

"A lizard!" Ligeia shrieked. "Kill it—someone *kill* it!"

Polymnia stood up. Half caught in the dream, she moved toward it—but Asterion was there first, leaning in, lifting a finger to touch. "It's white," he said, "but there were ones like it, at Knossos. Ones with spots." His voice was strained. His hand trembled.

It scuttled away from him, up almost to the place where the wall curved to meet the ceiling. "No," he said breathlessly, and reached for it with a clawed hand.

Polymnia crept up beside him. She started to sing before he could turn to her—but the lizard turned immediately. Its blunt, eyeless head swung and its translucent claws flexed as her voice washed it with silver. It went still, as the notes streamed on. She reached out and grasped it around its smooth, scaled middle, and it didn't even twitch. She broke its neck quickly, and the silver ebbed away.

Behind her, Ligeia made a disgusted sound and Zenais made a pained one. Beside her, Asterion breathed as raggedly as if he'd been running. She couldn't look at him.

"My brother," he gasped. "He used to . . . he'd sing to creatures and calm them. You were marked by the same goddess—by Artemis."

She felt him lurch and slide and looked at him, at last, crouched by the wall, shuddering. His horns were so bright that she couldn't see his face clearly. His breathing was wet, now. *Hunger filling his mouth*, she thought, and hunkered down next to him. She set the dead lizard on the ground next to one of his bull's feet and watched his boy's hands clench. She wanted to say something to him—something comforting and certain. Instead she rose and said, to Ligeia, "We'll go that way and wait for him," and, to Zenais, "Lean on me, now . . . More than that; I'm stronger than I look." The words flowed from her as songs did; she felt dizzy and light.

She glanced over her shoulder, as they moved off down the corridor. She watched as Asterion picked up the lizard; she heard him whimper as he put it to his mouth, and then she heard him groan. A few steps later, when he was out of sight around a corner, he roared.

Later she lay on her side, staring at the phosphorescent spray of a plant on a wall. A constellation she could have touched, but didn't. She was thinking about how she'd cowered, when her father had hit her for not singing quickly or loudly enough; when Asterion's voice whispered, "Thank you," from right above her, her stomach seemed to leap into her throat. She didn't stir, though, which made her feel a brief flare of pride.

"I was hungry," he went on. He was speaking quietly, and Zenais's moaning was echoing around them in waves that made his words even harder to hear. "But I couldn't have killed the thing myself. So thank you."

She longed to roll over and look up into his face—to be as bold as her words to the others had sounded. But she stayed as she was, and after a moment she felt a curl of wind above her, as he left.

———— · ————

Zenais had counted eight days, then four, then nine when they found the altar room.

Kosmas was carrying her as he did all the time, now, at the front of their little line. Ligeia walked behind him and Polymnia behind her, digging lines into the walls wherever she could. Asterion was well back. His ragged breathing was so loud that Polymnia didn't have to look over her shoulder to make sure he was still there. In fact, his breathing was like its own sort of song, which made her forget the hunger and the heat. *Walk . . . gently . . . walk . . . forever . . .*

Kosmas's first cry was garbled; the second was, very clearly, "Food!" A moment later, Ligeia was standing beside him, howling at the space beyond in her wolf-voice. Polymnia stumbled toward them. Even with all the other noise, she could hear Asterion's hooves on the stone behind her, jogging in their not-human rhythm.

She tried to see everything at once—every single, wondrous thing. *It's the last picture that boy Amon showed everyone, with his godmark*, she thought—and it was: the enormous circular space, the painted stairs up to the vast, round altar stone, which seemed to writhe with carven snakes. The urns. But there was more than there'd been in his image: two latrine seats, as grand as thrones, set between columns; two rings of jars, all of them as tall as the youths were, and all overflowing—one with figs, one with salt fish, another with honey cakes.

As she ran forward, her arms already outstretched, she heard water, and daylight plucked at her vision from above. She stopped running, swayed with one foot on the first step up to the altar. She craned her head back. Daylight, yes: six wavering shafts of it, slanting from what looked to be polished black pipes, ranged in an uneven row a very long way up the endless rock walls. Slightly lower down, but still a head-spinning distance from the ground, was a stream—more a waterfall, really, that foamed from a band of red stone and plunged a hand's breadth away from the wall. Polymnia followed it with her eyes—down, sunlit to shadowed, to where it hit the ground. In any other place it would have pooled there, deep and fresh and cool. But this was the Goddess's mountain, and her breath was so hot that the water turned to hissing steam where it struck.

Salt and sweetness; things that stuck in Polymnia's teeth before she swallowed them, so convulsively that she nearly gagged. She heard the snuffling and choking of others around her but didn't look at anything except what was in her hands. When she could eat no more (suddenly so full she felt sick), she stumbled to her feet and over to the water. She stepped into its stream and leaned her head back. Water on her face and running down her head and back; water in her mouth, so fresh and cool it almost hurt her, and distant sunlight in her eyes.

When she finally backed away, Kosmas was behind her. He smiled at her, before he took her place, just as he'd smiled at her when he'd made the first mark with his obsidian flake. *Very well*, she thought this time. *You can have your hope, now that we're going to survive a little longer. Some of us, anyway*—and she glanced at Zenais, who was slumped against the wall by the corridor they'd come in from, with Ligeia kneeling beside her.

Asterion was crouched between two of the jars. He was chewing slowly, frowning as if he were in pain. Polymnia thought, *Be brave; speak to him* and walked over to stand above him.

"Is something wrong?" she asked. She could feel the sweat crawling across her skin already; salt water gnawing away at fresh, as if she'd never stood beneath the stream.

He lifted his eyes, which were wide, and darted from her face to the food and over to the mouths of the three other corridors that led out of the chamber. "This food won't be enough for me. Not forever." His voice was low and rough; she hadn't heard him speak since she'd killed the lizard for him, and she had no idea how long ago that had been. "I'll need more." He stared back down at the fish in his hands: pale grey, bumpy with salt, shredded into long, thin pieces by his teeth.

"What will you need more of?" she said, though she knew. She remembered his roar, after he'd tasted the lizard. Remembered what he'd said, after their fall: "I might hurt you."

"Fresh meat." He tossed his head; she saw the golden hair around his horns go thick and dark. His lips were darker too: purplish-brown, straining into a different shape. "They put me here because they knew how much it would hurt. The heat, all the time . . . My body will always be trying to be the bull's. It's only been a little while, but the hunger . . . it's . . . it's ridiculous, is what it is. Bulls eat *grass*—and yet this godmark is so strong that it makes me long for flesh." He put his head on his knees; she watched a shudder take him, from horns to shoulders to legs to cloven feet. She heard him murmur something—Chara, maybe, or Charis—a girl's name, in any case—and felt herself flush with sudden jealousy. *He's beautiful*, she thought, staring at his sweat-slick skin, with its latticework of scars. Her own skin rose in bumps, from arms to chest to the insides of her thighs.

"It's all right," she said, knowing it wasn't. "You'll find a way." *A way to* what, *stupid girl? You see: you should never, ever speak. If you must make a noise, just sing, like Father told you. Smile and sing and pretend to be strong.*

He raised his head and looked at her, though not really. "Said the jelly to the ray, 'You will always find a way.' And the ray said, 'I have charms—but I'll never have your arms.'" He smiled, though not at her.

Before she could think of something else to say,

Kosmas called, "Look—another message!"

This one had been cut into the columns that flanked another of the corridor mouths. Polymnia read the words, with Asterion behind her.

Take some comfort here, Athenians.

"He didn't know I'd be here too," Asterion said, so softly that only Polymnia heard him. "No one told him—not my father, not my sister. Master Daedalus would never have let this happen to me. Icarus would never . . ." He stumbled back to the altar and sat down with a moan on the lowest step.

"Comfort," Ligeia said with a snort. She was kneeling beside Zenais, waving a fig beside her gaping mouth. "Yes, that's what I'd call this. Comfort. Come *on*, Zenais: try to eat. Just a bite?"

Zenais ground her cheek against the wall (a row of looping vines and flowers: green, scarlet, gold) and mumbled something. "Come *on!*" Ligeia shouted, and stuck the fig between the other girl's lips. Zenais's body lashed and she vomited a thick, dark stream of something, down the front of her already filthy robe.

"Enough!" cried Kosmas. He pulled Ligeia's shoulders until she fell back against his legs. She clawed at his hands, panting and snarling. Asterion moaned again. Zenais cried in thick, wracking sobs.

"Help me," Kosmas said to Asterion. They tipped one of the smaller storage jars carefully onto its side, emptied it of oatcakes and shuffled it between them to the place where the falling water struck the floor and vanished. They positioned it beneath the stream. It was full before the shafts of sunlight had dimmed above them. Kosmas pulled off his robe; Polymnia watched Ligeia's eyes as they leapt over the gleaming ridges and hollows of his body. He angled the water jar so that water poured out in a steady stream, onto the cloth. When it was soaked, he took it over to Zenais and ran it gently over her cheeks and across her forehead. She whimpered and strained toward the cloth. When he laid it against her wound she screamed.

Not long afterward, when everything was quiet, the last of the outside light ebbed away. Other light bloomed: green-blue sprays of glowing plants, maybe moss or lichen—*Something short and fuzzy*, Polymnia thought as she sank down beside Zenais. *Something that would make my fingertips smell like earth. Something the colour of the dress my mistress gave me after I calmed that calf that kept trying to bolt from the altar.* Other lights flickered up the length of the columns and along the carved walls: golden specks that seemed to weave like fireflies, blurring in the steam from the falling water.

"We should never leave here," Kosmas said.

The shadow of Ligeia's shaking head leapt up the wall behind her. "We'll have to. We'll go mad if we don't."

"What does madness matter if the other option is to get lost and starve?"

Kosmas stood and stared upward. Asterion leaned forward, rocking slowly.

"There has to be a way to reach those pipes," Kosmas said. "We could stack the jars, or collect rocks—big ones. We could use some of the stalactites in that huge chamber of them, if we could find our way back there. And we could: we marked it."

"No," Asterion said, without raising his head. "We'd need fifty jars, and some way of attaching them so they wouldn't fall. And anyway, the pipes are like glass, and they're on an angle; even if we *did* reach one of them, there'd be nothing to hold onto. We'd slide right back down again and break our necks. No: Master Daedalus made this place for survival, not escape."

Ligeia had begun pacing around them all in long, loping, scuffing strides. Zenais's breath was rough and wet in her chest. *Stop!* Polymnia wanted to cry. Instead she sang. They turned to her. They went still. Her godmark wove silver threads into the flickering gold and the dark.

CHAPTER EIGHT

"She's dead."

Ligeia was hunched over Zenais. Ligeia's shoulders were shaking; none of Zenais was moving at all.

Kosmas fell so heavily that Polymnia imagined she heard his knee bones cracking. She wasn't looking at him, though, nor at the others. She was watching Asterion, who was crawling behind the row of jars. His head was down, and the tips of his horns were drawing lazy sparks from the altar's stone.

A long time later, Kosmas said, "We'll have to do something with her body." His voice shook a bit.

Polymnia shifted her gaze in time to see Ligeia drag a hand under her nose. She was bubbling and sniffling, holding Zenais's wrist in her other hand. *Yes*, Polymnia thought. *Be sad.*

"The bridge," Ligeia said. Somehow her voice didn't shake. "We should throw her over. We have to."

"Yes," Kosmas said. "But we can't send her to Hades like this."

When he put his hands on the remains of Zenais's robe, the cloth fell away. He tore the skirt of his own robe into strips and dipped them in the water urn. He used them, one at a time, to wash her: her stubbly head, her face, her neck, her breasts. Ligeia gave a half-hearted snort when he reached her belly.

"What's the point, if you're just going to throw her off a bridge?"

He didn't answer. He washed Zenais's thighs, then stopped, the cloth strip poised and dripping above her calves. Her wound gaped, dark and ragged, still oozing. Polymnia could smell it, even from halfway across the chamber. At last he laid two strips over the wound. He pressed them flat, very gently, as if he were afraid of hurting her. He washed her feet, set the soiled strips aside, and lifted her. Her head lolled; he raised his shoulder so that she was lying against it.

Asterion moaned, behind the jars.

"You're doing it now?" Ligeia said. "Already?"

Kosmas was walking toward the corridor that would take him to the bridge. "Why would we wait?" he said over his shoulder. He glanced from Ligeia to Polymnia. "Are you coming?"

Polymnia shook her head, but Ligeia said, "Yes: wait!" As she did, Kosmas stepped into the corridor, and the world split apart in metal screeching and grinding stone. He drew sharply back into the altar chamber as the corridor's mouth disappeared, its firefly-lit darkness replaced with a dead-end wall. The wall didn't stay, though: it crawled down into a hole that had opened in the ground, as invisible gears shrieked and invisible chains pulled. Polymnia whirled to look where Kosmas was looking: at the second doorway, and the third, and at the changing spaces beyond them.

"What's happening?" Polymnia thought Ligeia was probably screaming, because her mouth was gaping and the tendons in her neck were standing out—but her words were barely audible. By the time the other noises faded, moments later, Ligeia was on her knees in the bloodied spot where Zenais had lain. "What," she said again, her chest heaving, "is happening?"

Kosmas's arms were shaking—perhaps from shock; perhaps just because Zenais's body was heavy. "This must have been the plan," he said slowly. "To give the Goddess's victims some rest, some food, then take all that comfort away by changing everything. Asterion: does that sound right? Does that sound like your Master Daedalus?"

Asterion didn't uncurl himself from behind the jars. From where she was standing, Polymnia saw one of his horns, dipping and swinging. "Maybe this is the best place to be," he said in a tight, dry voice. "Maybe he wanted people to stay here and not go wandering back out again, where they might come to harm."

Kosmas blew out his breath and set Zenais back on the ground. He sat down beside her and let his shoulders lift and fall. "Whatever the reason: I don't know what to do, any more. I thought it would be enough to mark our path—but now the marks are gone."

"We stay here for a bit," Ligeia said. "The beast's right: this is a good place."

Don't call him that, Polymnia thought, but didn't say. She edged around the steps so that she could see Asterion's lowered face and rounded back. His spine jutted. Muscles bunched in his thighs. His scars, purple, pink and white, were like the marks she'd watched her mistress's scribe make on Egyptian paper, but far more beautiful.

"Fine," Kosmas said. "But we'll have to go out there and see what it looks like—because we'll have to take care of Zenais's body somehow, and soon."

"Of course," Ligeia said. Polymnia couldn't see her, or Kosmas, or the thing that had been Zenais. She saw only Asterion, who had wrapped his arms around himself. He dragged his head up, and she shrank from the helpless fear in his round dark eyes.

———— · ————

Polymnia woke that night to more of Ligeia's screaming. *Another lizard?* she thought muzzily—except that this scream rose and rose and ended in a wolf's howl.

At first, blinking and squinting, Polymnia saw nothing but a blur of silver. A few blinks later, she saw Ligeia on all fours, straining her head and shoulders upward. It was the godlight pouring from her mouth that was turning the air and stone to silver. The air, the stone—and the horned beast crouched over the shadow of Zenais's body.

Asterion's head was the bull's, but his hands were the boy's. They were tearing, tugging, lifting things to his muzzle: long, wet, slippery things.

Ligeia's howl stuttered and died, and Kosmas yelled into the silence. The bull-boy raised his head. He dropped what he was clutching and flexed his fingers, which fused immediately into hooves. His back arched, and fur spread from shoulders to back to buttocks. He pawed at the ground and gave a bellow that thrummed through the altar stone and up through Polymnia's feet.

"Monster!" Ligeia's voice was still partly godmarked—rough and low, as if she were in pain. She had risen into a crouch, brandishing her obsidian shard. The bull bellowed once more, and she sprang forward.

"No!" Kosmas cried, and lunged for her even as the bull lowered his head and charged. Ligeia screamed in her own voice as the bull bore down on her. She dodged, and one of his horns grazed her side. Her robe tore; blood branched from a jagged cut on her ribcage.

"Ligeia—run!" shouted Kosmas from the doorway farthest from her. He turned and looked wildly at Polymnia, who'd retreated to another doorway. *No,* she told herself. *You can't leave Asterion. You're the only one who understands him. He needs you. And yet,* she thought, as he spun and charged again, and Ligeia whirled and made for the third doorway, *he's beyond you, for now. He'll only know you when his hunger and rage have passed and he's a boy again—so run—*

"Run!"

—go, and return as soon as he's quiet—

Ligeia disappeared beyond her doorway. Kosmas cast one more frenzied look at Polymnia and ducked away into darkness.

She turned to face the bull, who was turning to her. His breath was whuffing, and she imagined she could feel it, despite the broad expanse of ground between them—she could feel it, hot on her face and stubbly head.

For a moment, one of his brown eyes was on her and they were both still. She had time to think, *He does know me!* before his horns dipped and one of his hooves struck sparks from the stone. He let out another bellow and leapt, and she stumbled backward into a corridor. *It's all right: he won't fit; I'll just stay here for a bit.* Except that, as he made for her, she saw that he *would* fit—and at last she dragged her body around so that she was facing a dim, strange tunnel, and she ran as his hooves and breath pursued her.

This new tunnel was thick with steam: scalding jets of it, which filled her eyes with tears and her throat with coughing. The walls glowed with splotches of green light, but they were smudged and diffuse and showed her almost nothing. Steps fell suddenly away beneath her and she sprawled onto a polished floor; he was close, closer, as she struggled to rise. *Why does it matter? You're going to die in here anyway—so stop. Give yourself to this god. Nothing matters except him.* But she was up once more, slipping along the floor—obsidian, she saw, in the blurry green spaces between the steam.

She heard his hooves clatter and slide and continue, closer.

The path forked; she saw another opening, which was very tall and narrow. She moaned as she threw herself toward it and wriggled in, sideways. The bull was only moments behind her; he wheeled and tipped, righted himself with his head facing hers. He was all darkness, except for his horns, which lit the steam with shifting silver and gold. He thrust his head into the opening and pushed until his nose was a hand's breadth from her face. It stuck there. She watched his nostrils flare; she saw that they were slick with blood, and that the fur below his chin was matted with it. She felt his breath, and it was as hot as she'd known it would be. It lapped at her cheek, calling her out to him, and she dug her fingernails into the rock and her teeth into her lip. *No*, she thought, as he pawed and grunted. *I don't want to die. I want to be with him.*

Her heart hammered in her chest and behind her eyes. Sweat flowed in rivulets from her scalp and down across all her skin. She itched, inside and out. She felt her own breath, caught and squeezed by the rock walls and his closeness. They stood for minutes or hours or forever—until a wolf's howl rose and twined between them, with the steam.

The bull snorted and wrenched his head from side to side. *Don't go*, Polymnia thought, even as he withdrew from the opening and relief turned her limbs to water. *I'll find you*, she thought, as the sound of his hooves faded and she eased herself out. *I will find you.*

As it turned out, she barely found her own way back to the altar chamber. The moment she stood and stepped into the bank of steam that filled the corridor, she heard gears catch and grind and felt the obsidian floor beneath her shudder. She ran a few paces, crying out helplessly, knowing that it was too late.

A smooth marble wall had descended from the ceiling where the doorway to the altar chamber had been. She pounded on it, thinking *Asterion* every time her skin hit the stone—thinking only about him, and not the jars of olives and figs and water. Not the holes that poured sunlight and fresh air down into their prison.

Enough, she thought at last. She leaned her cheek against the marble, which was deliciously cool, and craned up at the ceiling. The steam was thick, and it took a moment for some deep, hot thread of wind to trace a clear path through it. She saw a metal loop hanging directly above her head, and reached up to pull it before she could wonder whether she should. Wood creaked and whined, and she scrambled backward as a ladder unfurled and swung heavily where she'd been.

She stared at it, shaking her head as if it had spoken. *Go a different way*, she thought—because maybe there was some other, faster path back to where he was. But there wasn't—of course there wasn't; there was only another wall, this one bumpy with carvings of nautilus shells and cresting waves that looked as if they were moving in the sickly green light.

The rope of the ladder was coarse against her palms. She clutched it as she swung, close to the ground but abruptly dizzy. When she felt steadier she pulled herself up the eight rungs. There was no steam at the top; she gazed down at it, roiling and dense, and almost laughed because she seemed to have no body except for her grasping hands and her sweat-slick head. Above her was a jagged hole filled with light that was as bright and rippling as sun. Her heart raced as she tilted her face toward it, even though the rest of her knew it was just more of Master Daedalus's godmarked work. She took a breath and hauled herself up. Her already tattered robe snagged on the hole's teeth, and she grunted as she tore it free.

The sun was an enormous glass globe filled with golden flames so bright that she couldn't see how it had been suspended. She closed her eyes a bit, so that she could imagine that it really was the sun, hot and low, surrounded by a sky that was made of air, not rock. *Enough*, she told herself, opening her eyes as wide as she could. This *is your place now. Yours and his.*

She set off into the light. Tiny, hard things cracked under her bare feet; she guessed without looking at them that they were the bones of white cave creatures like the lizard she'd caught for him. Perhaps these had died fleeing the false sun. When she reached a wall with three doorways in it, she leaned over to brush the creatures' remnants from her skin. The tunnel beyond one doorway was dark, and another was a sickly yellow; the last flickered with fire she knew was real. She chose the last.

After only a few steps she wondered if she'd chosen wisely; heat surged against her flesh and into her lungs in stifling waves. *He'd be all bull in an instant, if he were here with me*—but this thought made her ache with longing and fear, so she concentrated on her own tight breathing, and the way the tunnel's earthen floor was sloping down toward the light. She was soaked with sweat by the time it opened into a cavern vaster than any she'd yet seen beneath the mountain. A cavern of rock that looked red, because its floor was a lake of fire with a scorched black island at its centre.

She stood where the ground fell sharply away and rubbed sweat out of her eyes. The fire bubbled beneath her; plumes of it rose and subsided into steaming dimples in the lake. A few paces took her to a stone bridge that arced above the flames. She walked onto it and slowly across. The heat was unbearable, but she bore it. She thought of him: his scars, and fresh blisters rising on his skin. She glanced from side to side at the popping, hissing liquid and sucked in her breath when a shower of sparks fell on her shoulders and arms. *You're just like Asterion*, she thought. *You're brave.*

She was blind with heat and dizziness. When she paused she felt earth beneath her feet again, and turned to look back. The bridge was already several paces behind her. The doorway she'd come from was wreathed in steam. She wriggled her toes in the black soot, which was scattered with obsidian shards. She tried to avoid them, as she walked on, but there were too many: they pierced her flesh, and she knew that she was leaving twin trails of blood, though they were invisible against the black. The pain of the heat was so great that she couldn't feel the pain of the cuts.

Four three-legged tables stood in the middle of the island; a circle of clean, white stone had been set among them. Polymnia half-stepped, half-stumbled onto the stone, which was flat, and much cooler than the ground. Through the bright haze of fire and sweat, she saw words, carved in a spiral:

*Pray, Athenian, for you have reached the
Great Goddess's heart.*

She stared down at the words, and at her blackened, bloodied feet. She stared at the tables, which had been covered in tiny, painted statues: the golden-skinned Goddess with crimson snakes coiling around her arms and over her naked breasts; the green Goddess with a bright blue double axe clasped in her hands. Words, flesh, and paint trembled in Polymnia's vision.

Pray, she thought, in some faraway place in her head. She knelt on the white stone and closed her eyes and the world was a bit stiller, a bit firmer.

"Great Goddess," she whispered. Her voice was splintered and faint, and she wondered, briefly, when she'd last used it. For a moment, no other words came out of her mouth, because there were too many in her head.

"Great Goddess," she said again, at last, and this time she felt her voice filling her throat and the scalding air. "He can hear my words. Please let him hear my song, as well. Please let me comfort him."

She stood up slowly, and swayed, and opened her eyes. Another bridge shimmered before her, and she set off toward it, singing his name into the smoke.

———— · ————

She was aching with hunger and weariness when she finally reached a place she recognized: the vaulted cavern lit with stars that weren't stars. The glowing green constellations spun as she did; she held her arms out, laughing as if she were already strong again. Because she knew that she'd find the mark of an obsidian flake, on the wall at the foot of the staircase that curled around the thickest of the stalagmites. And there it was. She ran her finger along the groove, which grew thready and thin wherever Kosmas had hesitated (maybe Zenais had been hanging off his back?), or wherever the flake had grown too weak. It led her out and away, and back.

Gears ground and corridors shifted and settled, and she stood once again in the altar chamber—though she didn't stand so much as hunch. Her bones felt as if they'd melted and fused, and her skin was tight. But she thought, *I'm back; I'm home.*

She heard something, in the silence. A pattering that was so familiar and so strange that she was as breathless as she'd been by the lake of fire. She forced her head up, imagining how he must feel, dragged down by horns, and she looked at the floor and walls and saw water. Rain. It was flowing down the pipes, dappling the walls and floor with darkness—but there was light too, seeping and muddy. She remembered what rain was like, during the day; how it would wash the slaughterhouse blood from her hands and arms and clothes, when she slipped away. How the water made her close her eyes a little, so that the blossoms hanging over the wall across the street looked like smears of paint.

Enough, she thought. *That life's done, thank all the gods and goddesses.*

She pulled her tattered robe off, after she'd eaten and drunk, and spread it out on the altar. She lay on her side and closed her eyes. The rain was like mist on her bare, filthy skin. She fell asleep quickly and woke slowly. The rain had stopped, and there was no light at all, from above. Her limbs were heavy, but there was a strange weight on her back that had nothing to do with sleepiness. She rolled her head carefully up to look over her shoulder—and she saw an arm. A dangling hand. A bare, filthy hip.

Asterion was curled against her. His human knees were drawn up into the space behind hers. The bone of his cloven bull's hooves was cool on her ankles and heels. She felt the point of one of his horns digging into her shoulder blade, and for a moment she thought he was trying to hurt her—but then she realized that he was simply breathing, as he slept. Her own breath burned in her chest because she didn't want to let it out. *No breath no motion of any kind be so still he'll never ever wake up because the moment he does he'll go away.*

An itch crept along her shoulder and then her spine. She tried to imagine that it was a beetle that would skitter across her and away—but that single itch spread into innumerable itches. Sweat eased down her face and pooled beneath her cheek. A muscle stiffened painfully in her calf. A cascade of sensations, each of them intolerable: she eased herself away from him and onto her back, so gradually that she hardly felt it herself. He twitched and sighed. She could see him now: his sideways-turned body, and his head. His face was pointed up at the roof; his horns wouldn't let him put his cheek to the ground. His features were frozen somewhere between bull's and boy's: a nose and mouth that jutted, though the lips were Asterion's. Hollow human cheeks coated in fur. A slender scar wound from the fur to his chin and her fingertips tingled with the need to touch it—it, and all the others that puckered his skin, as if someone had been trying to mend him.

She didn't feel the sneeze coming: it simply did, with a force that drove her up onto her elbows. The sneeze ended in a sob—because he was twisting up too, of course, his brown eyes opening and rolling over her and everything around them, his hands scrabbling against stone and air. "Ari?" he cried, and "Chara?" Polymnia froze for a moment, shocked by the sound of his voice—but when he fell backward, she threw herself after him. "No!" Her own voice was much too loud, and it hurt her throat. "Asterion—wait!"—but he was already past the jars and down the steps.

When he reached a column. he paused and turned back. She watched fur spread across his face and down his neck, then over both shoulders at once. His nose and mouth were all bull now, and his nostrils flared. He tossed his head and huffed. She didn't speak again, didn't move except to lift her hands and hold them out to him. *Come back come back please come back . . .*

He edged slowly over to the water jug and hunkered beside it. She knotted her fingers together and squeezed so hard that tears filled her eyes. *Now stay stay please stay . . .* She eased herself down into a crouch and smiled at him. He tossed his head again, and scuffed the floor with a hoof.

He stayed.

——— · ———

Polymnia started measuring time with obsidian flake slashes on the altar chamber wall, where she could see sunlight turning to darkness—because she was often deep inside the mountain, and saw no lights except Daedalus's fireflies and little lamps. The first of the marks seemed to wobble up from the floor; the ones after that were deeper and straighter, which made her proud. She sometimes remembered Zenais murmuring, "It's been two days . . . five days . . . seven . . ." as her leg frothed and her red eyes squinted and rolled.

Polymnia had just carved the fiftieth mark on the wall when a sound like distant thunder rumbled from the sky beyond the chamber. *Lord Zeus sends a storm*, she thought, and her belly lurched with excitement because the other rain had been so light and brief. The sunlight in one of the openings wavered, but that was all. She glanced at Asterion, who was sitting in what was now his favourite place: by the water jar, his legs and arms outstretched to catch spray that might be cool. He was all boy, except for his horns and one foot. His eyes were closed; they remained closed, even when the rumbling stopped and a new noise began: a rat-a-tat bouncing that was faint, then louder, then all around them. She threw up her hands as the source of the sound rained down around her: hundreds, thousands of fat, moist figs.

She imagined Kosmas beside her, craning up, narrowing his blue eyes. "How is that happening?" he'd ask her. (Though he wouldn't have asked her: he would have thought of an answer himself.)

"Probably just someone shovelling," she imagined replying. "Though who knows how they got up that far. It doesn't matter: it's fresh, and we were running low on everything." She heard Asterion's hoof drag; she knew he was pulling his legs up under him so that he could stand. Maybe he was looking at her now, or maybe at the figs that bounced and scattered as they hit the ground.

Imaginary Kosmas turned to her eagerly. "So a person could slide down to us, too!"

"And break all the bones in their body?" she said, shaking her head. "Why? Why would anyone even try?"

"Maybe to help *him*." A thumb crooked in Asterion's direction. "Maybe someone up there won't like that he was shut in here. Maybe that's why there's food coming down at all. Why would anyone want to feed us when we were supposed to *be* the food?"

The stream of figs thinned to nothing. A moment passed before it was replaced by a thumping that turned out to be round loaves of bread. She whooped as she dodged them. "All ours!" she sang. "Ours and only ours!" She sang and she spun, and then she caught a glimpse of Asterion, and stopped.

He was holding a fig to his mouth, staring down at it as if it were something horrifying. He let it fall and sent it halfway to the altar with a swift kick of his hoof. He shook his head so violently that he fell backward, and lay where he'd fallen, curled and small.

So small, she thought—and suddenly she saw him as she hadn't allowed herself to see him, for all these weeks. His shoulder blades and spine jutted from sallow skin; his neck looked too slender for his head; the fingers on his human hand were more like claws.

So much food, but he's starving. He has to eat again. Not bread or figs or salt fish: fresh meat. He told me, all that time ago: meat and blood will be the only things that will give him strength here. It's been too long since Zenais. I have to find him something else, somehow.

Three days later, something found her.

CHAPTER NINE

Polymnia recognized Kosmas's voice, even though it was doing nothing but moan. His ankle was broken, or maybe his leg. She knew this even before she saw him: she heard his foot dragging, as he moaned.

She slipped behind a column.

She might have recognized his voice, but when he finally lurched into the altar space, she didn't recognize *him*. His face—which the Princess Ariadne had slavered over, in some other lifetime—was streaked with blood and dirt. His eyes were pinched smaller with pain, so Polymnia couldn't see their vivid blue. He was an injured animal, an old man—something that stank of weakness and promise.

"Polymnia?" The word was splintered and faint, but it echoed from the walls. She drew herself deeper into shadow.

Asterion's body stiffened. Kosmas wouldn't be able to see him; the bull-boy was lying behind the wide, squat fig jar. He lifted his heavy head off the floor. One of his horns whined on the altar's stone but Kosmas didn't seem to hear it over the sounds that were coming out of his own throat. As he advanced she could see them both. She had a sudden desire to sing to them—to wrap them in silver until they lay down next to each other, sleepy and slow. But no: Asterion was hungry, and Kosmas was bleeding.

Asterion rose and crouched, bobbing a little on his

human feet as his bull's head swung, looking. Kosmas paused where his corridor met the chamber's wall. Gears ground, somewhere close, and each of them froze, waiting—but floor and corridor mouths stayed still. The grinding echoed and echoed and stopped. Kosmas resumed his lurching.

Asterion rose to his full height and roared.

A cry left Polymnia's throat before she could quell it. They didn't hear her. Kosmas's handsome head jerked up; Asterion scuffed the ground with his feet and leapt across the space between them. Polymnia could see the blue of Kosmas's eyes, spreading, brightening, filling her own eyes with their fear. *No*, she thought, *he saved you both, remember? Don't let this happen*—but then she thought, *Yes. Asterion: yes.*

Kosmas turned, somehow. She saw the bone protruding, glistening and jagged, from the skin of his calf, and yet he spun and ran. Asterion was only paces behind him; Polymnia wasn't sure whether he was grunting or whining, but whatever the sound was, it made Kosmas run faster. She followed them. They were in a tunnel carved with scarlet nautilus shells and dark green seaweed. The colours pulsed from dim to bright and back again. She heard whimpering and snuffling and the dull thudding of bare skin on stone. She saw Asterion lunge, in the strange, changing light. Kosmas screamed and fell, and she stopped short, panting.

"No." Asterion's whisper was thick, almost human. She hadn't heard him speak in months. He bent and touched and backed away. Kosmas's arms and legs lashed, and his back arched and strained. "No." Asterion turned, his horns shrinking, his fur becoming golden hair. His eyes narrowed and blinked sightlessly at Polymnia. He was no longer the bull; he was a young man, plunging toward the open space of the altar—plunging past her, so that she was alone in the corridor with Kosmas.

He was dying. She knew this as soon as she squatted beside him and saw his wounds: the gaping flesh and the blood, which was spurting in beautiful arcs and collecting on the ground like dark tidal pools. His eyes rolled past her and then back. He gazed at her. Blood streamed out of his mouth and he coughed; he choked and writhed and reached for her with clawed hands.

The first notes of her song were so soft that their silver shimmered in the air above him, thin as ocean spray. The godmarked light thickened as she sang; very soon she could hardly see his face through the film of silver. But she knew he was quieting. His limbs loosened and he sighed a long, slow sigh, and she sang on, weaving peace and surrender as she had so many times before. She put her hand under his head, which rocked and stilled. She held her breath and the silver curtain parted and she saw his eyes, steady and finished.

The obsidian was ready. She drew it from her belt; she drew it along his throat. He gurgled as all the sheep and cows and pigs had. He subsided as they had, with a hiss and a *thunking* of bones and a flopping of skin. Her voice dipped so that it was barely a murmur. "Quiet," she sang. "Be quiet and certain. Sleep, now and forever."

She stopped singing only when she knew he was dead. She looked into the fixed blue of his eyes and then she leaned forward and closed them, as she had the eyes of those sheep and cows and pigs. *And now?* She didn't need this question, but she wanted it; it reminded her of purpose and home.

The obsidian was sharp enough. She doubted this, when she set it to his armpit, but the flesh parted and the bone splintered and the pieces fell to the ground as she wished them to. Great slabs of flesh; quivering, wet bits, large and small, crimson and oozing, as much alive as dead. She set the head and hands and feet aside, as she always had before, in the slaughterhouse. She'd throw them somewhere: off her bridge, maybe, beyond sight or care.

The pieces were heavy. She knew they would be, and yet she wondered, as she dragged them back to the altar room: *Why do bits of body feel like stone?* They were very red, on the altar. They shone and shook and steamed, a little, as distant gears spun.

She didn't see Asterion, as she stacked the meat. She thought she heard more whimpering, but she didn't look for him. Flayed thigh, shin, belly, chest; she piled Kosmas, remembering her father and sister and the blossoms that had waved at her from the wall across from the slaughterhouse. She didn't see Asterion, but he was there. *You're hungry. This is for you.*

When she was done she backed into one of the corridors. Long moments passed. She hadn't expected him to emerge right away, and yet she felt sick when he didn't. He had to be in one of the other passages; had to be close enough to smell the gift, at least. She twisted her sticky hands together and thought that she must wash them, and her shift, in the stream that sprang from the rock—and yet she couldn't move until he came.

When he did, he was crawling. His arched spine was covered in fur, and his back legs were the bull's, and his horns screamed across the floor, but the rest of him was human. *He's a patchwork god*, she thought. She pressed her hands against her knees to keep herself still, because she wanted to spring forward to him, to pass him the gift herself. But she didn't. She watched him advance, snuffling, pausing a few times to drag an arm across his sweaty brow and down over his cheeks. When he reached the pile of meat he leaned over it. His lips twisted and he squeezed his eyes shut.

Go on, she thought.

He leaned back on his bull's legs and picked up a piece of meat with his boy's hands. He stared at it, then raised his face and looked straight toward her hiding place. *He saw me! He was watching; thank the gods, he knows what I've done for him.* He looked back at the meat and threw it with a grunt that turned into a shout. The shout went on and on, echoing up against the bands of light and stone. She covered her ears but this didn't help—and anyway, she could see him; his mottled face and distended mouth, making sounds that weren't words.

When the echoes had died, he reached for another piece. This one was smaller—a forearm, she guessed, spread and halved. He brought it to his lips and bit. He jerked his head back and forth, clawing and wrenching, and some came away. His throat worked as he swallowed it. Immediately after he had, he coughed and gagged. The meat came back up and landed on the stone, along with a gush of fluid. He sobbed, his head hanging as if the weight of the horns were too great— only she knew it wasn't that. *"I don't want to hurt you but I will—I won't be able to help it."*

He lifted his head and took a third piece from the pile. He nibbled this one, at first, but soon he was tearing at it. He swallowed again and again. Blood branched down his hands and arms and dripped from his chin. She heard sobs, between bites, but he kept going. He'd eaten two entire pieces when he finally paused, gasping, chest heaving.

His eyes slid back to the shadows where she was. *Yes*, she thought, *look: here I am*—but before she could be foolish enough to speak or move into the light, a great blast of hot air rushed up from behind her and into the altar chamber. She saw it hit him; saw his head go back and his hands go out, as if he'd be able to ward it off. He changed almost immediately, and much more smoothly than she'd seen him do before. *Because he's eaten. Because he's stronger.* He roared and struck at the stone with his hooves: sparks spat and swirled. He tossed his furred head and ran—not toward her, but out between two columns and down the corridor beyond. As she moved to follow, metal shrieked and the corridor's mouth disappeared, as it had when Kosmas had first tried to carry Zenais's body away. When the grinding stopped, different walls stretched away into blue-lit darkness.

Polymnia screamed his name and other things she hardly understood, as if all the words she'd been too shy to say to him had been gathering in her throat, waiting for this fear to loose them. When her voice went hoarse and dry she pressed her lips together and listened to the quiet. The waterfall flowed. A bird called, very faintly, from the sky she couldn't see. The meat that had been Kosmas sizzled on the stone at her feet.

Patience, Polymnia, she told herself, as she tried to slow her breathing. *You're in the Goddess's home. She'll lead him back to you.*

———— • ————

Polymnia had always known how to be patient—with frightened beasts and her angry father; with dinner guests who took so long to eat that her legs ached as she stood waiting for them to finish so she could sing. Now she watched the corridors change and tried to determine whether there were reasons for their changing—but even after days and nights and months of staring and poking at the gaps between the corridors and altar room with obsidian and fingers, she still didn't know. Sometimes they shifted after steam burst from the earth beneath the altar chamber; other times the steam burst but the corridors stayed still. Sometimes she heard rumbling that sounded like distant rockfalls and waited for walls to go up or come down, but they didn't; other times they did, with absolutely no warning.

There's no pattern, she thought. *I'll never be able to know when or why or how—only the Great Daedalus and the Great Goddess know.* She closed her eyes as she thought this, and felt peace and surrender wash over her. Such calm: she imagined she understood, now, what beasts felt as they listened to her godmarked voice.

It rained as she waited. At first, drops spattered from the mouths of the pipes, but soon six thin, steady streams of water were flowing. Polymnia smiled at the way sections of them seemed to hang motionless in the air, while the rest cascaded and struck the stone and then sprayed up again. She held out her hands and stepped forward so that the spray hit her.

Twelve days had passed since his latest flight from her, and she was still alone. *Patience, Polymnia,* she told herself, the silent words a new sort of song.

He returned on the fifteenth day, part boy again. She put her hands to her mouth so she wouldn't make any noise, though she wanted to cry out his name— joyfully, this time. His head was the bull's. He walked to the altar steps, slumping under the weight of his muzzle and horns. At first he didn't look at her, and she was relieved and hopeless—but then he raised his sad, round eyes to her. His thick lips twitched, and she decided it was a sort of smile. A godsmile. The fur under his chin was dark and crusted with blood.

He knelt clumsily and she crouched behind him. She'd cooked the Kosmas-meat on the hot stone she'd found in one of the steamiest corridors, then rubbed each slab with salt from the fish: she knew how quickly meat spoiled. She'd drizzled the top piece in olive oil. It nearly slipped out of her fingers as she tugged it free and set it on the ground by his hand (also bloodstained; she'd try to lead him under the waterfall as soon as she could). He pulled his hand back convulsively. Extended it again, as the breath rasped in his enormous nostrils.

Go on, she almost said. She shuddered with the need to touch his scarred shoulders and back—his skin, his fur; anything, everything.

When he lifted the meat to his mouth and ate, she wrapped her arms around herself and sang a quiet, happy song that only they would ever hear.

——— · ———

The marks of her days stretched almost halfway around the altar chamber: rows of them, some straight, some angled, like patterns she'd seen painted onto clay in

Athens. She counted them silently every morning when she made a new mark, at first simply because she needed to remind herself that the days were passing, and then because she forgot how many there'd been. She was often surprised, as she murmured the numbers. Ninety . . . One hundred seventy-two . . . Two hundred fifty-four . . . Sometimes, after Asterion had returned from yet more wanderings, he stood at the wall beside her and stared at the marks, his gaze dipping and rising, his lips moving, as if he were counting too. He never spoke, and neither did she.

She dreamed of people, on the five hundred sixtieth night. Her mistress, her father, her sister, the boy who'd always frightened her with his godmarked teeth, which looked like a rat's and could chew through anything, even metal, or the leather of her belt: she dreamed that they were all falling. Some of them flailed; others held their limbs out straight and still, like starfish on a rock. As they got closer she saw their gaping mouths. They were silent. All she heard was wind, filling her ears as if she were the one falling. When her sister's blood-smeared hands were about to graze Polymnia's face, she woke with a gasp and dragged her own hands through her tangled hair.

I need to be ready, she thought as she scrambled to her feet in the empty chamber. *I need to know exactly how to get back to the mountain's door, because more Athenians will fall, someday soon, and we'll need them. He needs them* now—*he's weak; he chokes down dates and fish but they're not enough; it's been too long since Kosmas—and why* why *have I found no one else?*

When she closed her eyes, she remembered how they'd first approached the altar room—she, Kosmas, Zenais, Ligeia, Asterion. The corridor had been low, with a crystal roof and walls. Kosmas's head had brushed it, as had Asterion's horns, which had made an awful, slow, screeching sound. Polymnia had tipped her own head back and seen the blurred underside of something moist and wide, with tapered ends: a slug, perhaps, the size of her hand, oozing a dark trail along the crystal above her. They'd emerged between the two columns that were carved with bees and butterflies—a part of her had noticed them as she was running to catch up with Kosmas, who'd been shouting about food and water.

She went to stand between these columns and laid her fingers on the butterflies' blue-and-red painted wings. The corridor beyond wasn't made of crystal: it was stone, with a fissure that ran through its floor and seeped golden light. So she waited. After a time, she went back to the altar and ate a fig. She sat on the top step and stared at the corridor. Asterion's hooves clattered, and she straightened, turning to see if he'd appear—but he didn't, and the sound faded. She remembered with a smile how the old, frightened Polymnia had thought he'd never return, after Kosmas. Asterion left the altar chamber all the time now, but *this* Polymnia knew to be patient. It might take him days or weeks, but the corridors always moved in a way that led him back to her—or perhaps it was his god who showed him where to go.

The sun faded as the sound of his hooves had; the six shafts of light wavered farther and farther up the walls, until they vanished and the tiny bits of sky beyond the pipes went dark. The sun was back again when the corridor finally changed. She felt the stone beneath her thrum as invisible gears began to turn, and she returned to the columns, which vibrated beneath her palms. As the crystal corridor eased into view she wondered again how Daedalus had done it: perhaps walls and ceilings and floors spun like great wheels, one within the other, measured precisely to meet the altar chamber's doorways? Perhaps the corridors swung on cables that loosened and tightened? It made her head hurt to think about.

When the gears had stopped moving, she stepped into the hallway. She saw Kosmas's obsidian scratches immediately, because they were as clear as if he'd just made them. She imagined that the old Polymnia might have thought about what his face had looked like as he'd dragged the point along their path— thought about his intent blue gaze and his half-smile. This Polymnia didn't need memories.

The scratches wended along the crystal walls, then painted stone ones; they led her up the ramp Ligeia had led them down, long ago. This ramp was rough stone, not polished, and, though she scuffed her palms and knees, she had no trouble crawling up it. In the chamber above, she stood for a moment and remembered the only important thing: Asterion, a boy except for the horns, stepping timidly into their midst. Ligeia had called him a monster. Not long after, he'd cried out Polymnia's name, and she'd followed him, though she hadn't thought she would.

She followed the scratches into the blue corridor she knew would end in a row of jars. It seemed to take longer to walk back to them than it had to walk away—but maybe she was just tired. Maybe her fear, right after the fall, had made everything seem blurry, outside of time. *Be stronger*, she commanded herself. *Walk faster. You're better than that other Polymnia was.*

At last the jars were there, in their perfect row—but

the sections of ledge weren't. She wrapped her hands around the lip of the jar Zenais had held onto and gazed up the wall. The little golden lights shone on the undersides of the ledges, very far above—except that all the pieces looked like one, from here. She let go of the jar and seized one of the cables that ran up the wall. She tugged, though only half-heartedly; Master Daedalus had devised a method of getting the pieces back up, and she wouldn't be able to get them down on her own—and maybe not even with help. No—it would be the new Athenians who'd make them move again. All those frightened, wounded Athenians.

Polymnia didn't notice that she was grinding her hand along the metal cable, and she didn't notice when she started to bleed.

——— · ———

She was sleeping, when the door in the mountain opened.

She'd wondered how she'd know, or if she'd know; after all, the altar chamber was very deep within the stone. But the shuddering ran even deeper. She sat up, pressing her palms against the floor. The chamber was bright with morning light. The water glinted as it fell. She was alone; the bull-god had been gone for days. She'd heard him bellow once or twice, and another time she'd heard the drumming of his hooves. Now she stood up on trembling legs and heard only gears and stone and, threaded through these, screaming and sobbing. *So close*, she thought, even though she knew it wasn't true—that the Goddess and Daedalus had seen to it that sounds were never where they seemed to be.

The crystal corridor shone beyond the columns: the *right* corridor. *Thank you, Great Goddess—thank you—I will sacrifice to you very soon.* . . . To the air she sang, in a voice that didn't tremble at all, "Come back, my dearest god! Come back; I'll just be hunting." She slipped her tattered robe on and was away before the song's silver tendrils had dissolved.

CHAPTER TEN

Polymnia had counted on at least three Athenians, but had dreamed of four or five. Instead, though she could still hear screams and cries all around her, there was just one girl, hunkered on the ground by one of the ledges, clutching her ankle. Her cheeks were streaked with oozing cuts. Polymnia gazed at the blood as the girl gazed at her, silent and gaping. *This will do for now,* Polymnia thought. *There will be more. I simply have to be patient.*

"Don't be afraid." Polymnia's voice was raspy; it almost hurt, leaving her throat, though she'd started speaking the numbers of the days aloud, to try to remember how speaking felt.

The girl threw herself at Polymnia, sobbing and grasping her robe with blood-smeared hands. The stubble on the girl's skull prickled Polymnia's skin but she didn't shiver. She smiled.

"Hush, my sweet," she sang, and the girl went still and heavy in her arms. The silver of Polymnia's voice wrapped around them both.

"What's your name?" she asked, when she'd finished singing.

The girl sniffled. "Korinna," she murmured.

"Well, Korinna, I'm Polymnia, and I'm going to take care of you. No need to fret."

It was easier than she'd thought it would be. She was back in her mistress's house, comforting her mistress's child, making guests sigh and sit back in their cushioned chairs. Polymnia was dressed in the finest dyed linen, her belly full, the last of the sun turning her unbound hair to fire. The wind smelled like flowers.

Korinna said, "But I broke my ankle, I think." Her words were slurred: pain, shock, the sudden, sweet lethargy of a godmarked melody.

"That's fine, little one. That's fine. I'll take care of you. Come, now: up and lean on me. Yes: just like that. Lean on me and we'll walk to a place I know, where you'll forget your pain."

"Thank you," Korinna whispered.

———— . ————

When they came to the lake of fire, Korinna's eyes went very wide. Polymnia had decided, after months and years of consideration, that it would have to be here: she didn't want to soil the altar chamber, and many of the corridors were too narrow and dim. Also, this was the heart of the Goddess. Master Daedalus's words said so—and Polymnia would have known, in any case.

"What is this place?"

Polymnia could hardly hear the girl. She remembered the first time she'd seen the fire. She remembered how she'd hardly been able to breathe because of the smothering heat; how she'd hardly been able to drag herself across the bridge to the blackened island.

"Hush," she said—and this time Korinna looked at her with terror, not relief. She whirled away from the passage's end and tried to push past Polymnia, but Polymnia grasped her clean, smooth robe and pulled her in close.

"You'll forget your pain. I promise." Her tongue was so clumsy, so unaccustomed to making words; she just repeated ones she'd already said, as if this would be easier.

Korinna struggled a bit, when Polymnia began to tug her toward the bridge. By the time their feet touched the hot stone, the girl had gone limp. By the time the bridge gave way to black earth, Polymnia was carrying her. She felt as strong as a priestess bearing a calf across her shoulders; she felt the Goddess and Artemis beside her, within her, making her greater than she'd ever been.

Korinna didn't make a sound when Polymnia laid her on the circle of cool, white stone that sat atop the soot and obsidian flakes. The girl's head rolled back and forth near the spiral of words.

Pray, Athenian, for you have reached the
Great Goddess's heart.

Polymnia smiled. "You are my prayer," she said to Korinna, who moaned and squirmed weakly. White bone glinted from the torn skin of her ankle. "Just like Zenais," Polymnia said—because now her voice was as strong as the rest of her. "Like Zenais, except that you'll suffer no more than this."

Korinna seemed so weak—and yet when Polymnia raised her obsidian blade she flung herself sideways, screaming a thin, piercing scream, and Polymnia had to drop the blade to grab her. "Be still, little dove," she sang breathlessly, "be still and go to sleep; for you there'll be no need of morning."

Korinna's body sagged. Her eyelids dipped. They

fluttered a little when her throat opened—but only a little.

———·———

Polymnia's father had taught her so much about dead things. She remembered him now, as she hadn't in a very long time. The smell of fresh blood made her think of him. She remembered his face as he bent down to shift her hands on the haft of the skinning knife. She remembered *his* hands, which were always slick with blood, but somehow never slippery. The light had been muddy, in the slaughterhouse. She'd had to do so much by touch.

"Be firm," he'd told her in his low, whistly voice. "Be sure, before you cut, where the blade will lead you. Otherwise it will cut *you*." And he'd hold his left hand up, and she'd see his three fingers and two stubs wiggling at her in the murky air, and she'd nod and bend to the carcass.

"Over here, girl," he'd say. "This one's restive." She'd leave the skinning tools and go to where the cow was, stamping and bellowing and tossing its head so that no cut would have been clean.

She was always embarrassed, at first. They weren't alone, after all; there were other people in the room, skinning rank, fresh things that hung or lay in patches of filth that would suck at your heels and trip you. But her father would brandish his three fingers and his long, curved knife and flash his crooked teeth at her and command her over and over to sing, and she would, in the end, because everything frightened her until she was singing, and because he'd beat her if she didn't.

Silver came out of her mouth. It came out in ribbons that turned to sheets like summer rain. It swept through her body, as cool and clean as the blood was warm and filthy. The cow would go still and quiet; it would make no sound at all, even when the knife made its long, deep cut.

Later, as they worked side-by-side, her father would say, "Now sing again. The gods didn't mark you so you'd sit skinning dead animals—but you're doing that for now, and you should get their attention. Remind them, so they take notice and lift us both out of this muck. Sing, girl."

Her hands moved on the wet flesh beneath her but the rest of her was far away—too far for embarrassment or fear. Artemis and Apollo had *both* blessed her, folk said. They'd sung their marks into her ear when she was born.

"You're too good for us," her father said, gesturing from himself to her little sister, who was unmarked and always sick and had no skill at butchering. "Your godmarked voice and your fine red hair—someday your gods will see to it that we're all taken away from here." Leaning over dead beasts in the slaughterhouse, she'd wanted to believe him. She hadn't, though. She'd doubted Artemis and Apollo and her father.

Now she leaned over rank, fresh things and thought how wrong that old Polymnia had been.

She traced the girl's blood into Master Daedalus's words. She traced entirely new patterns, too: other, smaller spirals and lines of bull's horns, crimson on the white. She sang of Daedalus and Asterion, Kosmas and Zenais and Korinna. She sang of cattle and pigs and sheep. The flames around the island flickered with her godmarked silver.

When she was finished painting, she slid out of her soiled robe and spread it out on the stone. She stacked as many pieces of meat in it as she thought she'd be able to carry and tied the cloth ends together. Korinna's clean robe she plucked carefully up and wedged beneath one of her armpits, where it would get only a little dirtier. She set the rest of the meat in long rows across each of the bridges. By the time she returned for it, it would be cooked. *He'll like that*, she thought. *It'll be such a treat.*

When she returned to the altar chamber, he was waiting for her.

———— . ————

In the months that followed, Polymnia searched every tunnel and chamber she knew, and several she'd somehow missed, in her other wanderings. In the chamber of stalactites she found four Athenians so frightened and wounded that she had to sing to them right there, instead of luring them to the Goddess's heart. It took days to bring the first three, bit by bit, to the altar chamber. When she was nearly finished her last trip with the fourth, the corridors took so long to reshape themselves into the familiar pattern that everything she was carrying had spoiled by the time she set it down on the snake altar. She raged, ripping and tearing, retching at the smell—and he didn't come, of course. In the end she gathered it all back up and tossed it into the lake of fire.

As she was leaving the lake, she heard a wolf's howl. *You*—but the name wouldn't come, wouldn't . . . *Ligeia,* she thought at last, with a rush of relief and anger. *Where have you been hiding, all this time?* The howl climbed and climbed, then trailed into a whine, and silence. *I'm glad you're still alive,* she thought. *I'll enjoy hunting you.*

In a low, tiny chamber she'd never seen before, she found a body that had obviously been there for a long time: just bones, with bits of hair and cloth hanging off them. There were gnaw marks on the bones, and she wondered whether they were from his teeth—but no, he'd never have been able to fit into the space, not even if he'd been mostly human. *Who, then?* she thought with a stab of anger. *Who stole this from my bull-god's mouth? And where are all the others? Fourteen each time, and I've found only a handful of these.* She imagined tiny white lizards burrowing into flesh and re-emerging from nostrils or ears. She imagined tiny white spiders picking their way daintily over whatever was left, when the skin was gone.

She began to wedge stones and thick shards of broken pottery into the spaces where there were cables, between altar room and passages, and passages and other doorways. Sometimes the gears ground and stone moved and her bits and pieces held; other times they didn't, and the corridors changed with even more shrieking, and a rat-a-tat popping of rock and clay.

By the time she dug the thousandth mark into the altar chamber wall, there were many more pieces of stone to move around. He always dislodged some, in the frenzy of strength after he fed, and when she went to put them back, she always seemed to have more than she'd started with. She imagined that she was the Great Daedalus, as she worked—him, only greater. Her materials were far more interesting than his: she had large rounded stones, which added a wonderful sort of texture to the walls, and smooth, slender branches that wove snugly. She'd run her hands over them, once they were firmly set, and imagine that her old mistress was beside her. Her old mistress, and King Aegeus too.

"Such artistry!" the king would say, and her mistress would nod.

"Indeed—two godmarks—have you ever heard of such a thing? I've decided not to sell her, after all. Child: come, now, and we'll walk by the sea, and you'll sing birds down into our hands, and I'll shower you with gold and bright dyed cloth, and you'll never, ever leave—no—you and your Asterion will stay here with me forever."

———— · ————

Polymnia no longer counted the marks on the wall, after she'd made a new one. When she tried, her vision and fingers faltered—and anyway, she was starting to forget some of the words that went with the numbers. When she gazed at the marks, though, she knew that the door in the mountain would soon open again— so she kept digging her obsidian into stone, day after day.

She sang and cut. She cooked and stacked. She carried and stacked again, as rain pattered or sun wavered. She gathered up the figs and loaves and fish when they fell. She watched him—she always did, whether he was feeding (his fingers the only human things about him), or hunkered down with his furred head in the waterfall, his thick tongue lapping. She waited for him when he wasn't there; she arranged figs and salt fish and bread, while she waited, and nibbled some herself, when she remembered to. Sometimes pictures from another world bloomed behind her eyes: the sun setting over a harbour crowded with ships; a kitchen full of cooks and slaves and steam that smelled of soup and roasting meat. She saw the pictures, but she was forgetting the names for what she saw, just as she was forgetting numbers. She smiled and sang and stopped trying to count or remember.

— . —

For a long time he came and went, as he had since the beginning. He fed and slept, paced the perimeter of the altar chamber, gazed at her with his god-eyes, then disappeared for time she was able to measure as weeks. She never spoke to him, not even when he had a human mouth and could maybe have answered, and he was silent too, and always distant, even if he was close.

Until one night. She assumed it was spring, because the world above was often stormy. It had just stormed, in fact: thunder outside that the mountain seemed to answer with its own rumblings, and lightning that turned the chamber's stone ceiling white. Polymnia had closed her eyes and smiled because she could see the white behind her lids, flashing just before the ground shook. She looked for him, between flashes, but he wasn't there. When the storm passed, she stretched out on her robe and slept.

She woke to his hands on her skin. He was mostly a boy—but not a boy, anymore: a man, so much taller and broader than he had been when they'd fallen together—and he was straddling her, touching her breasts and belly with his hands while his foot-hooves jittered on the stone. His bull's head dipped and she felt hot breath on her face and whimpered, because she was so full of hunger for him that she felt no fear. He pawed at her hair, so long and smooth again, and flattened his palms on it, on either side of her head, so that she couldn't move it at all. He raised himself up and thrust into her and she cried out and wrapped her hands around his scarred, straining arms.

Just that one thrust—and he changed. His bull's muzzle shortened and his fur turned to flesh. In a moment he was a man, gazing down at her with his head bobbing and swaying under the weight of his horns. "Son of Poseidon," she said raggedly, and he groaned and pulled out of her and away. He crouched with his arms wound around his knees, panting, staring at her with a man's eyes.

"God's son?" she whispered.

His eyebrows rose and his eyes widened and he laughed a short, sharp laugh. Before she could reach for him he scrambled and stood. He ran from her, beneath a high-up blur of light that might have been the moon.

——— · ———

This time she wasn't patient, and she didn't wait for him to return. She went down corridors and into every chamber she could find. She cursed the gears when they shifted and kept her away from the altar chamber, because maybe he'd gone back there while she was somewhere else—but she kept looking, imagining that five days, six, seven, had passed. Imagining weeks. She heard nothing of him—no hoofbeats or breathing that might be close or far away—but she could feel him with her, a silver spark beneath the mountain, whirling just beyond the light her own spark made.

When she finally found her way back to the chamber, it was empty.

There were no more storms. Summer, then. The old Polymnia had hated summers in the slaughterhouse, when the heat had made the regular stench and sweat unbearable. The new Polymnia drew the Goddess's heat up through her skin and into her head. She thought about the god's body on hers, in hers, and knew that that could not be the only time. *My love,* she thought, as her chest ached with tears. *Why did you run from me?*

He still hadn't come back when the door in the mountain opened again. *Two more years,* some part of her thought; *I knew it would be soon.*

She rose. She shook with the need to run to them— to the newest Athenians, whose cries she could already hear, snaking through the Goddess's tunnels like blood through veins. But the corridor wasn't right. She waited. She washed in the waterfall, her skin puckering, and brushed her hair out with her fingers as she stood drying. She slipped Korinna's robe over her head and thought, *Lucky there's a fresh batch: I'll be needing a cleaner one of these.*

She was calmer by the time the corridor changed, three days later. As it settled, she slipped her obsidian blade into the cloth belt at her waist and stood up very tall, pulling her shoulders and head back. *I'll hunt for you, again, my god,* she thought. *You must be so hungry; this will bring you back.* She said, as if they were already in front of her, "Greetings, Athenians." She cleared her throat. "Greetings, Athenians. I am Polymnia. Do not be afraid."

She smiled and stepped between the columns.

—BOOK—
THREE

CHARA

Third Athenian Sacrifice

CHAPTER ELEVEN

Chara didn't mean to scream. She knew where she was going, after all; she knew she was going to fall. But the sound came from her throat anyway, as the mountain darkness seized her and pulled her down. She screamed and flailed, and fear dissolved any strength she might have felt on the other side of the great metal door.

Ariadne came to her, as she fell. Ariadne, not Asterion—and even breathless with wind and terror, Chara fought against this. But there she was: the princess, scowling, wrenching at all the tiny knots Chara had just made in her hair. The princess, simpering at Karpos; raising her hand to strike Chara; crying out Chara's name as she ran into the labyrinth.

All these images vanished when she landed. She lay on her back gazing up into an explosion of gold and crimson sparks. Her fingers clawed at something that felt like moss, and something else that felt like stone. She flexed her toes and rotated her ankles, as she began to hear again. Sobbing, very close, and screaming, farther away—or maybe the sounds were coming from the same place; all of them leapt and blurred.

"Quiet, now: Sotiria will help," Chara heard someone say, from right beside her. But when she took a deep breath and sat up, she was by herself.

All right, then, she thought as she looked around. *Here you are.*

She was on a ledge that was indeed thick with green-brown moss. Above her stretched a wall glowing with tiny Daedalus-lamps and gleaming with Daedalus-metal—cables, which began to move before she could decide what to do next. The ledge lurched beneath her. It moved down, down; she stretched to peer over the side, though her bones and skin hurt so much she wondered how she could move at all. She saw darkness, and steam that coiled up toward her. Her hands slipped; her body was running with sweat. The steam thickened and scalded her cheeks and lungs as the ledge crept lower. She tried to swallow and couldn't; she retched and vomited a string of bile onto the moss.

Asterion, she thought. *Asterion, Asterion, O all the gods and giant clams—Asterion. . . .*

When the ledge bumped against floor, she pushed herself to her feet. The world tipped around her, but only for a moment. She was aching and bruised—but that was all. She stood and breathed smoke and heat and slow, new calm.

Her ledge had come to rest in a corridor. There was a smooth wall to her left; to her right, the corridor stretched away into more steam-clotted darkness. Urns were set along it at intervals—one fallen and cracked in half, and past it two more, upright. Beyond the second, Chara saw people.

"That other ledge!" said the same voice that had spoken before. "It's down! Maybe Sotiria's on it—she has to be—we need her—Sotiria? Is that you?"

Chara pushed herself away from the wall and stepped off her ledge. She walked a few careful paces, into the flickering light of the wall lamps. A girl gaped at her. A boy was kneeling beside the girl, cradling his left arm. And Theseus was near them both, his golden brows drawn together in a puzzled frown.

"Who are *you*?" the girl demanded.

Before Chara could answer, Theseus said, "I remember: you are the Princess Ariadne's slave."

"Yes," Chara said. "I'm also Chara, daughter of Pherenike."

The girl lurched for her and grasped her robe, twisting it tight in her fists. "How did you get here? Where's Sotiria? *Where is Sotiria?*"

"Melaina," Theseus snapped. "Enough." He stepped forward and put his hands over hers; he held them until she let Chara go. "Explain, Chara," he said, and suddenly she heard him in her mind too, speaking words that she could feel all the way down to her bones: ::*Daughter of Pherenike: tell us why you are here.*::

She was shaking. She wondered how long she'd been shaking. Somehow, though, her voice was steady. "I arranged with Sotiria to take her place. I need to find Asterion."

Melaina scowled and opened her mouth, but Theseus spoke before she could. "Asterion. The monster."

"No," Chara said, and swallowed around a hard knot of tears. "Asterion, Pasiphae's son, and Poseidon's, and even Minos's. Princess Ariadne's half-brother. My friend."

Theseus's eyes gleamed as he looked at her. "The Princess Ariadne told me nothing of a half-brother— only that this was a vile, murderous creature; she begged me to come here, promised me aid, so that I might rid the world of him."

"She begged you for something else, too." Chara

wanted to curl herself into a dark corner and sleep. She wanted to run somewhere, everywhere, shrieking Asterion's name until he called back to her. "I wrote the letter to you," she went on. "For Ariadne. I know she asked that you take her away from here, once you'd killed Asterion. I know she expects you to someday make her queen of Athens."

The hum of Theseus's mind-voice splintered and crackled, and Chara closed her eyes for a moment.

"Well, well," Melaina growled. "How very interesting. Tell me, O Prince: are you intending to do as the Cretan whore wishes?"

The boy blinked and slid his wide-eyed gaze to Chara. His mouth was wide too; he looked so much like a fish that she felt a laugh push away the tears in her throat. She bit her lower lip hard enough that she tasted blood, and both laughter and tears vanished.

"I intended," Theseus said, his own voice slow and deep, "to kill the monster that has been killing Athenians."

Chara shook her head, half expecting tangled curls to fall across her eyes, as they always did—except that no, of course, her skull was rough with stubble and razor cuts. "You can't. My Lord—Theseus—please trust me. If he's . . . if we find him still alive, please let me go to him before you try to use that knife Ariadne gave you."

"Ah," Melaina said, "so she gave you a knife, did she? And what else?"

Theseus's eyes were on Chara again, as narrow as the boy's were round. "Tell her," Theseus said. "Since you were there when the princess gave me these things."

Chara sucked the last of the blood from the inside of her lip and looked at Melaina. "A ball of string."

She watched the other girl's lips twist into a sneer. "A ball of string fashioned by the great Master Daedalus, whose godmark is in everything he makes. Perhaps the prince will show it to you."

Careful, she told herself; *he* is *a prince—the prince of your enemies, no less—don't be rude.* Then she thought, with a rush of something like abandon, like hope: *It doesn't matter. We're all prisoners, here.*

Theseus let the sleeve fall away from his right arm. The ball of string was attached to his bicep, the hooked end of it looped around and through the rest of the ball. Chara imagined him squeezing it between his arm and body, as the priestesses prodded him toward the mountain door.

Melaina reached out a finger, touched the string, pulled the finger sharply back. "Yes," Chara said, "it's warm, and it vibrates. I used to think it was alive, somehow. It goes on and on and on, even when you're sure the other end will have to appear soon, because you've trailed it all through the palace." Asterion and Icarus laughing as they ran around corners and down steps, holding the hooked end; Chara panting, trying to catch up, holding the ball that grew smaller but didn't ever run out.

"We'll secure it here, somewhere," Theseus said. He walked back to the wall and craned up at the invisible door.

The boy, who had been very quiet, said in a quavering voice, "It won't help, though, will it? There's no way of getting up there again, even if the string did lead us all the way through the labyrinth and back."

"There would be," Chara said. "The hook on the end— it's weighted, and when it finds nooks and crannies it clings. You can climb it." She remembered Icarus sending the string whistling through the air to the top of the waterfall outside Knossos. She remembered him climbing swiftly, and Asterion trying to go after him—except he'd fallen with a *thump* that knocked his breath out, so that his laughter sounded like an old man's wheezing. "We'll be able to get up there."

Theseus tossed the hook; it fell back toward him and he had to leap aside so that it wouldn't hit him. The string whined as it re-spooled itself.

Chara cleared her throat. "Would you like me to do it? I've had some practice with it."

He grunted and handed her the ball. As it warmed her palm she forgot all the times she'd watched Icarus use it successfully; all she could see was him standing beneath the polished black pipes on the slope above and outside where she was now, spinning and throwing, spinning and throwing, uselessly. *And now here I am, my poor, lost friend*, she thought with a sickening surge of fear and giddiness. *Inside.*

The corridor was only wide enough for her to swing it in arcs, rather than full circles—and yet the first time she let it go, it flew and stuck in a spot far up the wall. Theseus grunted.

"Excellent," Melaina said, "but now what? Will we wait another two years for the door to open again, then charge out with the bull-thing's head and hope everyone lets us pass?"

Chara glanced at Theseus, who smiled a little. "I suppose you know this part too, slave of Ariadne?"

"No. But I can guess. You'll call Ariadne with your mind-voice, when you're ready. And she'll come with her sister, the Princess Phaidra, whose godmark lets her open locks. Either that, or she'll get the key from her father—assuming Daedalus even had one made."

"Yes," Theseus said. "Something like that."

"Except you'll do this without the bull's head."

He shook his own head. "That cannot be. It is my task. I have promised."

"Promised Ariadne, who lied to you, who didn't tell you what he was! Please—"

"Enough!" the boy cried. His voice cracked. "I'm hurt, and so are you, Melaina! We can't stay here forever—we need to find food and water. I heard there'd be food and water, for the beast!"

Melaina grunted and took two steps away from them, favouring her left ankle. "Alphaios speaks sense, for once. Pull on your godmarked string, my Lord, and let's be off."

A long, silent look passed between Melaina and Theseus. At last he said, "You are hurt; let me carry you."

"No." The word wobbled, just a little. Melaina turned away from all of them and limped off into the corridor.

Theseus followed her, and Alphaios—after a glance over his shoulder at Chara—followed him. She took as deep a breath as she could of the hot, thick air. Before she moved, Theseus's mind-voice was in her again, drumming like bull's hooves on packed earth.

::*I will think on what you have told me. I can promise you nothing more.*::

Thank you, she thought, even though she knew he couldn't hear her. She went after them, into Asterion's mountain.

———— • ————

"What's that?" Alphaios whispered. They'd been walking for hours—or so Chara's body was telling her, with its hunger, thirst, and weariness—through chambers and corridors, into dead ends that sent them shuffling back again, along the length of Icarus's string. Only one of these places had been utterly dark, forcing them to crawl around on hard-packed dirt, looking for doorways that ended up being only knee-high. Every other space had had light sources of some kind: darting ones that looked like sparks or fireflies; small gold ones that flickered, set in rows. But the light that Alphaios was gesturing at, reflected on a wall at the end of their corridor, was the bright white of noon sun on stone and didn't flicker at all.

"Perhaps we have already come to the centre of Master Daedalus's creation," Theseus murmured. "Perhaps the monster awaits us here." He turned to Chara. "Hold this," he said as he handed her the string. "I may need both of my hands."

She wrapped her fingers around the ball. Its humming turned into a buzz when she closed both her hands around it. *No*, she thought. *Asterion's not there; I'd know if he was.*

Theseus crouched and reached under his robe. "Ah," Chara said, when his hand emerged holding Daedalus's blade. "There it is."

Melaina gave a low whistle as the blade snicked to its full length. "And a most impressive gift it is. I'm glad we won't have to saw at her brother's neck with a shard of—"

"Stop talking," Alphaios hissed, and, though she shot him a spiteful look, she did.

They flattened their backs against the corridor's

wall—rough, unfinished rock, veined with crystal that caught the white light and spun it into tiny rainbows. "Stay behind me," Theseus murmured, "except for you, Melaina. You must be ready to cast your darkness on whatever waits for us."

"Yes, my Prince," Melaina said, too sweetly. *Gods and mussels*, Chara thought, *Ariadne would have flogged me senseless, if I'd spoken to her like that.*

Theseus and Melaina edged closer to the corridor's turning. "You next," Alphaios said to Chara, and she thought she saw him flush, in the passage's strange, underwater glow. She smiled at him and went after Melaina.

"Ready?" Theseus said, craning back to look at them. Melaina nodded; Chara tightened her hand around Icarus's string; Alphaios was motionless. Just as Theseus was putting out his foot, they heard a sound.

"Someone's crying," Melaina said. Sniffling and sobbing, a gulp, more sobbing. "Godsblood," she said, much more loudly, "it's *Phoibe*."

"No," Alphaios said, "that's not her light: it's never steady like that, and never white—it's some sort of trap, and—"

Chara stepped past them all. She'd narrowed her eyes in anticipation, but the light was so blinding that she had to put her hands over her face. By the time she'd let them fall and blinked the world back into focus, Alphaios and Melaina were already past her, kneeling on either side of the crying girl, who was almost invisible within her own glow.

"What happened to your godlight, Phoibe?" Alphaios said, but the girl wasn't looking at him: her gleaming white eyes were fixed on Theseus.

"Oh, my Lord: I'm so glad you're here!" The words stirred the light, like fish making paths in water. "I don't know what happened to my godmark—it must be because I'm so afraid; it's stronger, and it hurts, and I was all alone—and I *heard* things; things coming to hurt me . . ."

"Quietly," Theseus said, and again Chara imagined his mind-voice, thrumming in Phoibe's bones and blood, warming and steadying. The white trembled around them. Silver forked within it, thin, then spreading to streams that ran together. Within moments, the white had become a soft, fading gold— and moments after that, all that was left were silver ribbons, rippling lazily in the air above Phoibe's head. She gasped and fell forward, and Theseus caught her.

"We will be triumphant," he said quietly, one hand on either side of her face, gazing into her eyes (which, Chara saw, were brown). "The Princess Ariadne has risked her own life to help us: she has given me two gifts that will see the beast dead and us away from here."

No, Chara thought, *no, no: not that first one.*

"All hail the wondrous Cretan princess," Melaina muttered, but Theseus didn't move his gaze from Phoibe's.

"You will help us, Phoibe: your godmark will see us safely through any darkness we may find." He smiled. "And you won't be alone anymore."

"Oh, noble Theseus," Melaina warbled, clasping her hands beneath her chin—and Theseus rose, very suddenly, and twisted to seize her by the shoulders.

"Melaina," he said, in a cold, flat voice Chara hadn't heard before, "this place, it seems, is full of light: Daedalus's, and now Phoibe's. It seems we have no need of someone who offers only darkness. So," he went on, gripping her chin as she tried to turn away from him, "take care, or you may find your*self* alone."

Chara could hardly hear Melaina when she spoke, also in an unfamiliar voice. "But my Lord—you promised me—"

He let her go, and she stumbled backward. "Those of you who wish to continue on together: follow me."

He took Phoibe's hand and lifted her to her feet. She leaned on him, and they walked the length of the oval chamber, to a doorway framed by two black columns. Alphaios scrambled to his feet and went after them.

"Melaina?" Chara said. The girl stared at her—through her—and didn't move. Chara walked to the columns and hesitated there—and suddenly Melaina was behind her.

"Faster, slave-girl," she snapped, "or we'll leave you behind." She brushed Icarus's string, as she swept past Chara, and it made a long, tremulous sound. Chara followed it.

CHAPTER TWELVE

There were so many sounds. A dripping that made Chara's dry mouth drier, as she imagined water. Hissing steam. Skittering pebbles—and, once, a different skittering: the claws of white lizards surging up and across the corridor's wall. Phoibe shrieked and kindled her godlight. Melaina laughed. Theseus lunged for the creatures, his mind-voice shouting wordlessly in Chara's head as they flowed away from his hands and vanished.

One day or night, a wolf howled.

They were standing close together, because the chamber they were in was so small. The ceiling was low and rough with tiny stalactites; Theseus had to bend his head to his chest so they didn't catch at his hair. The walls, though, were ringed with squat, smooth columns. Phoibe's soft light showed that the walls between them were painted with images of the sea: waves rolling into a harbour, with birds perched atop them; writhing octopus arms and plants beneath. Tiny bright buildings lined the harbour.

"Great Goddess," Alphaios whispered as the howl faded. "What was *that*?"

Chara watched Melaina slip her hand into Theseus's, watched him shake his free and edge away from her.

"We should really have a blade," Phoibe said in a rush. "All of us should—not just you, my Prince."

"Of *course* we should." Melaina rolled her eyes as

she spoke. Phoibe's godlight trembled for a moment—long wavering lines that grew and broke against the stone.

Theseus was leaning against a column, now. Chara saw him nod.

"I suppose that's me, then," said Alphaios. He got onto his knees and scuffed his way into the circle of light, his hands patting at the chamber's hard-packed earthen floor.

"Something that once lived but's now dead," he murmured. He was smiling, leaning forward into the silver-orange glow. He plucked something from the ground. "This'll do."

Melaina clutched his hand and pried it free. "An empty snail shell? Maybe the great Master Daedalus wished to mock us, by putting it here with these paintings. Maybe he wanted us to despair."

Or maybe he was thinking only of Athens, Chara thought. *Of his home, and yours. Because the buildings in the paintings aren't Cretan.*

"I've never seen such a big shell," Phoibe said. It *was* big: apple-sized, with a pointed tip that cast a formidable shadow on the earth-and-stone wall. *I'd have given it to Asterion*, Chara thought, *like I gave him all those other ones, at the summer palace, when he'd turned back into a boy again after being a god.*

"Hush." Theseus's body didn't move, but this one word stilled them all. "Let Alphaios use his godmark in peace."

Alphaios took the shell from Melaina. He set it on the ground in front of him and laid his palms on it. *Now for the silver*, Chara thought—and there it was, coursing from his skin just as it did from every other godmarked person's. *I've never been jealous before, but now I am, because they have godmarks and I have nothing at all except some rhymes and hope born only of myself— and look where we are.*

The shell warped and twisted in his hands. It was molten metal, then writhing vines; it twined between his fingers and onto the earth, where it bubbled like a pool of silver lava. Melaina leaned closer; Phoibe drew back. Theseus pushed himself away from the column, very slowly, and stood above them all.

Alphaios whimpered. His eyes were wide, staring at a place beyond the rest of them. The silver curled and grew, straightened and tapered to a glinting point. Edges sharpened. Chara let her breath out noiselessly, between her teeth—not that anyone would have heard it over the grinding of the metal.

"Well," Melaina said, as the grinding stopped. "Look at that—Alphaios can actually *do* something. Why haven't you done anything before now? We could have used better food on the boat, and we could certainly use some—"

"Shut up," Alphaios whispered. His eyes were closed. One of his hands was on the knife—for it was that, or nearly. A long, thin blade with a lumpy pommel, which he curled his fingers around. The silver in the metal and his skin dimmed. He opened his eyes. "I can't make food—I told you that! I turn dead things into other dead things—"

"Well, dead cows are delicious," Melaina interrupted—and then the wolf howl came again, much closer.

The silver of Theseus's weapon shone as it turned from dagger to sword, one tapering section at a time. "Phoibe," he said, "make as much light as you can, the moment you see the beast."

Only it wasn't a beast: it was a girl.

She stumbled into the chamber, and her howl twisted into a human cry as Phoibe's light flooded over all of them. She doubled over, holding her arms above her head. Her hair was a dark, tangled mass; her robe was blackened with dirt and maybe blood.

"Enough," Theseus murmured, and Phoibe's light dimmed from blinding noon to starlight. He stepped toward the girl, who straightened and met his gaze.

"What is your name?" he said. Chara watched her eyes dart and widen and knew that he was using his mind-voice—the prince calming and awing his subject.

"Ligeia." Her whisper was so broken that it took Chara a moment to understand the word.

"Ligeia," Theseus repeated, and smiled—though Chara saw the fingers of his right hand tighten around the sword's hilt, and the fingers of his left around the ball of string. Melaina frowned and crossed her arms over her chest.

"When did you fall?" he said.

Ligeia thrust at a hank of hair, and it stuck out above her filthy ear. "With the first ones." Her voice was a little stronger, but still splintered. *She doesn't use it any more*, Chara thought, and felt a chill run through her, despite the mountain's heat.

Theseus's eyes were dark—with anger, Chara knew, because she felt him say, ::*You see? You see what your king has done to the youth of my city? You see why I am here?*:: The words dragged through her like claws. When he collapsed the sword back into a dagger, each *snick* made her start.

"How have you survived this long, here?" he said gently, motioning at Phoibe to dim her godlight even more. Phoibe did, with a small, tired moan.

Ligeia blinked at him. "I found a stream. The water's hot, but I know how to gather it."

"And what do you eat?" Melaina demanded, limping forward to stand beside Theseus.

"I eat . . ." Ligeia's brown eyes darted. "I eat dead things. The beast's dead things. What he leaves when he's done with them." She swallowed. "There are other things, in the round chamber, but I only go there when it's safe. The bits are mostly enough."

"What round—" Melaina started to say, but Chara interrupted.

"Have you seen him kill?" she demanded. Her chest was hot and tight and the blood sang so loudly in her ears that she could barely hear herself.

Ligeia's eyes swivelled to Chara. She squinted. "You don't sound Athenian," she said.

"*Have you seen him kill?*"

:: *Chara,*:: Theseus snapped, but she clenched her fists and didn't turn to him.

"No," Ligeia said. "But he leaves bits. In piles. Bits he doesn't want. I know it's him, though. I could tell he was trouble; I should've killed him in his sleep. Shouldn't have listened to *her.*"

"To her?" Theseus said.

Ligeia stared at him as if she hadn't seen him clearly before now. "Who're *you*? Why is your voice in my head?"

"Why, he's Prince Theseus of Athens," Melaina said. "Hadn't you heard tell of his wondrous godmarked mind-voice? The voice he uses to bind his subjects to his will? The one he apparently used to woo Princess Ariadne of Crete?"

THE FLAME IN THE MAZE

Theseus didn't look at her, and he didn't speak—not aloud, anyway.

Ligeia shrugged. "I've heard some of those things. A long time ago. And what's *that*?" she said, gesturing to the ball of silver string in Theseus's hand.

"Melaina?" he said, cocking his head at her. "Would you like to answer again?"

Melaina said nothing.

"I'll answer," said Chara, and saw the muscles in Theseus's arms tense. Her head was still pounding. "It's string fashioned by the Great Daedalus of Athens and Crete. It's godmarked—never runs out. Or never yet—and I've seen it tested since I was a child, when it belonged to my friend Icarus. The other end of it is attached to the wall beneath the entrance to this place. Once we find whoever else is in here," she went on, finally turning to Theseus, "we'll follow it back and use it to climb up to the door."

Ligeia cackled, on and on, until she had to bend over and lean on her own knees. Alphaios raised his new blade and held it shakily out.

"No," she finally gasped. "No getting out. And special string'll be useless, anyway, when the hallways change."

"Huh," Melaina said, as Theseus put his hand on Alphaios's and pushed his blade slowly down. "Well, then—no need for you to come with us."

Chara said, "No—*we'll* come with *you*. Show us where you find these 'bits' you say he leaves. Show us the places you've found. The water."

Ligeia sucked in her cheeks. At last she nodded, and pushed again at her mess of hair. "All right," she said. "I'll take you to the island."

Gears ground. "Wait," Ligeia said, and they did, in the blue and gold light of Daedalus-fireflies. Walls groaned and shifted. Dust fell. Tiny white spiders poured out of an old crack and into a new one; Chara heard the whisper of their legs, even though Phoibe was shrieking. When the walls settled, the fireflies were gone, and the corridor ahead of them rippled with reflected flame.

"Do things always change like that?" Phoibe whispered.

Ligeia nodded. Her right shoulder twitched, and she clamped her hand down on it, as if shoulder and hand belonged to different people. "Always. I never know when, but I know which parts leads to which. I know which parts danger's in, and when to stay away. No need for your string at all."

Theseus smiled and glanced back along the string's gleaming length. "Still," he said, "we'll keep it."

"But it can't show you," Ligeia said, sounding stronger, almost happy, "that the island is *there*." She pointed toward the red-orange light and smiled, and Chara saw black gaps where teeth had been.

Chara heard Alphaios gasp, when they reached the corridor's end. She stood beside him at the edge of a lake of fire. She wanted to gasp too, but couldn't—the heat leaned against her, and she against it, helplessly. *He won't have been able to bear this heat,* she thought. *Not as a boy. He'll always be the bull; he'll always be hungry and fierce.*

Theseus was the first to walk to the bridge that spanned the flames. "The island," he said, cocking an eyebrow at Ligeia. A droplet of sweat ran from his eyebrow to his cheekbone. The string in his hand looked as if it were on fire too.

She nodded again. This time her left shoulder twitched, and her right hand gripped it.

"Lead us, then, Ligeia," he said, probably with both of his voices.

She went first, and Theseus after her, then Alphaios, and Phoibe, though she whimpered about the heat, and being afraid. "Well, *slave*?" Melaina said to Chara, hands on hips, as the others shuffled up to the crest of the bridge.

"You first, my Lady," Chara said, bitterly—because instead of a bald girl in a torn robe, she suddenly saw Ariadne, turning, lifting her skirts and tossing her glossy curls so that they slid across her breasts and shoulders. Ariadne, Melaina: Chara followed, as the flames lapped at her skin and seared away her breath.

The island was a lump made of cinders, ash, and obsidian flakes. Chara guessed that the altar stone at its centre had once been white, but now it was covered in images, some dark red, others nearly black. Chara leaned closer and saw tiny, delicate spirals, and arcing rows of bull's horns. *Blood*, she thought, and, *Asterion: was this you? Gods forgive me for wondering—but now I'm here, and I see . . .* Was it you?

Ligeia bent and picked up a scorched piece of something. "Here," she said. "One of the bits."

Theseus took it from her and held it between his thumb and forefinger. It was mostly black, with some crimson beneath, and it looked like old, cracked leather.

"Eat it," Ligeia said. "You must be hungry. Or you will be."

Phoibe stepped forward and seized the thing. She

put it between her lips; Melaina made a strangled noise and batted at Phoibe's hand, and the thing fell.

"Don't you realize what you're eating?" Melaina said, and Phoibe frowned. "No, let me be clearer: don't you realize *who* you're eating?"

For a moment Phoibe's eyes were blank; then they went wide with horror. "That was a *person?*" she gasped.

Melaina laughed. "What did you think—that the monster was feasting on wild boar? Of course that was a person—an Athenian, no less—but by all means, eat."

Phoibe sat down hard on the altar stone.

Ligeia picked the leathery strip up and folded it into her mouth. "It'll be hard for you to find anything else," she said, chewing, as Phoibe whimpered and Melaina snorted. "Unless you go into the altar chamber. But I wouldn't do that."

"Isn't this the altar chamber?" Theseus said. He was walking to the offering tables that stood around the stone, picking up goddess figurines and setting them gently down, but Chara saw that he was glancing at Ligeia with half-lidded eyes.

Ligeia swallowed the last of the Athenian and shook her head. "Oh, no. No."

"Take us there," Melaina snapped.

"*Melaina,*" Theseus said. They stared at each other, still as statues themselves. Chara thought, *Gods, if only I knew what he was saying to her.*

He turned back to Ligeia. "Take us there," he said, evenly, and smiled.

She stared at him. Opened her mouth; closed it. At last she smiled back at him, with her yellow teeth and her no teeth. She lifted one of her feet and stared at its blackened sole. She set it down again, and walked slowly back to the bridge. The rest of them straggled after her.

Phoibe whimpered again, when she was halfway across the bridge. "I can't," she said breathlessly. "I'll die. We'll all die. There's light in this place—Master Daedalus saw to that. You don't need me. My Lord Theseus: let me lie down here. Leave me here."

Theseus caught Phoibe as she sagged. "We must be strong," he said, as the others came up behind them. "The Princess Ariadne has set me a task, and I will not disappoint her."

"The Princess Ariadne isn't here," Phoibe said—but she let him draw her up and shuffled on again, with his hand against the small of her back.

"The Princess Ariadne is not here, no," he said. "But she has helped us immeasurably—and she will be waiting for us. Thank all the gods for her—she has—"

The darkness came down suddenly. One of Chara's feet was raised, mid-step. She swayed so that she wouldn't stumble, and groped for the bridge's handrail. The fire's glow had vanished. The light in the corridor across the chasm had vanished. The only light was the faintest sheen of silver, rippling like slow waves in the black.

"Melaina!" Theseus called. "*Melaina*! What are you doing?"

Melaina had been mere steps ahead of Chara; Chara had heard the dragging of her injured foot. There was no sound at all, now—just silence, vast and silver-dark. Silence and then a rhythmic, metallic sawing.

Theseus bellowed into the air, into their heads; Chara doubled over, her own cries soundless beneath his.

Phoibe's godlight flooded the darkness, which thinned and squiggled away from them. Theseus was holding Melaina by the throat with one hand, and the ball of string with the other. Only her toes were touching the stone of the bridge. She was utterly still, except for one vein in her forehead, which pulsed with her heartbeat. Her eyes were on his; neither of them seemed to blink. A shard of obsidian lay glinting at her feet. Beside it lay one end of the string she'd cut.

"Explain yourself." A whisper, hoarse and ragged.

"You promised you'd marry *me*," Melaina croaked. "Remember? Remember how you did that, with your voice and your mind, the night before we sailed from Athens?"

What? Chara thought—and then she laughed. She laughed so hard that she fell to her knees on the bridge. "Quiet!" Alphaios said from behind her. She could see real fire again, blurring with steam and tears. When her vision cleared, she saw Melaina standing on her own, both hands splayed at her neck. Theseus was leaning on the bridge in front of her.

"I remember," he said. He leaned his forehead on his clasped hands. His shoulder blades, and the muscles that bound them and everything else, bunched and jutted.

"And?" Melaina's muscles and bones and skin were golden and smooth, so lovely that Chara thought again of Ariadne.

He straightened. "And you will knot the string together now, and hope that the knot holds."

She knelt very slowly, as he walked back to her, tugging at the ball, trying to find its end. Just before her fingers closed around the end that lay on the ground, it leapt out of her reach. She stretched to grasp it but it leapt farther, and farther yet, and then, with a piercing whistle, it sped away from her, back along all the paths they'd taken.

"Godsblood," Alphaios breathed.

Chara thought, *It always was like a living thing—like an earthworm, this time, cut in half, with both halves moving on their own. Oh, Icarus: I'm sorry*—even though it didn't matter. He was already dead, and she would be too, soon. For even if Ligeia *could* lead them back to the wall beneath the door, there'd be no way of climbing it.

Theseus walked past Melaina, who was staring at the place where the end of string had been. He went past her, past all of them; he stepped onto the ground above the reaching, sucking flames.

::*Where is Ligeia?*:: he said.

——— · ———

They waited for what must have been hours, Theseus pacing back and forth in the corridor by the fiery lake, while the rest of them sat against its walls. His shadow was always there, even when he wasn't.

"Why?" he hissed down at Melaina, on one of these passes. She stared back at him, her lips pressed together, and he made a snarling noise and set off again.

"She's gone," he snapped when he returned. "She's gone, and she could have helped us—not that we would have even needed her help, if you hadn't destroyed our only hope of escape."

"Yes, well, she probably would have left anyway," Melaina said, standing up to face him. "She was clearly mad. And anyway," she went on quickly, as Theseus drew a deep breath, "she obviously taught herself how to find her way around this place. Now so will we—without the *princess's* gift, which the wolf-girl claimed would be useless, eventually. If the gods truly favour Ariadne, and us, they'll show us another way out."

Chara thought Theseus's eyes would burst from his head. He strode away again. This time Phoibe and Alphaios straggled after him.

Melaina sat down heavily beside Chara and wrapped her arms around her shins. She pressed her face against her knees.

Because the sound of Theseus's steps was unbearable, and because the other girl was too still, Chara said, "I'm sorry." She'd said the same thing to Ariadne once, on her sixteenth birthday, when Queen Pasiphae had given Chara to her daughter as a gift. There'd been a storm, just before that; Chara and Asterion had been hunkered in the storerooms, feeling the thunder in the jars at their backs. "I'm sorry," Chara had said to Ariadne, who'd been small and sad and angry.

For a time Melaina made no sound. Only when Chara stretched her legs out, preparing to rise, did Melaina raise her head. "He used his mind," she said in a small voice. "He told me he'd never felt so drawn to anyone." She laughed a high, trembling laugh. "It was sunset. Goddesses of love and fury—how could I ever have believed him? And why did he even bother letting me think he'd give me this?"

Chara leaned back against the wall. "Maybe he meant it," she said carefully, evenly. "Maybe he means it every time he says it to someone."

Melaina dragged the back of her hand under her nose and gave a brief, hollow laugh.

"Why *did* you cut the string?" Chara said.

Melaina was silent for so long that Chara shifted, preparing again to get up. "I didn't intend it to . . . But no matter. I cut it because he believed in it." Melaina bit off another laugh. She stood and looked down the corridor at Theseus's shadow. She walked toward it— Chara counted eleven paces—and sat down. This time she stared straight ahead, her chin on her fists.

Alphaios hunkered down where Melaina had been. "She was poor, you know," he said, very quietly. "Really poor. When Theseus told her he loved her . . . well."

"Yes," Chara said. "Well." At last she got up. She walked past Alphaios and Melaina, all the way to where Theseus was standing, with his hands against the corridor walls.

"No more," she said. "No more godmarked string. No more proposing marriage to poor girls and princesses. Now it's time to save a god."

He raised his eyes to hers. ::*I do not save. I slay— both men and monsters.*::

"Take me to him, then," he said, and walked away from her.

CHAPTER THIRTEEN

They heard no more wolf howls, though Theseus and Alphaios called for Ligeia until they were hoarse, and the mountain rang with their voices long after they'd stopped. They heard only the dripping, and the grinding of gears that kept them from finding water.

"I'm so thirsty," Phoibe said once. They were in a cavern whose vaulted ceiling was impossibly high and covered in green points of light that looked like strange, sickly stars. The ground was a forest of stalagmites, some as tall as the grandest of the bull's horns atop the palace at Knossos, others tiny and needle-sharp against bare feet.

"So thirsty," Phoibe said again, and slid down to sit at the base of one of the large stalactites. Chara saw some of the little ones sink into Phoibe's skin, and winced. "I can't keep going. And I'm too weak to use my godmark, if I need to."

Theseus crouched next to her and put the back of his hand on her cheek. "We'll stay here for a bit," he said. "You'll feel better after a rest." Melaina sucked her breath sharply in through her teeth and took a few steps away from them.

Alphaios called then, from the far edge of the cavern. "Come and see this!"

Chara reached him first. He was drawing his finger along the smooth, lumpy black of the wall. "This mark," he said as she leaned closer, "someone made it. Look—it's even and fairly straight, and it runs all the way to . . ." He walked slowly, and Chara walked behind him, her own fingertip following the deep groove. ". . . here."

Their feet were touching the lowest step of a staircase. It climbed and turned, carved out of the thickest stalactite Chara had yet seen. She squinted up and up and saw that it became a bridge that spanned air and ended in a corridor whose mouth shone with crimson light.

"Maybe this line was someone else's godmarked string," she said slowly. Melaina came up beside her; Chara saw her flinch, even though she wasn't looking at her.

"Yes," Theseus said as he approached, with Phoibe clinging to his arm. "Another Athenian has given us a direction. But we cannot go there yet," he went on. "Not until Phoibe is feeling stronger."

"I thought you were all ready to charge about looking for the beast," Melaina said, and Chara winced at the weak, helpless anger in her voice.

Theseus was gazing down at Phoibe. "We wait," he said, and wiped gently at the sweat that shone on her closed eyelids.

Melaina gave a laugh that echoed around them, and limped into silver-flecked darkness that was partly of her own making. A moment after she'd disappeared, Alphaios said, "My Prince: shouldn't we go after her?"

Theseus looked up from Phoibe's face at the green lights that weren't stars. He said nothing. Another moment passed, and another.

In the silence, they heard singing.

It wound toward them like water—and even before she saw the song's silver flowing out of the rock above them, Chara knew whose it was.

"Polymnia." She could barely hear herself. "Polymnia!" she cried, over and over, as the others gaped and Melaina walked slowly back to them.

No, she thought as she shouted, *it can't be; she was so frightened, so sure of her own death*—and she saw the girl as she'd seen her four years before: lying in front of the mountain door, singing a frightened, hopeless wash of silver into the morning air.

There was no fear in this song. It teased—loud, soft, joyous, strong—and wrapped their limbs in silver thread. The threads tightened around Chara's arms and neck and the silver seeped into her blood, and she had to dig her fingernails into her palms to keep from lying down and staying there.

"Who's Polymnia?" Alphaios murmured, after Chara had shouted herself hoarse and the silver had faded back to silence. They were all blinking as if they'd just woken up.

Chara's throat had already been dry and sore; now she could hardly speak at all. "She was in the first group of Athenians. Ligeia's group. I spoke to her once, just before she was pushed inside. I was sure she'd die quickly."

"What a beautiful godmark," Phoibe said, almost dreamily.

"If she's survived this long," Alphaios said, "she knows her way around. Just like Ligeia. We have to find her."

Melaina scowled. "Such keen insight you possess, Alphaios."

"There is no way of knowing where the song was coming from," said Theseus. "Its strands appeared from the rock on all sides of this cavern, from low to high. All we can do is continue on and hope she sings again."

"And what of poor, weak Phoibe?" Melaina sneered.

Phoibe lifted her head and thrust her thin shoulders back. "I'm ready," she said, as Theseus took her hand.

———— · ————

Staircase to bridge to corridor; one corridor branching to two, to three; dead ends and turnings upon turnings—and still there was no song.

They found a trickle of water on a wall carved with octopus and flying fish, and lit by a blue light that streamed down through the crystal ceiling. They'd been taking turns following the same line that had led them from the stalactite cavern—and it was Chara who cried, in her low, ragged voice, "Water!", when her fingers passed through it, then fumbled back again. They pressed their lips and tongues to the wall, one after the other. Melaina was last; she drew back and gasped, "There's none left!"—and, somehow, there wasn't.

They were thirstier than ever, after that. Chara was so hungry that she felt only an empty sort of pain in her middle. She remembered how Ariadne had stopped her from eating sweets at feasts. "You mustn't get fat," the princess had said, holding a tray just out of Chara's reach. "I wouldn't be able to abide a fat slave." Chara remembered the figs and honey cakes on the trays, and the way the sunlight had turned Ariadne's hair to dark, burnished wood, and her skin to bronze. She remembered crouching under a table with Asterion, when everyone had gone except the other slaves, who laughed and gossiped and took no notice of them. Chara had whispered, "Honeyed cakes are in my claws," and Asterion had hissed back, brokenly, because he was laughing, "And now I'll put them in your jaws." He'd crushed the honey cakes against her open mouth and she'd choked, laughing too, heedless of the way the last of the sunlight had glinted from his horns. Heedless until now, when all she could do was remember.

The heat was increasing—or maybe it just felt that way because there wasn't any more water. They no longer slept soundly; they merely fell, when they couldn't walk any further, and curled up while the others straggled back to lie down near them. Phoibe clung to Theseus, sitting, lying or standing. Silver light flared from her skin whenever she was afraid, which was often. Melaina mocked her, but Chara saw her own eyes dart nervously whenever a strange sound came from the passageways and chambers that pressed down around them.

"Polymnia!" Theseus shouted once, his head thrown back, his fists clenched. *"Polymnia! Ligeia!"* The echoes of his voice lapped and died against the stone.

Still there was no song.

Strangely enough, it wasn't Phoibe who collapsed first. They were trudging along another corridor, this one twisting and narrow. Chara heard the dragging of Melaina's injured foot behind her and then, suddenly, she didn't. She turned and peered into the gloom, tinged green by glowing shells set into spiral patterns, and saw Melaina fall.

"Help!" Chara cried over her shoulder as she ran for the other girl. Chara lifted her off the ground and into her lap. Melaina's head lolled and her limbs were limp; she was as heavy as a block of marble. *Wonderful,* Chara thought as the others straggled up behind her, *we're all so tired that we'll go down in a big, heavy pile, and I'll be on the bottom, and Asterion will never find me, even if he passes by.*

"Hold her head up," Alphaios said, and Phoibe sobbed, and Theseus's mind-voice thrummed, ::*You are good, to have returned for her*::—and as Chara raised her head to command them all to be quiet, she saw a shadow shiver against the green-lit darkness.

"Look," she said. Even though it was a whisper, Alphaios did, and Theseus, and Phoibe, who backed up against the wall and raised her hands and poured silver godlight into the corridor.

A woman was standing a few paces away from them. "Greetings, Athenians," the woman said. "I am Polymnia. Do not be afraid."

"Polymnia?" Chara said—though it couldn't be: she hadn't been a woman, and she hadn't held herself this tall and straight. *But that was years ago,* Chara thought. *So many years ago; just imagine what* he'll *look like, now.*

Polymnia angled her head slowly, until her eyes were on Chara's. Her hair fell in glimmering red waves to her waist—far longer than it had been when she'd arrived on Crete, and far less tangled. Her hipbones jutted through her robe, which, somehow, was nearly white, and belted with a piece of torn cloth.

"Have we met?" Her voice was rough and rich. Chara tried to remember how it had sounded years ago, saying, ". . . Great Goddess's breakfast"—but all she truly remembered was her tears, and her godmarked singing.

"Yes!" Chara said, the word cracking. "We . . . the

morning you were sent in here. And Asterion with you." A long, silent moment passed. "Is he here too?"

Her belly and chest ached. Her ears roared with the rushing of her own blood—and yet she heard Polymnia when she said, "Yes. Oh, yes. The bull-god is here."

Theseus took a step forward and Melaina stirred in Chara's lap, but Chara didn't look at either of them. "And you know exactly where? You understand this place? You can take me . . . take us to him?" She was panting as if she'd been running or diving; her body was slick with fresh sweat.

Polymnia smiled. "Of course."

"Excellent," murmured Melaina. She tried to lift her head but it fell back against Chara's thigh. "Then you'll take us to him . . . Prince Theseus will kill him, as planned . . . and we'll figure out a way to get out of here. Yes," she went on thickly, waving a hand at Theseus, "you're right; shouldn't have cut that string."

Polymnia's smile had vanished. She shifted her gaze to Theseus. "Kill him?" she repeated, very softly.

"Yes," he said. As Chara drew breath to speak, his mind-voice lanced through her. ::*I told you I would think on this. I am still thinking.*::

Polymnia was still and silent for a moment. *She looks like she's listening to something*, Chara thought, and a cold prickle of dread made her feel abruptly, painfully alert.

"You will need food, then," Polymnia said at last, smiling again. "And water. I will take you to these things."

Melaina heaved herself out of Chara's lap and onto the ground. She twisted and thrashed, then lay on her back, gasping with laughter and tears.

"Great Theseus," she finally said, so weakly that they all had to lean forward to hear, "you'll have to carry me."

Polymnia went first, of course, and Alphaios after her. When the corridor widened, Chara moved up to walk beside him, and saw that his eyes were huge and dark, fixed on the sway of Polymnia's thin hips. "Alphaios," she muttered, "remember: we know nothing of her."

He swallowed. "I know," he muttered back, and shrugged.

Polymnia walked swiftly around corners and along passageways that branched and branched once more. In a chamber ringed with obsidian columns and only a single doorway, she pressed or pulled something set in one of the columns, and a ramp ground down at their feet. She led them up one ladder and down another. When they tired and straggled (even Alphaios, with his huge, dark, admiring eyes), she called, "Nearly there!" in a voice so cheerful and certain that Chara felt her steps quickening. When their way was blocked by a wall, Polymnia said, "This will move soon; the mountain tells me so"—and some bleary, blurred time later, gears ground and stone shifted and the wall did move.

There was sunlight in the vast, round chamber beyond. Chara counted six shafts of it wavering far, far up the chamber's walls, as Alphaios and Theseus and Phoibe pushed past her. Sunlight. Water. Figs and olives and oatcakes spilled onto the steps of an altar carved with snakes.

Polymnia put a hand on her shoulder and Chara felt

herself shake it away. "I'm sorry," she said, her tongue sluggish in her mouth. "I don't know why I did that."

Polymnia smiled. "Come," she said. "You're safe now."

CHAPTER FOURTEEN

Chara didn't want to sleep. *No*, she told herself, as she felt her clean, wet body relax against a column. *No, no, no: take care; be alert.* She tried to sit up taller and blink the heaviness away from her eyelids so that she could keep everyone in her sight: Melaina, spread out on her back between two of the jars; Theseus, propped against a wall with Phoibe's head in his lap; Alphaios, sprawled so close to the waterfall that a puddle was forming beneath his cheek; and Polymnia, standing with her arms crossed, gazing at each of them in turn, slowly, her own eyes narrowed. *No*, Chara thought, one more time—but only faintly, because her hunger and thirst were gone, and so was she.

When she woke, the sunlight was gone too. It seemed to take a very long time for her eyes and limbs to work—but her ears worked right away. She heard the water. Deep breathing and ragged breathing. A murmur of voices.

"Believe me: there are wonderful places here." Polymnia's words wove and wobbled before they took shape in Chara's head.

"Everything here frightens me." Phoibe's words trembled, but in a way Chara recognized. "I don't know how you've endured it, all this time."

Chara's vision was sharpening: she saw the dark shapes of Alphaios and Melaina and Theseus, exactly where they'd been before. Phoibe and Polymnia were side-by-side on the lowest of the steps that led to the altar. Phoibe was hunched; Polymnia was sitting up very tall.

"You'll learn," Polymnia said. "And you'll learn quickly; I can tell you're clever."

"Oh, no; I won't have to learn! Prince Theseus is going to kill the beast: that's why he came with us! He'll lead us out—with your help, I'm sure."

The water sounded very loud, in the silence that fell. Chara tried to swallow and realized that she was achingly thirsty again, but she didn't move.

"Well," Polymnia said after a time, "before any of that happens you'll have to rest more, eat more. Regain your strength and . . . fill out your skin. You're all far too thin." She put her arm around Phoibe's shoulders, and Chara pushed herself onto her hands and knees and gave a loud, false yawn.

"Phoibe!" she said as she got to her feet. "Come here; we should wash our robes before the others wake up"—except that they *were* awake now, as she'd intended. They grumbled and stirred, stretching their arms up toward the dappled light of fireflies and invisible stars.

"So, Polymnia," Theseus said a bit later, as he chewed on a strip of salt fish. "Tell me about the beast: its habits, say, and how I will find it. For I feel nearly strong enough to face it, now."

Polymnia's tongue glistened between her parted lips. Alphaios's own mouth fell open as he stared at her. Chara jabbed him in the side and he grunted.

"He is . . ." Polymnia began, and stopped. "He is never only a man. His head is always the bull's, and his hands and feet are almost always hooves. He is strong: the muscles bunch across his shoulders and down his back, whether he is man or bull." She rose from the step and walked slowly around the altar.

"And how will I find it?" Theseus asked. His hand was halfway to his mouth, as if he'd forgotten he was about to take another bite of fish.

Polymnia smiled at no one. "He has his own ways, and cannot be found. One day I hear the rumble of his hooves and his godmarked call, and I hide, and watch him as he feeds, or bends his great head to drink." Her faraway gaze lighted on Chara, who held it, and watched it focus. Polymnia frowned and looked quickly away.

Theseus put the fish down. "And have you seen it kill Athenians, before it feeds on them? Because your companion Ligeia had not."

"Ligeia," Polymnia spat, "has been no companion of mine—nor of yours, I see, because where is she now?" She turned her back on them, shaking her hands at her sides as if they were wet. Melaina rolled her eyes, and for the first time, Chara understood why.

"I have," Polymnia finally said, still facing away from them. "I have seen him kill."

"You haven't." Chara spoke quietly, despite a buzzing that had begun in her ears, and Theseus's mind-voice, which was pulsing in her, without words. "You're lying, and Ligeia was just wrong—neither of you have seen him kill because *he hasn't killed*. No, my Lord," she went on, holding a hand up as Theseus said her name, inside and out, "now I will tell you of him. Of him—because he is *he*, not it."

As she drew a shaking breath, Theseus said again, "Chara."

"No! Listen! You said you'd consider my words about him, and yet I've spoken hardly any. So let me tell you about Asterion—the boy. The boy who was always being burned for the glory of his father, Lord Poseidon, and all his priestesses. The boy who made up rhymes about sea creatures and laughed when I made up my own, until he had to scratch 'Stop!' into the dirt. The boy whose sister Ariadne set him on fire when he wasn't much more than two years old, and never stopped hurting him after that—never until now, because she's convinced you to do it for her."

Melaina's gaze was as wide as Alphaios's. Polymnia was looking over her shoulder, one of her eyes gleaming through the curtain of her hair. Phoibe was rocking a little, on her step. Theseus's expression hadn't changed: his broad brow was as smooth as ever, his lips as firmly set. Chara saw each of them very clearly because silver-grey light was seeping down above them. It was dawn, in the world outside the mountain.

"If he was so hurt already," Theseus said, "and had suffered so much for the sake of gods and mortals, this place may well have made him mad."

"Ariadne's the mad one. Unmarked Ariadne, whose beauty never really helped her. Until she sent you that wonderful little likeness of her that Karpos made—the one that smiled and blinked. I wrapped it up in cloth to send it to you, you know. And that was enough to make you come here—that, and your need to rescue her, because that's what you do, isn't it? You rescue beautiful young girls."

"Godsbled bastard," Melaina said, as Theseus's smooth brow furrowed. "Gods. Bled. *Bastard*."

Chara's head was spinning as it had when she'd clung to Icarus's waist and he'd swung them both back and forth above the waterfall near Knossos. Exhilaration and fear, and an odd little sadness, because she knew these other feelings would have to end. "Does Ariadne realize you'll likely leave her on the first island we get to, if we ever get off this one? Not that we'll even make it out of this mountain, unless you let me find him and speak to him. I have to do this, Prince Theseus. Please."

The water sang behind them. The wind sang, far above—and Chara remembered the black pipes that jutted from the mountain's peak, and thought, *Oh, Icarus: you tried; now so am I.*

Theseus said, ::*Daughter of Pherenike*—:: and then he stopped, because a roar shook the stone beneath their feet.

Chara wanted to sink down on the step next to Phoibe, who'd already started to cry, but she didn't: she stayed standing, listening to Asterion's voice. It was deeper than it had been, the day his father had thrust him into the mountain with the first group of Athenians. It was much, much louder—though maybe that was partly because of the rock walls. She knew it didn't matter that she recognized it, or that he'd been a boy named Asterion: this was the voice of the beast Theseus had come to kill.

"Can you find it?" Theseus said breathlessly to Polymnia, when the roar and all its echoes had faded. "Can you make it come to us?"

Her red hair fell over her face as she shook her head. "I have told you, Lord: I cannot compel him. He will come if he wishes to—and now I think he does not."

Do you really know so much about him? All of a sudden, bits of the dates and fish Chara had eaten so eagerly surged up and nearly into her mouth. She pressed her hand to her lips and swallowed desperately, over and over, until her belly stopped its clenching.

"Very well," said Theseus. "We will just have to wait for it."

They sat without speaking, as the sun changed its angle and colour. They all ate again, except for Chara. Polymnia sang under her breath—just a tune, which didn't tug at Chara the same way her song had, when it had flowed through the rock to find them. Phoibe nestled in against Theseus's side and dozed, her dark-stubbled head lolling. Alphaios used his godmark to turn the cast-off skin of a many-legged insect into a tiny yellow ball, which he bounced against each of the columns until Melaina snapped at him to stop.

It seemed as if the sunlight had barely started to warm the chamber when darkness took its place. Again Chara tried not to sleep, when her own head started to bob; again she failed. She woke this time to a yell, and more silver-grey dawn light.

"Where is she?" Theseus shouted, as Chara tried to rise. "*Where is Phoibe?*"

After a frozen silence, Polymnia said, "She must have wandered away. She seemed fearful, even here."

"She's always fearful," Melaina said. She plucked at Theseus's arm as he strode by; he shook her away without looking at her and kept striding. He stopped only to stare down into the corridors as if Phoibe might simply have been asleep in one of them, waiting to be seen.

"She didn't wander away," he said. "Or if she did, she wouldn't have gone far. How could I have slept so deeply? And for so many hours!"

Chara winced as his mind-voice growled inside her, low and harsh and wordless. Alphaios sidled up beside her and whispered, "He's so loud—his godmark—can we stop him?"

"I don't know," she whispered back. "Just wait a little. Let him calm down."

He didn't. When the sun's light was morning-gold, he grasped Polymnia's wrist and said, "I should not have waited so long; I will go after her."

"My Lord," she said, and put her long-fingered hand on top of his. "She is lost. The mountain has her. Stay here; stay safe."

"Safe?" he thundered, aloud and in their heads—in all of them, because they cried out as if they'd been a single person, doubling over and covering their ears, even though this wouldn't help in the slightest.

Theseus took Polymnia by the hair that hung at her waist and pulled her in close to him. "Come with me," he said. "You know these corridors; you will see evidence of her, while I might not."

"But my Prince, I will not know where—"

"Have these corridors moved since I slept? Have they?"

"No," she gasped, straining against his grip, waving her hands in the waterfall's spray so that they glistened.

"Then we go down this passageway first," he said, jerking his chin at the one they'd come from. "It is the closest to where she was sleeping. It is the one she had already seen. You will lead me there, and beyond, if we do not find her."

Polymnia stared back at him, motionless but breathing, as beautiful as one of Karpos's godmarked statues. "Very well," she said, just as Chara was about to throw herself at both of them and scrabble at their eyes or their perfect chins. "But do not expect to find her."

"So what do you think?" Alphaios said to Chara, a long, silent time after Theseus and Polymnia had disappeared down the corridor.

Melaina snorted and threw a piece of fish against the wall. Shards of it fell to the ground and glittered there, salt and light and old, dead flesh. "*I* think that he should die a death that no one will ever hear of, in Athens or anywhere else." She smiled, but her lower lip trembled. "I think he should suffer."

Chara cleared her throat and glanced at Alphaios, who shrugged back at her. "He may be our only chance of getting off the island," Chara said. "He's going to call that ship's captain with his mind-voice, remember?"

Alphaios frowned. "But we'll have to get out of *here* first. Which won't be possible, now that there's no godmarked string."

"Oh please," Melaina said, "as if that was actually going to work! A trinket from a whore of a princess. No—Theseus won't be the clever one, this time. That Polymnia person will be able to help us find a better way. She'll show us where to gather big rocks, or we'll all crack stalagmites off of the floor of that cavern and stack them up to those openings. We'll build something. We'll . . ." Her voice trailed to silence. She sat down heavily beside the jar of figs, with her back to them.

Sunlight rippled on the walls. Chara stared up at it; she tried to imagine cloud and wind, and couldn't, because the stone pressing against her was so hot, and the air so heavy. She remembered hanging upside down from an olive tree in the grove near the waterfall. She and Asterion both, of course, side-by-side like bats, spying on Glaucus as he tried to kiss the farmer's daughter. She'd pushed him away and said, "I don't care if you're a prince; you look like a toad!" and stormed off down the sloping row of trees.

Asterion had swung down from the branch, laughing. "Toad!" he said—and then Glaucus looked at him, and Asterion stopped laughing. "Glau—I'm sorry. You're really quite handsome. Isn't he, Chara?"

"Don't pretend just to comfort me," Glaucus mumbled. Chara handed him his painted stick. At first he crossed his arms and glared into the distance—but after a moment he took it, and sighed. When Asterion put his arm around the prince's shoulder, he didn't shake it away. They walked off together, the three of them. The silver-green leaves rustled and dappled the sun on the earth at their feet.

Trees, Chara thought now, as she wiped at the sweat that was seeping from every bit of her skin. *What if I never see one again?*

Hours after Theseus and Polymnia had left, the corridors shifted. *If Phoibe were here, she'd yelp*—but the screaming of metal and grinding of stone didn't frighten Chara anymore. Alphaios crouched next to her. "Polymnia will lead them all back to us," he said, as a stone wall lifted on the corridor Polymnia and Theseus had gone down. There was a different one there now, which wavered in its own green glow.

"Careful, Alphaios," Chara said, as Melaina snorted. "We don't know anything about her."

"You said you did." He crossed his arms across his chest and scowled.

"Please," Melaina said, "she's not even that beautiful."

"She is. She's far more beautiful than—"

Chara snapped, "Alphaios: catch," and tossed him the tiny yellow ball. He caught it in one hand and squeezed so hard that his veins darkened and bulged beneath his taut skin. Then he stood and walked up the steps to the altar and threw it against each column in turn, pivoting and diving when it sailed over his head. Melaina paced from doorway to doorway—limping only a little, now—and peered into the corridors beyond. Chara watched them. She thought, every so often, that she must have slept, because the sunlight had changed without her noticing it.

The light had just turned a dusky bronze when Theseus's mind-voice howled. Chara straightened with a cry; Alphaios spun blindly; Melaina hunched over, clutching her head. The howl was wordless, and it tore at Chara's insides with claws she could almost see, behind her closed eyelids. When she opened them, the world was a crimson-stained blur. *Am I seeing what he's seeing?* she thought. *Gods and fishes—make it* stop.

"What was that?" Alphaios gasped when there was silence in her head and her vision had eased back to normal. Chara tried to swallow, tried to speak, and ended up shaking her head.

"My Lord Theseus," Melaina whispered. "Oh, my love." She put her back to the column that was carved with bees and slid until she was sitting. She closed her eyes.

Chara and Alphaios crouched next to one another with their backs to the jar of olives. The yellow ball sat near his toes, but he didn't touch it. The light above them vanished, and Daedalus's fireflies sparked and guttered to life in its place. They slept, their heads drooping toward each other.

It was dawn when footsteps woke Chara. She

nudged Alphaios and they fumbled to their feet. Melaina was already up, standing very straight with her hands against two columns.

"You see?" Alphaios said. "I told you Polymnia would bring them back"—but the words quavered, and he wouldn't meet Chara's gaze.

Polymnia emerged first—and not from the corridor Alphaios, Chara, and Melaina were facing. As they shifted, Theseus walked out behind Polymnia. He was stooped, carrying something Chara couldn't see, but she shivered anyway. He walked up the steps to the altar and laid the thing down. Chara and Alphaios drew up on either side of him, glancing at each other over his bent back.

Chara recognized cloth, though it was soaked black with blood. When he unfolded a corner of it she recognized none of what lay within: strips and ribbons and pieces, some of them wet and red, others jagged and yellow-white.

"What is that?" Alphaios whispered.

Theseus unfolded another corner. A hand seemed to grope up toward them—a perfect, bloodied hand attached to nothing.

"Phoibe," he said.

CHAPTER FIFTEEN

"I wanted to leave her there," Theseus said, as Alphaios vomited half-digested dates and fish onto the altar. "What was left of her. But I also wanted proof, Chara. For you."

She put a hand on Alphaios's back and turned to look behind her. Polymnia's hands were clasped lightly; her lips were very slightly curved. There was a streak of blood on her forehead. Her long fingernails were dark underneath: more blood, Chara knew, and turned back to Theseus.

"It was not Asterion, my Prince." Her voice was thin. *It wasn't*, she thought, *it* was not—and she felt sick, too, as certainty and doubt knotted together in her gut.

Melaina gave a sharp laugh. "'Not Asterion'—surely you must be starting to see how foolish your devotion is."

Chara shook her head. "No," she said. Polymnia smiled at her as the word leapt around them. It was a warm smile—almost delighted—and again Chara felt herself shiver, without understanding why.

"I will not wait," Theseus said, rising from the ruin of Phoibe. "I will hunt him now." ::*I am sorry, Chara. I believe what you have told me of his past—but he is beast now, not boy. And he must die.*::

Polymnia touched his arm. "Best let him come to

us, my Lord. He will—I promise this. He will come here to drink and sleep—he does it every few weeks." She gestured at one of the walls, which was covered in marks Chara hadn't noticed: Long, straight carvings, with bull's horns scored at intervals among them. "See: it has already been two weeks since he was last here. He will return soon. Eat, Prince Theseus. Rest. I shall dispose of *that*—I shall give it to the Great Goddess, on her island in the fire."

"No," Theseus said, reaching for the bundle and its dark, wet contents, "I must do it, for I was the one who failed her." His mind-voice was still in Chara's head, higher-pitched than usual, as if he were keening.

"My Lord," Polymnia said quietly. Melaina was staring venomously at her hair, which looked to Chara like a shining fall of red silk. "In Athens you are a prince. Someday you will be king, there. Here, though," she smiled gently, "beneath the mountain, I am queen. Heed me now, as I will heed you later."

For a long moment, Theseus gazed at her. *Finally,* Chara thought. *He'll see it too; he'll see how* wrong *she is.*

"Very well," he said at last, straightening. "Give her to the Goddess."

———— · ————

Chara was still awake when Polymnia came back. It was deep night, and everyone else was sleeping—even Theseus, who had paced and paced, fists clenched and brows lowered, until the sunlight wavered and died. Asterion roared once, and even though the sound was farther away than it had been, Theseus whirled and brandished Daedalus's dagger-sword. Many hours passed, but at last he sat at the centre of the altar, the sword across his knees. His head and shoulders drooped.

Hours after that, Polymnia returned. She crept in silently, but Chara saw her: a shadow except for her hair, which glimmered in the fitful blue and green light of the fireflies. She slid the jar away from the stream of water and knelt with her hands on the ground, where the water was already turning to steam. She looked over her shoulder at Melaina's sleeping form, and Theseus's, and Alphaios's. Chara was closest; she'd settled nearest the spray. Polymnia glanced at her last, and by the time she did, Chara's own eyes were almost completely closed.

From beneath her lashes, Chara watched Polymnia slip her robe over her head and hold it, and herself, beneath the water. *Good thing Alphaios isn't seeing this*, Chara thought. Polymnia was thin, but muscles clenched in her belly and thighs as she moved, and her breasts were full. *How perfect she'd look beside Karpos's statue of Androgeus*—and the thought of Knossos's stone and sky nearly made Chara groan aloud.

When Polymnia had washed every bit of cloth and skin, she sang. Chara couldn't hear anything at first, but she saw the silver seeping out from between her lips, and leaned forward a bit, very carefully. Polymnia's eyes were closed now. She was smiling, as she sang. The others shifted in their sleep and Polymnia sang louder, until they settled again—even Theseus, who had begun to lift his head. At last Chara heard melody and words—but she was so weary, and the godmarked song was so lulling—that at first she paid them hardly any heed.

"Patience, singing girl . . . patience, god-born son . . . I'll bring them all to you, but only one by one. . . ."—and suddenly Chara was awake again, gasping as if she'd been about to drown.

Polymnia was in front of her. Her gaze was steady, as dark as her smile was bright. "Chara?" she whisper-sang. "What is it, freckled girl? A nightmare?"

"Yes," Chara whispered back, desperately trying to smile, herself. "I think so."

"Listen, then—and lie down—there, just like that—and do not fret: I will comfort you."

This time Polymnia's song was about wind in leaves and sunlight on sea, and even though she fought not to, Chara fell asleep.

———— · ————

Days passed, and Asterion didn't return. He bellowed, now and then, but the sound was very far away, then very close, then far away again. Theseus stopped leaping to his feet whenever he heard it, though his hand still went to Daedalus's dagger-sword. Polymnia smiled, as she listened; Chara watched her and thought, *Asterion: I don't understand; don't find us until I do*—and though she longed to shout for him until he came to her, she didn't.

"Eat," Polymnia urged them all, many times. "Another food delivery will come soon: eat everything you can now, so that there is more room in the jars."

"I'm not hungry anymore," Melaina snapped once. "Stop trying to fatten me up."

On the fifth day, Asterion's roar was farther away than it had been yet. Polymnia didn't smile, this time;

her delicate brows drew together and she gnawed at her lower lip.

"He is moving away from here," Theseus said, his hand once more on the blade as he stared at Polymnia. "Though you said he would return."

She said, "He will, my Lord, he will. In the meantime, there is a place near here where lizards gather. I know you will think it unpleasant, but very soon you will need their meat: it will strengthen you as all this food cannot. Come with me, Alphaios. I will show you how to draw them out and catch them."

Alphaios sprang to his feet, and so did Chara. "I'll go with you," she said quickly.

Polymnia shook her head, holding a hand to her face to keep her hair away from it. "I thank you, Chara, but two will be enough—any more will frighten the creatures."

Alphaios grinned at Chara over his shoulder as he followed Polymnia into a corridor made entirely of crystal. Chara didn't smile back at him.

"Looking for lizards," Melaina said. "How original."

Theseus said, "But won't young master Alphaios be glad"—and Melaina rounded on him and snarled, "Yes, won't he? Because mustn't it be *nice* to have a lover?" Theseus frowned; Chara thought, *Chiding her with his mind-voice*—and then, as Polymnia and Alphaios disappeared into the crystal's glow, *Enough of the prince and his cast-off betrothed.*

"I'm going after them," she said as she walked toward the corridor.

"Oooh!" Melaina cried, "How naughty of you to spy! But I suppose that's what slaves do."

"Chara," Theseus said, and, ::*What are you planning, daughter of Pherenike?*::

"Not what am I planning," she said, "what is *she* planning." And she stepped onto the crystal floor as his words hummed and faded in her bones.

She expected that one or both of them might come after her, but they didn't. She also thought she'd have to go slowly, since Polymnia and Alphaios would be only a little bit ahead, but they weren't: the corridor glinted before her, empty. She walked slowly, glancing up now and then when shadows fell on her—a long, sinuous one that was a snake or worm, and a flurry of smaller ones that looked like frogs—though how could there be frogs, so far from water? She wondered briefly what she would look like, to someone below, and imagined Glaucus sniggering, and Asterion swatting him with the stick that Glaucus had always pretended was a sword.

Asterion, she thought, for the thousandth time, *I'm here; I'm really here, and so are you.*

She quickened her pace and nearly missed the entrance to a smaller passageway on her left. She stopped and peered down it, bending because it was so low. The walls gleamed in the crimson light that shone from hundreds of tiny holes scattered across the ceiling. She ducked into the passageway—so narrow her shoulders brushed either wall—and took one step, then two, three.

She froze.

The walls weren't made of earth, obsidian, marble, crystal or rock: they were made of bones. Long and short, thick and slender, stacked and woven snugly together. A perfect ribcage bulged against Chara's right elbow, held in place by leg bones that had been driven into the hard-packed dirt. Some of the bones were a glossy yellow; others were covered in dark patches that looked like moss, but weren't.

She walked slowly down the passageway—because she had to see all of it—and soon she was at a place where the bones ended. The real walls continued past them, smooth, painted with rows of temples whose friezes were of temples, and on and on, dizzily into scarlet-speckled darkness. She blinked and focused her gaze on the last piece of bone: a skull that was a deep, wet, fresh red, and whose jaws gaped with a fear Chara recognized.

"Phoibe," she whispered, and, louder, "Alphaios!"—and she whirled and stumbled back to the crystal corridor.

She managed to be quiet, despite her hurry. *She can't know you're coming*, Chara told herself. *She might do something sudden—if she hasn't already.*

The corridor ended in a small, circular chamber with chalk-white walls and a perfectly vaulted ceiling. Alphaios was there, facing away from Chara; Polymnia was behind him with her hand resting lightly on his shoulder. "That's it," she was murmuring, "seize it by the neck"—and Chara saw that his hand was hovering over a lizard that was almost invisible: white against white. As she hesitated in the doorway, Polymnia's other hand crept up. Obsidian glinted: black against white.

"Alphaios!" Chara cried. He turned to her, his eyebrows arched and frowning at the same time. "Get away from her! Get away from her *now!*"

"Chara?" Polymnia's tone was puzzled, but she walked toward her purposefully and swiftly. "What are you going on about?"

"Show him the obsidian in your hand! Show him!"

"He knew I had it," Polymnia said patiently, holding

the shard up, still closing the distance between them. "I *was* going to teach him how to kill lizards, remember?"

"Not lizards: people! Us, and the ones who came before us—and don't say that was Asterion, because it can't have been. He's a bull now, all the time—you told us this yourself; he could never have arranged the bones in that passageway back there."

"Chara?" Alphaios said, as if she were the mad one. "What are you talking about? What's wrong with you?"

Polymnia was very close to her now, and there was no way that Alphaios could have seen Polymnia's hand, blurred with speed, jabbing the shard at Chara's belly.

Chara cried, "Alphaios: just get away from her!" and she spun and ran.

Polymnia shrieked. She was right behind, panting, her bare feet drumming on the crystal. She shrieked again—and Asterion roared, so loudly that Chara could almost feel his hot breath on her skin—but she didn't let herself falter, though surely he was nearer than he'd ever been, since they'd stood together outside the mountain's door.

When she was only steps from the altar chamber, gears began to grind. The floor beneath her lurched, and she sprawled into the chamber. As she was hauling herself up, Alphaios sprinted past her. *Good*, she thought, with a numbing flood of relief, and *Maybe the corridor will stop her*—but just as the crystal passage screeched its way up toward its next position, Polymnia dropped down between them.

"What—no lizards?" said Melaina from one of the steps to the altar.

Theseus strode toward them. Chara had to squint to make him out: the light was halfway between dusk and night. "What is this?" he demanded. "Chara: what—"

Chara was choking on her own moist breath, but managed to say, "She's mad! *She's* the killer of Athenians!"

Polymnia came silently up beside her. As she did, Asterion roared again. They all turned toward the sound—and suddenly there were hoofbeats too, pounding, louder and louder.

Theseus said, "Did you see evidence of Polymnia's treachery, Alphaios?"

"No." Alphaios's eyes were darting from Polymnia to Chara to the mouth of the tunnel from which the hoofbeats seemed to be coming. "I was looking at the lizards; I only turned around when Chara called my name."

Chara's chest burned. Her breath burned. She hardly heard herself when she said, "She sang about bringing us to Asterion one by one. She killed Phoibe: I found her skull in a corridor made of bones."

Polymnia was shaking her head. "Oh, Chara. I am sorry you are so confused."

"No." Chara reached a hand out for Theseus. He looked as if he were far away, and he started when her fingers touched his arm. "Believe me, Prince of Athens. Asterion didn't kill Phoibe. He didn't arrange all those bones."

The hoofbeats were nearly upon them. "He is coming, at last," Theseus said, putting one hand over Chara's and reaching for the sword with the other, "and you would say anything to sway me from my purpose."

"No! I'm *telling* you . . ."

The sword snicked to its full length. Melaina ran up the steps and hunkered down behind the tallest of the jars, where she picked up the dagger Alphaios had made. Alphaios ran for the jar next to hers and stood peering around it, his hands clasped beneath his chin.

Chara walked to the mouth of the corridor.

::*Daughter of Pherenike: step back.*::

She looked over her shoulder at him but didn't move any more than that. She watched him raise the sword. She watched Polymnia wrap her fingers around it and she frowned, just as he did. Polymnia pulled, and the blade trembled and bobbed lower, and blood seeped between her fingers. She was smiling, her gaze fixed on the corridor. Theseus opened his mouth— but before he could speak with either of his voices, a shadow loomed in the passageway and roared one last, ringing cry.

"Asterion," Chara whispered. He was coming toward her—enormous and distended, his bronze horns shining in the strange, rippling light. Chara stumbled back because he was moving so quickly; because for him to see her clearly, she'd have to be away from him.

I thought I'd cry I thought my legs would go weak and I'd fall I thought he'd know me but none of this is true

She saw, as he galloped out between the columns, that the fur of his muzzle was matted and blackened. She saw that his nostrils were wet, and that there was a long wound on his front leg that was also wet, and pink inside. She saw that he wasn't anything like a boy.

The bull stopped running when he was fully inside the chamber. His great head swung, and his round eyes rolled. Mere steps away from him, Theseus wrenched his sword from Polymnia's grip; she snatched at it again, with her bloody hand, her gaze steady on Asterion.

"Asterion!" Chara's voice shook, so she called again:

"Asterion!"

He pawed at the floor and sparks spat from the stone. The light above was dimming, and the fireflies had only begun to come out; she saw their green, blue and pink reflected in his eyes, but she couldn't be sure that he was looking at her. She wasn't sure—until he lowered his horns and charged at her.

Theseus bellowed into the air and into Chara's mind, and she fell to her knees. She held her head and hands up, and all she could see was one of Asterion's horns, brighter and larger than anything else in the world. It swooped down toward her, and she wanted to scream—but instead she sang, in a thin, trembling voice, words that rose up from a day of sun and wind and laughter:

The hermit crab's got pretty clothes
Alas, he hasn't got a nose . . .

Too quiet, she thought, as her stomach twisted and sickness surged into her throat. *He won't hear*—but the bull pulled up short, directly in front of her, his wide nostrils flaring.

"Asterion," she said, steadily this time, despite the pounding of Theseus's mind-voice within her. "It's me. It's Chara." She lifted a hand but couldn't reach him. He gave a snort and tossed his head.

"No!" Polymnia cried. "My Lord! My Bull-god— Poseidon's son—see who I have for you! A boy, two girls, a prince: my Lord, a *Prince of Athens*! They are yours, O Great One! And I shall slay them for you, as is my duty"—and Chara turned at last, because she felt Polymnia move toward her.

Obsidian flashed, far closer to Chara than Asterion's

horn was. Before it could touch her, though, Alphaios leapt between them and knocked it away. Polymnia screeched and flailed, clawing at Alphaios's eyes. Behind them, Theseus was gaping, the sword drooping in his hand.

Chara turned back to Asterion. She rose into a crouch, and this time her hand brushed the fur at his neck. It was coarser and thicker than she remembered—but of course: it had been so many years, and so much had changed. So much; so little.

"I know it's hot here," Chara said, as the bull's head began to swing again. "I know you feel as if you can't change back into a boy—a man. But you can. You must. You must, Asterion. Don't be afraid."

An eye staring into hers. Breath on her forehead. It stank of meat but she didn't turn away.

"Asterion," she said—and he spun, tossing his head, roaring a broken, shaking roar, and galloped toward one of the doorways. Theseus got there first, and raised the sword between them.

"No!" Chara cried, scrambling up, running and tripping, hardly hearing her own panting over Polymnia's and Melaina's screams. The bull halted just short of the blade and stamped his front feet; she skidded around his bulk and grasped Theseus's wrist.

"No! *No*—you've seen! You've heard! She . . ." Chara gestured at the other side of the chamber, where Alphaios was holding Polymnia against him. She was writhing, scrabbling at his forearm, which was across her throat. His eyes met Chara's; somehow the bleakness in them made her calmer.

"My Prince: Polymnia was the murderer. Asterion . . ." She glanced at the bull, who was still pawing, his head cocked. "Asterion was a boy whose sister hated him and connived to put him here, where his godmark would hurt him. I wrote that letter to you, as she spoke the words. Gods forgive me, I helped her convince you he was a monster, because I thought she or you would lead me to him." All of a sudden the words went hot and dry as cinders in Chara's throat. She reached for Asterion's muzzle; he spun once more and clattered over to the steps to the altar. He huffed, head down and facing away from Chara.

Theseus stepped past her. He cut the sword through the air in a sweeping arc; she shrank from its wind. ::*The princess lied. Polymnia lied. How can I know that you do not?*::

"Wait. Wait, and I'll show you."

He swung the sword again, then lowered it so that its point was resting on the floor. He said nothing with either of his voices. After a moment, Chara walked slowly by him and circled all the way around the altar, so that she could approach Asterion from the front. She knelt before him, just out of reach of his horns, and put her hands on her knees.

"It's Chara," she said. His head tossed and his huge body swayed.

"My Lord!" Polymnia called, the words so high and cracked that Chara could hardly understand them. "My Lord: I am your servant! I have fed you! I have sacrificed to the Goddess for you, and prayed for your strength—and I have *tried* to use my godmark to bring you peace. . . ." She started to sing, raggedly. Silver left her mouth in thin ribbons that fluttered and faded before they reached Asterion. Alphaios's arm tightened, and the silver vanished.

The bull walked slowly to the waterfall. Polymnia hadn't replaced the jar beneath it; he stood in the stream of it, until his head and shoulders were soaked. He shook himself, and water sprayed, lit by the fireflies' colours.

"My Lord!" Polymnia managed to choke the words out, despite Alphaios's grip—and Theseus strode over to them, wrapped her long red hair around and around his hand, and pulled her face in close to his.

"We should kill her," Alphaios said in a hard, flat voice that sounded like someone else's.

"No," Theseus said softly. "No: we will bring her to justice in Athens."

Her lips curled in a sneer, and she spat, "As if any of us will ever see Athens again."

Theseus tugged once more on her hair, savagely, and she gave a cry—and Asterion heaved himself to his feet. He struck the ground with his front hoof three times, quickly, and lowered his head, and Chara yelled, "*No!*" as he charged.

She rose and ran, or tried to: she felt as if she were slogging through mud. Asterion was halfway to Theseus, but she'd been closer; she reached him as he turned, his sword already up. Asterion was right behind her. She whirled just as the blade was about to pierce Asterion's chest, and Asterion's horn was about to pierce Theseus's. She called, "Asterion!" into his great, dark face, and he stumbled. The sword sank into his shoulder, and his horn screeched along the ground as he swerved away from them, wrenching the weapon from Theseus's grip. Asterion's legs buckled and he fell with a dull, echoing *thud*.

Chara ran the three paces to him. She knelt and put one hand on his heaving side and one on his head, between his ears. Theseus leaned over her and pulled the sword out. Asterion bellowed and lashed, and Chara had to sit back so that his hooves wouldn't strike her. Blood gushed from his flesh, coating his fur and pooling on the floor. He bellowed again, but this time she heard a voice beneath the bull's—a higher, frightened voice.

Beside her, Theseus raised his blade.

"No," she said, not taking her eyes from Asterion. "Wait. Please"—and everything faded around her—Polymnia's screams, Melaina's whimpering, the water sizzling on the stone—as Chara sang:

"Nearly time" the small fish cried
And tickled bigger fish insides. . . .

Asterion's eye rolled and stilled. He looked at her. His breath whistled as he panted. He rocked his body a bit, as if he were trying to rise, and fresh blood bubbled. This time his roar broke and turned into a keening sound she knew.

"Asterion," she said.

He lashed again, differently, because his back hooves were lengthening, flattening, splitting into toes, and his front ones too, and his fur was retreating into skin that was dirty and bloody and covered in scars. His newest wound gaped and frothed beneath his right collarbone.

His head was the last thing to change. It seemed to take a very long time. A slow, groaning noise that wasn't from his throat, but from somewhere deeper, made her suck in her breath, and tears along with it. When the change was done, and only the bull's horns remained, smaller, but still bright, she smiled down at him and sang:

"I've missed you," clicked the crab
And the fishing crane clacked, "Me?"
"Why yes," crab said,
"You showed me
That there's sky as well as sea."

He lifted his head, then let it fall. He gazed at her and wet his cracked lips with the tip of his tongue, which was also bleeding.

"Freckles," he whispered, and closed his eyes.

CHAPTER SIXTEEN

Asterion slept for a very long time. *Maybe he isn't sleeping*, Chara thought as she watched him. She longed to touch his cheeks and forehead, his lips and hair, but a strange, new shyness kept her hands at her sides. *Maybe he's unconscious. Maybe his god is finally granting him rest that will help him.* She stared at his wound, which Alphaios had dabbed at with a wet, almost-clean corner of his robe, and remembered Sotiria, who could have healed it.

She started when Alphaios said, "Chara?" She glanced up and saw bright daylight on the rock above. "Do you still have Master Daedalus's string? Theseus wants to tie *her* up with it." He jerked his head toward Polymnia, who was slumped against a wall, her chin to her chest. Her arms were limp on either side of her, her bloodied palms up.

Chara eased Asterion's head from her lap to the ground. He moaned, and his eyes moved beneath their lids, but he didn't wake. "Let me," she said.

The ragged end of the string cut, as she wrapped it around Polymnia's wrists, and more blood smeared both of their skin, but Chara didn't falter. "If I'd known what you'd do," Polymnia said in a dull, dead voice, "I would have tried to kill you, that morning outside the mountain door. My hands were bound then too, but I would have tried anyway."

Chara said nothing, and looked only at the string.

"Wait," Alphaios said after she'd knotted it. He leaned forward to cut it with the blade he'd made himself, from the shell. "I want to do her ankles."

He wound the string even tighter than Chara had, and Polymnia gasped and reared back, hitting her head against the wall. Melaina laughed and drifted over to them, not limping at all now, carefully avoiding the place where Asterion was lying. "Difficult, isn't it?" she said loudly to Alphaios. "When desire turns to hatred. When love becomes a rage so strong that you could *kill*—"

"Melaina," said Theseus wearily, "enough."

She ignored him and bent down over Alphaios's shoulder. "She's not even all that beautiful," she said, and patted him on the shoulder.

She is, though, thought Chara. *She really is*—and she remembered, with a rush of dread, how Asterion the bull had charged, after Polymnia had cried out— protecting her? Defending her? *All these years; what were they, to each other?*

Asterion still hadn't woken up by nightfall, though metal and stone screamed as two of the corridors changed, and Alphaios and Melaina shouted at each other about who should bathe first, until Theseus commanded them to be silent. They retreated to opposite sides of the altar stone, and Theseus settled against the wall beside Polymnia. Asterion's head was back in Chara's lap. She tried to stay awake, and thought of that other time when she'd tried, and failed—and she failed again, because her weariness was too heavy to throw off.

She woke to Polymnia's voice, and air drenched in silver. She tried to spring to her feet, but couldn't: only her ears seemed to be working. The song was enormous, everywhere; it had so many words that she couldn't make out any of them. She heard blood in it, and night or ocean, endless and consuming.

She dragged her eyelids open.

Polymnia had managed to get herself to the middle of the altar. She was kneeling there, her bound ankles behind her, her bound wrists in front, her head thrown back to the moonlight. The silver flooded from her mouth in a spout that fell back on itself and down around her, and all of them.

Alphaios and Theseus were staring, motionless, at her. Melaina was lying with her face turned to the wall, so Chara couldn't tell if she was awake.

The song squeezed Chara's throat. It reached down into her chest and squeezed her heart. When Asterion stirred against her, she felt it, but only barely. She heard herself groan as she urged her gaze down to him.

His own eyes opened. He frowned at her—in confusion, not pain. He sat up and looked around the chamber, blinking at the silver, and rose. He gaped at his hands and feet, tipping forward slightly.

He didn't remember he'd turned back, Chara thought muzzily, and, *Her godmark's not affecting him; I don't understand.*

He straightened and walked slowly toward the altar. Polymnia's song faltered as she lowered her head to look at him. The silver broke into foam around her.

"No!" The word was thick and loud, from beast's throat and man's. Asterion stopped at the foot of the steps; Chara heard him panting, and saw his naked back heaving.

Polymnia strained against Daedalus's string, and fresh blood seeped down her hands. "How dare you?"

she screamed—and the others began to squirm and stretch, as the song's light dissipated. "How dare you help mere mortals when I helped *you* become a god? Answer me! *How dare you—*"

Theseus sprang past Asterion and crouched behind her. He pressed his hands against her mouth. "Alphaios," he said, "bring me a strip of cloth."

After Theseus had pulled the gag tight, Polymnia sang a few notes—but no words came, and no silver. She sobbed in great, dry heaves as he walked away from her.

"You were trying to kill us!" Melaina shrieked, struggling onto her hands and knees. "You *whore's* daughter!"

"Stop," Asterion said, so quietly that no one seemed to hear him.

"We should do away with her now," Alphaios said dully, his eyes on something far above them. "Why even bother imagining that any of us will get to Athens? She's right about that, anyway."

Theseus said, "We will return to Athens, and she will be judged according to the law of my father, King Aegeus."

"And what about the head of the beast?" Melaina hissed. "Won't you have to bring that back to your father King Aegeus too? Hmm, great prince?"

Chara leapt to her feet, her head suddenly clear. She was about to stride over to Melaina and perhaps seize her by the neck when the mountain shuddered, and gouts of scalding steam billowed into the chamber. Melaina fell, and Alphaios and Theseus stumbled. Chara was propelled forward, nearly to the steps. Asterion didn't stumble or even sway—but as she righted herself, next to him, she saw his arm twitch, and twitch again, and sprout thick brown fur.

He turned to her, his eyes wide. "I need to be . . . away," he gasped. "Come with me?"

"Of course," she said, and took his shaking hand in his, just as his fingers melded into hard, ridged hoof.

"Are you just going to let them leave?" she heard Melaina cry as Chara gathered some food into a piece of her own robe. "*Are* you?"

"Yes," Chara heard Theseus say, and, ::*Come back soon, daughter of Pherenike; Chara who spoke truth*::— and then she and Asterion walked together into the darkness.

———— · ————

At first she tried to pretend that they were weaving their way through Knossos—the underground part, of course, where they'd hidden themselves as children. But there were no chambers lined with olive oil jars here—no other slaves to dodge and greet, or flights of stairs that would lead them up to golden sunlight and the red of the courtyard's earth and the silver-green of olive trees. Just close, hot spaces, and stairs that led only to more of these.

She held his hand, and sometimes he leaned on her. He shook, and his breath hissed between his teeth. When the altar chamber seemed far behind them and they'd shuffled along at least three corridors, he tripped over something and sprawled, pulling her down with him. He made a guttural sound and clawed at her with hands that had started warping into hooves. His eyes were unfocused and darting. "Crabs and oysters," she blurted as she held his shoulders, which were twitching, trying to broaden. "Crabs and oysters and *pearls*, Asterion: imagine them!" He was still shuddering, but he blinked and blinked again, and saw her. "Big round pearls," she went on, more quietly. "Imagine that we're stringing them on thread Daedalus has made—wonderful soft humming thread that glows in the light—the kind of light that shines at noon in the summer: almost white."

He was nodding, holding onto her forearms with hands now, not hooves.

"So hot," he said, even as smoke coiled around them. "Can't help it. . . ." A moment later he said, "Daedalus. Icarus. What happened to them?"

She tipped her head up because she felt tears and didn't want him to see them. The ceiling above them was vaulted in a long series of arches, lit by criss-crossing veins of dark red light—*Like we're inside an enormous fish*, she thought. *Oh Master Daedalus: why did you have to make it all so beautiful?*

She looked back down at Asterion, who was frowning, now. "They died." Her voice wobbled, and she cleared her throat. "King Minos freed them and put them on a ship, and it was attacked, and . . ."

"Naucrate too?" Before she could reply, he said, "Of course Naucrate . . . too."

She drew her finger from his cheekbone to his jaw to the thick tangle of hair at his neck. "Where are we going?" she said. "Not that I care, mind you. But."

He raised himself up on an elbow and touched the tip of her nose with his. "It's close," he said. His breath still smelled of meat, though maybe not as strongly. "It's cool. Usually. It's . . ." He squeezed his eyes shut. "Icarus," he said. "Oh, gods: you make no sense."

They passed beneath the arches and onto a ledge above a wide space of nothingness. Chara peered down and thought she saw fire, flickering very far below them, but she pulled herself back before she could be sure. Across the chasm, another tunnel mouth gaped in rock. A soft, white glow lit it.

"Is there sometimes a bridge?" she said. "Or another bunch of ledges that come down from above, that you can walk across?"

Asterion smiled. "You know . . . Daedalus." She watched his smile falter as he thought of what he'd said, and what she'd told him. He knelt and leaned into the empty space, patting at the stone beneath them. As he did, she thought, *I can't believe he's right here. Can't believe I'm talking to him as if all those years didn't happen. Can't believe I could touch him now.*

He gave a tug, wincing as his shoulder wound stretched. A rumble ran up through her feet. Metal ground out from the ledge: like Daedalus's sword, it emerged in pieces that gave way to smaller pieces, all of them patterned filigree that reminded her of the stone spirals on Ariadne's dancing ground. When the last piece was out and touching the opposite wall, Asterion rose and turned to her.

"I'm the only one who . . . knows about this." He swallowed and shook his head, frowning. "My voice isn't . . . right. . . ."

"Of course it isn't," she said. "You haven't used it in ages, have you? Anyway. You're the only one who knows about this place—this bridge."

He swallowed again. "I found it early, when I was still . . . mostly a boy. Couldn't move the lever after that. I used to . . . stand here, when I couldn't. Used to look at the light."

He stared at the other corridor. His body was stiff, his shoulders high and hunched. As she watched, a shudder rippled down his naked spine and along his arms. She touched the small of his back and heard him suck in his breath—but when he looked at her, he was smiling.

He stepped onto the first section of the bridge. "Like walking on the edge . . . of the falls," he said over his shoulder. Her laugh turned into a gasp as she went after him. The metal thrummed and bounced, no matter how gently she set her feet on it.

"Right," she said in a voice that was as wobbly as the bridge, "just like that."

"Be glad Deucalion . . . isn't here to call up a wind, like he . . . used to."

"Until Glaucus begged him to stop." She was speaking through gritted teeth, hardly listening to herself. She wanted to drop and crawl, clinging to whatever she could, but instead she stared straight ahead. *If he can make it on two legs, after everything, so can I.*

There *was* a wind: hot, slow breath that eased up around her, then seemed to tug at her as it receded, like waves at wading feet. Halfway—the third section of bridge, ever-narrower; him leaping and turning to her from solid rock, waving.

Why a chasm under *a mountain? Why?*

Last section, barely wide enough for her feet, placed shoulders'-breadth apart. A blast of scalding wind made her cry out and wave her arms for balance, and look down.

There was definitely fire, in a place so deep that it had to be where the world ended, or where it had been born, or both. Black smoke reached long, hissing fingers toward her and made everything smudge and run together. She had no breath; she had no body, which was a relief, because now she wouldn't feel the fall.

"Chara! You're nearly there. Look up, and jump!"

She did all of this before she could think. The space between the daintily tapered end of the bridge and the ledge was one she probably could have crossed in a single long pace, but fear, and his command, made her leap. She landed, sprawled, rolled onto her back, wheezing with laughter.

"Up, old woman," he said from above her, his hands on his knees. She struggled to sit— her bones had all gone soft—and struggled to breathe, because now, suddenly, she was crying.

Asterion's hands were on her shoulders. "I shouldn't have brought you here. The mountain is . . . different. There was never this . . . much wind or heat, before. I'm sorry. . . ."

She gulped and dragged her hand under her nose. "That's fine," she said, smiling shakily up at him. "But whatever's on this side had better be worth it."

CHAPTER SEVENTEEN

At first, Chara thought that the chamber was made entirely of crystal. There was no single source of light: it came from everywhere, rainbow and white; when she squeezed her eyes shut, she still saw its dazzle. If there was an end to the expanse, anywhere, she couldn't tell: no ceiling, no rock wall anywhere but at the corridor's mouth.

Asterion took three paces past her, to the place where hard-packed dirt became crystal. She couldn't see his face. "How long has it been since you were last here?"

"Don't know." He looked back at her: a stranger with inward-turned eyes. "How long since they put me . . . inside?"

Questions, she thought, with a shiver made of dread and relief. *At last.* "Four years. A little more than that."

"Ariadne . . . thought of it, didn't she? Of putting me in here? And the king did . . . the rest?"

"Yes."

"Who else knew?"

"Ariadne and your father were the only ones who weren't surprised. It was their secret. She'd have wanted it that way. Asterion," she said, wanting to touch him, but wary of his stranger's gaze. "Show me this place?"

He stared a moment longer, then blinked as slowly as one of Karpos's statues, and returned. "Of course," he said, with a twitch of his shoulders, and a shadow-smile.

A path wound through the crystal, which rose in blocks that were jagged or smooth, knee-high or far, far taller than Chara and Asterion were. She started every time she moved and her reflection did the same, distorted and close; she tried to look only at him, padding slowly across the slippery ground. The path branched and he led her right, without hesitation. *It's a labyrinth within a labyrinth*, she thought, and remembered Ariadne's puzzle box, with its tiny metal figures.

After they'd taken two other, narrower paths, Asterion stopped. She was behind—no room beside—and saw something dark on the ground just beyond him. He blew out a long, slow breath. "Well. Here we are."

She stepped after him onto a small patch of brown-red rock, fuzzed with moss so painfully bright that she thought, *How had I already forgotten green?* A trickle of water had carved a channel in the crystal of one of the enclosing walls; the trickle disappeared into the moss, soaking it almost black.

"Some of this light must be from the sun." She whispered, because she wanted to be able to hear the burble and drip of the water.

"I thought that too, when I first came here. It hurt me. It hurt that there was . . . still sun, somewhere."

She dug her toes into the moss—the dry green, then, paces later, the damp almost-black. She walked around the entire patch—thirty-two paces in all—and had taken fifteen steps across it when a piece of cloth made her stop. She hadn't noticed it before, because it was folded up into a very small square, and was so dirty that it blended in with the rock.

"That was . . . someone's," he said. "Kosmas's, maybe. *She* set it aside. I picked it up. I never had anything of my own; I was naked when I fell, because I was . . ."

"The bull," she said, "or mostly. I know. I was watching."

". . . And I took this because I thought . . . it might make me feel more human. To wear it."

He picked up the cloth and twisted it in his hands until his knuckles went white.

"Did it work?"

He shook his head. "But maybe now I could make a . . . loincloth out of it, anyway . . . Try again."

"No—don't," she said, and felt herself flush. "I mean, you're obviously a boy—a man."

He grinned. It shocked her as the green had; she thought, *I'd forgotten—O gods and snapping turtles, but he's beautiful when he smiles like that.*

"If I shouldn't . . . neither should you."

She slipped out of her own robe and dropped it at her feet. Her skin was blazingly hot; so was everything underneath it. *We've been like this before*, she thought, as if she could reason the heat away. *When we were children. He'd be naked after a rite; I'd be wearing only a loincloth—gods, but it bothered Ariadne, and her mother.* But this wasn't the same. Of course it wasn't.

She sat down by the damp moss with her legs drawn up under her chin. He knelt in front of her and leaned to put the edge of her robe in the water. He wrung it out over her shoulders and she gasped at its cold and its long, tickling trails. He dipped it again and squeezed it over her front, this time. When he sat back she saw the cloth tremble in his hands, and reached out to hold one of them. She shifted so that she was kneeling, and he put a hand on the back of her stubble-roughened head and pulled it closer to him—to his lips, which were dry and cracked and slightly parted.

If he kissed her, it was too quick for her to feel. What she did feel was him pulling his hand away, and bumping her shoulders with his as he thrust himself to his feet. She stood too, but he was already stumbling away from her. The crystal walls warped his shape and features; he wobbled, as if she were seeing him through receding veils of water. He took one path and then another, until he vanished into the glare.

She sat with her back next to the stream, even though she wanted to run after him. "No," she said quietly—aloud, because her voice made her feel steadier. "Leave him. He'll come back. Be patient."

Darkness fell around her, almost between breaths. All that was left of the blaze of colour and white was a deep blue glow far above, which seemed to pulse in time with her heartbeat. *The sky*, she thought. *The night sky above Knossos; the horns on the palace roof, darker than the sky. Ariadne standing up there, watching for her father's return from Athens. The same sky, nights later, when Asterion gored the king. The High Priest made lightning and thunder; the ground split open at our feet. And they took Asterion away.* Each word, each memory was thick and tangled with weariness.

When she woke it was still dark, except for the blue—but there was a shadow across from her. She saw him as the sleep cleared from her eyes: crouched, coiled, rocking. She didn't speak. After a moment he crawled over the moss to her, and she saw that one of his legs was dragging behind him, and that it ended in a hoof. His horns were longer than they'd been when he left.

He took her hand, and she flinched, though she didn't mean to. He guided her forefinger to some carved lines in the wall beside her, which she hadn't noticed. He drew her finger along them, slowly, his hand shaking a little. The marks meant nothing, at first—but then, after he'd made her trace them again, she felt the shape of his name and, right beside it, hers. She drew in a quick breath and turned her fingers around so that they were gripping his.

"I wanted to remember," he whispered. "I was afraid I'd lose . . . everything. I used obsidian to carve them. I . . ."

His belly hollowed as he sucked in his own breath.

She held herself still, though she wanted to draw him in against her. "Do you remember everything else?" she said. "Everything that's happened to you in here, when you were the bull?"

He slid himself away from her and lay down on his side. He was silent for so long that she thought he'd gone to sleep. "Yes," he said at last, and curled even more tightly into himself.

She sat with her hand on their names and waited for dawn.

———— · ————

He didn't leave again, in the days that followed, but he hardly spoke, either. One morning his hoof had turned back into a foot; the next, his arms were covered in fur, which became scarred flesh again by nightfall. She made her own way back and forth to the crevasse to empty her bladder and bowels of the very little food she was eating; when she returned he was always where she'd left him, silent, his eyes rolling away from hers.

He didn't eat at all.

She left a fig near his hand, as she ate one. She broke off pieces of salt fish and dipped them in water and placed some on the stone, while she ate the others. He didn't even glance at the food.

"You have to eat," she finally said, though she'd promised herself she wouldn't be the one to break their silence.

He was sitting cross-legged in the middle of the mossy patch, staring at nothing. "I don't," he said, and she started; she hadn't expected his voice.

"Here: have one fig. Just one. You need strength; your shoulder won't heal quickly enough, otherwise."

"No!" he shouted, and leapt to his feet. *There*, she thought dully, *now he'll go*—but he didn't. He paced, stumbling a bit with every turn he took.

"Why did you bring me here with you?" She tried to speak quietly, but the words cracked and came out louder.

He stopped pacing and stood with his forehead against the crystal, facing away from her. She saw his reflection—his closed eyes, his parted lips, blurred.

"It was wonderful, being . . . back. It was—at first. Now . . ."

He turned and walked to her and sat down with a *whoosh* of breath that sounded like the bull's.

She shook her head, though he wasn't looking at her. "I can't imagine what any of this has been like, for you. All these years. And I don't have any idea what to do now, myself. I was so certain I'd find you—but I didn't ever think past that."

"Because you knew . . . we'd both die in here."

She kept shaking her head, until her vision swam with crystal and light. "I don't believe that."

"And even if we did get out, and . . . escape . . . where would we go? How . . . would we live?"

"I don't know." She could barely speak over the lump that had risen into her throat. *We*, she thought. She wound her fingers together and squeezed, tight.

"You used to bring me things," he said, some time later. "After a rite. After I'd changed back."

"I did. So here—look: it's a fig!"

He made a snuffling noise that was almost a laugh and took it from her. He turned it over and over in his palm. "I can't eat yet," he said. "I'm sorry. For everything."

They didn't speak again that day. At night, as they lay against opposite walls, he said, "Prince Theseus was going to kill me."

She propped her cheek on her hand. "He was."

"He shouted . . . into my head. *Into* it. As he was . . . about to strike me with his sword. He called me . . . monster."

"Ariadne told him that's what you were. She lured him here to kill you, then take her back to Athens with her."

He snorted. "Ariadne, Queen of Athens."

"Yes. But that won't happen, now. He's seen what you really are."

"And what's that?" he asked.

A man, she wanted to say, but couldn't.

———— · ————

"I wrote to you," she said, on another, later day.

He turned to her. He was lying down; she was sitting beside him, close, not touching. "Really?" he said.

"While your sister was sleeping. I wrote and wrote— on paper, not clay. I hid it in that place we found—that loose spot behind the olive oil jars."

He squinted at her, as if the light were too bright. His cheeks were hollow and fuzzed with golden hair. He was all sharp edges and empty space; all scars upon scars upon flesh thin as Ariadne's Egyptian paper. "Why?"

"Because I missed you so much. And it helped to think that I'd read them to you, someday—that I'd read to you about how I'd planned to save you. Then I was afraid someone would find them and stop me."

"What did you do?" One of his hands came out and found her knee. She didn't move.

"I burned all of it. Took a lamp out to the waterfall— and then I worried that Ariadne would be waiting for me when I got back, just like she was that time we came back from there with Icarus and Glau."

"And was she?"

"No. It was the middle of the night, and you remember how she used to sleep."

"Tell me what they said? If you remember."

"I remember." She paused, then told him. Ariadne begging Karpos to marry her. Karpos and Deucalion laughing, their bare shoulders touching. Glaucus, with his painted stick that would never be a sword. Minos burning up the countryside while his subjects gossiped and cowered, or craned to watch.

Asterion's eyes closed, as she spoke—but when she

stopped his hand pressed her knee, and he said, "What about my mother? And my sister Phaidra?"

"The Queen continues as ever: beautiful and hard. Though she is always gentle with Phaidra. Phaidra, who is very, very beautiful, herself. As bright as Ariadne is dark. And very strong, though no one would've believed it of her, when she was the child you remember."

"I knew she was strong," he said. "I watched her rescue a toad from a snake, once. She was magnificent."

You're speaking normally, she thought, but didn't dare say. *You're coming back.*

He sat up and opened his eyes. "So have you eaten all the figs?" he said, and smiled, just a little.

———— · ————

"Theseus was right." The same night; perhaps the next. "Ariadne, too. I *am* a monster."

She sat up so that her knees were touching his. The blue glow was beating out the rhythm of her blood, far above them in the dark. "We're all monsters."

"You don't know. You can't understand." He sounded tired, not angry.

"You're also a man." She could say this now, to the Asterion who was back with her.

"I don't remember becoming one. I was a boy, the last time I was with you."

"I don't care what you are." A sort-of lie, but her voice didn't betray her. "You could be part lobster, for all I care. Though," she added, "that would make things—"

"Pinchy," he said. They laughed. She leaned toward him and put her forehead against his. He laid his hands on her head and dragged his fingers back and forth over the stubble there. She put her own hands over his and pressed them down, hard.

"At least you won't get tangled in my curls."

"I always loved your curls," he said, and slid his hands down to her cheeks and pulled her in and kissed her.

At first her head was full of words that kept her from feeling much: *He'll end this; he'll walk away again.* But he didn't. She was the one who pulled back—but just to see him, in the dimness. To trace his smile as she'd traced the marks of their names.

He lay down and she slid on top of him, holding him with her arms and legs; holding him as he slid inside her with a groan. He dug his fingers into her hips and moved her up and down against his, and she threw back her head and saw the crystal and the air that looked like sky. He pulled her back to him, and she eased her fingers and tongue along all the scars she could feel. When he shuddered and went still, she lay listening to the slowing of his heart.

She was nearly asleep, still sprawled on him, when he said, "Have you done that before?"

"Once," she murmured, "with a bull dancer who imagined himself quite wonderful."

"And was he?"

"Once, I said. That's all."

"I did it once too," he said slowly. "Or almost, anyway."

She was fully, abruptly awake. She eased herself off him and rolled over, and he fitted himself into the curve of her back and legs. "Polymnia?" she said. Her tongue felt swollen in her mouth.

"Yes. But I couldn't . . . I ran from her. I think I was

almost always the bull, after that. Chara," he went on, and one of his horns poked at her neck as he nuzzled her, "I feel as if my skin needs yours, now, so it can stay like this."

She swallowed. *Forget Polymnia. He's here; he's with you.* "You don't want to change again at all?"

After a long silence, he said, "I don't think so. I don't know. And it's not as if I have a choice, anyway. As long as there's heat, it'll happen."

She squeezed his arms, which were crossed over her breasts. "Icarus was jealous of you. We had a fight, at the top of the mountain, when I was sure there'd be a way in. He said he envied you, in here."

Asterion's breath was warm against her stubbly skull. "And I'm sure he hated himself for it."

"He did."

"Poor Icarus. Poor all of us."

His arms loosened and his breathing grew deep and slow. The sweat between their bodies dried.

::*Chara?*:: she heard, just as she, too, was falling asleep. ::*Where are you? It's been two weeks; come back to us.*::

——— · ———

She woke to the whine and snap of cracking crystal. Asterion was already on his feet.

"What is it?" she said groggily, rubbing a hand across her face as she sat up.

"Maybe the start of an earthquake. There've been a few, while I've been in here, but small ones. This feels different."

She stood up and reached for her robe, long-forgotten on the moss. "We should get back to the others," she said. Just then, Theseus's mind-voice filled her, much louder than the night before. ::*Chara! The Great Goddess may be opening a way for us. I have summoned the ship; it will be waiting.*::

The ground lifted and fell beneath them and they sprawled into each other, fumbling to stay upright. Behind them, metal shrieked. "The bridge!" Asterion cried, and they stumbled toward it through shards of falling crystal.

The bridge had pulled farther away from the ledge; its slenderest section was listing down toward the abyss, an arm's length away.

"We'll have to jump," he said. "Now, before it moves any more."

She crouched and rocked, rubbing her fingers into her sweaty palms. "Just like the waterfall," she said. "Right?"

He kissed the top of her head. "Just like that," he said, and she jumped before she could think, and falter.

She'd thrown herself down—too far down, because the filigree was running out, just beyond her reaching hands. She gave a cry and strained, her bare feet running in mid-air, and the rock behind and ahead of her grumbled and shifted in puffs of tiny pebbles, and then her hands found metal, and clung. She swayed at the end of the lowest, thinnest part of the bridge, the weight of her body pulling it down still more. Hot wind belched from the chasm; when she glanced down, the fire seemed closer than it had before, as if it, too, were reaching.

"Climb, Chara!" Asterion sounded very far away. She couldn't turn to look at him, because she had to concentrate on her hands. *Move*, she told one of them—and it did, in a quick, lurching dart. The other ended up above it; the first above that. She climbed until she reached the wider portion of the bridge, which was still in its original position. She hauled herself onto its relatively flat expanse and lay on her stomach, panting.

"Don't stop!" Asterion called. She got to her hands and knees and crawled, no longer looking at the glow of the fire or the crumbling stone. All she saw was the ledge where the bridge ended. It seemed to get no closer, and she whimpered in frustration—but at last her hands were on solid ground and her arms collapsed and she lay for a moment with her face in the dirt.

She sat up when Asterion shouted, and turned just in time to see him hurl himself from the opposite ledge. He landed on the drooping section of bridge with a *clang*. As he did, the earth gave another shudder, and the metal shrieked and twisted, and more hot air came gusting up from the chasm. Even she felt it, up on her ledge, but Asterion took the full force of it. She watched him writhe against the bridge. He lifted his face to hers, and she saw the terror on it. He yelled again, and the yell became a roar, and his lengthening horns flared silver-bronze.

One of his hands slipped as its fingers began to fuse.

"No!" she cried, leaning out into the space beside the bridge, digging her own fingers into the ledge. "Asterion: keep climbing! You're so close—don't stop . . . ." His head was pressed against the bridge; she couldn't see his face any more. "Asterion: think of the falls. You told me to—do it yourself, now. The water, so cool on your skin. Your skin, Asterion. The water.

The air—the cool wind that throws spray against your cheeks—you have *goosebumps*—"

His fingers weren't yet hoof. He lifted his head; she still saw terror, but his eyes, seeking hers, were steady when they found her. She called out more words she hardly heard, though she knew that "cool" and "chilly" and "water" repeated, repeated—until he pulled himself up. The scars on his shoulders and back darkened and contorted as he moved. He glowed with sweat, and fresh blood from his shoulder, and his hands lost their grip a few more times before he dragged himself onto the broader section of bridge. He stood up, as she hadn't, and ran.

When he reached her, he kissed her brow and lips and neck. Between each kiss was a word: "Thank . . . you . . . Freckles. . . ." She gasped, this time with laughter.

"Lead us back, my Prince," she said, and felt him pull away.

"Not 'my Prince,'" he said, in a cold voice that reminded her of his mother, Queen Pasiphae's. "Not that, or 'my Lord' or 'Bull-god.' None of that. Ever."

She put her hands on his cheeks, which were grimed with rust from the bridge, and ash blown up from the abyss. "Very well, Asterion," she said. "Let's go."

He shivered and blinked, as if he'd been far away, and smiled at her, and looked eight years old, not eighteen.

Thunder rolled beneath their feet. The bridge screeched and warped and tore free of the rock. Chara watched it fall toward the fire that was not so distant any more, and then she turned back to Asterion, and they ran together.

The tunnels were like living things around them:

roiling with rock or plaster dust, tipping, bending. A row of columns cracked and crashed behind them; an ocean frieze exploded in painted fragments that tore at Chara's skin; a doorway collapsed just as they threw themselves beneath it. Her breath tore at her too, in hot, stinging jabs, and her muscles—almost unused, in the crystal chamber—felt white with pain. But she kept up with Asterion, who darted and leapt as if he'd always been only a man. He finally paused when they reached the entrance to the altar chamber. When she came to stand beside him she could see the chamber, between the pillars: its jars, some toppled; the steps and waterfall and the shadows of people who were rising, stumbling, to meet them.

"Thank the gods," Asterion said, between heaving breaths, "it's the right door."

She took his hand, and they passed through it.

———— · ————

The earthquake didn't seem to end. Even when the worst of the shaking and heaving had passed—churning up the stones of the floor, sending the obsidian on the walls falling like needle-sharp rain—new gouts of steam and flame still leapt out from the corridors that remained, and from fissures in the ground. The heat was almost unbearable. Asterion's feet and one of his hands were hooves, and his horns were long, and the golden fuzz on his cheeks turned brown and thick. He was still mostly Asterion, because the trickle of water remained (though it was warm, now, even before it hit the fractured stone), and because Chara gazed at him, and made him gaze at her, and whispered old and new rhymes against his human lips.

"Oh, please," Melaina snapped, days after their return. "It's bad enough that the Goddess is trying to consume us—must we put up with your *love*, as we prepare to die?"

"We will not die," Theseus said, before Chara could reply. He was standing with one leg on a block of stone. Polymnia was propped against the same stone, sideways, bound and silent. The only sound Chara had heard her utter was a broken, trailing cry, when she and Asterion had come back. He hadn't even glanced at Polymnia, then or since—or not that Chara had seen, anyway.

"Remember: I have called for the ship," Theseus went on. "The mountain could yet shift enough for some of us, at least, to escape it; if the gods are good, we will reach the sea and the ship will be waiting to return us to Athens." As he spoke, a section of the wall above him disintegrated in a streaming shower of rock; he ducked and ran a few steps, over the buckling ground. Polymnia hardly flinched as the rocks struck her.

"Escape," Melaina scoffed, shaking her head. "Oh, my Prince: the mountain will keep shifting, yes, and we'll all be crushed. *This* is where the gods will have us end—not Athens."

"No," Alphaios said, "he might be right: if the ground keeps moving like this, and if we can stack more rocks on top of each other, we might be able to—"

Flame spewed from one of the corridors, and Alphaios had to leap out of its way.

"Yes," Melaina said loudly, over a hiss of steam, "we obviously have so much *time* to build this rock ladder of yours."

"Is it wrong to hope?" he demanded. Melaina made

some retort, but Chara didn't hear it; she was looking up at a strange, flickering shadow. *One of ours*, she thought, *all twisted and stretched by the firelight*—but as soon as she thought this, she knew it wasn't.

"Quiet, all of you; look!" she cried, and pointed. All of them looked, except Polymnia.

"It's from *outside!*" Alphaios said, as the shadow grew on the crumbling stone at the top of the chamber. "It's coming in! *Down!* What . . . ?"

Chara clutched Asterion's slippery hand with her own and waited.

—BOOK—

FOUR

ICARUS

First Athenian Sacrifice

CHAPTER EIGHTEEN

Icarus had never known such darkness. He'd always been able to find the sky, when he'd been too long indoors and his flesh prickled with longing and feathers. And the sky had never been this dark: there were always stars and sometimes moon, sometimes lightning, and drifts of silver cloud that taunted him because he couldn't reach them.

When he and his parents had been seized during the attack on the ship that was supposed to bear them away from Crete, they'd been thrown into the hold of a different ship. It had been dark there, but some sunlight had crept between the timbers; Icarus had been able to see his father's teeth, bared in the smile he wore whenever he was puzzled, and his mother's slender fingers, wrapped around his own downy arm.

"If they're pirates," she murmured, "they'll soon find out that none of us have anything to take."

"Not pirates," Daedalus murmured back. "Not sure what, but not pirates."

The sunlight was gone by the time the ship docked. Shadowy figures blindfolded them and bound their wrists. "Icarus?" Naucrate called as someone tugged her away from him. "Don't be afraid . . ." He wanted to call back, "Mother, I'm not a child—I'm not afraid!"— except that he *was*. His legs shook so badly, when he was finally pushed out onto solid ground, that he thought he might fall. His calfskin boots had come unlaced, and they slipped off his feet as he shuffled to stay upright.

What do *they want with* us? *I don't even have my boots, any more—though Mother might have brought a few of her alabaster jars?*

Even with the blindfold, he could see things: tiny orange blurs that must have been lamp- or torchlight; darker smudges that might have been people, shifting in and out of what passed for his vision. He stumbled where he was driven, by hands and harder things, maybe the wooden ends of spears. The first place was part slippery sand, part knobbly stones—probably a beach. The next was a staircase up a cliff; he knew this because, when he listed, someone growled, "Straighten up, man, or you'll end up in the sea," and because he could hear this sea, pounding and hissing to his left, spattering him with spray. Just as his lungs and legs started to burn, the steps turned into a path that was flat and hard-packed. "No stopping," the same voice growled, as whoever owned it thrust at him again, sharply, between his shoulder blades. *Pirates would have killed us as soon as they found out we had nothing to steal*, Icarus thought, his chest tightening even further.

They ripped his blindfold up over his head so quickly that he felt strands of hair go with it. His wrist bonds fell away at the same time. The world lurched around him; he flapped his arms and tipped forward, into what he saw too late was an abyss made of sky and water. "Whoa, there: that's not the way down," said the same voice, as hands wrapped around his arms and tugged him away from the cliff's edge.

Daedalus was at Icarus's right shoulder, blinking at the white-crested waves far below. His teeth were still bared, but not in a smile. Naucrate was beside him; as Icarus tried to catch her eye, she rounded on one of the six men who stood behind them in a ragged line. "Explain yourselves!" she spat.

The one nearest Icarus laughed, and the rest of them did too, loudly, as if they were making up for not having done so immediately. Their loincloths were plain, their weapons unadorned, but Icarus thought he recognized two of the faces. Before he could try to puzzle this out, a new voice bellowed, "Silence!"

King Minos strode into the glow of the torches.

Daedalus's laugh was high and wavering in the quiet. He didn't turn to look at the king. "My old friend," he said, when he'd finished laughing. "I wondered why you'd let us go so graciously."

Silver-orange fire kindled beneath the skin of Minos's neck. Icarus watched it spread up beneath his jaw, pulsing under the dark hair of his beard. "I couldn't let you go at all," he said. "Old friend." He waved a smoky trail through the air. "Take them down," he said, and there were hands on Icarus again, pushing him to sit, prodding him to turn and flatten so that the stone of the edge ground into his belly and his legs flailed in empty air. He lowered his legs and poked at the cliff with his bare toes and found an indentation that was barely a step—but the man above him said, "That's it: down you go," and Icarus went, groping and shaky. He tried to ignore the wind that buffeted him, but couldn't: he sprouted feathers as he always did, when his body felt called to the sky. The ones on his arms tickled his cheeks.

Another pair of hands steadied him, as his feet settled onto something that felt like ground. The hands turned him so that he was facing the chasm once more—and he saw that he was on a narrow ledge. "Here," the man beside him said, and pulled him along for a few paces. Icarus pressed his back to the rock as his father descended, then his mother. "Steady, now: wouldn't want you taking a tumble before you get to your fine new quarters." The man grinned—or perhaps it was more of a leer. His face was pockmarked and sallow in the starlight.

"Theron?" the king called from above them, and the pockmarked man shouted, "Ready, my Lord!"

A strangled shout drifted down; a body followed it, and another, another, until all six of Minos's men had fallen, flailing, past the ledge and into emptiness. Icarus didn't hear their bodies meet the water; the waves were too loud. His own voice, circling wordlessly in his head, was too loud.

Minos dropped onto the ledge with a grunt that Icarus did hear.

"Monster," Daedalus said, quite calmly.

The king shrugged. Silver-red light bloomed on the curve of his shoulder. "The fewer people know about this, the better. Do you not agree, Theron?"

Theron bent his chin to his chest. "I do, my Lord."

"Lead on, then!" the king cried, as gaily as if he were summoning his people to a feast. Theron grasped Icarus's arm and shuffled along the ledge, and Icarus followed. He kept his eyes on his own feet; if he'd looked at his parents, his dizziness would have pitched him into the sea.

After only a few careful paces, Theron said, "On your knees."

Icarus eased himself down, his back to the emptiness. He saw a low, rounded door in the cliffside. Rusty bolts; rusty lock, already unlatched.

Push him, Icarus thought. *Turn around and push both of them: nothing good is waiting behind this door.* But he couldn't move—not until Minos said, "In you go," and Theron set his hand on Icarus's head and pushed *him*.

Theron's torch flickered off a low, curving ceiling and root-encrusted walls. Icarus crawled until he reached an open space: a cavern with a soaring ceiling that glittered with crystal veins and hardened drippings of something that looked gold. There was a low, flat rock in the centre, and an opening that might have been a jagged doorway beyond the reach of the flame—he saw it for only a breath before his parents pressed in behind him.

"Theron?" Minos said. His teeth glinted in his beard. "The bonds."

"Back on your knees," Theron said to Icarus. Icarus glanced at his mother, who shook her head helplessly, and then at his father, who was rocking a bit, his eyes closed. Icarus knelt. Theron crouched behind him and tied his wrists behind his back. As Icarus thought, *Gods and gulls—so tight—my wrists must be bleeding*, Theron thrust him onto his side. He lashed once, twice, like a fish in a net; the third time he felt his feet hit something hard, and heard Theron grunt.

"Stop," snapped the king. "It will go even worse for you if you struggle."

There's nothing I can do, Icarus thought, and went still. Theron bound his ankles. With a jerk that made Icarus's teeth knock together, Theron tied the ankle and wrist bonds with yet another length of rope. Icarus gasped as his back bowed inward. His hands and feet were already prickling; soon they'd be completely numb.

Naucrate cried out and Daedalus bellowed as if

someone had hurt him, but Icarus couldn't see either of them. He blinked grit out of his eyes, and the king's legs swam into focus. The king's legs, bending; the king's face, angled sideways so that it was level with Icarus's. Minos's cheeks were glowing with pinpoints of fire—stars scattered on flesh. He put out a finger and stroked the feathers that had sprouted along Icarus's shoulder. *Don't move*, Icarus told himself, as his insides roiled and squirmed.

"Your god has made you a monster," the king murmured, "just as Asterion's made him. May you both think on this, in your deep, dark holes."

He rose and swivelled on his heels. Icarus craned and saw him staring down—at Naucrate and Daedalus, no doubt. He stared for a very long time. At last he arched his brows and waved an orange and silver hand languidly. "Sleep well, children," he said, and laughed. A moment later the torchlight was in the passageway, twisting the men's shadows; a moment after that, the door clanged, and all the light was gone.

———— · ————

No time and all time passed, in this darkness Icarus had never even imagined. No one spoke, and all of them did, in hushed, urgent voices.

"Even your underground workshop wasn't this dark," he whispered to his father. He could smell Daedalus beside him: sweat and urine and blood. He tried to remember that workshop, which had always frightened him, a little. It had been hot—the air, and the water that lapped over his feet, stirred by the beasts that lurked beneath it. But there had always been daylight, above and behind him; if he held his arm up, its hairs and feathers turned gold.

He couldn't lift his arms, now; couldn't even feel them, except when he ground his wrists together. He did this several times, because the knife-cut pain reminded him that he had a body.

"No," Daedalus said, after a silence. The word was vague and soft; Icarus wondered if his father even knew that he'd said it.

After a longer silence, Naucrate said, "They're not done." Her voice was raw. Icarus had seen her cry only once, when he was five, and his sister had been born and died, in the same day.

"The king—he's wanted to hurt us since I spurned him, all those years ago. His plan for us will be terrible, cruel beyond anything we can imagine. I'm sorry," she breathed, and this time it was Icarus who said, "No."

He rolled from his right side to his left, gasping at the pain. That was all he could do. There was no way he'd be able to get to his knees, let alone his feet—not trussed as he was. He rolled again. Dirt and stones stuck to his cheeks and lips; he spat and spat, but the grit was between his teeth, coating his tongue. He tasted blood.

No time and all time; nothing but the dark. He felt the weight of sky, pressing at the rock above them, and at the rusty metal door. He *heard* it, pressing on his ears—and then he heard the screech of lock and hinges.

Light wavered at the edge of the chamber.

"Turn away," Daedalus said. "Don't look at him." The three of them lurched and scuffed and lay still, in a tight, curved row. Icarus stared up at the stone wall nearest him. Its bands of ochre and grey glistened with moisture that made his throat constrict with thirst.

"Go closer, Daughter," the king said. "Go and see this secret that is now ours."

Icarus turned his head toward the king's voice and had to close his eyes against the brilliant blur of orange, gold, silver and red. When he opened them and squeezed his tears away, Minos was standing by the flat stone.

He rolled his head and saw her: towering, too bright, too beautiful.

"Ari." He hardly recognized his own voice. He felt a bead of fresh blood well between his lips. He flexed the talons at the end of his fingers and heard them scrabble weakly at the dirt.

Ariadne turned to her father. "The pirate attack," she said. "Was there one?"

He smiled down at her. "Oh, yes. The ship went down—after my men got these three off. Just before it burned. It sank, and everyone else with it. But these three . . ." He was smiling down at Icarus and his parents, now. "They deserved more."

Daedalus lifted his head and spat. He'd probably meant the mucus to land on the king's feet, but instead it clung to Daedalus's chin. "And now," he rasped, "you have come to give us this 'more.'"

Minos's laugher echoed off the cavern's walls and up into the emptiness above them. "I have," he said. "And my daughter, who deserves to know this secret, will be here to watch."

A sour taste surged into Icarus's mouth as Minos spun on his heel and strode back toward the cavern's opening. "I thought about starting with Naucrate," he said as he picked something up from the ground there, "but I have reconsidered. I believe I will start with the great and clever Daedalus."

He walked back. His hand was wrapped around a hammer—one that Daedalus or Karpos might use to work their colossal blocks of stone. Minos's other hand closed around Daedalus's collar and hauled him up and over to the low, flat rock. Daedalus choked, and his bent-back body lashed like a worm in a beak. Icarus groaned.

"Now, then," said the king, and drew a dagger from his boot. He cut the rope that attached Daedalus's wrist and ankle bonds. "Let us get you settled properly. You are an artisan, after all; arrangement and order matter to you." He pulled Daedalus's bound hands onto the rock and pinned them there, pressing down on the rope around his wrists. His fingers jerked inward as if he wanted to make fists, but Minos adjusted his hold and flattened them out.

"Little Queen," he said. "Come and help me."

Ariadne walked to her father, who took her hand. Her head and shoulders were very straight.

"Kneel behind him. Yes. Now press here on the rope, as I did. Good. He will try to move, in a moment. Use all your strength to keep him still."

She licked her lips. "Yes, Father," she said.

Daedalus turned his head so that one bright eye was on her. "Ariadne," he said, in a low, rough voice. "Minnow."

"No. Don't call me that. Do not." Her knuckles whitened as she tightened her grip on his wrists.

Minos raised the hammer and brought it down on Daedalus's right palm.

His hands flapped and a tremor went through the rest of him—it bent his spine, from buttocks to skull. He hardly moved, otherwise. He screamed, but only once. As the hammer came down on his other palm and all his fingers, one by one, he dug his chin into his chest and shuddered. Bones cracked in skin. Icarus was shouting; he didn't know when he'd started, but it filled his ears now, along with the cracking bones and Naucrate's wailing.

When Minos was done, he laid the hammer down and crouched in front of Daedalus. "You will never make anything again, old friend," he said, shaking his head regretfully. Red light glowed behind his teeth. Cinders drifted between them and into his beard. "Surely this will be a relief: first exile, then endless seeking for things you could never quite touch; your art has only ever caused you pain."

Ariadne let go of Daedalus's wrists.

"Little Queen," Minos said, rising, "would you agree that it is not just the great Daedalus's hands that have caused unhappiness in our palaces?"

"I would agree," she said firmly. "He has also *spoken* wrongly—yes; I remember the feast at which he said my noble brother Androgeus's name over and over, in defiance of your command."

Minos nodded. A blotch of flame appeared beneath his flesh, at the hinge of his jaw. Icarus watched it wriggle up past his ear to the pouch beneath his left eye, where it stopped and pulsed, perhaps in time with his heart. "Precisely, dearest. His words have wounded us. What else, then, might we do to him?"

The knife was in his hand. His fingertips stained the haft with coursing, molten orange.

Icarus's talons were still scritching at dirt and pebbles; he couldn't seem to stop them from moving. Naucrate was whispering Daedalus's name over and over.

"We might cut . . ." Ariadne's voice shook, just a

little. "We might cut out his tongue," she went on.

The king smiled at her. He thrust Daedalus onto the ground, fell to his knees beside him, pried open his jaws—which stayed open, gaping, fish-like—and with that same hand he pulled Daedalus's tongue out between his teeth. With his other hand he raised the knife and set it to the tongue and sliced.

Icarus stopped moving. Naucrate stopped murmuring. The only sounds were a far-off, steady dripping and the low moan that bubbled from Daedalus's weeping mouth.

"Minnow."

Naucrate spoke softly, but the cavern's rock caught the word and made it louder.

Minos dropped the wet, dark tongue onto the dirt. Ariadne turned to look behind her.

"*You* will not call me that, either." She sounded both calm and threatening.

Naucrate was holding her head up as best she could, but it was trembling, bent at an angle. Tears had made clean streaks on her skin. "Princess," she said, "I loved you. Even as I watched you grow and change and scheme, I loved you, because when I looked at you I always saw the little girl who used to bury her face in my lap and cry. The little girl who ached for her life to be different."

"I do not know why you expect me to feel mercy. I do not know why you even try. After all, I am my father's daughter."

Naucrate's head sagged back onto the ground. Her eyes were wide and fixed on nothing. A long, tangled strand of hair slid across her forehead and nose. It rose and fell gently, with her breath.

Minos pointed at her. Sparks hissed and fell from

his forearm. "Look here: the beautiful, brave Naucrate does know how to fear!" He went to stand above her. More sparks fell; they lit and lingered on Naucrate's hair. Icarus smelled burning, through the clot of tears in his nostrils. "You have never feared *me* enough," he said, suddenly quiet. "Even when I took you as my lover, you never trembled. I would have killed you then, except that I grew too bored with you to bother. And I am glad. For this, now, will be far more pleasing."

Naucrate's head came up again. Her lips parted and the singed strand of hair sank between them, but she didn't seem to notice. "I have always hated you," she said in the cold, flat voice Icarus had heard only a few times before, "but I have never feared you. So do this pleasing thing. Do it quickly or do it slowly. It will not matter. And remember: I hate, but I do not fear."

Minos made a growling noise deep in his throat. The fire that had lit him from beneath throbbed brighter and higher until it leapt from his skin and out into the air. It fell on Naucrate like a sheet of rain. Her hair, her neck, the grimy cloth stretched tight over her back: all of it kindled and glowed. She thrashed until she was on her stomach. Minos chuckled as he bent down and cut all of her bonds. The stench of filth and burning was still terrible.

Naucrate rose, somehow. She wrenched herself around and up, streaming, screaming, and reached her blazing hands out to Icarus. He felt his body curl away from her and her terrible heat. She reached for Daedalus, who was crouching with his hands swollen and limp behind him, his mouth still dribbling blood. He tipped toward her but she was already past him, stumbling for the hole that led out to the sky. Minos held his hands up and sent flames after her. It didn't matter: she was gone, leaving smoke and skirling sparks in her wake.

Ariadne stumbled after her.

For a moment there was quiet in the cave. Then Icarus heard a long, high, warbling bird cry, swelling and dying over the sea.

When Ariadne ducked back into the cavern, Icarus found his voice. "What now? How will you break *me*, great king?"

Minos didn't turn to him, but Ariadne did. Icarus didn't look at her.

"Poor bird-boy," the king said, still smiling at Ariadne. "He cannot fashion anything—certainly not wings that fly, despite the mark his god has given him. I shall let him stay here to keep his father company." At last he looked down at Icarus. "Perhaps you will chirp while he gabbles?"

"Ari. Ari, please. Your father listens to you. Don't let him do this."

She crouched beside him and reached for him slowly with her pale, steady hands. They found the ball of string where it always had been: wrapped up under his belt. He flinched when she put her fingers on the cloth, and again when she drew the hook out of the end of the ball and pulled it free. She sat back on her heels and tossed it up and down as if it were a child's plaything.

"Ari—no—leave me *something*." He felt himself shrink with every weak and pleading word.

She laughed. "Oh, Icarus: why would we leave you with this, when it might help you escape this cave? No—you have no more need of it. Not ever."

As she rose, Minos said, "You will find that the walls, deeper in, run with fresh water. Do not imagine you will be able to follow it out; it comes from rock and returns to rock. One of my men will come, once a month, with food and wine. Take care not to eat and drink too much."

Icarus looked away from Ariadne at last. "My King," he said, "why not kill us and be done with it?"

Minos walked toward the exit. His feet left black impressions in the dirt. "I may yet have need of you," he said over his shoulder. "And also, gods enjoy the suffering of mortals. That is simply the way of things. Daughter: cut him free."

Minos tossed a knife to the ground next to her. She picked it up and set it to the rope around Icarus's ankles. They took a while to part, but the ones around his wrists were quicker. He shifted and writhed, watching her stand and tuck the knife into the hem of her open bodice. She threaded the ball's hook next to it. Minos walked back toward the passageway, and she followed him.

Daedalus made a sharp, agonized sound, and Icarus yelled. He scrabbled for the tunnel on hands and feet that were nerveless—but then the blood rushed back into them, and the pain of this made him falter. He brushed the sole of her foot; she kicked out and crawled faster, whimpering. Minos was leaning in from the outside; he pulled her free and she cried out, and he slammed the rusted metal door home with a *clang* that echoed over the sound of Icarus's scream.

CHAPTER NINETEEN

Daedalus's keening sounded like wind trapped in stone. *Because that's what it* is, Icarus thought as he stroked his father's head and gritted his teeth. It had been days, surely. Days and days sunk within this stone place, listening to broken bones and heart and voice.

His father's hair had grown, at least a little. Maybe it had been weeks, then. Everything stank enough for it to have been weeks. Icarus had tried to wash both of them, after he'd groped to the passageway and found the water Minos had spoken of (though it was not truly a passageway: more of a cleft, so narrow that he had to squeeze his way in). Thankfully, he'd found the water almost immediately, trickling down the wall. He'd licked some off the rock; it was cool and fresh. He'd taken off his loincloth and soaked it; he'd groped his way back to his father and pressed it against one of his cheeks.

"Drink," Icarus said. "Drink, and then I'll get more and wash you, then myself."

Daedalus sucked at the wet, filthy cloth for a moment, then gagged and moaned and turned his face away.

"Father." Icarus's voice was quiet and hard and helpless. "I know it must hurt—your . . . where your tongue was. But you have to drink. You have to."

Daedalus shifted away from him and lay down in the

darkness. When Icarus untied his father's loincloth, Daedalus didn't move. Icarus soaked it in the tiny, silent fall of water and fumbled his way back to his father with it. Daedalus didn't move when Icarus pressed the cloth gently against his forehead and nose and chin, and on his curled-in shoulders.

Icarus leaned down close to his father's damp, stinking skin. "Don't leave me here alone," he whispered. One of Daedalus's shoulders lifted and fell—and that was all, for a time that might have been days.

Thirst was constant; hunger was slow. At first, when it finally twisted in Icarus's belly, he didn't recognize it. The moment he did, he imagined fresh bread and fresh fish, plump dates and olives drizzled in their own oil, and he writhed on the ground, clutching at the pain and longing at his centre. Icarus felt his father's hand on his back and thrust it away.

Thirst and hunger and darkness. The rise and fall of Daedalus's keening, or silence—until Icarus woke from another dark, muddled sleep to the door screeching open.

"Father!" he said, reaching for him, wondering whether he were dreaming. "A month—it must have been a month."

Theron's lamplight arrived before he did. This time it wasn't just lamplight, though, not just the orange-gold: there was blue, too, pulsing to a deeper gold and back. At first Icarus had to close his eyes and cover them—but even then the light seeped in like a glorious mist.

"Thank the gods," Icarus rasped, when Theron was standing above him. He was holding onto the long rope handle of one of the crab shell lamps from Daedalus's

Amnisos workroom. Daedalus's keening had stopped. He gazed at his own creation, which threw lurid, moving shadows on his filthy face.

Theron stared at them, his eyes cold and almost unblinking in his scarred face. "Do not think the king was mercifully minded, when he ordered me to bring this to you from Master Karpos's workroom," he said. "No—it is just that he wishes you to be able to see the sad wreckage of your lives from this moment on, all the time. And he wishes you to eat, now, so that you will continue to live these sad, wrecked lives."

Theron set the crab shell lamp on the flat rock where Minos had shattered Daedalus's hands. The guard smiled and held up a bag. *Linen*, Icarus thought. *So clean.* The cloth bulged, and as it swayed he smelled things—so many impossibly wonderful things: bread, dates, fish, both fresh and salted.

Icarus stood up slowly. The space around him felt vast and strange; he was wobbly, erupting with tiny, soft, seeking feathers. "We might not eat," he said. His own voice sounded very far away. "We might deprive the king of the pleasure of our continued torture."

Theron's laughter bounced from walls and invisible ceiling for far too long. When he was finally finished, he let the bag fall. It thumped against the dirt.

"Oh—and there's one more thing," he said. He drew a spade from his belt and tossed it down next to the bag. "You'll want to dig a hole. For your shit. You see? The king is a thoughtful man."

Icarus took a step toward him and raised his hands. *I'll strangle him; I'll thrust my knee against his throat and press him into the dirt, never mind that I'm as weak as a newborn.* Theron drew a knife from his belt. He spun it lazily; its silver reflection swam across his skin and the stone behind him. He laughed again, quietly, and Icarus crumpled. He sat on the dirt and swayed, because his bones so badly wanted him to run and fly.

"Until next month," Theron said, and left the chamber.

After the door had clanged shut, Icarus didn't move—not his legs or arms, and not his eyes. They were on the bag. Its rope tie had come undone; an end of bread was protruding from its neck. The bread shone—with honey, he knew. His mother had made this, of course; she'd made everything, from the meltingly sweet to the richly spiced. She'd sung in her bird voice as she did. He'd hunkered between the columns of the kitchen, listening, watching, barely able to keep from springing up to dig his hands into the flour. And yet he'd stayed still, watching sunlight slant, catching the red in her dark hair and the jewelled gold within the honey.

He crawled to the bag because he found he couldn't walk. He pawed at it until it fell fully open, and he pulled out the bread. His hands shook; he dug his fingers into it and smelled a surge of sweetness.

"Father," he said, and crawled to where Daedalus was crouching. Icarus tore a piece free and swallowed a sudden rush of saliva. He tugged the soft flesh of the bread away from the crust and rolled it between his fingertips.

"Here, Father," he said. "Eat. If you can't manage this, I'll soak it in water."

Daedalus swallowed once and turned away from the bread. His face was gaunt and stark in the soft light. He gazed at the lamp, almost without blinking, until Icarus almost wished that Theron hadn't brought it at all.

—— · ——

Icarus stopped himself from overindulging: he had some bread, two dates, two olives, and a sip of the wine he found in a little stoppered jug at the bottom of the bag. And yet he was giddy and nauseous and, when he finished, shakier than when he'd been starving. Because he couldn't bear to be still, he grasped his father's lamp in one hand and crawled some more, this time along the passageway to the door.

It locked inside as well as out. Icarus stared intently at the mechanism, which was set just beneath a ring handle. He touched the lock; rust flaked beneath his fingers, but the bolts were firmly embedded in the metal of the door. There was a tiny space between the lock and the rest of the door, but, though he tried for a long time, he couldn't wiggle his talon-nails very far down into it. He slid their pointed tips into the keyhole, but the talons were too short to reach the mechanism within. *Father could have fashioned something*, he thought, sitting back on his heels. *If he still had his hands. If they still turned silver when he touched things.*

When he returned to the chamber, he set a rolled-up bit of bread between his father's lips. Daedalus's throat worked, and the bread fell deep into it, and he choked and gasped. "Good," Icarus said. "Have more. And listen: there's a lock on the door—on the inside. It's strange that it's there at all, obviously." Daedalus was digging at the earth with his toes. Icarus wondered whether he could urge his father to try using his toes instead of his hands; surely his godmark wouldn't know the difference? Daedalus's toes scrabbled clumsily at pebbles and dirt, and no silver came—but he kept scrabbling anyway, then and later, as if he might dig his way to the sea.

"I think this must have been a pirate cave. They'd have kept their spoils in here, and would've needed a door that locked from the inside. For when they were in here *with* the spoils, wanting to keep people away." He stopped tearing at the bread. "So they'd have made sure there was another way to the outside."

He set the loaf down and rose. He paced the length of the cave twice—stronger, steadier—then knelt again before his father. "I followed the other tunnel before, but only a little, because it was so narrow and there was no light at all. It's time for me to go there again. There *must* be a way out."

Daedalus's toes stilled. His gaze wandered over Icarus's face. His lips parted but he made no sound.

"I'll feed you some more, now. I'll make sure you're comfortable." Icarus lifted the glowing crab shell from the ground and looped its rope around his neck. The light flared blue, then eased back to gold. "I hope I won't be gone long, but it might take a while to find out what's down there. You'll be without light again while I'm gone." Icarus touched his father's brow. Daedalus closed his eyes and nodded.

When Icarus had been in the passageway before, in the absolute dark, he hadn't been afraid—just nervous about getting stuck. Now, when he squeezed inside and past the trickle of water, his little light flickered, and his breath came faster and shallower. *Be calm. Think only of the way out. Of coming up into open sky. Of leaping off boulders, even if you still can't fly. Open sky. That's all. Open sky; the king's chest, also open. A sword? Glaucus's walking stick? Won't matter. Ariadne's face crumpling as her bones do, beneath my fists.*

He stopped walking and pressed his forehead against the wall that was right there, at his shoulder. His breathing had turned into a sobbing that ground at his throat and ears. *Stop. Be calm. Think of Chara—* already he was quieter—*and the time you both got lost in that cave, looking for Asterion. Remember the way the dawn light looked, when you finally found the entrance. Remember how you laughed.*

The ceiling was so low that he had to crouch, and the walls were so tight around him that they held him up. He eased his way forward, the light no longer swinging at all. No time and all time passed. His mind was empty of words—until, at last, a thread of fresh air touched his cheek, and he thought *Yes yes yes, oh, all you gods and goddesses, yes.*

There was a fissure, where the top of the wall met the ceiling. Even if he hadn't felt the air, he would have noticed it. He forced his body straight and ran his hands along its lip. It was barely wide enough for him, but he squirmed and thrust his way up and inside it. He had to remember to keep breathing as rock pressed and plucked at him. The shaft angled gently upward. He scuttled like a lizard, pausing sometimes to taste the air. It made him want to cry again, because it was sweet and close and not enough.

His groping hands hit stone. For a moment he was dizzy—*Which way am I pointing—up or down?* He wriggled until the light from his lamp fell on the stone. It was a different colour than the rest: black instead of red-brown. It had been placed in the shaft, its edges measured and set with care, so that only the thinnest thread of air could twine between it and the wall. And it was scored with marks. Icarus lifted a trembling finger to trace them.

King Minos was here before you.

Icarus laughed until his voice and tears were gone.

——— . ———

When Icarus returned to the cave, Daedalus wasn't there.

"Father?" The word cracked. "*Father?*"

They came for him while I was away. The king decided to have him killed after all, and next time they'll come back for me—or maybe they won't—maybe they'll just stop coming and wait for me to die.

As he crumpled to his sore, scraped knees, Daedalus crawled out of the tunnel that led to the door. He didn't look at Icarus. He rose, shuffled over to a wall, and laid one of his broken hands against it. Icarus went to stand beside him. The light breathed scarlet over them both.

"Father. What is it? What were you doing?" But he knew. He could almost see Daedalus crouching in the darkness, lifting his fingers to the lock. His fingers that could make nothing, but that could feel. The rust; the tiny crack between lock and wall. The keyhole. All this Icarus could imagine—the actions, but not the thoughts. "What?"

Daedalus leaned forward so that his nose was nearly touching a spray of translucent threads that clung to the stone. The threads were alive, somehow, without sunlight or wind: Icarus could see this. They'd put out buds that looked like minuscule mushrooms—and maybe that was what they were. Cave mushrooms. Daedalus ran his nose and forehead across the web, then lurched a few paces, until he was standing beneath one of the stalactites that hung from the ceiling. He tipped his face up to it. Raised his right arm.

He's thought of something, Icarus thought. *He's still godmarked, even if he has no hands and no mouth.* But his father stood there for so long, motionless and staring, that at last Icarus thought, *Maybe not; maybe he's just confused,* and took a step toward him.

Something dripped from the stalactite's point and landed on one of Daedalus's bulbous knuckles. It was a swift, tiny movement, but Icarus saw his father's body begin to tremble. His wide, shining eyes found Icarus's.

"What?" Icarus said eagerly. "What have you thought of?"

Daedalus pointed his chin at the moisture that gleamed on his finger, then at the strange plant webbing on the wall.

"Yes, yes: I see these things. What of them?"

Daedalus held both his hands up beneath the stalactite. He waved them, mimed something urgent and sweeping. Icarus shook his head.

"I'm sorry—I don't understand. But you do. I see that you do. That's enough."

It wasn't, though. There was no other way out, and no silver flowed, any more, from Daedalus's fingers, and Icarus didn't understand. He sat down and watched his father holding his hands toward the invisible sky as the air breathed blue and gold.

—— · ——

It took Icarus far too long to understand. He stared as, hour after hour, his father raised one arm and then another beneath the stalactite. He stared from the knob of drippings that had grown beneath the stalactite to his father's twisted hands and still didn't understand—not until, one day or night, the pulsing light caught the wet glint on Daedalus's skin.

Icarus leapt to his feet, dropping the bread he'd been tearing into bits. "New fingers," he gasped as he strode the four steps to where his father was standing. He seized one of Daedalus's wrists, turned it more gently so that he could see his hands. The broken, lumpy fingers were coated in dampness—but beneath that were other layers that shone more dully, as if they'd already dried.

"Do you think . . ." *Will Great Creator Zeus take pity on you and give your godmark back to remade hands?* There were so many things Icarus didn't dare say out loud.

"Ech," Daedalus said. He waggled the fingers of his right hand. His lips curled, and Icarus thought for a moment that his father was going to cry—but then he realized that he was smiling.

For a long while, Icarus watched Daedalus every time he stood beneath the stalactite. This very quickly made him insane with impatience: the dripping was so slow, and his father so motionless, except for the shifting of his arms—it was unbearable. There was a measure of relief whenever Daedalus shuffled over to the section of wall that was covered with splayed, translucent plants—because he was moving, at last, and because when he wound the sticky plant threads around the hardened drippings it seemed as if he was making sudden, swift progress. But he wasn't. The fingers hardly seemed to grow. They thickened a bit, but even after Theron's fourth visit to the cave they hardly extended past Daedalus's actual fingers.

Around this fourth month, though, Icarus's impatience smoothed away. Time didn't matter, after all. Better to grow the false bone carefully, to be sure of its strength, so that it wouldn't snap the moment Daedalus touched the lock. *Ariadne and Minos will still be there, above, whenever we get out. Imagine their surprise. Imagine her eyes as you hurt her.*

Patience settled over him, breathing like the constant, changing light in the empty dark.

——— · ———

Daedalus drew pictures in the dirt.

Icarus recognized some of them: Levers, a sun with rays, rising steam, gears. Water pouring from bulging bladders that Icarus knew were made of cows' stomachs—because he'd seen them. He'd been beneath the Goddess's mountain, watching as the corridors grew beneath pick axes and shovels and his father's machines and glowing hands. Icarus had seen the gears as they turned for the first time, moved by gouts of steam or falling water, so deep within the stone that he could barely breathe. He'd stood at the centre of the altar, his hands on the brimming food jars, and stared at the corridors that changed with a screaming of stone and iron, and no man's hand upon them.

He hadn't understood how any of this happened. He still didn't. But when Daedalus drew pictures in the dirt with his stone fingers, Icarus recognized everything.

One day or night, Daedalus's hand faltered as he was drawing circles. He'd already drawn five, and Icarus knew what they were: the polished black pipes that brought sunlight, wind and rain down into the altar chamber.

"Are you sorry?" Icarus said, as his father's strange, pointed finger hovered over the pebbles and earth.

Daedalus's eyes were closed. Icarus watched him squeeze them tighter, and swallow convulsively.

"Father?"

His eyes opened slowly. "Eaeeun," he said.

"Yes," Icarus said. "Asterion."

"Eh . . . eh . . . Ah-hee. . . ."

"And Athenians. Yes." And suddenly, from nowhere he'd expected, he felt rage. It rose into his chest and mouth, so hot that it hurt him. He saw himself grasping his father's wrists; saw himself squeezing until his own tendons bulged, as if they'd break. "Asterion and Athenians. And you've killed them—for what? For *what*?"

Daedalus opened his eyes. They were darting and wild—Icarus remembered all the times they'd been like this when he'd been a boy, and how afraid they'd made him. Now he gazed into them and said, "Well?"

His father gazed down at the markings he'd made. He leaned away from Icarus and traced more lines— these ones sunlight or maybe moonlight, streaming down onto the carved snakes that Icarus knew writhed motionlessly over the Goddess's altar. When Daedalus was finished, he let his hand fall to the ground. He turned to Icarus and opened his mouth wide, so that all Icarus could see was deep, wet darkness, and the ruin of what had been his father's tongue.

"Yes," Icarus said—calmly, because the anger had

gone. "Yes, I suppose the gods have punished you." *And me. And me, because now I'll never fly.*

Daedalus's shoulders were heaving. His false fingertips scratched at the pictures, smudging them to nothing but dirt and pebbles.

"Father?"

Daedalus choked. His chest heaved, and he pitched forward. Icarus caught him before he fell and wrapped his arms around him to keep him steady. "I'm sorry," Icarus whispered. "I know you had to. I know Minos was . . . I know. Father—please don't cry"—but he was crying too, thinking of Asterion and the others, trapped with levers and steam and gears; thinking of his father, who'd thrown his head back and laughed as he carved tiny bulls into the golden stone of Knossos for the Princess Ariadne.

"I'm sorry," Icarus said again, into Daedalus's stinking, matted hair.

CHAPTER TWENTY

Almost four years. Icarus knew, because he counted Theron's visits and held the numbers in his head with effortless desperation. Forty-four months passed before Daedalus said, "They're ready."

Part of Icarus didn't believe the number. *I lost track at some point*, he thought, more than once. *I added months because it's felt like so long since we were shut up in here. Or maybe Theron's changed the pattern of his visits, and he's now coming twice a month, and it's only been two years.* But the rest of Icarus knew: Theron's routine hadn't changed. Icarus's mind had been clear, every time he'd put a scratch on the wall after one of the visits. His mind was clear, and his hair fell between his shoulder blades to the middle of his back, and his father's hair was just as long and all white.

Almost four years without wind, sun, stars, moon, cloud; without other voices that spoke words that weren't broken. Icarus understood the broken words, though. He heard Daedalus say, "They're ready," though what his father had really said, with his tongueless mouth, was, "Ay eh-eey." Icarus understood. He would have understood even if Daedalus had made no sounds; if he'd only waved his new claws and rolled his wide, anguished eyes.

Icarus leaned forward and reached for Daedalus's hands. His father flinched but let Icarus touch them. Long, hinged digits that looked like fleshless bone.

Little bits of cave, grown from stalactites and sticky plants and time. Their tips were thin and sharp as needles.

He remembered when Daedalus had tried to tell him what he'd do, as he gestured up at the dripping stalactite. It had taken Icarus a very long time to understand—and when he finally had, all he felt was fear, because what if Theron saw them, and understood more quickly than Icarus had?

"Good," he said now. "And good timing: Theron won't be back for weeks. We'll have some time, if we . . ." *If we manage to get out*, he thought, as the words lodged in his throat.

He touched the place on Daedalus's right hand where flesh ended and stone began. White, almost transparent threads bound the two parts together, strung like spider's web, loose but clinging. Icarus remembered, too, the first time he'd seen these same threads on the cave walls, nearly four years ago. They'd filled him with hope—them, and the tiny mushrooms that poked out from crevasses in the rock. Growing things in a place of stillness. He wondered if the thread-veins on his father's hands would someday sprout tiny mushrooms.

"Let's go, then," Icarus said.

Daedalus stared at him and didn't move. Icarus's own limbs felt as heavy as they had when he'd nearly drowned after throwing himself off a waterfall. (What did waterfalls look like? How did sunlight strike the mist and turn it into rainbows? Sometimes he could almost see.)

"Come on, then. To the door!" Icarus stood, still holding his father's new hand. "To the door that we will *open*, despite King Minos's best efforts!"

After a long moment, Daedalus leaned into Icarus and rose. They'd done this countless times, over the years, but his father's body felt especially frail now—so bony that Icarus's fingers grasped for skin and found only tendon. *How strange that I'm the strong one*, Icarus thought. They ducked into the low tunnel that led to the door. Icarus had lain here, the day Minos and Ariadne had come and gone. He'd curled up and pressed his face into the dirt until his open eyes stung and rocks scored his cheeks. He'd listened to his father's moaning, and the silence that came after. He'd held the king's and princess's faces in his mind for a bit, then covered them both with red until they were invisible.

He and Daedalus never used this tunnel anymore; only Theron did, when he brought them their food. But Icarus thought of the last time he'd been here, and knew precisely what he'd see now: the rusted lock; the ever-so-slight space between it and the rusted door. Daedalus had seen these things too, that day years ago when Icarus had gone looking for the pirates' other way out. Daedalus had seen, and known immediately what he'd do.

The door seemed even rustier than it had before: salt mist and fog and waves brushing it, always. Icarus put his ear to it but couldn't hear the waves—just a dull silence.

Talons longer than his own stroked his back. "Ihus."

"Yes," Icarus said, drawing away from the door. "I know. It's time." *I just had to delay a little longer, because if this doesn't work, we'll both go mad.*

Daedalus didn't delay. He slid one of his new fingertips into the lock, as confidently and smoothly as if he'd practiced the motion here before. He hadn't,

Icarus knew. He'd sat or stood, growing stone and fungus threads, and had never once gone to the door. Now he leaned forward, his brows drawn together, his back hunched so that his shoulder blades looked like sharp little wings, and moved his finger slowly within the lock.

Nothing.

Icarus tried to quiet his own breathing, which was all he could hear. Sweat was easing its clammy way down his spine, flattening downy feathers as it went. He could feel the prickle of other feathers starting, and he could see them, too: in the half-darkness, his skin was speckled with points of silver. It was as if his blighted mark could sense the open air.

Nothing.

Daedalus bent his head to his chest for a moment. Icarus shifted on his knees so that he'd be ready to touch his father, if necessary—restrain him, or catch at his flailing claws. But Daedalus lifted his head and raised his other hand and closed his eyes.

Silver light kindled along the length of one finger, then along all the others, until his hand looked molten and the tunnel seemed flooded with moonlight. *A true crafting*, Icarus thought, not caring, any more, that his breathing was so loud. *A machine like all the others he's made: godmarked and strong—O gods and goddesses, please.*

The silver began to fade, as it always did, once the machine was ready. Daedalus slid another fingertip into metal. He closed his eyes again, and so did Icarus.

The lock clicked.

For a moment there was silence. Then Icarus made a sound that was part whoop and part sob. He scrambled the short distance to the door and put his hand next to his father's on the ring that would open it.

Daedalus didn't move. He was gazing at his new fingers, pressing his lips into a line that was neither smile nor frown. Icarus remembered, suddenly, how his father had been in his workshops; how he'd bounced on the balls of his feet, or danced from one table to another, or laughed as he chiseled a shape into marble, waggling his brows to make Icarus laugh too.

"Father." His voice shook. "Move just a little, so I can open it."

Daedalus lowered his head to Icarus's shoulder with a sigh that shuddered through them both. His hand slid away from the ring, and Icarus's tightened on it.

The door screamed as it always did, though it was much louder, this close. It opened inward, so Icarus and Daedalus shuffled back on their knees to make room for it. Daylight followed them: a swift cascade of it, which made Icarus cry out again and grind his fists against his closed eyes. He rubbed at tears and turned to his father in the sun.

"You first," he said. Daedalus nodded and shuffled forward again. He set his palms on the ground so that his stone fingers extended like crab's legs, touching nothing but air. He crawled under and out, and Icarus did too, and they sat side-by-side on the ledge above the sea.

Icarus saw only a blur of colours and light, at first: the white-blue of the sky, the dazzle of the water, the brown and green of a shape that slowly resolved itself into an island that hunkered below them, not far from the cliff. Once the island snapped clear in his vision, so did other things: streaks of cloud; gulls wheeling high, from cloud to open blue; gulls wheeling low, diving and surfacing with fish gleaming and lashing in their beaks.

Nearly four years, he thought.

Feathers hissed up through his skin, from his neck to his ankles. He felt his mouth and nose warping into beak for the first time since Minos had put them in the cave, and he whimpered at the pain, and his hunger for it.

The ledge was very narrow; Icarus hadn't known how narrow, before, because the king had brought them at night. Now he watched his father lean his back against the edge of the open door and swing his legs out over the long drop to the sea, and he forgot his pain and laughed like a child.

"Come," he gasped, when he'd had enough of laughing (though not enough of the wind that bent his feathers and lashed his hair around his face— never enough of that). "Let's go up."

He stood, but Daedalus didn't move.

"Father?"—and the last of his laughter died as Daedalus looked up at him.

"Uh-er," he said. "Rah-hay." *Mother. Naucrate. Running from the cave and leaping from here—from this place, with her hair and skin on fire, singing as she fell.*

Icarus sat back down. He said nothing. He stared at his father's face—at the lines that had been invisible in the cave, branching like deep, dry riverbeds across his skin—and tried to remember hers.

After a time Daedalus stirred. "Let's go now," Icarus heard him say.

Icarus remembered where the chiseled steps were, but they were so shallow, so indistinguishable from the cliff face, that it took him a few moments to find them. When he did he set his taloned, bristly hands to them and glanced at Daedalus and said, "Come on!"—clearly enough, despite his part-beak and his shrinking, thickening tongue.

Daedalus didn't move. Even his legs lay still against the stone. His eyes were fixed on the island. Icarus followed his gaze and saw a dead tree among the green ones. An eagle was perched on a nest there, snugly wedged between two thick, bare branches. Its young were craning up, crying and gaping; Icarus could hear them, could see their straining pink gullets. His own flesh rippled as his shoulder blades tried to turn into wings. He wrenched himself around, away from the sight of the nest.

"Father?"

Daedalus tipped his head up. His eyes shone with light.

"Here: look! The steps up: we'll follow them and see where we are." The words were difficult, squeezed in his changing throat, but that wasn't why he stopped speaking. His father's eyes stopped him. His eyes, and the thin, hinged claws he lifted and held in the bright air between them. His lips, forming sounds that would never be whole, but that Icarus understood.

I can't climb with these. And if I could climb, I wouldn't. Theron would tell Minos we were gone. We wouldn't be able to leave the island. Everyone watching. We're supposed to be dead! The king would hunt us. He'd kill us, this time.

"No." Icarus's beak was easing back into lips. The salt spray stung them terribly. "You have to try. If your fingers break I'll push you from below—I'll get you to the top, and we'll just look around a little—we'll go back to the cave afterward to decide what to do."

No. Daedalus didn't need to thrust out any more

slurred words. Icarus heard them all in his own head. *If the fingers break we won't be able to grow more for months, for years. We won't be able to lock the door again, let alone open it. We'll be stranded, in hiding, waiting for Minos to find us.*

"I'll go up," Icarus said, quite clearly. "Just for a bit, this time. I'll come back as soon as I've seen what's up there. I promise. I'll come back very soon."

"Ech," Daedalus said. *Yes. Take care.*

"I will," said Icarus. He bent and kissed the tangled white hair at the top of his father's head, and then he set his hands and feet to the steps.

He was dizzy by the time he reached the top, and the effort of easing his forehead and eyes over the edge made all his muscles tremble. Grass tickled his nose. He squeezed his eyes shut, then opened them wide, stretching up so that he'd be able to see above the grass. He saw more grass, and a bush with white blossoms. *Spring*, he thought. *The green and flowers. The coolness of the wind. Spring—by all the gods and fishes, as Asterion and Chara might've said.*

Icarus pulled himself slowly up over the cliff edge and rolled onto his back, panting. Four years in a cave, in the dark. Four years of sitting, stretching, crawling, lying curled up on threadbare blankets. Holding onto his father's hands when he tried to pummel his own face with them. And now this climb, this light; he had no idea how to keep moving. If Theron had loomed over him with a sword, Icarus would only have spread his feathered arms against the grassy, stony ground and waited.

But Theron didn't loom. A gull did, at Icarus's left shoulder. *Spring*, he thought again, blinking at its patchy black head. *In summer its head feathers will be glossy black. I remember this.* It took one of his own feathers in its black-banded beak and tugged. He whistled sharply at it—clumsily and incoherently. *Mother would've known exactly what to say to a gull,* he thought, and for a moment he saw her there above him, smiling and reaching, and he could hardly breathe.

When he finally stood up, the world tipped around him. He laughed and bit his lip to stop himself; what if there were people standing just beyond the bush? There weren't, of course: there was just a vast, sloping expanse of grass and blossomy bushes and tumbled stones. No roads, or even paths. He and the gull were the only living creatures about—and when he turned to it, it waddled and flapped its way into the sky, where it soared so gracefully that he wrenched himself around again, away from the sight of it.

He set off walking, though it was more like a stumble. He was still dizzy: too much space; he felt tall and tippy, not bowed and small as he did in the cave. The ground unfurled beneath him, rippling like cloth. *Chara,* he thought. *You'd let me lean on you. Glaucus would lend me his staff. It never did make a decent sword. Ariadne swore a hundred times that she'd break it across his head.*

The thought of Ariadne flooded his head with a white rage that cleared it. For three paces he felt stronger and steadier, but his right ankle crumpled on the fourth. He teetered, his arms flailing. As he righted himself he felt yet more feathers thrusting out from his flesh—from forearms and thighs and the tops of his feet, all of them glowing silver at their roots. His godmark, awake again; his man's body weak. He stood gasping, staring down at himself and the ground, because the sky's light hurt him, now.

Next time, he thought as he let himself slowly down to the ledge, *I'll be stronger. I'll go farther.*

His father was still sitting with his legs dangling and his gaze fixed on the island.

"I'm sorry," Icarus said. "It was difficult. I couldn't . . ." His throat was rough and sore, as if he'd been shouting, or trying not to cry.

Daedalus leaned his head back and smiled. He looked at Icarus; his smile vanished, and his eyes widened as they traced the lines of feathers, up and down, down and up.

"I know; they just burst out of me the moment I got up there—as if my godmark's been waiting for open air, saving up all the feathers that used to take ages to grow, under my skin. Saving them and making them grow much faster. Maybe it's why I'm so tired." *And hungry. Gods and magpies, so hungry: next time I'll find food; something other than salt fish and stale bread.*

Daedalus wriggled backward and lurched to his feet. He leaned close to Icarus's forearm, which (Icarus saw with a start) had grown longer, thinner, tapering toward the talons. The feathers on it were as lush as if he had been mostly changed for months. His father gestured from the feathers to his own arms to the island, over and over again, as Icarus shook his head. At last Daedalus blew out his breath and cried, "Ah fai air! *Ah* fai!"

Icarus sagged against the cliff wall. *I'll fly there. I'll fly.*

His father spoke on—more words than he'd uttered in a year, tripping and melding so that Icarus shouldn't have been able to understand them. Only he did.

"I can't climb without breaking my fingers. So we

won't go up: we'll go down. You'll be able to glide at least as far as the island. If I build a framework for my arms, just like I built my new hands—if your feathers keep growing, so there are enough for both of us—I'll be able to glide there too. You could steal a fisherman's boat; you could come and get me."

Icarus was still shaking his head. His skin and bones ached. "There has to be another way," he said when his father's words dribbled to silence. "There has to be. I could make a sling for you just as easily as I could steal a boat—maybe *more* easily. I could let it down from above, pull you up, and we would . . ." He didn't say the words he heard in his head: *We would end up trapped on the big island, when that small one down there would get us close to open sea. Down would be quicker and safer than up.*

Daedalus lifted one of his stone hands. Two of his crab-claw fingers closed gently around a feather on Icarus's shoulder. The stone and paste and flesh pulsed with silver. His wild, hungry eyes met Icarus's.

"I understand," Icarus said. "Another way wouldn't be enough for you. It's your godmark telling you to do this. The Great Daedalus, who needs to make things." He shook his head slowly. "But I can't. It already hurts so much—and remember when those boys pulled my feathers out, years ago, to see me cry? Please don't ask this of me."

His voice cracked. He couldn't bear to look at his father's eyes, but he had to: they hadn't burned like this since the workroom at Knossos. "No," he whispered. "I *can't*"—and he ducked out of the light, back into the gloom of the tunnel and the smothering darkness of the cavern. He squatted with his forehead pressed against stone, next to a clump of mushrooms.

He rocked a little, as if his mother's arms were around him. He heard the door squeal and *clang* shut. He heard his father crawl into the cavern behind him, and then he heard nothing except his own shallow breathing.

He dozed. When he woke, the cavern was bathed in silver: from his feathers, bristling thick and layered from his skin; from his father's lumpy, hinged fingers. The little island seemed like a dream. The bare tree with the eagle's nest, the waves that broke on sand and stone, the bright emptiness above that had no end.

Daedalus was standing beneath the stalactite. His hands (both silver) were at his sides, though his head was tipped back. He didn't look down until Icarus said, "Father."

Daedalus's eyes still burned. Icarus took a silver hand and lifted it to his own silver arm. Daedalus's fingers closed once more on a feather. He blinked and Icarus nodded and the fingers pinched and pulled. Icarus gasped and squeezed his eyes shut so tightly that he saw points of multi-coloured fire spinning in blackness. When he opened them, they were dry. They stayed that way, even as Daedalus plucked and plucked, and feathers drifted, soft and silver, to the ground.

——— · ———

The next month, after Theron left, Icarus followed him. He waited a good long while before he gestured to his father to open the door; it would all be over if Theron heard the screaming of the metal. They waited so long, in fact, that Icarus feared he would be out of sight—and he was, but it didn't end up mattering.

This time it was night. Icarus had brought the light, just in case, and its pink and gold played over the ledge and the stairs. He gazed past its glow at the stars, which were everywhere: in the water and the sky and spinning behind his eyelids when he closed them. The moon hung among them, nearly full. Feathers thrust through his skin the moment he felt the wind and saw the stars, and the emptiness below him. *Father*, he thought, *you'll have so many, when I get back.*

When he hoisted himself up off the last step, the first thing he saw was the path. The moon plucked it out for him: a narrow, sinuous line that led through the silvered grass and out of sight. *Theron walks here every month*, Icarus thought. *His feet fall on the same ground every month. I can't see him now, but I can see where he's been. Thank you, O Terrible Theron.*

Icarus ate, as he walked: a handful of figs and an oatcake, taken from the latest delivery. It was strange: he wasn't hungry, though the feather-plucking usually made him ravenous. Nerves, perhaps, because this time he intended to reach something—a palace, temple, a hive of sleeping bees—he *had* to find something and bring the news of it back to the cave.

The path wound down hills and around olive trees and ended, quite suddenly, in the middle of a pasture. He pushed at the cropped grass with his toe-talons and felt a seam, almost immediately. One seam, another, another: a hinged door, with grass on top. He was sure of this, even without bending to scrabble at it; he knew, now, about small, secret doors. He wanted to scrabble, though—to haul the door up and throw himself inside the tunnel that had to be there, beneath. He wanted to follow it to wherever Theron ended up, when *he* followed it. *No*, he thought. *There'd be nowhere to go, if someone was already in there. So it'll be overland for me, not under.*

He went to the edge of the pasture, where it met rockier ground. Here he found another path, this one lined with stones, and obvious enough that he slipped the light beneath his filthy shirt, in case there was someone close enough to see it. This path led him up toward a peak that loomed blackly against the stars. Icarus was so transfixed by the peak that he almost walked right past the hut—but he caught himself, fell back, stared.

A beehive-shaped hut—a shepherd's, he was sure. An open doorway with nothing but darkness beyond it. *Maybe not nothing,* he thought. *Maybe something I can use.*

His heart thudded as he ducked inside. Star- and moonlight seeped in after him, and in a moment his eyes had adjusted. He saw a shelf, high up on one of the curving walls. An empty, overturned trough on the hard-packed earthen floor. A staff of gnarled olive wood.

He reached up and patted his hand along the shelf. He felt a wooden cup, which fell over and made a hollow, rolling sound. *Good,* he thought, imagining his father holding it between his palms, rather than leaning awkwardly forward to drink from their bowl. Then he felt cloth. He pulled it down: a cloak, hooded and thick; the kind shepherds wore to protect themselves from rain and gales. It was far too big for him—the hood came down nearly to his lower lip, and he could have wrapped it around himself twice—but he felt safer in it.

He sat in the doorway until the light of his lamp dimmed and died against the grey-blue light in the sky. The sun rose, just after that, and he knew which way to go: south and west, because that's where the summer palace had to be.

His head was filled with words, which tripped and rushed as his feet did: *Only the slaves, acolytes and apprentices will be up. I'll use the entrance that leads to the priests' quarters, and I'll pull my hood down. Maybe I'll see Chara—because it's summer—the heat and the colours tell me so—and the royal family will definitely be there. Chara! You'll turn pale when you see me; your freckles will·look so dark.*

But his feet slowed, long before he reached the palace. He'd begun to recognize his surroundings: rocky outcroppings he'd jumped from years ago, flapping his useless boy's arms. A stream Glaucus had dropped his stick into by accident; the thing had snagged among rocks halfway down a waterfall, and Asterion had almost fallen in, reaching for it. Icarus stood where Asterion had, that day. He closed his eyes and felt the spray on his lids and brow. He saw the water that trickled down the wall in his prison. He saw his father crouched in the unnatural light, weaving feathers onto the branches Icarus would soon gather from the bushes on the cliff.

No, Icarus thought. *Not the palace—not yet, or maybe ever. Think only of him: keeping him strong and safe; getting him onto the little island. Getting away.*

He turned back the way he'd come.

When he finally crawled into the cave, Daedalus was crouched in the unnatural light, his stone fingers splayed beside three neat, curving rows of feathers. Icarus knelt in front of him. His hands shook with weariness. The shepherd's cloak weighed on him as if it were made of iron. The stench of the pit they'd dug, which he tried to cover with dirt every time either of them used it, was even viler because he'd been away from it.

"Here," he said. "Look what I have for you." The wooden cup. Four slender branches: three very long, one shorter. Three ripe lemons. A handful of thyme. And feathers, layers and layers of them, covering him from neck to ankles.

Daedalus nodded and smiled, then went to lock the door again.

CHAPTER TWENTY-ONE

Icarus and Daedalus were laughing, when the door opened. Later, Icarus tried to remember what they'd been laughing at, and couldn't.

Theron's visit had happened only a few days earlier: the fresh bread was teetering in one stack, the salt fish in another. Icarus had just carved a fresh scratch into the wall, where it joined four years' worth of other scratches.

Their eyes met: *Not Theron—*

Icarus seized his father's wings. The layers of feathers were thick and glossy; the frame was huge but light. He thrust the wings into the tunnel behind them and sat down beside Daedalus just as someone stepped into their cave.

"Icarus?" a strange voice called. "Icarus: it's Phaidra. Where are you?"

Not a strange voice, after all—but not a girl's, either. And she'd been a girl, the last time he'd seen her: a thin, long-legged, golden-haired girl. *How old is she now? Sixteen?*

He glanced at Daedalus, who lifted one of his long-fingered hands and shook his head. Icarus shook his own and slipped into a crouch. "Phaidra," he said, and went forward into the guttering light.

This new Phaidra took two paces and held out her hands to him. He rose, stumbled, took them. He touched his forehead to hers, hardly needing to bend because she was so tall. "Phai," he murmured, "gods, how you've changed." Then he called up the red he'd been holding within him for years, and spun, and cried, "Ariadne! Show yourself!"

Phaidra pulled her hands free and backed away from him. Ariadne stepped forward. "Here I am," she said.

Icarus heard himself shout—a sound that was just a pale, weak echo of the red. Ariadne was smiling as she took three more paces and stood before him, bathed in the light that was green now—new olive leaves, or the pool below the waterfall where he'd leapt as a child, trying to fly.

"Icarus," she said. "I am sorry it has taken me this long to return to you."

He felt very clear-headed, somehow. He felt as if he'd seen her only yesterday; as if he were accustomed to speaking to people other than his father. "Ah, Princess. Imagine how sorry *I've* been, not to have seen you all this time! For when last you were here, you took my ball of string—oh, and you broke my father's hands with a hammer, and watched as *your* father cut his tongue out—oh, and then you watched my mother throw herself into the sea."

Phaidra gave a wordless cry.

Ariadne held out her hands. "I have longed to visit you, and why not—for how well you speak! The palaces have not been the same since you left them."

She was going to say more, but Daedalus's raspy, moist breathing stopped her. He drew himself up from the floor, and suddenly Icarus saw him as Ariadne and Phaidra would be seeing him: as a hairy, ragged, filthy creature that didn't look much like a man. For a moment Icarus remembered how tall his father had been, and how his hair had been a neat, close-cropped black, threaded with white.

He sprang at Ariadne with his remade hands extended.

Icarus threw himself between them. "No, Father," Icarus panted. "You leave her to *me*." He clutched Daedalus's warped hands and turned back to her. "Princess," he said, as calmly as if he wasn't actually himself. "Why are you here?" He was dimly aware that Phaidra had retreated and was standing by a rock, and that his father had curled up on the ground.

"My old friend," Ariadne said, "I need you."

Icarus laughed. His head spun with so many words that he couldn't choose any.

"Yes. I need you—for my father is mad, and intends to give himself to godmarked fire at the door to the mountain. The door *you* made, Master Daedalus"—she slid her gaze to the man at their feet—"and I cannot bear the thought that the place will be destroyed, because there may be people living within: Athenian sacrifices, and my brother, of course . . . And only you." She drew a deep breath. "Only you and your father can show me how to find them so that they may be saved."

He couldn't laugh, this time, and he still couldn't speak. At last he said, "You cannot bear the thought." He drew a shuddering breath. "You, Princess Ariadne . . ." Laughter bubbled in his throat again, and he spun in place, feathers rustling and whining in the wind that was hardly a wind. One of his feet sent the lamp scudding into the rock where Phaidra was; the light went from pink to blue to gold to green in a breath, then died entirely. Ariadne held up her own lamp, whose glow seemed very dim.

"You wish to save them," Icarus gasped as he

stopped spinning. He pointed his taloned fingers at her and waggled them. "The Athenians whose entry into the mountain was so dull to you that you watched the sky instead. And your brother! The boy you set on fire when he was, what? Two years old? Yes, Chara told me—and she told me much else, besides. About how much you hated him. And now you can't bear the thought that he might die?"

Phaidra had sunk into a crouch. Her hands were clasped; her eyes darted between Icarus and Ariadne and Daedalus.

"I am glad you mentioned Chara," Ariadne said, her voice catching a little. "Because she, too, is in the labyrinth. Yes," she went on, as he felt his mouth-beak fall open, "she is. She disguised herself as an Athenian, and I noticed her too late—as she was leaping through the doorway. A month ago, Icarus. And in barely two more the mountain will be on fire."

He went to Phaidra and hunkered down in front of her. "Phai," he said quietly. "Is it true?"

Phaidra nodded. "Though I didn't," she began, and cleared her throat, "I didn't know about Father's plan."

They gazed at each other, as unblinking as Minos, until Ariadne said, "So, Icarus?"

He glanced over his shoulder at her. "Your mother will put the fire out."

"She will try. But this will be like no other fire. Her power may be no match for his." She put her lamp on the ground and walked around Daedalus. She set her hand on Icarus's hair. He didn't flinch, though he wanted to wrench himself free of her, and of the old hunger that had begun to stir.

"It should not matter why I want in," she said. "You should not care." She drew her fingertips down through his hair and he shivered. "Four years ago you would have longed to do my bidding."

She knelt behind him and wove her arms around his chest. She pressed her skin against his and breathed slowly. His own traitorous breath shuddered and rasped. *You don't want her*, he thought. *You can't. Remember the last time she was here; just remember her hand holding his down as Minos shattered it....*

He stood, drawing Ariadne up with him, and turned in the circle of her arms so that he was facing her. She smelled unbearably sweet: fresh air and clean skin, and the perfume she always dabbed behind her wrists, which reminded him of grass and honey. He straightened. "And what will you give me, if I help you?"

She flinched a bit. She slipped out of his arms and took two paces back. She undid the clasp of her jacket and pulled it open and he couldn't help it—he felt his eyes travel from her face to her breasts.

Phaidra rose and ran for the mouth of the corridor, and Daedalus stirred and moaned, but Icarus hardly noticed. Ariadne lifted her hands and ran her middle fingers around her nipples, and as they hardened she began to untie the girdle at her waist. *O gods and goddesses you've punished me enough though I've done nothing wrong please please do not make me suffer any more than I already have please lend me some of your own strength—*

"No," he whispered.

Just then the outer door screeched open and clanged shut. *Phaidra*, he thought, and felt something else—a different kind of desire.

"No," he said again. She cupped her breasts lightly as she stepped toward him. They weren't smooth, as they had been when he'd last seen them (shining with oil, as she danced): they were patchy with scars, as were her arms and even her hands. The scars didn't disgust him, though he wanted them to—especially as her thumbs made languid circles on her own skin. *Phaidra*, he thought again, and remembered how firm and cool her forehead had been against his, and felt stronger.

"Yes, Icarus. You will have me here, now—perhaps again at the mountain, under the open sky? Put your hands on me and—"

He walked to where she was and stopped with his feather-splotched chest almost touching her. "No," he said, and smiled, and walked away from her.

He knelt beside Daedalus, whose eyes were closed. She whirled to look down on them both. "So your hatred of me is stronger than your desire to help your friends."

Icarus shrugged. "The gods will see to their fates. And yes."

Ariadne fumbled with the clasp of her jacket. "Then your father will help me, because I'll make sure neither of you gets any food; I'll starve you, and he'll beg to show me the labyrinth—you will both—"

"Starve us?" Icarus said. "In the two months before the king gives himself to the mountain?"

Daedalus moved abruptly, straining up from his knees. "Ihoh," he said, with his tongueless mouth, and Icarus knew that the word was "Minnow." "Ihoh"—beseeching, sad, not quite hopeless.

Ariadne picked up her lamp and walked, very slowly, to the corridor.

Icarus's strength left with her. He hunkered down and rocked back and forth. He rocked for a long time, as Daedalus blinked at him from across the cave. *Who's moaning like that?* Icarus wondered; a moment later he thought, dully, *Oh—that's me.*

He stared at nothing, but what he saw was Ariadne's smile; Ariadne touching her bare, scarred breasts with her fingers; Ariadne pressing herself against him. He'd imagined, over all the years that had passed since she'd last come, that he'd kill her, if she were ever in front of him again. He'd imagined wrapping his hands around her throat. Slamming her head against a rock. Gouging at her eyes with his talons. And yet there she'd stood, in front of him, and he'd done nothing except say "No" to her, as the blood pounded in his head and his groin.

Phaidra, he thought at some point, because this had chased Ariadne from his eyes, before. *Phaidra.* Tall and slender, smiling at him from the woman's face she hadn't had when he'd last seen her. Taking his hands in hers, which were warm and strong. He imagined lying down with his head in her lap; he knew she would have stroked his hair and spoken to him in her newer, deeper voice.

He stood up thinking of Phaidra's face, but hearing Ariadne's voice. *"So your hatred of me is stronger than your desire to help your friends."* He'd said yes—but other words had been tumbling through his head: *Chara . . . Chara under the mountain . . . Chara and Asterion . . .* These words returned now and circled, circled until they drove him over to his father. Icarus dropped to his knees before him.

"We have to go in there," he said. His voice wobbled, then smoothed. "We have to rescue them."

Daedalus sat up and reared back as if Icarus had struck him.

"If you can open this lock, you'll be able to open the other one too. Won't you?"

Daedalus shook his head wildly. He grunted "No," over and over, then gabbled something like, "Too hard; not the same; no way I'd do it."

Icarus said, "I'll to go Phaidra, then—she'll help us with the lock. And you and I are the only ones who could find our way in and back out again. So we'll do that. We'll get them out—whoever's in there—before the king's mark-madness destroys the mountain."

Daedalus rose and staggered to the stalagmite. He stared down at it, his palms turned up, his long fingers twitching.

"I know you didn't want to go back up, ever," Icarus said. "That you wanted to use the wings you're making to glide down to the islet. But I also know you're ashamed," he went on slowly. "That it haunts you— that place, where Athenians have gone to die. So this is a change of plans. Let's go end it now."

He remembered the way his father had looked at him, years ago, when Icarus had said, "How can you do this to your own people?" They'd been standing on a bridge, both of them coursing with sweat; the labyrinth had been belching hot steam. Daedalus had gazed at him—through him, really.

"The king is always watching me," he whispered. "With godmarked men who record my work after I've done it and relay their findings back to Minos."

"But you're stronger than they are," Icarus had said, glancing over his shoulders at the workers' shadows, bending and stretching on the walls behind them. "You could make another door somewhere and they'd never know; you could—"

"No." Daedalus's voice was splinter-thin. "I won't

waste time with pity. I won't risk my freedom to help children from a city that rejected me."

Icarus had put his hand on his father's arm. Their skin slipped and stuck. Daedalus was panting. "The gods will decide," he said. "They'll decide everything, for all of us. In the meantime, I do the king's will and await my freedom."

"Let's go end it," Icarus said again now, as his father continued to stare at his own ruined hands. "You said once that the gods would decide—and they did, when Minos took your freedom away. But it's not too late; the gods have given us a way. You can let me out of here, and I can go and find Phaidra. We'll come back and get you up the cliff, and then we can go back into that place."

Icarus set his fingertips on Daedalus's lumpy palm and Daedalus twitched. "And whatever Ariadne wants," Icarus said, "whatever she might be trying to do by getting in there herself—we'll stop it. We'll stop *her*—that bitch."

Daedalus put his other hand on top of Icarus's. "Ech," he said, and Icarus heard, "Yes," and tried to smile.

CHAPTER TWENTY-TWO

It was supposed to be easy: a few days' travel along a well-known path; a careful approach to the summer palace, his identity hidden by the shepherd's cloak; a whispered word to a sympathetic slave, or perhaps to Phaidra herself, if he could find her alone.

He hadn't counted on the storm.

The sky over the sea was clear, when he climbed up the cliff steps. But as he took his first few eager paces inland, he saw that clouds were massing above the mountains. Mere moments later, lightning lit them a boiling purple, and he felt thunder buzzing against the soles of his feet.

"No," he muttered. "No, no, no: Sky God, don't do this; don't keep me from this."

The rain didn't start gently: it sheeted from a cracked-open sky. He saw only what the lightning flashes showed him: his own talons, on hands and feet; flattened grass and churned red mud. *Stop walking*, he told himself. *Wait this out. If you get lost you'll end up losing time.* But he didn't stop. If anything, he moved faster: the storm's power and the vastness of the hidden sky called feathers up from his skin in prickly waves, from his ankles to his neck. He heard a gull scream and tipped back his head to answer it. *No*, he thought faintly, *you're losing yourself.*

He tried to fly once, when he ran into what his hands and then the lightning told him was a rock outcrop.

He scrabbled up its slippery ridges and threw himself off, and for a moment the wind lifted his wings and silver filled his eyes—for a longer moment than ever before, surely—but no: he fell, and lay panting on the muddy ground.

After that he simply wandered. He had no idea where his taloned feet were leading him. His belly ached. His arms and legs bristled with feathers that hadn't sunk back into his flesh because they were still growing. All that plucking? A mark soon, at last, to be fulfilled? He didn't know; he knew only that his hunger was so vast that it swam before his eyes like an extra layer of rain. He stumbled and righted himself and hardly noticed. *Meat*, he thought, the palace and Phaidra and the Goddess's mountain forgotten. *Too hungry; I need* meat.

The storm passed, after a time. The sky went from purple to yellow to blue. The clouds thinned and scattered. Hours since he'd left the cave; maybe days. He remembered darkness. He remembered lying down in wet grass and slurping mud. Now he lay blinking up at the sharp, wheeling shape of a bird. Wind raised goosebumps among his feathers. He felt so sick that he didn't want to move—and yet he remembered. He had to get up.

The landscape was completely strange to him. He was on a flat place among jagged peaks; he'd climbed without knowing it, probably to be closer to the sky he couldn't ever reach. He thought he recognized the shape of the Goddess's mountain, but wasn't sure— his vision was blurred—o gods and finches, where *was* he?

As he stood there, dizzy and helpless, he smelled blood.

He followed the smell, though he didn't see where he was going. It was like the storm: his feet led him, though his eyes were blind. His belly was the sky, yawning and reaching, the only thing he knew.

The bleeding creature was lying in a stream. The water was so icy that he started, as if waking from a dream he'd thought was real. He was kneeling in the water, which was shallow and quick and full of boulders. There was a sheep caught between two of these boulders. It was sprawled, limp and wet, its wool turned pink with blood. Icarus crawled toward it, wincing as smaller stones tore at the skin of his knees and calves. He stood to reach down for the sheep— and then he saw the boy.

He was eight or nine, with a thatch of dark hair and enormous eyes that went even wider when they saw Icarus. The boy tugged desperately at his own leg. His ankle, Icarus saw with sudden clarity, was trapped beneath one of the boulders.

Must eat, Icarus thought. He said, "Don't be afraid."

"I'm not," the boy said in a high, quavering voice. He swallowed. "Even though you look very, very odd."

Icarus imagined what the boy was seeing: a man-shape covered in feathers of various lengths. A mouth distended and pointed into a fleshy beak. Fingers scaled and hinged like talons. Mad, ravenous, round little eyes.

"Yes," Icarus said. Words would keep his hunger at bay, at least for a time. "I'm glad you're not afraid, because that means you'll let me help you. What's your name? Mine's Icarus." *Why did you tell him your real name?* he thought. *So hungry; so careless.* The boy swallowed again. "Manasses. I'm nine, but I'm small for my age, so you'll be able to pick me up, even though your arms are very odd." He bit his lower lip. "I already said words like that, didn't I? Papa says I talk too much. He likes silence, but 'Tiria seems to like it when I talk. My foot hurts a lot. I thought the water would freeze it, but it still hurts."

The smell of the sheep's blood was making Icarus feel ill, now. His throat was dry. When he stooped to lift Manasses, his vision went briefly black, but as soon as the boy's arms went around his neck, the world returned.

"Where's your home?" Icarus asked, thinking, *Please, all the gods, not far: I need to get to the palace; need to find Phaidra and head for the Goddess's mountain.*

Manasses gestured at what looked like a very distant peak. "Will you fly me there?"

Icarus settled the boy on his hip and took a few steps, each less wobbly than the last. "No."

"Why not? You have feathers. And a sort-of beak. You're a man-bird; you should be able to fly."

"I . . . cannot." His breath was already rasping. He was so hungry. "I have only part . . . of a godmark."

"You're lucky. I have none. Papa's mark comes from Athene: he can see as well as an owl, at night. He told me that my mother could turn brown grass green from beneath. She died birthing me. I guess the sheep have never had such good pasture since."

Icarus made a huffing noise.

"I don't mind being unmarked. Papa doesn't either. He says the gods can still favour or punish unmarked people. He says no one even needs priests or priestesses to explain things. Are you angry that your god didn't make you a real man-bird?"

"Sometimes," Icarus gasped, and then, "Manasses . . . I can't talk while I'm . . . carrying you . . ."

The boy nodded. "All right," he said, and shifted in Icarus's arms so that, for a brief moment, he felt lighter.

"I hope Papa isn't angry at me because Thirsty Girl died. He and 'Tiria were in the cheese-making hut by the lower pasture, and he made me be in charge of the flocks—the sheep and the goats—and I was so tired! But I only fell asleep for a minute. And I knew where the ewe had gone as soon as I woke up—she always wanders off to the river. That's why 'Tiria calls her Thirsty Girl. Papa's never beaten me, but he makes me do extra chores when he's angry. This hill seemed shorter when I ran down it! My foot feels like it's really big. Big and hot. Look—there's the path! Follow it and you'll see the upper pasture, and our hut is just there, too. I hope Papa isn't angry at me. . . ."

The hut looked like the other one Icarus had found: an enormous beehive made of rough-hewn slabs of stone. A fuzz of blossom-spotted grass covered its pointed tip. Through a haze of dizziness and dancing black spots, he saw a man standing in front of the open door, squinting into the light of the sun that was setting behind another distant peak. Behind the man was someone wearing a skirt and jacket, so she had to be a girl—and yet her hair was as short and fuzzy as the grass on the roof. She and the man ran toward Icarus, the man silently, the girl calling Manasses's name.

The man took the boy carefully from Icarus, who crumpled to his knees. He blinked up at them and saw Manasses wrap his arms and one leg around his father. The other leg, with its injured ankle, dangled. The shepherd didn't look away from Icarus.

"His name's Icarus," Manasses mumbled against

his father's neck. "He's a man-bird but he can't fly. He carried me all the way from the river. Thirsty Girl fell on the rocks in the river and so did I, and she's dead, and my ankle hurts a lot. Please don't beat me."

The man continued to stare down at Icarus. "Thank you," he said at last. His voice was quiet, rough-edged as the stone. Manasses whimpered, and his injured foot twitched. "Come inside," the man said, and Icarus stumbled to his feet. He thought of saying, *No—there's somewhere I should have been, days ago.* But when he imagined what would come after—another long, dizzy, famished walk—he followed.

The hut was cool and dim and smelled of cheese. At first Icarus held his breath to keep the smell at bay, because it turned his stomach as the sheep's blood had, once the fever of his hunger had passed. But when he sat on the bench at the table and saw a bowl there, full of curds and honey, his hunger returned.

"Eat," the girl said as she slid a wooden spoon to him. Her eyes seemed huge because she had so little hair. He ate, wishing she weren't watching him fumble with the spoon—and then she wasn't; she was watching the father bend over Manasses, on one of the two sleeping platforms. Icarus lowered his head to the bowl and used his talon-tipped fingers to shovel the cheese into his mouth. His head and vision cleared. He could see the swirls of honey in the cheese; the whorls of wood grain in table and spoon; the muted reds and blues and yellows of the coverlet on the other sleeping platform.

"Let me see him." Her voice was barely a whisper, but Icarus looked up. The girl—Tiria, he assumed—was standing behind the shepherd. Her hands were clenching and unclenching at her sides. Her fingers and palms were pulsing with silver godlight. "Alexios. Please. I need . . ."

Alexios turned to her. His eyes reflected her silver as they widened. "Sotiria—what is this?"

She knelt beside him, clasping her hands in her lap. "I can't help it—it's my godmark—I have to heal him. Asclepius demands it."

Manasses's eyes were wider than his father's. "Why didn't you tell me you could do that?"

"I thought my god might let me live without it for a time. I was foolish." Icarus saw her straighten her shoulders as she looked at Alexios. "I will take the pain away from him and take it on myself. I likely won't cry out; I've borne worse. Although my own ankle will be broken, you won't be able to do anything to help. My body will take care of itself."

Icarus's heartbeat stuttered, then raced. He hardly felt the new feathers that thrust suddenly at his skin from beneath.

"Your scars," Alexios said slowly.

She smiled. "The ones you've never asked about. Yes. It's a difficult mark, but it gives me great joy."

Alexios lifted his hand and laid it lightly against her cheek. She leaned into it, her eyes closed. *He loves her.* This thought cut through all the others crowding Icarus's head. *And she loves him. She must be seventeen, eighteen; he, no younger than thirty, though perhaps the lines on his face are from the sun, only.*

The silver was spreading from her hands to her elbows, brighter than the dying light outside. Silver veins branched from shoulders to neck to cheeks; silver hairs lifted along her arms.

Icarus hardly breathed as she wrapped her fingers around Manasses's ankle. The boy started but made no sound. She was still—*A statue*, thought Icarus, *though not one of Karpos's, of course, which seem to move.* All the sun was gone now, and Alexios didn't get up to light the lantern that was sitting on the table. Godlight rippled into the darkness in long, lingering waves. Silence throbbed in Icarus's ears—until Manasses gave a whoop. He scrambled to sit up, grinning, waving his leg in the air.

"It's better!" he cried. He leapt off his sleeping platform and jumped up and down. "You made it better, 'Tiria! It hardly took you any time at all!"

The last of the silver waves quivered against the stone and vanished. Icarus was gasping as if he'd been trying to fly. He saw nothing but shadows and remembered, suddenly, that Alexios could see in the dark like an owl. As Icarus's own eyes adjusted, the shepherd lifted Sotiria. She wrapped her arms around his neck as Manasses had. Alexios carried her past Icarus, and he saw her eyes, black and white and shining with tears.

Alexios set her down on the other sleeping platform and said, "There must be something I can do to ease your pain. Though you say there is not."

"You could get me some wine," she said. "That's all."

Alexios gave Icarus some too, in a cool, lumpy clay cup. "Stay here tonight, if you wish," the shepherd said.

Icarus took a quick, bitter sip and coughed. "Thank you," he said when his throat was clear. "I will be gone before the sun is up." *And not alone, if the gods are good. Which they often aren't.*

Alexios lay down beside Manasses and drew a blanket over them both. The boy murmured something and giggled, and his father hushed him. There was silence for a time, until Manasses said, in a dramatic whisper, "'Tiria, could you have healed Thirsty One?"

Icarus could see her shadow on the ledge above him. It didn't stir even a little as she said, "No. Just people."

Icarus listened as Alexios's and Manasses's breathing slowed. He couldn't hear Sotiria's at all. When he rose, his thigh feathers made a hissing noise that he was sure would wake the child, at least. But the sleep-breathing continued. He straightened slowly, wincing; his latest attempt to fly had raised the usual bruises. He leaned carefully toward Sotiria's sleeping platform, and as he leaned, she sat up.

"Icarus." He tried to draw back but she reached out and closed her hand around his wrist. No silver; just her fingers digging invisibly, inexorably into his flesh. "Take me outside, now," she murmured, "so they won't hear."

The sky was blue-black and full of stars. He craned up at it for a moment, as he carried her away from the hut. *What will you say?* he thought. *Decide, because you have to say it soon, now, before she—*

"I'm from Athens," she said. He'd set her on a flat bit of ground, and she was sitting with her back to him, her head raised to the cool night wind. He wanted to walk up beside her, to look down at her face, but he couldn't. He wanted to ask her why she was here, in this mountain pasture so far from her home, but he couldn't. "People tell stories there, about Master Daedalus, who was exiled to Crete because he murdered someone. Daedalus and his son, part bird, who was born on Crete."

She turned to him. The starlight made her skin white. He stared at it, and at her mouth, which looked like octopus ink brushed onto the white. "They died four years ago," she went on. "Or so the stories say. Attacked by pirates. Yet here you are."

He opened his mouth but no words came. He'd felt like this with Ariadne—but no: he felt no anger before Sotiria. He was silent, not lost.

"Your need is so clear to me. For healing, but not your own." Her voice was weary, sad. "And because I feel it, I can't deny it. My god makes sure of this. But there's also this: you're Athenian. Your father is Athenian. So perhaps I wouldn't deny it, even if I could."

The moment she stopped speaking, Icarus stammered, "I don't . . . will you . . . what are you going to do?"

Sotiria smiled a weary, sad smile as she gazed over his shoulder at the hut. "I'm going to go with you," she said. "To help Master Daedalus."

"They're old wounds," Icarus said in a rush. "Old, broken bones—maybe you won't be able to heal them. And there's more: there's the labyrinth. The Athenians in the labyrinth—and my friends Asterion and Chara, who are in there too—"

Sotiria raised her hand up and laid it on his chest. Even though there was no silver bleeding from it, it felt warm and steadying. "Chara?" she said, and he nodded, not wondering why she'd repeated the name; knowing only that she'd said yes to him.

"Chara, and Asterion—the one the Athenians are being sacrificed to, except that he isn't killing them; he *can't* be." He cleared his throat so that his voice would come out more steadily. "So there'll be a lot of pain, probably. Maybe you shouldn't; maybe you should just—"

"Icarus," she said, very quietly, "I will come with you."

CHAPTER TWENTY-THREE

Sotiria told Icarus nothing about herself. "I'd rather not," she said after he asked her to, on the first day. She was bouncing against his back: though her ankle was healing remarkably quickly, he'd insisted on carrying her. *An Athenian girl with recently shorn hair, living in a hut with a shepherd and his son. The Athenian sacrifices had their heads shaved.* He shook these thoughts away. *She'll tell me soon. When she trusts me.*

By the third day, she was walking as swiftly and smoothly as if she'd never been hurt.

"You're very lucky," he said. "To have such a strong godmark—to heal and help, even if it causes you pain. You must be—"

Only when she moaned did he realize she wasn't beside him anymore. She was behind, kneeling, her hands pressed against her ears.

"What is it?" he said, crouching next to her. "Is your ankle hurting?"

"I hear him," she murmured.

"Who?"

Her hands ground against her ears. "I hear Theseus."

The air was abruptly hot and thick; Icarus struggled to draw a clean breath. "Theseus," he managed to say. "Son of the King of Athens."

She didn't answer. Her eyes were squeezed shut.

"Sotiria." He put his hands lightly over hers and held them still, when they began to tremble. He was careful not to dig his talons into her skin. "Sotiria," he said again, as she opened her eyes and raised them to his. "Please tell me what's going on."

He watched her swallow hard. Her gaze swung from his face up to the sky, which was empty and blue. "I was one of the Athenians from the last group." She sounded half-asleep. "So was Prince Theseus. He disguised himself as a commoner so that he could get into the labyrinth and kill the bull-beast."

Asterion, Icarus thought. *Chara.*

"His godmark," Sotiria said, rubbing at her cheeks so that they went splotchy. She already sounded much more awake. "You might know of it. He can reach out and put his voice into people's heads. Even when he's not saying anything, it's there—like a hum. Another heartbeat. It went quiet, a few weeks ago. I could barely hear it. But just now I heard him again: words, not just hum. And I saw what he was seeing."

Icarus felt himself nodding, as if this made sense; as if he weren't cold with dread and shock. "And what *did* he say? What did you see?"

She stood up as slowly as an old woman. He put out an arm and she gripped it. "I saw a dark place, and frightened people, and a monstrous . . . something." He watched her look past him at the shape of the Goddess's mountain—its ragged sides and splintered peak, looming, though it was still so far away from them.

"I had friends," she said. "Tryphon and Phoibe and Alphaios and the rest—even Melaina, though she was mostly unbearable. My friends—those who are still alive, anyway—are under the mountain with Prince Theseus, and they're all in danger. I should be with them. I should be taking their pain away, as my god would command me to. I'm a coward. I must find a way in."

Icarus squeezed her hand, which was still holding onto his arm. His feathers prickled up between her fingers. "You'll come with us. You already know that."

"Yes," she said, "but it'll be impossible: how will we find our way, once we're inside? If I'd only stayed with them, I'd be able to help."

"You'd be in danger," he said. "As they are. And as for finding our way: my father knows. I know. He built the labyrinth, Sotiria, because King Minos forced him to. He built it, and I was with him when he did."

He watched her gaze slip somewhere very far away. Watched it return to him, clear and focused.

"Let's hurry, now," he said. "We're nearly there."

———— · ————

Icarus yelled himself hoarse and hammered on the rusty metal, but the door above the sea stayed closed.

"I don't understand this," he said to Sotiria, who was pressing herself against the cliff wall, her fingers spread wide and white. "He's usually waiting. He usually hears me right away." *But this time's different*, Icarus thought, and felt a sudden sickness rising from his belly. *This time he knows I'm going to make him go to the mountain. But he doesn't know about* her.

"Please," he said to Sotiria, "shout for me. Tell him your name, and what you're here to do."

She knelt carefully beside him. "Master Daedalus!" she called. She glanced sidelong at Icarus, who nodded at her. "My name is Sotiria—I'm one of the Athenians who . . . I'm Athenian. I'm godmarked. I can heal wounds."

Icarus put his ear to the door. He heard nothing but the waves; somehow they sounded louder. Nothing, nothing—and then a scrabbling, and the familiar screaming of metal.

If Sotiria was disgusted by the cave's smell or Daedalus's, she didn't show it. She stood by the dripping stalactite and looked around her with a calm, steady gaze. The pink light painted her hair and skin, and her teeth, when she smiled at him. He dipped his head as if he couldn't look at her, or was bowing; it could have been either or both, Icarus couldn't tell.

"Master Daedalus," she said in a much quieter voice than the one she'd used outside. "Your son and I have travelled together. He has told me much of you. Please give me your hands."

Daedalus raised his head and looked at Icarus. "I've seen her heal a broken bone, Father." He could barely speak over the anticipation in his throat. "This will help us get to the mountain together. Not in the way we expected—but it'll be even better."

Daedalus twitched. He dragged one of his false fingers through the bird's nest of his hair; some of the webbing snagged, and he growled. Icarus watched Sotiria's eyes follow the fingers. Her face was still composed and calm. *She must have seen some terrible things*, Icarus thought, as his father turned his palms up and extended them to her.

She sucked in her breath. She drew his hands toward her chest and blinked down at them; traced the lumps on his palms and then the knuckle-knobs of limestone, with their clinging, binding webs. He closed his eyes and didn't move. After a moment she closed her eyes too. *Come on*, Icarus thought. *Heal him. Heal him* now.

"The damage is very old," she said at last. Her eyes opened and found Icarus's. "As you told me. I won't be able to heal both hands—not without crippling myself."

So do that, he nearly said. *Make him right; I don't care what happens to you.* Except that he did. He met her clear, steady, sad gaze and said, "So you'd fix one? Because that would be enough to help us get him out of here. Enough for him to open the mountain door. I think."

She nodded. "Yes. I'll fix one—if he tells me to."

Daedalus's throat constricted, beneath the chaotic growth of his beard. "Ech," he said. Icarus was about to tell her that this meant "yes," but then she smiled at his father and said, "Very well, then. Sit down with me, Master Daedalus."

Icarus started to tremble as soon as the silver kindled in her fingers. When his father's fingers began to glow silver as well, Icarus wrapped his arms tightly around himself. Feathers thrust their way between his own fingers, just as they had when Sotiria had healed Manasses. This time, though, the godmarked light was so bright, the power so palpable, that Icarus's feathers pushed thicker and thicker through his skin, until he thought, *He could make another set of wings right now, with these.* He could see the wings, tilted against the cave wall: their sheen of feathers and the dull, solid lines of the branches that made the harness. *But there's no need for any wings, now that she's here.* Another, very faint voice said, *Oh really? And what do you intend to do after you've rescued everyone, and you're all huddled by the mountain?* He shook the voices away.

She'd healed Manasses silently and swiftly. Now she moaned. The tendons in her neck tightened; her brow shone with sweat; her silver hands shook and clutched at Daedalus's. He made no sound, but his own brow furrowed as he squeezed his eyes shut. Moments passed. Icarus took three paces away from them, then turned back. More moments. He wanted to shout, to fling himself off the cliff and fly, because surely he'd be able to: the godmarked power in the cave was tugging fiercely at him, promising him sky. He stayed where he was, as she moaned and struggled, until the silver flared and blinded him, and he fell to his knees with a cry.

Someone was weeping: a dry, wracked sound that seemed to come from everywhere. Daedalus, Icarus realized, and crawled toward him. Daedalus, hunched over his left hand, crying but also laughing, flexing fingers that were all flesh and nail. His false fingers lay between his knees and Sotiria's. He raised the hand and wiped at his wet eyes. When he'd done that, he leaned over and touched her cheek.

She was crying too, soundlessly. Her right hand was cradling her left, which was twisted and swollen, its palm as lumpy as Daedalus's had been. She was staring at him, hardly blinking, despite the tears.

"Ank oo," he said. She nodded once and drew in a noisy, shaky breath.

"Yes," Icarus said, "thank you." He thought, *Don't ask her for more. This is enough. Have some pity.* But he went on anyway, his heart hammering, "What about his mouth?"

His father rounded on him, shaking his head so wildly that hair fell in front of his eyes. He pushed it away with his good hand. "Oh," he said. "Oh ee."

"No need—how can you think that? You'd be able to speak! You'd be closer to being as you were." He swallowed and looked at Sotiria. He felt sick again; his voice was strained and thin. "I'm sorry. I don't want you to suffer, of course—I just . . . it's beyond wondrous, what you've already done. It makes me want more, for him."

Sotiria spoke so softly that Icarus could barely make out her words. "Even if he wanted it, even if I could try now, it probably wouldn't work." She smiled at him. He felt a surge of shame, and imagined all the skin beneath his feathers flushing scarlet. "The flesh of his tongue isn't just injured—it's gone. And my godmark isn't commanding me to try. Which means it probably can't be healed."

Daedalus shook his head, slowly this time. He said words that meant, "No—this is enough."

She rose, holding her left hand up and away from her body. She swayed, and Icarus leapt up and took her by her other arm, as gently as he could. She sagged against him.

"I wish we had wine to give you," he said. "Like Alexios did."

She pressed her head against his chest and made a snuffling noise that reminded him of the one Chara made, when she was trying not to laugh. "It's fine," she whispered after a long, quiet moment. "I'm fine, as long as you don't ask me to carry anything. And give me just a little while, before I try to climb those cliff stairs with one hand."

It was dark when the three of them finally emerged onto the ledge.

"We should wait," Icarus said. "Do this in the morning." But his feet shifted and his fingers twitched on the cloth that was full of food he'd carried out with him, and Sotiria said, "We've already lost too much time. Our friends need us. So let's try."

They all stared down at the door, after Daedalus pulled it shut. *He could probably lock it from the outside too,* Icarus thought. *But there's no need. We're not hiding that we can do this, because we're* never coming back.

Sotiria went first. Two feet, one hand, rasping, ragged breaths—Icarus called, "Careful!" then bit the inside of his lower lip so that he wouldn't say anything else.

"I'm up!" she called down at last. Her head was a darker shadow against the sky.

Icarus turned to Daedalus, who was still gazing at the door. When he looked away, Icarus saw that his eyes were full of tears, again. "Eye ings," he said.

"Forget about your wings. You won't need them now: we'll find another way to get off this island, once we've rescued everyone. Come, now. If she can get up there, so can you."

His father's climb was even slower than hers had been. When he was halfway up, one of his feet slid off a step in a shower of dust. He gave a garbled shout and lay flat against the rock for what seemed like forever. "Go on," Icarus murmured, his own hands and feet already on their steps. "Hurry—*hurry.*"

"Now you!" Sotiria cried, and he climbed. He'd done this before, almost without thinking—but now it was the last time, and he panted with desperation, the food banging against his back. Hands came down to pull at him, but he shook them away and hauled himself onto the grass as he always had—though he didn't roll over onto his back and look up at the stars.

"The shepherd's hut first," he said as he stood up between them. "Because he'll need a place to rest, before too long. Then the Goddess's mountain."

Their eyes were on him, gleaming and steady. They said nothing, but he nodded as if they had. He turned and walked, and they followed him.

———— · ————

They'd been at the shepherd's hut for only a few minutes when the earth began to shake. It took mere moments for the stone blocks above them to loosen and rain down; Icarus gave a yell and pulled both Daedalus and Sotiria out of their path, toward the door. When they were clear of the falling stones, he ran, Sotiria right behind him—but Daedalus stumbled and fell onto his hands with a strangled cry that Icarus could hear, even above the cracking of earth and rock and the sudden screaming of the wind. *He's not used to open space*, Icarus thought wildly as he whirled to go back. *He's helpless; he's weak; his hands must hurt.*

"Come," he gasped as he set his own hands under his father's arms and pulled. "Use your legs, Father; *try.*"

The ground opened into a jagged, mud-clotted mouth beneath them. Icarus leapt sideways, shouting as he felt his grip on his father loosening; shouting again as he gave a great heave, and Daedalus fell, nearly on top of him. He stared at the crack—an abyss, from so close, easily wide enough to have swallowed all three of them.

Daedalus struggled into a crouch and hid his face against his knees. Icarus remembered another earthquake, when he had been about ten, at Knossos. A crack had opened in the earth then, too, tearing his father's outdoor workroom in half. Daedalus had knelt on the edge of the fissure, pawing at severed vines, muttering and smiling. He had bent in so far that Icarus had screamed. "It is nothing to be afraid of," his father had told him, as Naucrate wrapped her arms around both of them. "I am simply examining what the gods have revealed: the insides of the world."

"Father," Icarus said now, to the man who was hiding his face. "Come away from there."

Daedalus didn't move, not even when the olive tree beside the hut tore free of the earth and slammed down an arm's length away from them. As this sound faded, so did the wind. All Icarus could hear were pebbles trickling down the face of the newly-opened crevasse.

Sotiria was sitting at the bottom of the slope that led up to the hut. Icarus picked his way over the fresh rubble to her. "The mountain door may have broken open," he said. His voice was quiet but sounded loud. "We might not even need Father's godmarked hands, now!"

She nodded and frowned at the same time. "But what if it hasn't?"

"I'll go find Phaidra, at the palace: she'd be able to open the door with *her* godmark. But we need to leave now, in case we need the extra time to get her. Father!" he called up the slope, where Daedalus was still crouching. He cocked his head up. His arms tightened around his knees.

"Get up, Father! It's time!"

Daedalus didn't move. Icarus walked to him with Sotiria beside him. She hunkered down in front of Daedalus, whose eyes wobbled and slid before settling on hers. After a long moment, she said, "You aren't going to come, are you?"

Icarus looked from one to the other. His mouth

opened and shut with a snap, like a beak. "What? Father—is she right?"

Daedalus's own lips sagged apart. Icarus looked past them to the wet darkness where the ruin of his father's tongue was. He waited for a grunted word he'd understand; a denial; a reason. There was only silence. Except for a bird's call, far, far above—only silence.

———— · ————

Sotiria spoke at last, a long while after they'd started walking. "You mustn't blame him. You can't. He's in such pain—too much for even me to take away."

He felt himself swallow. Took a breath and let it out again. He wanted to turn to her and ask her whether she could feel his own pain, but he didn't.

"Icarus," she said, when he said nothing. "It's all right. You'll go back to him when this is done."

He stopped. "How can you be so sure?" His voice sounded splintered and faint. "This may be the end of all of us. Who knows. Maybe not even the gods know."

"Maybe the gods don't," she said. "And maybe we can't. But I didn't come all this way with you for nothing. The earth just moved. Now it's our turn."

He looked down at his feet, which grasped at summer-stiff grass, and his taloned fingers twitched.

"You're right," he said, after a silence. When he started off again, toward the Goddess's mountain, she had to lengthen her own stride to keep up.

CHAPTER TWENTY-FOUR

It was late afternoon when Icarus and Sotiria stepped onto the mountain path—or tried to. The earthquake had turned it into a line of waves: red-gold earth, churned and chipped, tumbled into shapes that poked at the soles of his feet. They walked in the yellowed grass at its edges, though even that was sharp. The light around them was burnished, but the sky ahead was blurred with smoke. Icarus glanced up at the sky once; after that he kept his gaze on his feet. *So close*, he thought, and he imagined Chara and Asterion singing nonsense rhymes into the smoky air, and he walked faster.

When the shattered path sloped upward, he thought, *Not close:* here.

The door hadn't broken open. It loomed as it always had, the small one nestled in it, both of them snug and locked. Tendrils of smoke wove like floating snakes in front of the metal. More smoke billowed from the mountain's peak—but it made him dizzy to look up that far, so he kept his gaze on the door.

"What now?" Sotiria said.

No idea, he thought—and then he heard footsteps. He turned back toward the ruined path. For a moment the world slid out of focus—because there was Phaidra, with Ariadne behind her. They'd seen him: Ariadne's eyes were narrow; Phaidra's were wide. He tried to take a deep breath and couldn't.

And so the gods have delivered you to me outside, and I am strong. The moment he thought this, he felt the feathers that dusted his skin retract with sharp, wrenching motions; felt his long hatred turn to sickness in his belly.

"Sweet hands of Aphrodite," Sotiria whispered. "I remember them: the princesses."

"You," Ariadne said, when she was close enough to reach out and touch Icarus's cheek—or claw it, more like. He stopped looking at her because he knew he'd claw at her first, and there was too much else to do. Instead he looked at Phaidra. Her eyes were so bright that he wanted to close his own, but he didn't. *You're here*, he thought, feverishly, and forgot about the bile of Ariadne. *I see you so clearly—for the first time, after so many years.*

Ariadne rounded on Phaidra, her eyes alight with rage. "And *you*! You let them out after all!"

He shifted his gaze and stepped toward Ariadne. "She didn't. We got out ourselves. We planned it for years." He laughed suddenly, tipping his head up at the mountain's peak. The smoke was white against the darkening blue of the sky. "We thought we'd fly together to the island, then away." *Years and years, and see, now: no father. No long, slow glide to the island beneath our prison. Just you and another prison, my Lady.*

"And you still may," Sotiria said.

"And who are *you*?" Ariadne snapped.

Sotiria's eyes rose to Ariadne's. "Sotiria."

The princess frowned. "I remember . . ." She sucked in her breath. "You're an *Athenian*—Chara and I visited your cell the night before the procession! Your hair was long and tangled then." She laughed almost as Icarus had. "She switched places with you. She went to you to plan it, even as I went to him."

"To him?" Icarus repeated. The second word cracked—because he already knew. Prince Theseus: of course, of course, though Icarus didn't yet know why or how.

Ariadne reached up and touched the edge of the lock. Her filmy sleeves fell away, revealing an arm that was taut with muscle, and brown except for its scars. "And why did you come here, bird-*man*?"

He tried not to sneer back at her. Phaidra's face was still there at the edge of his vision; when he spoke, it was to her. "The earth moved. I thought . . . I hoped the lock would have broken. I hoped the door would be hanging open; that we'd be able to go inside and find them."

"And it isn't," Ariadne said, waving her free hand. "It isn't hanging open. So we need to *get* it open, and see whether Zeus's earth-shaking has made a way for us, inside."

"Why so desperate, Princess?" Icarus said, and Phaidra said, calmly and coldly, "Yes—why, Sister? I'm not sure you really answered, when I first asked you this."

"How *dare* you?" Ariadne said. Her hand clenched, on the lock. "How dare you ask me to explain myself? You—"

"Stop." Sotiria spoke quietly, but they all turned to her. She was looking back down the path, and they followed her gaze. The sky behind them was pulsing with orange.

"The procession," Ariadne said. "The king. Already." She reached out and gripped Phaidra's wrist; dragged it up to the lock. "Open it *now*."

Phaidra glanced at Icarus, who smiled at her. She smiled back, then stood up on her toes and placed her palms and fingertips on the lock. The silver flowed immediately. It coursed over the metal and into the air around it; it turned her golden hair to white, and the lock to liquid, before it sprang open. The low door opened too, with a muffled *clang*.

"Yes!" Ariadne tugged on it until it swung wide. She knelt, her hands out, seeking air, and the others crouched behind her.

There was no air. No opening. The doorway was blocked by three slabs of stone that might have been placed deliberately, so neatly did they fit together. No space atop or around them; no spaces between—just seams to show they were separate pieces.

"No," Icarus heard himself say. He put a hand on Phaidra's back and pressed. She was so slender, but so strong and solid. She didn't move.

Ariadne lunged forward with a shriek. She pounded her fists against the stone, growling and panting.

"Stop," Sotiria said again—loudly, this time. She hunched over, curling her fingers (even the broken ones) into her palms. *She's in pain*, he thought. *Ariadne's pain—and I can't do anything at all.*

Ariadne kept hammering at the blocks. "I need him!" she cried, and the stone darkened with her spit. "Gods*blood*—let me in! *I need him!*"

Yes, he thought. *Suffer. Bleed.*

Phaidra turned and took Icarus's hand in both her own. She was cool; he wanted to pull her closer, to feel the coolness everywhere, like windy sky on flesh and feathers. To forget.

He nodded once. "We have to go," he said.

Phaidra nodded too. "Where?"

It came to him at last, in an image so clear that it blotted out everything else. Chara scrabbling at the mountain; Chara's lips moving as she begged him to throw his string up, because surely they'd be able to climb it? "There are lava tubes near the top—pipes. I tried to reach them once, with Chara, and it didn't work"—blood under her nails; the string a useless silver pile around his feet—"but the earthquake may have loosened things, up there. It has to have *somewhere*." He glanced back down at the orange stain in the sky. "Yes," he said, still to Phaidra, "We go up."

Ariadne was in front of him, just as she had been in his prison. Near enough to touch. "And," he said, "we leave your sister here—because if I have to have anything more to do with her, I'll probably kill her."

Phaidra didn't smile, but she glowed anyway, somehow. "Let's go, then," she said.

———·———

Ariadne followed them, of course, but she was silent, and only Sotiria glanced back at her. Icarus stumbled on stones and earth, but Phaidra's hand was there, and he grasped it, holding on as if he were drowning, as King Minos had told everyone he had.

It didn't seem to take very long before they were beneath the black pipes that still seemed to gleam, despite the thickening darkness and the darker pall of smoke.

"No," he said—and it was just like it had been years before, with Chara, only worse. Worse, because this was the end. The mountain was shuddering beneath them; the mark-mad king was closing in behind them. *Father*, Icarus thought, helplessly.

Phaidra let go of his hand, and for a moment he was afraid he'd fall over. He turned to her, straightening and shrugging at the same time. He was just about to say something that he hoped would sound wry, rather than defeated, when she leaned forward and kissed him. He pulled away quickly, before he could really feel the warmth of her lips, and stammered, "Phaidra— don't tease me; don't—" She smiled and put her hands behind his head and pulled him back to her again.

Never, he thought, as a humming filled his ears. Ariadne made a disgusted noise, but she sounded very far away. *This was never going to happen to me.* Phaidra said, "Icarus: don't be sad. There's a way." He didn't hear her say this; he felt the words passing from her lips to his. He drew away just enough that he could see her—though she was mostly a blur, gold smudged against blue-black, like one of Daedalus's paintings— and then *he* kissed *her*, over and over, gasping with breath and laughter in between.

Feathers pushed up through his skin so suddenly and swiftly that he stumbled backward. He cried out as the bones of his arms and legs lengthened. He hadn't changed this quickly since he was a child—and he'd never changed so completely. He watched it happen, with vision that was his and wasn't. He looked up from his own body, at the people around him. Ariadne was crouching, staring up at him with horrified eyes. Sotiria was pressed against the mountain, her own eyes huge, her mouth open. *I wonder if she feels this pain?* he thought as it burned its godmarked silver through his blood and flesh. She had to be: it was spilling out of him—pouring from the ends of feathers and beak and flexing, grasping talons. He beat his wings to shake it off; closed his eyes to pull it deeper.

Phaidra's whoop brought him back to himself. He peered down at her. Down. *Down?* he thought, and the word echoed strangely in his silver-soaked head. None of him was touching the ground. None. He was stretched out with his fingers and toes dangling; he could have brushed the top of her head with them.

He gabbled meaningless words and fell. Only when he hit the ground did he realize how the air had felt: *slippery and cool, like water*—except those words didn't touch the truth of it. He gasped and clawed at the earth, which was too hard, too dry; it crumbled and scattered.

Phaidra was beside him. Her hands flattened his feathers. "You can fly!" she said, and laughed a deep, rich laugh. "You can fly up there and get inside—Icarus: *you can fly!*"

"Yes," he said thickly, as his beak stretched back into lips, "but I think you'll have to kiss me again."

She did.

This time he knew what was going to happen. He was on his feet before they turned into talons; he was flapping his arms before they were fully wings. Ariadne snorted, and he glanced at her. *Why did I ever think I loved you?*—and with this thought he surged upward, calling with his new voice—his mother's voice, a bird's, full-throated and soaring. He saw Phaidra raise her arms, in the moment before the sky tilted and he tumbled and rose at the same time. The smoke that was the Goddess's breath was above him, below him, slinking in around him like arms that couldn't hold him.

Nothing he tried to think was right. Nothing was enough.

He remembered Asterion above a waterfall, saying,

"You know, it's heat that makes *me* change. Maybe there's something like that for you but you just don't know it yet." Icarus angled his wings and dipped and saw Phaidra with her head tipped back. The rest of her was flattened and shortened, with distance and nightfall—but he could see her eyes and the curve of her lips. He sang to her, with his new voice.

Her mouth was moving. He spun until he was dizzy. He dipped wildly, and his stomach didn't lurch. He was, at last, himself.

"Icarus! The pipes!" The wind took Phaidra's words and twisted them, flattened them as her body was flattened—but he heard her. "Don't go too high—not yet!"

The sky above him was endless: he could see a layer of blacker darkness there, could sense a crushing cold lying atop the air he'd always known. When he looked back down, he saw a throbbing bruise of light, and knew that it was fire. He felt waves of humming that reached into the sky from beneath the earth, and knew that the mountain was changing.

"The pipes, Icarus! Asterion and Chara!"

The pipes were ranged like tiny gaping mouths below him. He swooped, because he could—and because he remembered Asterion, despite the cold wind and the ribbons of cloud that wove above the smoke.

He didn't choose: the pipe simply appeared before him, larger and darker than anything around it. He managed to hover. Every feather felt as if it were the only one. Every feather felt as if it were part of a whole that was larger than his body.

He flapped his wings, then tucked them in against his sides as smoothly as if he'd always been doing it. The small space within the pipe grew larger. Phaidra called his name and he called hers back—or thought he did—and plunged into the mountain.

BOOK

FIVE

ALL

CHAPTER TWENTY-FIVE

"Quiet, all of you; look!" Chara cried, and pointed. All of them looked, except Polymnia.

"It's from *outside!*" Alphaios said, as the shadow grew on the crumbling stone at the top of the chamber. "It's coming in! *Down!* What . . . ?"

Chara clutched Asterion's slippery hand with her own and waited.

The shadow grew, and then it plummeted. Wings splayed and flapped and tucked in close to a slender, feathered body. Chara let go of Asterion's hand and stepped forward, though she was suddenly dizzy and far, far too hot. The body landed clumsily on its side, and started making a shrill, skirling noise. She drew closer.

The noise was laughter.

Her shriek was louder than the laughter. She threw herself onto her knees just as the slender, feathered creature was drawing itself up; their shoulders bumped and their arms tangled, and now they were both laughing, clutching each other with hands and talons.

"Icarus?" Asterion said from behind them, and they drew breathlessly apart. Icarus rose as clumsily as he'd landed. He spread his wings wide again and drew Asterion in against him.

"You died." The words were muffled. Icarus loosened his wings and Asterion gazed at him with wide, shining eyes. "Chara told me: you, your father and mother—you all died."

Icarus's cheeks were covered with feathers too, and his mouth was somewhere between beak and lips—a strange hybrid of a face, but Chara could still see the pain on it. "My mother died," he said in a higher, more pinched voice than he'd had before—though she recognized it as his. "Not the way the king said she did. We were all imprisoned—by the king—and Ariadne knew." His chest heaved and his finger-talons flexed convulsively. "There's too much to tell, and the king's close, and he's going to give himself to his god here, in fire, and I don't know how much time I can be a bird for, so I have to get you out *now*: Phaidra's up there waiting, and Sotiria, and . . . Ariadne."

A huge chunk of rock smashed to bits on the floor by the bee column, but no one seemed to notice: they were all gaping at Icarus. He cleared his throat. "She and Phaidra came here together, and there's been no time to think about how to deal with her."

"How will you be able to carry us?" Chara asked, into the silence. "The pipes are too narrow for you to fly inside them—and aren't they terribly slippery?"

He shook his head. "They were, but the earthquake shattered a lot of the obsidian—the gods granted us this much good fortune, at least. I'll carry each of you up to the pipes and we'll crawl to the top, and then I'll fly down with you." He held up his hands; Chara saw blood dripping from beneath the feathers. "Wrap cloth around your hands and knees, though, if you can: it'll be a rough climb."

Melaina walked up to him and put her arms around his neck. "Take me first," she said softly. "I would see this Princess Ariadne before anyone else does."

Icarus glanced at Chara, who shrugged and turned to Theseus. His eyes were on Melaina, steady and dark. *I don't care what he's saying to her*, Chara thought, and felt fresh laughter pushing into her throat. *Asterion and Icarus and maybe a ship that will take us away: that's all that matters.*

When Icarus dropped back down again, Theseus said, "Take me next. I do not wish her to be where I cannot see her."

It took three tries for Icarus to bear Theseus up; just one to take Alphaios. In the quiet after he'd gone, Asterion began to make his way over to Polymnia, who was still slumped against a piece of rock.

"What are you doing?" Chara said. "Leave her!"

"I can't." Asterion picked up the same piece of obsidian that Melaina had used on the string. He knelt in front of Polymnia, who was humming around her gag: silver wound into the darker smoke above them. Blood beaded on her face, where bits of shattered obsidian and rock had grazed it. Her eyes were closed.

"Asterion." Chara put her hand on his arm and squeezed. "Think of what she's done to you—to so many people."

He shook his head and she drew back as his horns swept by her. "No. Yes. I know. But I can't bear this. We both suffered." He cut the gag away.

More chunks of stone fell from the roof and exploded into splinters around them. Chara felt them cut her shoulders and arms; she heard Theseus bellow, from far above, "Chara! He is coming back now—hurry!"

"Asterion," she said again, "you shouldn't feel—"

"I don't want to go." Polymnia's eyes were open and nearly black. She was gazing at Asterion, who'd gone very still.

"You must," he said, so quietly that Chara could hardly hear him over the hissing steam and cracking stone.

Polymnia smiled. The smile was beautiful; *she* was beautiful, despite the dirt and blood on her skin.

His head dropped and swayed from side to side, as if it were as heavy as the bull's. For a moment Chara was afraid he'd start to change again, but instead he looked slowly up at Polymnia. The shard of obsidian glinted. "At least let me cut your bonds."

"What for?" That smile; Chara wanted to claw at it until it was shredded flesh and chipped teeth.

He opened his mouth but said nothing. He shrugged, helplessly.

Icarus fell toward them.

"Fly away, my dear one," Polymnia sang, and Chara forgot her rage in the spiral of silver that wove around them all. "The sky is full of stars . . ."

The obsidian fell from Asterion's fingers. He took a step backward. Something whistled by Chara's ear and she stumbled back too, reaching for him. He took her hand and she held it tightly, even when a gout of flame leapt up from the earth between them and Polymnia.

"Gods grant you peace," he said to her, and turned away.

— · —

She watched them go, through a shimmering haze of fire and smoke. Chara, who had spoken to her when no one else would, years ago, before the sacrifice. Chara, who had ruined her.

The bird-man carried Chara up and out of sight.

O gods of all—O Poseidon and Great Mother, let the bird-man not come back; let your bull-god stay with me.

But he was not a bull. He was standing on two scarred legs. He was tall—though his shoulders were rounded—and his horns had shrunk, and he spoke in a man's voice, as if he'd never roared.

The bird-thing (too clumsy by far to be a god) dropped down once more, stirring smoke and sparks with his wings. He waited on what remained of the altar where her god had come to her, and run from her.

"My Lord!" she called—not to stop him, anymore; just to make him look at her. He didn't. He put his arms around the bird-man's neck. *He's bigger,* she thought; *they won't be able to leave the ground.*

They rose, very slowly. Arms slipped from neck to waist—*Yes! Fall; I'll tend you, if you're hurt*—but they kept rising.

Close to her, or far away, a wolf howled.

"Asterion!" she cried, just as they drew up to the pipes. At last she saw his eyes, through the haze. She saw the clean paths of tears on his cheeks. And then she saw nothing but fire.

———— · ————

Icarus didn't so much set Chara down as let her go, when they were still above the ground. She tumbled and rolled; she pressed her cheek against dry grass and earth and started to cry. She was choking on tears and yet more laughter by the time she flipped onto her back. The tears made it nearly impossible for her to see the sky, so she rubbed at them until she could.

Darkness—but not the darkness of stone. Deep, soft darkness—some, but not all of it, filled with the mountain's smoke, which was grey, out here. *Out here.* Stars were scattered across the black beyond the smoke, and clouds stretched thin between the stars.

She sat up only when Icarus and Asterion came down, like a strange, meandering patch of shadow. She heard voices behind her but didn't look at anyone except Asterion, who huddled on his side where Icarus laid him, near the mountainside. She was afraid her legs wouldn't hold her if she stood, so she crawled to him, across the crackling summer grass.

"Asterion." She touched his quivering shoulder. "Look up."

"I can't." His voice was muffled because his face was tucked into the crook of his elbow. "Can't look . . . at anything."

"Look at me," she said. "To start with."

He eased his face away from his arm and blinked up at her. She watched his pupils grow and shrink as they tried to adjust to this new light. He raised an arm and wiped at the tears on her cheek, and she smiled into his cupped palm. "Now," she said, "*look.*"

He gripped her hands as he sat up, and then he let them go. His breath rasped and whistled and he flattened himself against the rock, scrabbling at it as if he were afraid of falling. "Gods and fishes," he hissed between chattering teeth. "Fishes and gods and fishes and . . ." His gaze swung from the sky to the mountaintop that jutted above him and, at last, to the people who stood watching him.

They were gathered in a ragged half-circle, Chara saw as she, too, finally looked at them. Theseus and Alphaios and Melaina, of course—but also Phaidra, and Sotiria—*Sotiria!*—and—

"Sister." Asterion pushed himself away from the rock and took three wobbly paces toward the group. "Ariadne." The strength of the words seemed to give strength to his legs; he was striding by the time he reached her, in five more paces. Chara followed more slowly, watching the princess's eyes dart from Theseus to Asterion. *Is* this *what she looks like when she's frightened?* Chara thought.

"Asterion," Ariadne said. "Godsblood, but you look remarkable—so—"

"Alive?" he said.

"And Chara!" Ariadne went on, craning past him as if she hadn't heard him. "Look at *you!*"

"Also alive," Chara said. "My Lady." She was next to Asterion now, her arm resting against his. He was still shaking.

"I hope," Ariadne stammered, "I hope you understand, both of you, that I—"

Asterion took one more step, which brought him so close to her that she had to crane up to see his face. Her eyes flitted from it to the scars that nearly brushed her own.

"I don't care," he said quietly. "Not about what you were going to say. Not about you." He flung his head back and laughed, his arms up, his horns glinting in the starlight. "Isn't that amazing?" he asked the sky, and spun so that he was facing Chara again, and fell to his knees.

Phaidra ran to him and wrapped her arms around him from behind. "Brother. Oh, Asterion—thank all the gods."

"And fishes," he added, and smiled at Chara.

Everything around her blurred then, for a time. Warm wind came and went across her skin. Clouds changed from sheets to ribbons. Stars flickered. Voices murmured.

"We mustn't stay. He's very close, now."

"Wait a moment, at least. Look at them: they're in no shape to run."

"A ship? Well if that's true—tell the captain there's an island: just a small one, but he'll see it, if he's coming around that way."

The lash of Ariadne's familiar, angry voice brought Chara back. "Is there something I can do for you? Your gawking would suggest so."

Chara discovered that she was sitting with her knees pressed against Asterion's. She looked up at Ariadne, who was glaring at Melaina. *Oh no*, Chara thought muzzily.

Melaina shrugged. Between them, Alphaios swallowed hard.

"I'm merely taking in the beauteous Princess Ariadne—the one Theseus intends to rescue from this benighted island and marry, instead of me."

Ariadne turned to frown at Theseus, who was standing beside her. "Who is *this*?" she demanded.

He waved a hand at Melaina. "She is of no account— just a girl whose godmark the king and I imagined would be useful, in the labyrinth."

"I see," Ariadne said. "Of no account. Good." She was turning away from him when Melaina lunged toward her, suddenly and silently. Metal gleamed, in the instant before she brought her godmark down upon them all and turned the darkness even darker. Alphaios's blade, Chara knew, and she wondered stupidly, in that first blind instant, where Melaina had been keeping it. Ariadne shrieked, and Alphaios shouted—but Theseus's yell was loudest.

Melaina's godmarked black lifted quickly, leaving a shimmering gauze of silver that faded in a blink. Chara struggled to her feet, leaning on Asterion, straining to see Ariadne and the dagger and the wounds it had made. But the princess was standing where she'd been before—beside Theseus, who was grasping at the dagger in *his* chest.

His eyes were wide, his lips pressed tightly together. His yell was done—but now Chara's head and bones and veins echoed with the screaming of his mind-voice. She knew the others heard it too: they cried out together, in their different voices. Melaina leaned in against him, moaning. Chara could no longer see the blade—but she did see blood. It flowed over Melaina's hand and down her arm, making gently curving lines in the dirt on her skin.

::*No!*:: Theseus's left hand scrabbled and sought at his waist, and then it was holding Daedalus's blade; it was slashing, slashing, opening Melaina's dirty skin until she sagged away from him, to the ground.

Chara's head was full of Theseus's screaming, but she still heard Sotiria's. *Her godmark*, Chara thought dimly. *She's feeling everything—how can she possibly take on all that pain?*

She took on Theseus's first: she fell to her hands and knees beside him. Chara heard her whimpering, but her hands were steady. She tore at the hole in his tunic until his chest was bare—smooth, golden-brown, stained dark. She set her left hand on his wound, and her right on top of her left. Silver flickered like tiny branches of lightning, which spread and spread, until his chest and arms glowed—until the air glowed, as if dawn were coming. She lifted her right hand slowly to her own chest. Her eyes closed; her lips parted. Chara heard her moan, as the silver flowed from his skin to hers. The moan went on and on, even after Theseus had slumped to the ground. Sotiria swayed, and then she cried out, and fell.

Icarus knelt and lifted her head into his lap. Ariadne knelt too, and pawed at Theseus's shoulder. "No," she said. "No, no, no—you were supposed to rescue me; you were supposed to take me back to Athens and make me *queen*."

Sotiria raised herself up, very slowly. Her eyes were wide and unfocused—though just for a moment. They cleared, as they found Melaina. They burned, and swam with tears.

"Stop," Chara said, "Sotiria: stop—you're not strong enough."

Sotiria threw herself toward Melaina, who didn't seem to be breathing, who couldn't possibly be saved—and yet Sotiria scrabbled at her wounds with hands that dribbled silver, at first, and then nothing.

"No," Icarus said as she sagged, hands reaching, sticky with blood. "Please."

She stopped. She went still, her limbs splayed and stiff.

Theseus gasped and sat up, clutching at the place on his chest where his wound had been.

Ariadne screamed a laugh.

Icarus pulled Sotiria up against him. She was limp

now; she slipped over and through his arms, like a sheet of flowing water. Chara said one more useless, "No," remembering the other words she'd said to Sotiria, three months before: words that promised safety and escape.

"Gods!" Theseus rasped, and lurched to his feet. He retched, doubled over but still standing. He lifted his hands and squinted at them, in the starlight.

Ariadne stumbled as she rose, crying out words Chara didn't understand. Maybe they weren't words— just noises that only *seemed* to have form. Theseus braced himself on Ariadne's shoulders for a moment, before he took three unsteady steps back.

"I'm fine." He smiled a shining, trembling smile as he pushed her away. "Fine! Praise the gods and goddesses: I live."

"Look," Phaidra said in a quiet, measured voice. "My father—the king—he's getting closer." The sky beneath them was filling with scarlet and orange and voices.

"We can't just leave her," Icarus said. His mouth was fully human again. One of his hands twitched on Sotiria's hair. "I'll fly; I'll carry her back to where she was when I met her—there's a shepherd there, and his child; they loved her—"

Phaidra put her hands on Icarus's shoulders and her chin on the top of his head. Chara bent down beside him. "No," Chara said. "If the king's coming, we need to go. And she's already gone."

"A priest would say that her god is welcoming her." Icarus's lips twisted even more than usual as he bit the inside of his mouth.

"I don't know anything about gods," Chara said.

She glanced up at Asterion, who shrugged and smiled, just a little. The helplessness in this smile made her stomach knot.

"I don't either," Asterion said, and put his own hands over Phaidra's. "There's nothing you could do for her, Icarus, even if you did carry her away from here. Let's go get your father."

Ariadne glared down at all of them, gesturing at Icarus. "Leave him, if he insists on grieving for her here. I, for one, intend to get off this accursed island."

Chara stood, already turning to Theseus. "Will you be able to keep up?" she asked.

"I will," he said. He looked down at Sotiria's body. "I feel very strong. Thanks to the grace of those gods you claim not to understand. Thanks to her."

"Yes," Ariadne snapped, "beautiful—now let's *go*"—and she began to pick her way over the stony ground.

Icarus let Phaidra draw him up. He ground his head against her shoulder; Chara saw the feathers on his neck rise and ripple.

"You're tired," Phaidra said. Chara thought, *Gods and sea snails, when did she get so beautiful and tall and old?*

"Yes," Icarus said as he raised his head. "And so are they."

Chara almost said, "I am not! I could run and run, because there's nothing to stop me"—but then she saw that Alphaios was leaning over with his hands on his knees, and Asterion was stooped, as if he could hardly bear the weight of his horns—and she knew that her own body was just as weak as it was eager.

"I wish I could carry each of you to the sea," Icarus said. "But I imagine I'll have to carry you once we get there—to the ship Prince Theseus says will be waiting.

And flying's new to me, so I'm not sure—"

"Icarus," Chara said. "We'll walk. Or run, if we can."

"But you?" Phaidra asked him.

He shrugged a bristling shoulder, a little sheepishly. "I think I might fly again. A little."

Phaidra's smile was broad, and it made her look like a girl again, just for a moment.

"Of course," she said, and kissed him.

"Head straight for the cliff above our old prison," he said as his feet left the ground. He turned to look down at Ariadne, who'd stopped to wait for them. He smiled, which looked very strange; his mouth was caught somewhere between lips and beak. "I believe you know exactly where that is, Princess."

She scowled at her own feet and said nothing. Phaidra called, "We do—now fly!"

———— · ————

King Minos stood before the mountain door. His hands sizzled as they traced the lines of it; the metal buckled, and gouts of it fell like incandescent tears and burned for a moment on the earth.

"Already open," he said.

Pasiphae and Karpos glanced at each other. "Yes," the queen said, "the earthquake, surely—or the gods making the way clear for you to enter—"

"Not clear enough," the king said slowly. He laid his palms on the blocks of stone that barred the way inside, and a cloud of smoke rose and hid both blocks and hands from view. Fire slid up along his spine, beneath his skin. "But the door's metal has not buckled. It is open because someone opened it." He turned and swept his empty eyes over the people ranged behind him. "Where is Phaidra?"

Someone cried out, in the silence. A shadow lurched into Minos's glow and folded in on itself—a girl, gasping, whimpering as she clutched at the long, ragged wounds that covered her.

"She was here," the girl whispered up at the king. "Gone, now."

Minos reached for the girl with one chipped, blackened hand. "Who are you?" he said.

She rolled her head on the earth. A trickle of blood ran from the corner of her mouth and pooled beneath her cheek. "Melaina. Of Athens." Her voice was so faint, and his crackling skin so loud, that he had to lean down next to her. Her eyes wandered, half-lidded, from his face to the sky, which was lightening from blue-black to blue-grey.

"And where did Princess Phaidra go, Melaina of Athens?"

"Not just her," Melaina said thickly. "Ariadne too. The Prince of Athens. Icarus."

She reared up on her elbows. The trickle of blood became a gush. Deucalion knelt and eased her back down.

Flame sizzled and spat as Minos breathed. "*Where did they go, child?*"

"They were all here. They . . . are going to . . . the sea. To get Daedalus. To escape. From you."

"Icarus," Minos said. "Daedalus. Theseus." The crowd murmured and shifted.

Melaina's eyes were closed, now. Her own breaths were shallow, with long pauses between.

"Which way, Melaina?" Deucalion said. He wove a net of silver wind across her face and she smiled, a little. "Melaina? Which way did they go?" Karpos bent over his shoulder, frowning, one hand on Deucalion's back.

Her smile looked sleepy. "There," she murmured, waving limply, maybe at the east. "And Icarus flew."

Pasiphae stepped closer to her husband—as close as she could get, without touching the plumes of flame that were rising from his tattered skin. "He flew?" she snapped.

Melaina gritted her teeth. More blood frothed between them. She squeezed her eyes shut and grasped at the grass and dirt with clawed fingers.

"*Girl*," the queen said, and Karpos said, "My Queen—she's dead."

Minos threw his head back in a steaming, spitting arc. Sparks gushed from his mouth when he laughed. Deucalion took Karpos's hand and held it tightly, as they watched the king.

"And so the gods set me on a new path," Minos said.

"Husband?" Pasiphae's voice was a growl.

The king spun so that his body and his fire blurred. "I shall kill those who must die," he said as he spun. The words rippled and hissed. He lifted his arms and sent plumes of fire up from his fingers and forearms, so high that the mountain's peak and the darkness above it were lit brighter than day. The glow lingered and spread, pulsing with a web of silver lightning.

He stopped whirling as suddenly as he'd started. "We go to the sea," he said. "I shall make a few more offerings to the gods, before I give myself to them."

He set off down the path, past the crowd, which did not murmur, now. Pasiphae followed, and Deucalion and Karpos. Only Glaucus lingered, for a moment, leaning on his stick in the livid glare of his father's godmark, gazing down at the dead girl on the ground.

CHAPTER TWENTY-SIX

Daedalus was a small, dark shadow in front of the shepherd's hut. *He heard my wings*, Icarus thought, then: *Don't cry, for gods' sake; you'll fall out of the sky even more clumsily.*

Daedalus was crying. He wiped at the tears with the backs of his hands and moved his mouth soundlessly. "I know," Icarus said breathlessly after he'd landed and sprawled and laughed. "I know," he said again as his father touched his feathers, still cool and moist from the wind. "It was Phaidra—she did this—" and he told him quickly of the mountain rescue, and of Sotiria, and the people who were coming, even now, to the cliff above the little island.

"So we have to go," he finished. "Now. We have to see whether there *is* a ship, at least, so that we can give them some sort of warning, if we need to." He paused. "I'll carry you there," he said in a rush. Daedalus cocked his head and frowned. "Yes, it's tiring—but you weigh barely more than a child, Father. Here: put your arms around my neck, and climb onto my back."

The thought of Phaidra was enough to carry them both up off the ground and into the sky that was full of dawn, now so bright that Icarus felt his eyes shift and focus in an entirely new way. He wheeled higher and higher and angled his glide so that he'd be able to show his father the way he'd come. Daedalus made a high, keening noise that was so unlike anything Icarus had ever heard from him that he assumed it must be laughter.

He craned to find his friends, with this new vision that was so keen it almost hurt him—and he found fire instead. The king, who was made of flames that reached up like incandescent, rippling fingers. Black smoke wreathed him, with the fire, but Icarus could still see the solid lines of his limbs and skull. Ranks and ranks of people followed him, but at some distance. He flowed out ahead of them, scoring a smouldering trench into the earth as he went.

Where are they? Icarus thought, dipping wildly, hardly hearing his father's shout—and then, through a wisp of cloud, he saw them: six small, flattened shapes. They were struggling: bending, lurching, a couple falling behind the others, forcing the rest to slow, too. King Minos was closer to them than he was to his own people. *They're too weak—of course they are*, Icarus thought. *I have to help*—but even as he tucked his head down and prepared to dive toward them, he knew it would do no good. *You'd save Phaidra, maybe one other, and then be too tired yourself to save the others. No. It cannot be your choice. Go back; see if there's a ship. Gods and gulls, let there be a ship.*

He sang warning and strength to them, as he turned away. He sang, "Faster, friends," and other things that weren't words, and barely even thoughts. As he did, his head swam with dizziness and the skin under his feathers lifted in a long, cold shudder. Daedalus tightened his hold, which made the dizziness subside—but as Icarus flew back toward the sea, he felt fear settle like stones in his belly.

The water was white-gold with rising sun so bright

that he could see nothing except flatness that curved a bit, where his vision ended. As his eyes adjusted to the dazzle, he saw wave ripples on the sea—and a tiny, solid patch of darkness caught among them.

"There it is!" he cried up to Daedalus, not sure if words or song were coming out of his mouth.

The ship was well up the coast: long and low in the water, shaped like the Athenian models his father had made for him to play with, as a child. Twig oars bristled from its sides. A white sail was lashed against its mast.

The moment after he'd called, a tremor of exhaustion shook him. He sucked at the wind and imagined Phaidra's arms and lips, and the angle of her neck, beneath her hair—but his weariness dragged him down toward the ragged line of cliff. He spun, and Daedalus's arms and legs slipped and squeezed. *No no no*, Icarus thought. He flapped desperately, and flexed his legs and talons because the ground was whirling up to meet them and he had no idea what else to do.

The force of their landing threw them apart, and nearly over the cliff's edge. Daedalus scrambled to sit, his legs dangling; Icarus lay for a moment longer with his cheek in the grass and dirt. Already some of his feathers were withdrawing into his skin, leaving trails of pain in their wake. He watched one of his slender wing bones warp and thicken, and he moaned because it hurt, and because he *couldn't* change—not yet.

"Uh," his father said from above him. "*Uh.*"

"Fine," Icarus said, "Up, yes." His voice was changing too, or maybe his ears; maybe both. As soon as he was standing he had to bend over again to retch up a thick, yellowish ooze that tasted like rot.

"The ship," he gasped, when he'd finished, and

wiped his mouth on the feathers that still covered the back of his hand. "It's well away from the island— too far—I wanted to be able to fly you there right away, but now I'm so tired . . . I should be flying back for *them*, but I can't, and the king is so close behind them."

Daedalus put his hand on Icarus's. "Wait," Icarus heard him say, through a buzzing that had started in his ears. "Nothing to do except wait."

And so they did, as the sun climbed over the sea. Icarus tried not to look too often at the ship, which seemed to be crawling south, toward them; he fixed his gaze on the island instead, with its tree and eagle's nest. He remembered how he'd longed to reach it, before his wings had worked. Before Phaidra—and then he remembered her tiny, helpless shape and the king's fire, and he stood up to wait, facing the way she and the others would come.

When they finally did, Asterion's horns were the first things Icarus saw, flashing in the sun that was now almost directly overhead. The horns, and his hair, and Phaidra's—and then all of them were in sight, moving far too slowly toward the cliff. Icarus ran to them, though his legs didn't feel as if they belonged to him: they were slow and leaden, and he stumbled over his own feet, which ended in both toes and talons.

"He's so close," Phaidra gasped when her arms were around him and her head was on his shoulder. Feathers prickled instantly, reaching for her.

"I know." Icarus buried his face in her hair and breathed in a scent which was new and already beloved. "But the ship's nearly here. I'll get all of you onto it before the king catches up."

Alphaios crumpled, when they got to the cliff. He

lay on his side, his eyes closed as Ariadne stood above him, stooped, sweatier than Icarus had ever seen her, even after a dance. Theseus knelt with a hand on the bloodied place where his wound had been. His brow was furrowed; Icarus assumed he was speaking to the ship's captain with his mind-voice. Chara limped past everyone and sat down heavily, slipping her legs over the ledge. She held up a hand and looked over her shoulder at Asterion—but he wasn't looking at her. His muscles twitched and strained as he dragged himself toward Daedalus, who was waiting with his gaze cast down.

When Asterion reached him, Daedalus's eyes flickered up and over his naked body, with its streaks of scars, sweat, blood and dirt. Then, slowly, Daedalus knelt and bent his head.

After a silence that seemed very long, Asterion said, "No." His voice shook; so did the hand he set on Daedalus's head. "Stand. Stand with us."

Daedalus did. He made noises that Icarus understood, and that he knew Asterion would not. Icarus said, "He had no idea what the king and Ariadne were plotting. Had no idea they'd put you in there too. He's hated himself all these years, for what happened to you, and to the Athenians. He—"

"Enough," Asterion said gently to Daedalus, whose noises sputtered into silence. "Please." He paused and tipped his head up to the white-golden-blue above.

I can't imagine how he feels now, looking at the sky, Icarus thought. *Even I can't imagine this.*

Asterion sucked in a breath that made the space beneath his ribs go briefly hollow. His eyes were back on Daedalus. "Do you know, Master Daedalus, what I have always thought of first, when I've thought of you? That night when you filled the room at Knossos with all kinds of mechanical beasts—when you spoke my brother Androgeus's name, even though you knew it would enrage the king. That night."

"Icarus," Phaidra said quietly, into the silence. They all followed her pointing finger; they all saw the shimmer of heat that was warping the air, and the drift of black smoke that was rising.

"We should go down to the ledge," Phaidra said.

Icarus shook his head. "I won't have enough room there—I'll need to run"—*because I'm so horribly tired, so dizzy; gods, I just want to lie down with Phaidra and sleep.* "Father," he said, "let me take you first."

Now Daedalus shook his head, wildly. "No—not me—me *last.*"

Ariadne, who couldn't possibly have understood him, said, "Asterion should go last: he's the only one strong enough to fend off the king."

Asterion sucked in his breath. Chara said, "No. He's not changing—not again. And anyway, he may be too weak to."

And so Asterion went first. "He's survived this long," Chara said as Asterion and Icarus were hovering, Asterion's feet just above her head. "Do *not* drop him." Asterion's grin made Icarus feel suddenly stronger.

"I'll be careful," he said, and launched them off the cliff.

Waves, sun, reflected sky and real sky—the world spun around him. The ship dipped and wobbled. He remembered the clarity of his first flight, only hours earlier, and tried to believe that this, now, was the same vision, the same muscles and feathered skin. The ship wobbled nearer. He saw men on the deck, some standing, some bent over, rowing. They bobbed as if the deck were water and they were seabirds; he blinked and focused only on the weathered planks. He wheeled, dived, and fell. His vision went white, and his ears filled with a piercing noise that drowned out every other sound.

Asterion's hand on his shoulder brought him back. "Think of Phaidra," Icarus heard him say. "Think of her *now*, Icarus: you need to go back."

He did. He cleared the cliff, but only barely.

Minos's smoke was much thicker, now. The heat-warped air was red.

Chara was next. Twice Icarus swooped dangerously close to the waves—once because he was so tired, and her grip kept loosening, and once immediately after that, because they were both laughing so giddily that he couldn't stay aloft. "Gods, I missed you," she cried, and he sang joy back to her in his mother's voice before he bore her down to the ship.

Back on the cliff, Alphaios stepped toward him. "No," Icarus panted, "Ariadne now"—*Because she mustn't be alone with my father.* But Daedalus waved his good hand at Alphaios and grunted another stream of broken "*nos.*"

Alphaios felt far heavier than he had been at the mountain—and suddenly the leaden sensation was back, more intense than ever. Alphaios tumbled off Icarus's listing back well above the deck. *I've killed him,* Icarus thought dimly. *I'm a danger to all of us.* He heard himself screech fear, when only moments before he'd been so happy—and he heard Chara call, "He's fine, Icarus! Go on, if you can: go on." Phaidra raised her arms to him and he straightened up and went.

The first thing he heard, after he slammed into the earth, was shouting. He didn't look toward it, when he staggered to his feet. Why would he, when he knew what he'd see?

He was so dizzy he could barely make out Ariadne and Daedalus—but they were both there: she hadn't pushed him off the cliff. "Father," he whispered. "You now." But Daedalus shook his head as he had before and gestured at Ariadne. Icarus had no will left to argue.

"You'd have left me here," she said. She was very close; he could feel her breath. "If I'd been last."

"Maybe," he heard himself say. He wondered if he were feverish.

"You won't drop me into the sea, will you? Icarus. Think of how much we share. Remember: we were children together." Her voice was shaking.

"Yes," he said, trying to get his breath, to slow his heart. "I remember everything. Are you sorry, Princess? For any of it?"

In her silence, Minos's voice rose above the others— shouting his children's names, one by one. Shouting Icarus's name too, and Daedalus's. The words were garbled, but Icarus understood each of them.

His vision cleared a bit; he saw Ariadne's scarlet lips, slightly parted, and her bright, steady gaze. He said, "I won't be the one to decide your fate. That's up to Theseus, or the gods, or Chara. I suppose you'll think me weak for this, too."

Phaidra, he thought—but it was barely enough. He strained his way back into the sky. The wind pulled him sideways and up and down; he gulped as if he were swimming, not flying.

The deck was cool against his cheek. Phaidra's lips were cool. He clasped her hands to his chest, which was part feathers, part flesh. "My love," she said. "There's just your father, now. Just him—and then we're free."

Icarus blinked, after he'd tumbled back onto the cliff's edge. The blinking was very difficult, and seemed to take a very long time.

"Up," Daedalus said, as he had before.

Icarus rose. He was crying: everything wavered in tears he couldn't feel. Everything, including Minos. The king was close enough that Icarus could see his smile, through the smoke and flame. The white, white teeth in his blackened skin.

"I can't do it, Father," Icarus said. "Can't carry you. I'm so sorry."

Daedalus was holding something—Icarus noticed this only now. Wings. The wings his father had made, month after month, from branches and his son's plucked feathers.

Behind them—so close—Minos cackled and snapped.

"Up," Daedalus said again.

They turned and leapt together into the air above the sea.

———— · ————

Chara hadn't been able to draw a deep, clean breath since the wind had taken it away, over the water. She still felt like laughing, but she couldn't. She wanted to gabble all the words that were crowding her throat, where her breath should have been, but she couldn't. She turned to look at Asterion; she put a hand in his thick, warm hair and smiled at his smile.

Daedalus and Icarus were small but distinct, on the cliff. *I love them both*, she thought. When she turned back to the deck behind her, she thought, *I love all of them*—even Ariadne, somehow. Even the princess, who was gripping the side next to Theseus, her bright, hungry gaze on the open sea.

Everyone started, when Icarus and Daedalus jumped. Phaidra gave a strangled cry—because the moment their feet left the ground, Minos was behind them on the ledge. He was a swift, flaring, stilling blur that lit the sky around him to a brightness beyond noon.

Daedalus was gliding—too high, which was better than too low. *How does* he *have wings?* Chara thought. The feathers matched Icarus's, but they glowed, too, with the silver of Daedalus's godmark.

Above him, Icarus weaved and dipped.

Pasiphae was on the cliff, now. Deucalion. Karpos. *Farewell, all of you*, Chara thought, as Asterion's hand clutched convulsively at hers.

"What's that?" Alphaios said hoarsely. "What's the king holding?"

It looked tiny, from the ship. Tiny and slender, shuddering with firelight as the king drew it off his shoulder.

Daedalus's silver-feathered glide ended in a plunge. He was in the water by the ship; men swarmed to the side, reaching with hands and oars.

Still too far above, Icarus rose and spun and sputtered.

"It's a bow," Asterion said. "Oh, gods. *It's a bow*."

Minos raised the bow, which was burning. He loosed an arrow. It coursed with his flame, as it arced down into the waves.

Phaidra screamed, "Icarus!", and for a moment he

was flying again, straight and true, toward her. But then he twisted, spine to the waves, face to the sky, wings churning.

Minos loosed another arrow, and it caught him in the chest.

So many voices rose, but Chara hardly heard them. The sound in her ears was white and red, and it spread out beyond her and changed the colour of the sky. The only clean, clear spot was where Icarus was falling. She could see every point of kindled flame, every feather that blackened. She could see his beak becoming nose and lips, and his wings becoming hands. At the last, she could see his eyes, dull and fixed on nothing.

He landed far from the ship, with a splash and a hissing of water and steam.

Phaidra's voice shattered Chara's white and red. "Get him out! *Get him out!*" She was leaning too far out over the boat's side, her arms flailing, only one foot on the deck. As Theseus pulled her back, Chara rose (she hadn't even noticed that she'd sat) and stumbled over to her.

"He's dead," Chara said, gripping Phaidra's wrist. "He died as he fell."

Phaidra's mouth was gaping. Spittle dripped down her chin and scattered in the wind. Her hands were like claws on the wood.

A flaming arrow lodged in the deck behind them. Men shouted and stamped at it as another arrow hissed over all of them and into the water off the stern. Suddenly there were gobbets of fire among the arrows: bits of spinning, streaming flame that sent everyone on deck sprawling or dodging.

"Turn about! Turn!" someone shouted.

"The wind isn't right!" shouted someone else. "We'll

never come around in time!"

Chara felt Phaidra's arms slacken and caught her as she slumped. Chara crouched, holding her hands, and gazed back up. Minos was nearly invisible within his own fire. She saw his fingers, extended above his head; she watched sparks detach themselves from them and grow, grow, until they hung above him. His fingers closed, and the fire sped out and down, toward the ship: so much fire, turning the sky to a boiling, blazing sea.

The figures on the cliff trembled in heat and maybe, Chara thought, her own tears, but she saw the queen put one hand on Deucalion's arm and one on Glaucus's; saw the three of them step even closer to the edge. Silver poured from their mouths and swept out into the flame.

A new wind rose, and the current beneath the waves shifted. "No!" someone near Chara yelled—for the wind was bearing the king's flame toward them even more quickly. Before it reached them, the sky above the cliff darkened, behind his glow. Heavy black clouds took shape from nowhere; heavy black rain poured down in sheets that advanced behind the fire and doused it, and then the ship.

Chara rubbed her eyes clear and whispered, "The princes' wind. The queen's water. They're *helping* us?"

The ship lifted and plunged, as it turned. The waves rose taller and taller, as dark as the rain beneath their foaming white tops. The last of the flame scattered and drowned, and the ship cut a fresh, clear path into the sea. The cliff was receding so swiftly that Minos looked like a blurry setting sun.

Asterion braced himself on the side next to Chara and raised both his arms. Through the rain and spray, she saw the tiny figures of Glaucus and Deucalion raise their own. She thought that Glaucus might be jumping up and down, but she couldn't be sure. It was all dwindling—the rain and fire, the cliff, the people, the mountain, the palaces and huts and waterfalls.

She felt Asterion leave the side and turned, herself. He was struggling up the slick, tilting deck to Daedalus, his horns catching the sunlight that was returning. *Oh, gods*, Chara thought. *You cruel, bloody gods*—and she followed.

Daedalus was lying on his side in the damp wreckage of his wings. As Chara crawled to him she wondered whether he'd even seen Icarus fall—but then she reached him and looked at his eyes and knew that he had. Asterion eased the bindings off one of his arms and started to pull the sodden feathers away, but his long-fingered hand lashed out and wrenched them back again.

"Master Daedalus," Asterion began. "Master—"

Daedalus rolled onto his back, pulling the remnants of the wings around him like a cloak. He stared past them at the empty blue of the sky as the ship bore them south and west and away.

CHAPTER TWENTY-SEVEN

For two days they sailed through calm, open water. The sky stayed blue; at night, it was thick with stars that also lit the sea. Dolphins leapt and chittered. Islands smudged the horizon, but the ship's course didn't change.

"This wasn't the route we wanted," one of the sailors said to Theseus. "I'm sorry it will take us so long to return to Athens."

"It cannot be helped," Theseus said. He smiled at the man, who stared at his own feet, shifting them awkwardly on the boards. *They love him*, Chara thought. *I'm sure he speaks strong, princely, reassuring words into their minds. Now that he's not in ours, anymore.* Even the hum of his mind-voice was gone—from her head and Alphaios's, at least.

Near dusk on the second day, she heard Alphaios say to Theseus, "What are we going to do with *her*? Surely you won't bring her back to Athens with us?"

Theseus didn't look over at Ariadne, who was standing very straight at the prow, where she'd been for most of the two days. She looked as if she were trying to smell Athens on the wind.

Theseus didn't answer Alphaios. Instead he sat down beside Phaidra and took one of her limp hands in both of his. Her gaze flickered up to his, then down again.

"What's wrong with him?" Alphaios muttered to Chara. "Why won't he *do* anything?"

Chara let out a long, slow breath and licked salt from her lips. "I don't know. Maybe he's waiting for the gods to decide for him."

"Or maybe," Asterion said, his eyes steady on Ariadne's back, "she frightens him, too."

The third day dawned grey and sullen. "When will we be there?" Ariadne said, to no one in particular. "When? Because I can't—"

"Look," Asterion said. The word shook.

Chara turned with the others, to face back the way they'd come. The horizon there was alight with a crimson that blossomed and spread upward within moments. "The Goddess's mountain," she whispered, as Phaidra cried out, beside her. "The king." *It took him this long*, she thought. *Three days. Maybe because he wanted more sacrifices, after Icarus—or dancing, singing, speeches. Maybe because it wasn't so easy, after all, to sacrifice himself.*

An explosion lifted the sea. The ship seemed to leap and hover, just as Icarus had; then it plunged back into the surging waves. Chara fell—they all did—and lay sprawled on the deck, gasping, gazing at Asterion. He was pale and wide-eyed, but he scrambled up first, and held out his hand to her.

The crimson sky was filling with darkness. *Smoke*, she thought, clutching and leaning as the ship continued to pitch. *Whatever's left of the mountain.*

"Polymnia," Asterion said—not to her, or anyone. She covered his gripping hand with her own and he pulled his away.

Theseus was on Phaidra's other side. He narrowed his eyes at the smoke, which had already consumed the fire. "The king has given himself to his god, at last," he said, turning to Phaidra. When he put his hands on hers she flinched and sagged against Chara, her eyes closed. Asterion grasped her forearm and she opened her eyes.

"Our brothers?" she whispered. "Our mother?"

As he shook his head, the ship surged up and tipped. For just a moment, Chara was in the air, touching nothing at all. *Not like when Icarus carried me, when I saw his feathers in the light, and the land, and the sea*—but now the sea was washing over the deck, over her, because she'd landed with a jarring *thump*. The water was cold, and it stung cuts she hadn't known she had. She scrabbled at the soaked boards and slid, Asterion beside her, his legs tangling with hers. Daedalus tumbled by them in a blur of sodden, trailing feathers.

"Row!" the captain roared from somewhere. *That won't help*, Chara thought: the ship wasn't levelling off or righting itself—it was bucking once more, sending them back into the air and onto hands and knees and bellies, slipping, helpless. A wind rose, as they struggled. It lashed at the sail, which sailors swarmed to tie down. It battered Chara's skin with scalding breath and cinders, and drowned all of their cries with its own howling. She lay with her arms over her head and pressed her eyes shut so that all she could see was darkness—but only for a moment, because the wind lifted and threw the ship yet again, and she tumbled, scrabbling and reaching for something that would keep her still. Up and down, sideways and down, in the screaming and the heat: ears that heard and skin that felt, but eyes that saw nothing but night. She tried to draw enough breath to scream—his name; she wouldn't lose him now—but something came at her in the night, and struck her so hard that she didn't have time for any more fear.

———— · ————

The silence sounded thick.

She opened her eyes and saw only sky. It wasn't black or fiery: it was a thick, sluggish grey. *Ash,* thought some part of her that was still able to think. *Whatever's left of the mountain.* She remembered having thought this before—not long ago? On the ship. Just before the storm.

Where am I now?

Before she could move to find out, a face eased into sight above her. "Told you she was waking up." The voice wobbled and warped. Chara rolled her head on the ground and felt water pop, unsettlingly deep in her head.

"This one is too," said another voice—very clearly, now that the water was gone.

The face dipped closer. It was a young man's: sun-browned, laced with wrinkles around the eyes, which were brown and wide with curiosity. He brushed a long strand of hair away from these eyes and said, "So—who are you?"

Chara tried to say her own name, but suddenly there was water in her throat too, and she choked and choked—no breath; no space inside her body for anything except thick, burning fluid. Hands took her by the shoulders and turned her onto her side. They pummelled her back, between her shoulder blades, and the fluid came out in a short, violent rush.

"Chara," she gasped. "And who are *you*?"

His smile filled her with such relief that she had to

close her eyes, just for a moment. "Diokles," he said. "And if you can sit up, you'll see Pelagia. And Xenon. Oh, and the people you already know, of course."

She sat up too quickly; Diokles grasped her shoulders again, as she tipped backward. Her vision swam with grey: sky and water; the sand that sloped down to the water and clumped between her toes. In a blink or two, the sand turned to a dull gold. She looked up and saw Asterion, who was sitting too far away from her, hunched over with his horns nearly touching the sand.

She tried to stand, but her legs were too weak. She crawled to him instead, past people she hardly saw, and said his name when she was nearly there. He lifted his head. His cheeks were as grey as the sky; his cheeks, and the rest of him, except for his horns. "Freckles," he said, and coughed until he was wheezing. He reached for her, when he'd quieted. Pulled her in against him and pressed his lips to her forehead. His skin was rough.

"Chara?" called Alphaios. His voice was high and quavery. She stirred and saw him reeling toward them. His face was also coated in grey, except for the blood that was streaming from his brow and down along his nose.

"Careful!" cried a woman from behind him. "You've hit your head."

"You have," Chara said, when Alphaios sat down with a *thump* beside them. "You're bleeding."

Alphaios grinned. "I know." He laughed then, and she did too, even though she wasn't sure why.

"You're both mad," Asterion said, but she could hear his smile.

They stopped laughing when Diokles called, "This

one's injured, too." He was bending over someone, and Theseus was standing above them both. Chara didn't recognize the prince, at first: he was even greyer than Alphaios and Asterion were. She finally glanced down at herself and saw that she was covered in the same thing they were—a mud-like substance that was cracking, now, as it dried.

Asterion rose, drawing her up with him. She leaned into him, and they walked very slowly toward Theseus. Every time her heels and toes met the sand, she felt stronger—strong enough to look around at the beach: at the sailors clustered near the shore, and the ones still lying on the ground; at the long arm of rock that enclosed the harbour where Minos and Pasiphae's storm had driven them, and the place where the rock gave way to hills patched with green that seemed too bright, against the grey. At Diokles and a woman who was maybe the queen's age, and Ariadne, splayed on her back near them, her eyes fixed and glassy.

"Princess," Theseus said. Chara saw Diokles and the woman raise their eyebrows at each other. "Ariadne. Can you hear me?"

She's dead, Chara thought, *thank the gods*—and her gut heaved, even though there was nothing more inside her to spew out.

"Ariadne?" Asterion knelt. Chara felt a different roiling in her gut as she watched him put his hand to his sister's cheek. He didn't leave it there: he slapped her so hard that all the grey mud flew off his arm in a stinging spatter.

Ariadne sucked in one rasping breath, and another, and coughed as the rest of them had. She blinked and opened her eyes even wider, and fastened them on him.

"I knew you wouldn't go so quietly," Asterion said. "Sister."

She struggled to sit up, and got as far as her elbows before Diokles put a hand on her shoulder to keep her still. "Gently," he said. "Look at your leg."

Chara looked too, and winced. Ariadne screamed. Her right calf was bent behind her, as if she'd been trying to turn around when she fell. She thrust at Diokles, who rocked back on his heels, and wrapped her hands around the ankle. With another cry, she wrenched it out straight. She gnawed on her lower lip as she pulled herself forward.

"Don't," the woman said, "I'm sure it's broken."

"Pelagia's right," said Diokles, "you'll only make it worse if you—"

"Who are you?" Ariadne spat, twisting to face them. "Other than fools who don't know who *I* am? I will get up; I will get back to the ship."

She did get up. She teetered, flapping her arms as she had when she used to mock Icarus. She tried to put weight on her right foot; Chara heard the hiss of her breath, in and out, and watched her fingers flex into claws. Slowly, hissing with every movement, she hopped down to the shore. The rest of them followed her, even more slowly. Chara kept her eyes on Ariadne's uninjured leg. *Go on—give out*, she thought, and, *No, no—stay straight*.

"I've never seen anything like her," Diokles said, so admiringly that Chara snorted—but then Ariadne reached the shore and gave a ragged cry, and Chara finally looked away from her, toward the water.

Except that it wasn't water: it was ash, as thick as the sky, choking the waves. A soup of it pushed sluggishly up onto the sand and retreated, leaving a long, thick, dirty line. The ship was on its side in what should have been the shallows. The mast had snapped; a forest of oars stuck up out of the sludge around it. There were bodies too, Chara saw, with terrible slowness. Arms sticking up as the oars were. Faces jutting above the grey, like rocks.

"The captain," Theseus said, gesturing at one of the faces. "I found him while the rest of you were unconscious. Him, and so many other friends from home."

Ariadne dragged her matted hair away from her face with both hands. "We'll never get there." Her voice sounded loud, even though she was barely speaking above a whisper. "The gods are angry at us. We'll never get to Athens."

"We?" Alphaios said. "*We*? Prince Theseus: tell her—"

A guttural sound tangled with Alphaios's words, and all of them except Ariadne turned toward it. Daedalus was crouched some distance away, where the sand curved to match the arc of the rock arm. His feathers were gone, as was his loincloth; he was naked, rocking slowly, his spindly cave fingers stretched in front of his eyes. Phaidra was sitting cross-legged beside him. *How did I forget about them?* Chara thought. *I should go to them now—I should try to help*—but they looked so far away, and she was so tired; she stayed where she was.

Alphaios cleared his throat and looked back at Theseus. "My Prince?" Alphaios said—but Theseus was walking away from them, weaving a little, his head slumped to his chest.

Chara shifted her gaze from Daedalus to Diokles. She put a hand on his arm and squeezed. "Please tell us what happened. Tell us where we are."

He exchanged another glance with Pelagia and nodded once, as if she'd used a mind-voice. "We will— but not yet. Let us take you to a place where we can tend to your injuries—where you can wash and rest."

Chara heard Polymnia's voice beneath his, promising them the same things—but it was no more than a fading echo.

Asterion said, "Is it far from here? Because some of us may not be ready for a long walk."

Diokles smiled at Ariadne, whose gaze had finally moved from the ship to him. "Don't worry. Xenon will carry them."

A giant of a man stepped forward and bowed. His legs, as big around as the boles of ancient trees, were ash-covered up to mid-thigh. *He went into the sea and brought us out*, Chara thought, and she remembered the flame and the wind and the wild tipping of the deck. She sank to her knees in the sand.

"No!" Ariadne cried as Xenon straightened and walked to her. "I have no idea who you are—do not *touch* me—"

"Take me first, then," Chara said. "I seem to be weaker than I thought."

The giant stooped, and she wrapped her arms around his massive neck. His cheeks bristled with black hair, though there was none on his head. His eyes were nearly invisible beneath the jutting bone of his brows.

"Chara?" Asterion said from below, and she waved at him.

"I'll see you there," she said. "Wherever that is." And she laid her head on Xenon's chest as he bore her away from the sea.

———— • ————

She fell asleep, as Xenon carried her, though she hadn't realized she was sleepy. One moment she was watching the landscape, thinking, *Olive trees. Rocks. Lemon trees. Rocks. Pine trees*; the next she was on her side with her fists beneath her chin. Her muscles were aching, and her tongue was so swollen with thirst that she couldn't do anything except moan. She forced herself onto her back. Once again she stared up at the sky, which was a much deeper grey now, shot through with sickly orange. *Where am I?*—and once again she felt dizzy with not-knowing and dread.

"Lean on me," said Asterion, very close to her. He smiled and drew her up until she was sitting against him. An old woman squatted in front of them, holding out a crude clay mug. Chara took it in her hands and gulped water that was colder than any she'd drunk before. When she was finished she looked past the woman and saw that they were inside the circle of a low stone wall. Shadow-people were leaning on the wall, staring down with wide, dark eyes.

"About time you woke up," Ariadne said, from across the circle. There was a hearth in the centre; the smoke from the fire twisted in the air between them. "They wouldn't explain anything to us until you did." Her last word ended in a yelp and a groan: Diokles was sitting beside her, winding cloth slowly and tightly around her injured leg, which had been splinted with a length of wood. "Stop!" she cried, and lifted her hand as if she'd strike him. He didn't flinch. His hands went still, poised over her leg.

"Truly?" the old woman said as she straightened slowly. She took two shambling steps. "Do you want to end up like me already, girl—with you still so young and pretty?"

Chara watched Ariadne swallow. "Fine," she said at last, gesturing at Diokles without looking at him. He arched a brow and resumed wrapping.

"So," Alphaios said. He was kneeling, as if he was about to leap up and go somewhere else. Theseus was standing beside him, his eyes on something far away. *The sea*, Chara thought. *The wrecked ship. Athens.* Then she thought, *Daedalus?* She glanced wildly around at the circle and found him, lying on his side, facing the wall. The knobs of his spine thrust against his skin. Phaidra was curled up with her head almost touching his, staring almost without blinking into the fire.

"One of you can explain," Alphaios went on. "Now that Chara's awake."

Pelagia crouched next to Chara and handed her a bowl of what turned out to be stew. "I'll begin," Pelagia said. Chara hardly heard her, over the sound of her own feverish chewing. The stew was rich and thick and maybe the most delicious thing she'd ever tasted.

"There was a storm," Pelagia said, and Ariadne snorted. "Unlike anything we'd ever seen before," Pelagia continued, ignoring her. "And we've seen our share of storms. We watched it come, driven by gods, or godmarks. We watched, and we saw your ship being tossed on the sea like a twig."

"Other ships have found us," Diokles said, "some by design, and others accidentally, driven by storms. We're used to going down to the beach to wait. Xenon usually waits in the water, because he can hold out against the current. But he couldn't do that this time: the waves were just too strong."

Chara followed his gaze and saw the giant looming on the other side of the wall, at the edge of the firelight.

Diokles turned back to the splint and Pelagia smiled at his bent head. *Maybe she's his mother,* Chara thought—because she remembered, faintly but without doubt, her own mother smiling like that at her.

"The sea tossed many of you directly onto the shore," Pelagia said. "You, Ariadne, looked as if you were flying. We'd never seen anyone land so far up on the beach."

Daedalus's shoulder began to twitch, over and over. Phaidra laid her hand on it, and it stilled.

Diokles said, "We waited for the sky to lighten a bit, so that we could see how many of you were alive. Many weren't. We watched the ash thicken in the water and trap the others. Xenon waded out, when the storm had blown over. It took him a long time, but he managed, and he pulled up a few who lived. He left the others."

"The rest I know," Theseus said, and Chara started at the hardness of his voice. "Tell me where we are. I am the Prince of Athens, and I command you to tell me this, *now.*"

Pelagia's eyes widened. Chara thought, *Ah, the mind-voice,* and the memory of its bone-deep thrumming made her shiver. "Prince of Athens," Pelagia said, very quietly, "you are nowhere." A strand of grey-black hair fell in front of her face and caught between her lips, but she didn't brush it away.

Diokles knotted the cloth beneath Ariadne's knee, set her leg gently on the ground, and rose. "You've washed up on an island that may never have had a name. The only names here are ours."

"And who," Chara said, "are you?"

His eyes glinted with reflected fire. "Exiles," he said. "Castoffs. The unmarked and the mark-mad and the children who've been born to them." He drew a deep breath and leaned back against the wall, crossing his arms over his chest. "Take Xenon, there. He came on a ship captained by one of those who knows where we are. He was chained; we saw the marks on his wrists and ankles, when he finally let us get close. He charged around the island for weeks, bellowing. We understood some of the words; others sounded like gibberish—but they weren't. We came to understand that his godmark was languages: too many for any other person to speak, or understand. Gradually he stopped running. And he stopped speaking."

Xenon didn't move. The darkness was thickening, so Chara couldn't see his eyes.

"What about you?" Alphaios said to Diokles.

"I was born here, and I'm godmarked: I can make fog."

"But no one ever needs fog," called someone who was outside the wall.

Diokles grinned. "Right. So I'm allowed to stay."

Silence fell, for a moment. The flames spat and leapt; Asterion drew back, away from the heat. Daedalus's foot drummed a dull, uneven pattern on the earth.

"Monsters," Ariadne said. Asterion's hand tightened on Chara's. "You're all monsters, to live like this, away from the world."

Pelagia shook her head. "This is *our* world. It's a fine one, too: we have sheep and goats, brought or given as gifts; we have bee hives and vegetables in rows, and nets that bulge with fish. You'll see all of this tomorrow, in whatever daylight there is."

Ariadne went on, as if she hadn't heard the woman, "The priestesses said there were those who wanted to send my father to a place like this, where his power wouldn't frighten anyone. *They* wanted to. But now it's me who's here. I'm a princess. A princess! I danced for . . . I . . ." She pressed her hand against her mouth with a gasp.

"And Agapios was a metalworker," Pelagia snapped. "Galene had four children. Everyone here has lost something. Everyone here is home."

As Ariadne opened her mouth to reply, silver-white light lit the heavy clouds above them.

"What's that?" Phaidra whispered.

Diokles glanced at her. "Zenobia. She lives in the forest that covers the highest hills. We leave food for her, now and then, because we're never sure if she gets enough on her own. She's like Xenon was, except that her mark-madness hasn't passed. Sometimes she fills the sky with white fire shaped like flowers or fish, or people's faces. There are others like her, who've chosen solitude over company. We tend to them if we can."

Ariadne lurched to her feet. Her hair was as tangled as Chara knew her own would be, once it finally grew out, but somehow the princess looked beautiful and fierce. "We'll fix the ship. Theseus! Surely there are enough of us left alive to fix it—we'll do that, and we'll leave this horrible, horrible place."

Theseus turned to Pelagia. "We will need you," he said. "For there are not enough of us left alive."

Pelagia raised a brow and smiled, a little. "We'll help you with your ship and your injuries, just as we've helped those others who've come, and then gone. We'll ask you no questions—though we might wish to, given your princess, and your young man with horns." She glanced at Asterion as she said this. His horns shone like molten gold in the firelight. "We'll see you safely on your way back to your world, whatever it may be."

"Good," Theseus said. "Thank you."

For a long time, no one spoke. Chara watched the white light, and waited for thunder that never came.

CHAPTER TWENTY-EIGHT

Alphaios counted out the days it took to fix the ship. Every morning before he set off for the beach, he placed a stone on the wall; every evening he checked on them, as if they might have fallen or been swept away.

"What's the count now, Alphaios?" someone would call, and he'd call the number back to them. "Three." "Five." "Seven."

For many of those days, Chara stayed near the huts that had been built against the hillside below the wall, which, Pelagia told them, might once have been part of an ancient temple. "Those were also here when I came," she said on the second day, pointing at two huts with conical roofs. "But I helped build that one, and Diokles was born in it, during a winter storm."

"Filled it up with fog, too," said Amyntas, Diokles's father, "when he was three. Likely doesn't remember now how we shouted."

"Oh, I do," Diokles said over his shoulder as he trudged away with Theseus and Alphaios and Asterion, and other men and women whose names Chara didn't yet know. "You made so much noise I thought you were dying."

Despite Pelagia and Diokles's warnings, Ariadne limped up and down the path that led from the huts to the grove of lemon trees at the foot of the hill, leaning on the crutch Diokles had made her from a gnarled length of tree root. Phaidra slept for hours at a time on ash-coated grass beside the stream that ran clear and cold from somewhere up near the hill's peak. Daedalus, though, didn't move from the place where Xenon had laid him, on the first day. He'd grunted and flailed, when people tried to lift him, and they'd left him, and he'd been motionless ever since. So Chara stayed away from the beach, at first because she felt too weak to be of any use, and then because of Daedalus.

"Drink, Master Daedalus," she said, over and over. "Eat. Please." She soaked bits of bread in water or goat's milk and held them to his mouth, but he only stared blindly up at her. "Close your eyes, at least. Sleep." He stared and stared and never slept, never saw her. His breath barely stirred the woollen blanket someone had put over him.

"Why do you bother?" said Ariadne on the fifth day. She was leaning on the wall, her chin in her palms. "He's given up. He's as good as dead already."

Chara sat back on her heels. The clouds had finally begun to thin, and the gold loops that hung from the princess's ears blazed with new sunlight. "Icarus would have wanted me to bother," Chara said. Her voice shook, and she squeezed her eyes shut. When she opened them, Ariadne was gone.

Chara walked, when she wasn't with Daedalus. She felt stronger with every day that passed, and went farther: down through the sun-dappled lemon grove and up another, steeper hill, into the thick shadows of pine trees; up, days later, to its top. Everything fell away from her there, in tiers of red earth and silver-green trees, down to the golden crescent of beach, and the tiny human figures on it. She watched them swarming around the ship, which was nothing more than a dark blot on the sand, and then she squinted past it, at the sea that seemed to have no end. There were other islands in it—small ones that blurred when she tried to see them better. *Not Crete, though*, she thought. *Not Crete, ever again*.

"It's so beautiful," she whispered to Asterion that night. "I'll have to show you"—but he was already asleep, his head heavy on her shoulder, one of his horns cool against her throat.

On the day Alphaios called, "Nine!" a child found Chara coming back through the pine forest. The girl was as fine-boned as a bird, and had a wild fuzz of hair, and reminded Chara of herself—or what she thought she'd been. "Diokles sent me to find you," the girl said. She was panting. "Something's wrong at the beach—the man Asterion's in trouble."

Chara hardly felt herself move, but within moments she was past the lemon grove and running away from the huts, her breath burning in her chest. *I'm too slow*, she thought, and stumbled—but even as she did, Xenon closed in on her left and swept her up under his tree branch of an arm.

The sun was setting, when he put her down on the beach. People were clustered by one of the many fires that speckled the sand—fires with pots of various sizes hanging over them. She ran the last few paces and all the people moved aside, until only one was left.

Diokles raised a shaking arm and pointed at the dark bulk of the ship. "He's there," he said—but Chara had already seen. Asterion was turned toward the ship. He was on all fours, pawing at the ground with a hoof that glinted with crimson light. His other arm was bent beneath him.

"He tripped," Diokles said. "He fell, and the pot tipped—it's my mother's pot; she brought it from Thera; it's never been stable, sitting or hanging—and the boiling pitch spilled all over his arm. I thought he'd faint, but he changed into that instead, and ran around and around, roaring."

She saw the marks he'd gouged in the sand. She followed them and knelt behind him, trying not to choke on the stench of tar. His hunched shoulders were covered in fur, and his horns were full and sweeping, dragging his head down. He'd driven the tip of the left one into a plank.

"Asterion," she said quietly. She put a hand on his back, where it was skin, not fur, and he flinched. "Show me?"

Very slowly, he drew his bent arm out. It was patchy with fur that looked singed. The flesh between was raw and pink, blistered and oozing. She eased up beside him, her hand still on his back.

"It was so hot," he said. His voice was low and cracked, and muffled because of the angle of his head. "I couldn't help it." One round brown eye rolled and found her. "I'll never be able to help it."

"I know." Her own words splintered; she imagined salt and tar and ash making paths down her throat, to her chest.

He put his good hand on the ship's side. "It doesn't matter where I am: my god won't release me. So where will I go?"

She stood up. "Back to the village, first of all," she said. "So that you can have those burns dealt with."

His fur was melting back into skin, and his hoof into fingers. "I would," he said, his voice entirely a man's, now, "except that I'm stuck." He gave a loud, clear laugh, and she gave her snuffling one. She leaned down and wrapped her hands around his horn, and they laughed harder as she tugged and he twisted. He came free so suddenly that they both sprawled onto their backs.

"Is everything all right?" Diokles asked, from above them.

"Yes," Chara gasped, as Asterion got to his feet.

"Yes," he said, and then, more steadily, "Diokles. I'm sorry. Even though Pelagia said, that first night, that you'd never ask us questions, I should have warned you. I should have told you how . . . powerful my godmark was. And the moment I saw the fires and pitch, I should have gone back to the village."

Diokles was frowning—*Though maybe just because of the light?* Chara thought hopefully. "Yes," he said. "You should have." He glanced at Chara. "Is there anything else you should tell us about the other godmarks among you?"

She rose. "No," she said. "But Alphaios transforms things that once lived into other things. Theseus speaks directly into people's minds. Phaidra opens locks. One of the sailors turns water into snow, though only for an instant, and another puts lines in wood without touching it, and I think there are a few more who are marked. Ariadne and I are unmarked." She closed her eyes briefly, against the deep copper of sunset. When she opened them she said, "And that's all. Truly."

Asterion nodded. "It's just me—I'm the only real problem, here. I'll stay away until the ship's ready, if any of you want me to."

After a silence that felt far too long, Diokles said, "We'll speak more of this, with the others—but come back with me, now. My father will tend to your burns."

——— · ———

When Chara went to Daedalus later that night, after Asterion had fallen asleep, Ariadne was there, and Daedalus was sitting up.

"Master Daedalus!" Chara cried, crouching in front of him—but he gazed at her just as blindly as he had before, as the light from the hearth fire flickered across his face.

"When did this happen?" she asked Ariadne, who shrugged and walked toward the break in the wall.

"Just before sundown. He also ate that bit of bread you left this morning."

"And *you* fed him."

"Well, there was no one else here to do it, was there?" Ariadne said, and vanished into the darkness.

When Chara looked back at Daedalus, he was blinking at her. At her—seeing her for the first time since Crete. He made a strangled noise and she leaned forward. His breath was stale, and his unwashed skin stank, but she didn't turn away. "Say that again, Daedalus. Please."

He made the same noise, and this time she understood. "Minnow." One of his hands reached for her, his stony, web-wound fingers grasping at air. "Icarus," he said.

She pressed her palm against his as tears seeped through the dirt on his cheeks.

——— · ———

"Fourteen!" called Alphaios from the wall.

Chara smiled at Daedalus, who was standing up to his shins in the stream. Asterion was sitting on the bank, splashing water onto his arm. The blisters had popped and the skin was less livid, but there were yet more new scars, over the old. She'd traced them, kissed them, spoken silly, rhyming words against them, as he sank his fingers into her hair.

They were sitting on the flat ground outside the wall, sharing a plate of olives with Phaidra, when the group returned from the beach. Some sat down near them, talking and stretching stiff limbs. Theseus stood, staring back the way they'd come.

"You are quiet, Prince Theseus," Pelagia said, holding a cup out to him. He took it but didn't drink.

"Fourteen days," he said. "Fourteen, and not many more."

Chara glanced at Diokles, who was also standing, holding a guttering torch.

"How many?" Pelagia asked.

"Two," Theseus said. "Three, perhaps. Our people have worked hard and well, together."

"That they have," said Amyntas. "Now, then: we'll provide some fruit and bread, some salted fish—but is there anything else you'll be needing for the journey?"

Phaidra stood, and Asterion, and Chara. Only Daedalus stayed as he was, the plate of olives forgotten on his lap.

"I thank you," Theseus said, "and I accept whatever you offer—but there is one thing that remains to be done." He turned to Alphaios. "I will need something—some proof to bring back to my father. He—all of Athens—must believe that I killed the beast."

Alphaios nodded slowly as people murmured. Chara had told the islanders their story, at long last, the day after Asterion had changed on the beach; they knew, now, about the labyrinth, and all the ones inside it.

"Come on, then!" Ariadne cried, thrusting her way through the people between Alphaios and her. "Make something!"

For just a heartbeat, Chara was back in the labyrinth: Alphaios was kneeling, and Melaina was mocking him, and Theseus was snapping at her while Chara watched silently, full of dread and longing for Asterion, lost somewhere in all the crushing stone. She shook her head and tipped it up to the sky, which was thick with stars.

Asterion put his chin on the top of her head and wrapped his arms around her. She pressed herself into his warmth as Alphaios plucked a fish skeleton from a plate someone had left on the ground next to him and bent over it. Godlight bloomed almost immediately from his hands. Someone gave a muffled cry; a child started to wail. Alphaios rocked and the skeleton juddered, on fire with silver. The bones flowed together—but not into a blade, this time: into something that grew bigger, thicker, darker. "More," he gasped. Someone handed him another fish skeleton, and another, and someone else passed over a clump of lemon seeds and a bunch of dried herbs. The light grew brighter and brighter, and Chara had to close her eyes, though she didn't want to. She opened them only when he gave a wrenching cry, and the light vanished.

He was on his back, panting, his arms flung out. The dark thing sat beside him, casting a strange, reaching shadow in the torchlight. Asterion let go of Chara and walked past her. He hunkered down beside Alphaios and touched him on the shoulder. Then he lifted the thing so that everyone could see it.

It was the head of a bull. It looked nothing like

he did, when he changed, but still: it had horns, and fur, and wide, motionless nostrils. He walked over to Theseus and set it in his hands. "Here," Asterion said. "I hope your father and all of Athens enjoys me."

He walked back to Chara and took her face in his hands, which were shaking. "I like your face much better," she said.

"Thank all the gods and fishes," he said, and kissed her.

———— · ————

On the evening of day fifteen, when Alphaios returned to the wall, he was carrying something. Chara, Asterion and Daedalus were sitting on top of it, facing in; across from them, Ariadne was leaning on it. Phaidra was sitting close to the fire. Chara had been singing: priestesses' chants with every "god" changed to "fish"; children's songs with no words at all. Behind and above them, the sky was washed in Zenobia's white, mark-mad pictures.

Chara's voice trailed off as Alphaios approached. He was walking unusually slowly, as if the thing he was carrying was very heavy. He didn't even glance at his line of stones as he passed it.

"Master Daedalus," he said, also slowly. As he spoke, Chara recognized what was trailing from his hand. She slipped off the wall. Daedalus didn't—but she saw, in the dark of his eyes, that he'd recognized it, too.

"Things from the wreck have been washing up on shore, since the water started to clear. These were there today."

Alphaios held Daedalus's wings up to him. The light from the hearth fire flickered along rows of feathers, and the latticework of branches where other feathers used to be. Phaidra rose and went to stand by Daedalus. She looked up at him, then back at the wings. She touched one of the feathers. He made a sound between a hiss and a sob, and slid down beside her.

"All the feathers are so clean," Phaidra said softly. "Not ashy at all. They look like they're still part of him."

Daedalus ran his hands haltingly along the branches. Godlight flickered in the seams of his palms and up along his fingers—the ones Sotiria had healed, and the ones he'd made. *He could fix the wings*, Chara thought. *His godmark* wants *him to fix them.*

Daedalus pulled the wings from Alphaios's hands and spread them wide. The gaping holes and bald patches were easier to see, this way. He lifted them high above his head and looked sidelong at Phaidra. She stretched up on her toes and laid both her hands where the feathers were thickest. When she eased herself back down again, she smiled at him.

"We'll get new branches for you," Alphaios said. "Tomorrow, when it's light. If you want."

Daedalus lowered the wings and walked past him, to the fire. He sat down very close to it, one wing splayed in his lap. He tugged a feather free of the frame and held its tip to the flames. It sizzled and blackened, and he leaned even closer and dropped it.

"No!" Ariadne cried as it curled to nothing. Everyone except Daedalus turned to her; everyone except him watched her wheel and limp into the darkness. Alphaios left a few moments later; Phaidra a few moments after him.

"Come," Asterion said to Chara, "let's leave him be." She couldn't stop thinking of him, as she and

Asterion lay watching Zenobia's white pictures bloom and fade. An eagle, a chair, a moth, a goblet—but all she could see was Daedalus, feeding Icarus's feathers into the flames, one by one, until they were gone.

CHAPTER TWENTY-NINE

The stone for day sixteen was almost perfectly round and entirely black, except for a tiny patch of crystal that winked in the light.

"It will be tomorrow," said Theseus. Behind him, the Athenian sailors cheered and clapped each other on the back.

"Tomorrow," Alphaios said, and grinned. "Asterion, Chara: can you imagine?"

They looked at one another. "No," Chara said. "I don't think we can." She glanced up at the wall where Daedalus was huddled, as he had been when they'd first arrived; she willed him to rise and come down to them, but he didn't.

She and Asterion slept through the hottest part of the afternoon, while the others were on the beach. Phaidra's cry woke them.

"Daedalus! Master Daedalus: wait!"

He was nearly at the lemon grove, walking steadily. He didn't turn when Phaidra called again, nor when Chara did.

"I couldn't sleep," Phaidra said. "I saw him leave the hill and I called to him, but he wouldn't even look at me. His face was very strange—I don't know what he's doing. . . ."

Ariadne narrowed her eyes. "Stupid child," she said, "he's leaving." And she set off after him, moving surprisingly quickly with her crutch.

Asterion, Chara and Phaidra followed more slowly. By the time they reached Daedalus and Ariadne, they were standing facing each where the lemon trees dwindled into pasture. Some of the sheep grazing there lifted their heads at the sound of voices; others didn't.

"How dare you?" Ariadne was saying. "How dare you try to leave us all, the day before the ship is set to sail?"

Daedalus arched his tangled brows at her, and turned and took three swift paces away.

"Wait!" Chara called, and she drew close to him as he hesitated. "Master Daedalus," she said, and he made a strangled sound. He shook his head so violently that his long hair brushed her cheek. He made another sound, and another.

"He's saying 'Not master,'" Phaidra said. He nodded and raised his hands, waggling them in front of Ariadne's face.

"Yes, yes," she said, "but you still have a godmark—we all saw evidence of it last night. Even now you have one, though my father tried to take it from you." He cackled, but she kept talking. "Why are you wandering off into the hills when you should be preparing to return with us to Athens? You *come* from there! Theseus has already said he'll see to it that you're pardoned. So, Master Daedalus: tell me why—if you can get the words out."

"*Ariadne*," said Asterion, but Daedalus waved his good hand at her and smiled. He opened his mouth very wide and waggled his stump of a tongue at her. And then he put his false right middle finger between the thumb and forefinger of his other hand, and ripped it off with a crack.

"No!" Chara cried. She lunged toward him but Asterion held her back. Beside them, Phaidra fell to her knees. Ariadne stood very still, her knuckles white on the knobby end of the crutch.

Daedalus ripped the rest of the fingers from his right hand. Silver flared briefly within them as they separated from his flesh, but the light was gone by the time they landed in the grass. He stamped on them until they lay in pieces—little bits of cave stone, dull in the sunlight.

He straightened and brushed at his matted hair. He gazed at his twisted fingers, and plucked at the strange tendrils that clung to them.

"Such drama," Ariadne said, "when you don't even need that one."

He slapped her hard across the face with his good hand. She stumbled back and her crutch fell and so did she, with a *thud* and a cry.

Chara stepped past her and touched both of Daedalus's hands. She said, much more quietly than before, "Mas—Daedalus. You don't have to go."

Daedalus tugged his hands free. He smiled at her—at all of them, even Ariadne—and turned away for the last time. They watched him cross the pasture, weaving among the sheep. They watched him disappear into the shadows between two hills.

Asterion dried Chara's tears with his thumbs. "There's somewhere I have to show you," she said.

——— · ———

It was almost evening by the time they reached the top of the hill. The island sloped away as it had before, except that this time it was burnished, half-dark, half-bright.

"You can still see the ship," Chara said.

"Yes."

She heard the hopelessness in the word. She waited.

"The other day, when I changed . . ." His breath shuddered. "There are things I want, when I change. Things I remember. Now you'll say you know," he went on, quickly, savagely, as she opened her mouth to say exactly that, "but you don't. You can't—and I'm glad of this, even though it terrifies me to be so alone. But Chara: I so badly want to be as certain as Daedalus was. I so badly want some sort of peace. "

She waited a bit longer. She watched the darkening sea. At last she saw his shoulders sag, from the corner of her eye, and said, "The other day you asked where you could go." She paused and licked her lips, which had gone as dry as the rest of her mouth. "Why do you—why do we need to go anywhere?"

He looked at her. She bent and drew her lips lightly along his newest scars. "Yes," he said, when she straightened. "If they'll have us, Freckles—yes."

———— . ————

"You're *staying*?"

Not even in the labyrinth had Chara heard Theseus sound so alarmed.

"Yes," she said. "We asked Pelagia and Diokles, late last night, and they spoke to the others, and—"

"And you waited until now to tell me?" Theseus demanded. He began to pace up and down in front of the ship, which was half in the waves now—quick, glittering waves, without a trace of ash.

Asterion cleared his throat. "We weren't sure when to tell you—we wanted to right away, this morning, but everyone was so busy and so excited. So we waited. Until now." He cleared his throat again.

"And you accept them?" Theseus said, stopping in front of Pelagia. "You accept *him*, despite the power of his godmark?"

She nodded. "We believe that Chara will soothe him, if he changes. And we've never turned anyone away, whether godmarked or not, if they wished to stay."

Theseus pursed his lips and cast his eyes to the sky, which was an empty, endless blue. "Very well," he said. "But do any of the rest of you wish to tell me you'll stay, now that we're here and the tide is turning?"

"They'd have to be mad," Ariadne said. "Now let's go."

"We should, my Prince," a sailor said, one hand spread on the ship's stern. "We don't have long."

Theseus nodded and turned to Phaidra. "What of you, Princess? You will not stay too, will you, and tell me only now?"

Phaidra looked at the ship, and what was beyond it. "Will there be many locks to open, in Athens?" she asked.

He gazed at her—speaking, Chara knew, in his other voice. Aloud, he said, "There will be, Princess. I am sure of it."

Phaidra walked to Asterion and he put his arms around her, and they stood, swaying a little, until she pulled away. Chara took her hand, which felt small and dry. "Be well, Phaidra," she said. "Please be well, and happy."

"How?" Phaidra said—but before Chara could try

to answer, Phaidra was moving back to the ship and scaling the rope ladder that lay against its side.

Alphaios laughed as he gripped Chara's hands and swung her up off the sand. "May the gods not lose sight of you, on this strange little rock," he said, after he'd let her go. She squeezed him until she had no breath, herself.

"And may they grant you fame or peace, in Athens," she said as she drew away. "Whichever you want more."

Once Alphaios had joined Phaidra on the deck, Theseus climbed. Two sailors followed him, the second panting beneath the weight of Alphaios's bull's head.

"At last it is the Princess of Crete's turn," Ariadne said. She smiled a wide, satisfied smile at Chara and Asterion. "Expect no farewell words from *me*."

Chara reached for Asterion's hand. It was shaking—or maybe hers was, too.

Ariadne limped toward the ladder, her head held high, her cane spraying sand. "Yes," she said, her free arm reaching for the ladder, "at last I—"

The rope bounced against the ship's side as Theseus drew it up. Its lowest rung dangled above her head, which she tipped to stare at him.

"My Prince." Her voice was louder than the waves. "No games—not now. Let me up."

When he didn't move, she dropped her cane and reached with both hands—and the ladder bounced farther away from her.

Chara felt cold wash from her belly to her toes. Asterion's nails dug sharply into the back of her hand.

"Theseus. *Let me up*."

For a moment he gazed down at her, and she up at him. If he spoke, it was with his mind-voice; his other was silent.

"No." This time Chara could hardly hear Ariadne. She jumped, or tried to: her injured leg gave way and she fell backward, hard.

Phaidra bent her head. Alphaios laughed.

Theseus shouted, "Push!" The sailors who were left on the beach braced their arms on the wood and their feet in the sand. They grunted and yelled, and the ship eased deeper into the waves. They scrambled up the ladder that was dangling low, again, and onto the deck. "Row!" Theseus shouted, and oars dipped, pulled, rose, and dipped once more.

Ariadne crawled in the boat's wake, until the water hid everything but her head and shoulders. Her hair swished like seaweed, in front of her and then behind, as the waves grasped it.

Chara let go of Asterion's hand and waded in after her. When she reached her, the sea came up only to Chara's thighs—but the current hauled and tugged, and she fought to keep her footing.

"The gods will punish him," Ariadne said, before Chara could speak. The princess's eyes were wide and nearly unblinking, despite the surging water.

Maybe they just want to punish you, Chara wanted to say. There was so much she wanted to say—years' worth of words clogging her throat—but the only ones that came were, "Princess. Come away."

Ariadne didn't look at her. "Another ship will come," she said. A wave crested and broke over her, and she choked and coughed but didn't rise.

"Ariadne," Diokles said from behind Chara. He passed her, glancing at her with one raised, hopeful brow before he looked again at the princess. "Let me help you up."

Ariadne shook her head. Tendrils of hair clung to her cheeks and neck.

"Fine, then," he said. "You get up yourself—but I'll walk beside you, at least. Back to the beach."

She blinked, over and over, and dragged a hand across her face. She rose, dripping, more beautiful than she'd ever been, and turned away from the sea and the ship. Another wave plucked her up and thrust her toward the beach. Diokles grasped her arm, when she righted herself, and she didn't shake it off.

Chara reached the shore before they did. She stood beside Asterion and watched Diokles and Ariadne step out of the water; everyone watched, as they made their way slowly along the sand. Her limp seemed worse, but she didn't take her cane, when he picked it up and held it out to her—and she didn't take his arm, either. She lurched past them all, toward the scattered trees beyond the beach.

Xenon took one long stride after her. "No—don't, Xenon," Diokles said, and the giant stood still.

"Ariadne!" Diokles called. She limped on. He made a wordless sound and followed her.

"Pelagia," Asterion said, and she looked at him with one brow raised, just as Diokles had looked at Chara. "It was wrong of Theseus not to tell you of his plan—wrong that he didn't ask for your permission."

She smiled, just a little. "Ah, but he did."

"So you . . ." Chara began, and stopped. She took a deep breath. "So you don't mind her?"

"I do," Pelagia said. "But she's lost—everyone is, when they arrive here. Some are found again."

They turned back to face the sea. The ship was smaller. Once it had passed beyond the long rock arm of the harbour, the sail—once white, now blackened with ash—unfurled from the straight new mast and snapped taut in wind. Chara leaned her shoulder against Asterion's arm. *Theseus didn't have a single word for* me, she thought. *After the labyrinth—after all those days and nights—not a single word or look.*

::*Daughter of Pherenike*,:: Theseus said, as the ship took to the open sea. ::*Chara: farewell.*::

———— . ————

Phaidra stared at the place where the island had been long, long after it had vanished. She stared until her eyes stung with salt from the spray churned up by the oars, and darkness hid everything except the stars.

She heard voices behind her, but didn't really listen to them. "My Prince! Will you speak to your father, with your godmarked voice? Will you tell him we're coming? For he said he'd wait for you every day, at Sounion."

"I will surprise him. The ship will surprise him, coming toward the cape—and he will rejoice even more when he realizes what his eyes are showing him. No. I will not tell him."

He was there with her, then, a shadow like all the others. "Princess," he said. "I will bring you with me to my father's palace; I will keep you by my side. You will be happy in Athens: I promise you this."

She had no heart to say, *It doesn't matter—nothing has, since Icarus fell.* She said, "Yes," instead, and let him take her hand.

EPILOGUE

Her eyes were open. She saw nothing but grey-black-white shadows that shifted and swam. She felt a deep thrumming around her but heard nothing. She smelled smoke. Seeing, hearing, smelling: she knew these. Remembered them.

She thought, *Who am I?*

The pain answered. It was strongest in her chest, where it burned with the white of a blade-wound. A blade. A chest. A man's cry.

Theseus, she thought, in a flood of memory and stronger, sharper pain, which threaded thorns through all of her flesh. *And I am Sotiria, who took his wound away. A wound that killed him—because here I am, in the darkness of the Underworld.*

The shadows began to part on some deeper, more frightening colour. The mountain beneath her was hot.

Not the Underworld. Though it seemed impossible—though the air and the heat told her otherwise—she knew this.

I'm alive.

Melaina? Theseus? Chara? But the heavy silence told her that she was alone.

She could see the sky above her now, thick with black smoke whose twisting made her so horribly dizzy that she had to look away. She stared down at her own body, at first just because it was there, and then because she realized she should be willing it to

THE FLAME IN THE MAZE

move. *Legs*, she thought. *Feet. Do something. Twitch? Bend? No? Fine: hands.* Hand—*only one works—I do remember that. Fingers. You start.*

Her thoughts felt as if they were whirling around in her head, and yet her limbs lay like a statue's. An old statue, fallen and forgotten in an overgrown courtyard like the one she and her brother used to run past, because they were afraid a creature would lunge at them out of the shadows. *All the time I imagined they were just dead stone—but did those statues think, like I'm thinking? What am I thinking? Gods and goddesses of sky and earth and sea:* why am I alive?

The first thing that moved was her shoulder. She'd been concentrating on everything but it, so when it twitched, all her spinning thoughts stilled abruptly. A moment later it twitched again. A laugh pushed up under her ribs and she commanded it to subside, because it hurt.

When she rolled onto her stomach, pain tore through her like godmarked silver, just as it had when she'd healed Theseus. She heard herself whimpering, though the inside of her head was full of screaming. She managed two lurches, fresh pain blossoming in the hand she'd ruined when she healed Daedalus. She lifted her head and forced her vision to clear. Surely the mountain's downward slope was far, far steeper than it had been when she'd come up it? *Just go.* Go, Sotiria.

The mountain grew hotter under her palms and knees as she went, tippy and slow as a snail. The earth was seeping steam; she watched it wind up between her fingers. *Oh, Goddess: why are you angry?* But then she remembered the king who'd been so close, when she and the others had been gathered beneath the black pipes. The king who was mark-mad and spewing fire.

Farther, Sotiria. You have to get as far away from this mountain as you can.

Days went by—or so she imagined. The sky grew even thicker with dark smoke and cloud that would have smothered any daylight. She panted with every lurch forward and forgot that there was still pain everywhere in her reawakened body. She was aware only of the ground beneath her, patchy with grass that singed black as she went, and earth that smoked and crumbled.

At last she rolled onto her back, trying to fill her burning chest with breath. She had to put her chin to her chest to see the mountain. *I'm off the slope*, she thought, and felt boneless with relief and exhaustion and a sudden, aching hunger. *I'm away.*

The mountain was veined with flame, from flanks to ragged top. The flame should have been running, but wasn't: it was flickering. She blinked and squinted. *The mountain's opening*, she thought. *It's cracking apart; the fire's inside it.*

She flung herself back onto her hands and knees. She scuttled, her back arched, no longer caring that she was leaning on her bad hand, certain that soon she'd be able to stand up and maybe run—but then a roar ripped the air around her, and the earth reared up and threw her into darkness.

———— · ————

Manasses had worried mostly about the donkey, at first. What if his father needed her, while Manasses was gone? Alexios didn't *usually* need her, except once a month or so, when he went to town—and he'd just been there. "He shouldn't need you," Manasses said as the donkey—Timo—bore him down stony hills and across rivers and pastures, toward the smoking mountain. "He shouldn't. And he'll understand, when we come home. He won't be angry then, even if he is now. Or maybe he'll be a *little* angry that I didn't ask him—but he'd never have said yes!"

After a day, he tried not to think about his father at all. "She's there, Timo," he said, slipping down a slope that was too steep for the donkey to manage, with him on her back. She blew out her breath, as she picked her way after him. "I'm sure she is. Maybe the bird-man, too. I'll invite them to come home with us. They're very kind—but of course you don't know that, because you were at the lower pasture when they came. But you'll know them soon. Once we've found them and led them away from that mountain. He carried me, you know. The bird-man did, when I hurt my ankle. And then she healed it. Healed it, Timo!"

The fire above the mountain dimmed, on the very first day of his journey, and was replaced by huge, thick snakes of black smoke that writhed their way across the sky, reaching for him. He said, "Hurry, Timo. Hurry! Something terrible is happening, and we need to get to them." He stopped only twice that day, to let Timo crop at some dry grass, and to eat some of the cheese and bread he'd brought. He didn't let them sleep until the stars were dimming.

On the third day, Timo started trotting, as if she sensed his excitement at being so close to the mountain. He could see the bulk of it, and the fire that ran through it. He made a triumphant sound and raised a fist in the air—and the mountain exploded.

Rock and fire flew up and out, toward them; the ground rose, and Manasses tumbled off Timo, who fell to her knees. He lay on his belly, covering his head with his arms. He cried out as the rock shards tore at him; he rolled and rolled to escape the fire, which pattered like rain and set the dry grass alight. *I'm sorry, Father,* he thought. *I'm so sorry—I shouldn't have left; I only wanted to bring her back to us because I knew you'd want this, even if you were afraid to say so.*

Just when he thought he and Timo would burn too, the rain began. He didn't believe it, at first, but very quickly his loincloth was soaked, and his skin, and Timo was making surprised, questioning noises beside him. He sprang to his feet and tipped his face up to the rain, which had already turned from fat drops to silver sheets. Timo was shaking herself and stamping her front feet.

"We're saved!" he shouted. He slid over to her, spraying mud, and threw his arms around her sturdy neck. "Timo: we're fine, and she's fine too—I'm sure of it!"

He wasn't so sure only a short time later, as they slogged across the coursing, sucking swamp that had replaced the solid earth. He thought of his father, pacing in and out of their sleeping hut. He saw him as if he were *right there*, wrinkling his brows in that way that meant he was very angry, or very sad. *I'm sorry,* Manasses thought again. He could barely lift his feet. *I'm sorry, but I'm not. I had to try. The bird-man saved me, and she made my ankle better, and she made you smile.*

It was Timo who found her. He realized that the donkey wasn't beside him, in the dark grey of the rain, and he turned to call for her—and there she was, nuzzling something on the muddy ground. He fell, as he tried to run to her, and ended up crawling, among and over the chunks of rock that had been the Goddess's mountain.

Sotiria's eyes were open, blinking away the water. They turned to him, when he knelt and leaned over her. Her lips parted.

"Manasses." He couldn't hear the word, over the rain, but he could see it.

"Yes!" he said, very loudly, so she'd be sure to hear him. "Yes—it's me! I've come to save you, 'Tiria! But where's the bird-man?"

She struggled onto her elbows and winced, and Manasses dropped down so that she could lean on him. Her arm was heavy and slippery on his shoulders, but he didn't flinch. "I don't know," she said, much more clearly. "But I hope he flew very far away from here." She moaned then, and closed her eyes, and put a hand to her chest. Manasses touched her hand with his own, which was much smaller than hers. Her fingers were twisted and bent, as if they'd all been broken. He moved the twisted hand gently aside, because he saw a dark, ragged mark, through the cloudy white of her wet bodice.

"Your hand—your chest: you healed someone," he said.

Her wounded chest heaved. "Yes."

"It was very bad."

"Yes."

He suddenly felt shy. He cleared his throat. "Will you come back with me, now? If no one needs you here?"

She was still for a moment, her eyes wide, despite the rain. Then she squeezed his shoulder and smiled. "Help me up, Manasses," she said.

She half-slept with her cheek against the donkey's mane and her arms wrapped loosely around its neck. *Her* neck: "Timo," Manasses had called her. The half-sleep was gentle. Sotiria felt the rain easing. Her eyes dipped open and closed, and she knew the smoke was thinner—grey, instead of black. Sometimes she saw the top of Manasses's head, and his fingers splayed on the donkey's neck. His nails were small and ragged and dirty.

"'Tiria?"

He hadn't spoken in days. She hadn't, either. "Mmmm?"

"We're nearly there. I'm . . . He'll be angry."

She forced her body straight. She gazed down into his eyes. "Not for long," she said. Her heart was thudding as if there were nothing else in her chest.

The hut was as it had been. The grass around it— just the same. No godmarked fire; no godmarked rain. Not here.

Alexios was running before Timo had even started to huff her way up the gentle slope to the hut. Sotiria wanted to look at him—only at him—but she looked instead at Manasses. His little hand was clenching and unclenching on Timo's hide, and he was biting his lower lip.

"Manasses?" she said. She could hear Alexios's feet, pounding the thick green grass. She could see his face, though she wasn't looking at it. She knew his cheeks would be burnished with the sun that had begun, finally, to break through the thinning clouds.

"I've never seen him run," Manasses murmured. "He only ever sort of *trots*, when he's going after a sheep that's wandering. He must be *very* angry."

"Not for long," she said again—and then Alexios was there, sweeping Manasses up under one arm and reaching for her with the other. His fingers flexed in her hair, which was soft now, not stubbly. He thrust Manasses onto his hip and the boy burrowed into his shoulder, clinging with arms and legs.

"Don't be angry, Papa," Manasses said, his voice muffled and wavering. "You should be—I know you should—but, look—I brought her back!"

"Manasses," Alexios said, in a growl that broke. "You shouldn't have gone."

He turned to look up at her, his chin wedged against his son's head. Sotiria leaned down and put a finger to his parted lips. As she did, images rippled in a place beneath her eyes: Athens' harbour, bronze and crimson at dusk. Her brother kicking up dust as he darted before her through sun-dappled courtyards. Her mother weeping after she cut herself gutting fish, and only then realizing what Sotiria's godmark was. Chara crouching in the dark by the Goddess's mountain, lifting the mask away from Sotiria's face; sending her on her way with coins that were supposed to buy her passage home.

She blinked. The images wavered but stayed, like a reflection of moon or sun on shifting water. She slid off Timo's back.

"Will it be . . ." Alexios began, hoarsely, his one hand still cradling her head, "will we be—will you . . ."

Sotiria looked up at the sky—at the blue that was showing, between the thinning clouds. Then she looked back at Manasses, who was smiling, and at Alexios, who was starting to.

"Yes," she said.

ACKNOWLEDGEMENTS

When *The Door in the Mountain* was published in 2013, ChiZine Publications put out a call to readers, in its final pages, to name the sequel. Readers responded. Two of the responses were particularly entrancing:

Charlene Challenger's *The Godmarked*
John Sebastian Rohrer's *The Dark Below*

And one was perfect: Kelly Robson's *The Flame in the Maze*.

Thank you, Charlene, John, and Kelly. Thanks to all who entered. You read my words and gave me yours, and I'm so grateful.

ABOUT THE AUTHOR

Caitlin Sweet is the author of three adult fantasy novels: *A Telling of Stars* (Penguin Canada, 2003), *The Silences of Home* (Penguin Canada, 2005), and *The Pattern Scars* (ChiZine Publications, 2011). *The Door in the Mountain* (ChiZine Publications, 2014) was her first young adult book; its sequel is *The Flame in the Maze*. Her books have been nominated for the Locus Best First Novel, Aurora, and Sunburst Awards; *The Pattern Scars* won the CBC Bookie Award in the Science Fiction, Fantasy or Speculative Fiction category.

When not working on her own books (which, sadly, is most of the time), Caitlin is a writer at the Ontario Government and a genre writing workshop instructor at the University of Toronto's School of Continuing Studies. She lives in Toronto with her family, which includes a science fiction-writing husband, two teenagers, four cats, a lop-eared rabbit, a hamster, a bunch of fish, and a passel of itinerant raccoons.

UNLEASH YOUR WEIRD

DID YOU ENJOY THIS BOOK? CHECK OUT OUR OTHER CHITEEN TITLES!

THE DOOR IN THE MOUNTAIN
CAITLIN SWEET

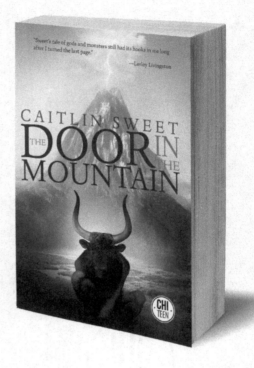

Lost in time, shrouded in dark myths of blood and magic, *The Door in the Mountain* leads to the world of ancient Crete: a place where a beautiful, bitter young princess named Ariadne schemes to imprison her godmarked half-brother deep in the heart of a mountain maze . . .

. . . where a boy named Icarus tries, and fails, to fly . . .

. . . and where a slave girl changes the paths of all their lives forever.

AVAILABLE NOW
978-1-77148-191-5

DEAD GIRLS DON'T
MAGS STOREY

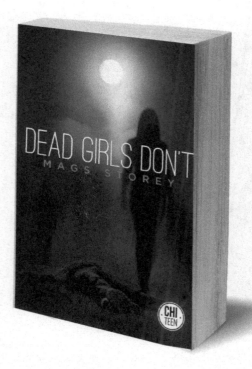

Liv might be in love with a serial killer. You'd think the fact she can talk to the dead would make it easier to discover who's really been slicing up her high school bullies. But all the clues have been leading back to Adam—the oh-so-hot fugitive she's been hiding in the funeral home. As the bodies pile up, she'll have to risk matching wits with the ghosts of her freshly-dead classmates—some of whom have deadly agendas of their own. Was the cute guy with the wicked grin really framed for murder? Or will Liv just end up the latest bloody victim at Rosewood Academy?

AVAILABLE NOW
978-1-77148-306-3

CHITEEN.COM

THE GOOD BROTHER
E.L. CHEN

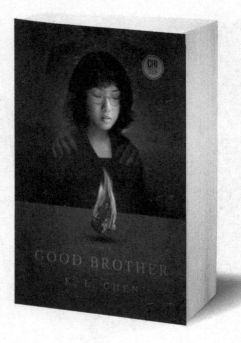

Tori Wong is starting over. She's fled her parents' strict home to live out of the shadow of her overachieving brother, to whom her parents always compare hereven though he's dead. But during Yu Lan, or The Festival of Hungry Ghosts, when traditional Chinese believe that neglected spirits roam the earth, Tori's vengeful brother Seymour returns to haunt her. And soon, Tori begins to despair that she too is a hungry ghost and has more in common with Seymour than she'd thought. . . .

AVAILABLE NOW
978-1-77148-345-2